Three's the nau[...]

Getting to the one-year mark is hard enough in a relationship between two lovers. For three, just getting through the day can be half the battle. Between Alice's headstrong insistence on pushing her sexual limits and Jay's need to confront an abusive former lover, Henry has his hands full keeping both his partners safe and happy. But despite all the challenges—and unexpected dangers that lurk in their hedonistic world—the three have formed a union that brings each of them to the edge of something new—something they may not be able to hold onto . . .

Books by M.Q. Barber

Neighborly Affection Series
Playing the Game, Book One
Crossing the Lines, Book Two
Healing the Wounds, Book Three
Becoming His Master, Book Four
Finding Their Balance

Her Shirtless Gentleman

Published by Kensington Publishing Corporation

Finding Their Balance

A Neighborly Affection Novel

M.Q. Barber

LYRICAL PRESS
Kensington Publishing Corp.
www.kensingtonbooks.com

Lyrical Press books are published by
Kensington Publishing Corp. 119 West 40th Street New York, NY 10018

All Kensington titles, imprints, and distributed lines are available at special
quantity discounts for bulk purchases for sales promotion, premiums, fund-
raising, and educational or institutional use.

Special book excerpts or customized printings can also be created to fit
specific needs. For details, write or phone the office of the Kensington
Special Sales Manager:
Kensington Publishing Corp.
119 West 40th Street
New York, NY 10018
Attn. Special Sales Department. Phone: 1-800-221-2647.

Kensington and the K logo Reg. U.S. Pat. & TM Off.
LYRICAL PRESS Reg. U.S. Pat. & TM Off.
Lyrical Press and the L logo are trademarks of Kensington Publishing Corp.

First Electronic Edition: March 2016
eISBN-13: 978-1-60183-547-5
eISBN-10: 1-60183-547-7

First Print Edition: March 2016
ISBN-13: 978-1-60183-548-2
ISBN-10: 1-60183-548-5

Printed in the United States of America

For those who plan and those who persevere. Your time will come.

Chapter 1

Alice abandoned work at noon Wednesday for tea at a fetish club. Her coworkers wished her luck at the dentist's office.

When she arrived home, Henry stood surveying a freshly showered Jay seated on the end of the bed. Dark hair damp, body nude, he enticed more than the promise of a dainty meal.

Hip hugging the doorframe, she fiddled with her blouse's top button. "Are we stripping down and skipping tea?"

Henry beckoned. Obedience earned her a commanding kiss and flushed her with heat.

Jay's eager whimper swirled around them.

"Don't tempt me." Caressing her throat, Henry slipped her first button free. "But do remove your clothes. The lovely summer dress is yours."

The dress hung over the closet door. Deep cream with green spiraling up the left side. Ivy? Knee-length, sleeveless, a slight A-line drape with a high neckline. Modest. Dark brown pants and a cream-colored shirt bracketed Jay on the bed. If his outfit included a tie, five bucks said he'd match her green ivy.

"Hey, stud." Working her blouse open, she bent and kissed Jay's cheek. "You leaving room in the waistline for all the tea-party snacks we'll be eating?"

"Fancy little cakes?" With a sly grin, Jay coaxed out her giggle.

"Absolutely." She shrugged off her top. "Do little cakes come in other kinds?"

Loosing a mocking growl, Henry tossed boxers into Jay's lap. "Behave, my dears, or you'll not eat any treats at tea."

Sock-footed, Jay stood and flowed into the shorts. Pants next, open and clinging to his hips while he swung the shirt around and slipped his arms in. God, fucking with that hasty, half-dressed thrill——

"Distracted?" Clasping her waist, Henry jolted her from open appreciation. "You've forgotten to undress." Fingers dangerous and nimble, he unhooked the hidden fastener and lowered the zipper. "Or perhaps you wanted me to take charge of you?" Pushed past her hips, her pants slumped to the floor.

Jay fumbled with his shirt buttons.

Henry traced the top of her panties. "Alas, you've worn underthings light enough for your dress, and we haven't time to indulge without reason."

Reason enough to never again wear a pale peach bra and panty set. If she'd worn the black ones, he'd be stripping them off her now.

Henry brought her the dress, unzipped the back, and helped her step in. As he lifted her hair from her shoulders, a few wheat-blond strands escaped.

Jay waited, tie in hand. Matching green. Called it.

"I've sandals for you beside the bed, Alice." Henry kissed her neck and patted her back before turning to Jay. "Formal for afternoon tea, I know, my boy."

He flipped up Jay's collar and looped the tie, fingers deft and sure as he formed the knot. Whatever Jay knew, she lacked a framework for what constituted formal enough—or too formal—for afternoon tea.

"Better overdressed than underdressed." Henry straightened the tie. Kissing Jay, he displayed more than a little possessiveness. Not for her benefit, but for Jay's. He deserved a calming reminder that every inch of him belonged to Henry. Tension melted from his lanky frame as he allowed Henry control. "And seeing you so attired pleases me."

Their desire tugged as a steady warmth in her chest rather than a thumping beat between her thighs. She ducked, hiding her smile as she closed the clasps on her sandals.

Henry herded them to the car. Ordering Jay to the front, he handed her into the back. The positioning suggested a deliberate attempt to prevent Jay from dwelling on the night they'd come home in tears. Being at the club without Henry, even not for play, would give him fidgets. Henry trusted her to take good care of Jay. Fuck up, and she'd burn in the self-ignited fires of coulda-shoulda hell.

After pulling the car into traffic, Henry settled his free hand on Jay's knee and stayed. "I'd like this afternoon to be an enjoyable experience for you both." The rearview mirror granted him authority over her, too, with his flickering gaze. "Mingling with other submissives outside of a dominant's influence will be an excellent opportunity to bond over shared hopes and attain deeper understanding."

She signaled her attention with a sharp nod. As if she'd ever ignored his advice or instructions. She'd listened Friday night, despite how he'd halted her lesson in anal play short of penetration and refused to blame her for her inability to relax. Failure stung hotter in the bright light of his generosity.

"Not all of them will be like you, nor will all of their relationships be like yours with me." Henry kneaded Jay's thigh and patted his knee. The constant comfort might seep inside and bolster his courage. "But you are likely to find commonalities, and those will be lovely places to start. So long as you make an effort to be social, I will be very proud." Pausing in stopped traffic to allow a car to pull out from a side street, he captured her gaze. "If you have difficulty, look to Emma for guidance."

Troublesome enough to reconcile Emma as Henry's friend—one who held uncountable secrets she'd never learn. No fucking way would she be bound to obey someone else outside Henry's presence. "Is she in charge of us?"

"No." His clipped tone left no room for confusion. "I would not hand over that control, Alice, and I expect you know that were it even a consideration I'd have spoken to you well in advance."

"I'm sorry." Her face heated. Her voice barely cleared the low music from Henry's favorite classical station. Twice in two weeks he'd been forced to pivot when tension and excitement rendered her unable to submit and relax for anal play, and now she challenged and snapped at him for an invented slight. "I know you wouldn't do that."

He hummed along with the soothing melody. "You're nervous, perhaps? Feeling out of place?"

"I've never been to a formal tea." The dress flowed as she crossed her legs at the knee and resettled her shoulders. "This is important. What if I get it wrong?"

Jay bobbed his head twice. Maybe he harbored similar worries.

A quick pause and a smooth twist later, the car rested in a parking space along a side street down the block from the club. After turning off the engine, Henry directed his full attention at her.

"Much as I appreciate your desire to assist in removing a predator, the responsibility to do so is not yours." Sharp and swift, he half-turned toward Jay. "Nor is it yours. The importance of this afternoon in such terms means less to me than your continued good health."

Henry swept rebellious black strands from Jay's forehead. "I believe forming friendships and listening to others discuss their relationships will be valuable for you both, but you will not have failed me or yourselves no matter the outcome. You are well-mannered, delightful partners at home. I expect you will be no less in a social outing despite its unaccustomed formality. But if you have concerns during the tea...." Eyebrow rising, he trapped her in his stare.

She scrambled to impose logical order on his implication. "We can look to Emma's example."

"Precisely." Henry granted her a gentle smile. "She has a great deal of expertise in these situations, and she's accustomed to mothering nervous novices."

Ugh. The uncertainty of inexperience dragged her down a gravity well. Needing constant coaching undermined confidence at a speed approaching light.

"You're likely to encounter a wide range of behaviors. Experienced subs in stable, long-term relationships. Newcomers too shy to lift their eyes. Attention-seekers who play at submission but in practice become demanding tops." A wisp of disapproval invaded his even baritone.

"Like me?" More than once he'd told her she wasn't altogether submissive.

"No, sweet girl, not like you." Through the gap between the seats, he gathered her fingers in a tender clasp. "You want to please me, and you trust I will please you in return. A dominant allows, even encourages, a certain amount of boundary-testing to foster that reciprocal dependence."

From the beginning, she'd fought her pull toward dependence. But he'd said reciprocal. As if he depended on her and Jay as they did him.

"The line is different for every dominant. Some submissives find childishness its own reward. Brats misbehave in an attempt to force their dominant to action." Frowning, Henry shook his head. "When the needs of the dominant and the submissive are properly balanced, such behavior is unnecessary." He patted Jay's knee. "We must move along if we wish to be punctual."

He stepped out and helped her exit as Jay followed suit. Lateness would mortify Henry and insult their hostess. The three of them covered the block at a brisk walk. No doorman stood guard outside, but the door opened as they approached.

"Daniel." Henry nodded to the man inside, who responded with a sharp "sir" and allowed them to pass into the lobby.

"Good afternoon, sir." The woman behind the front desk, like the doorman, hadn't been working the night things had gone to hell. "Signing in for tea?"

Emma made the schedules. Maybe different people staffed Wednesday afternoons than Friday nights anyway, but as a submissive herself, and Henry's friend, she'd avoid traumatizing Jay.

"Indeed. Cait, isn't it?"

"Caitlyn, yes, sir." She blushed and ducked her chin, presenting Henry with a veil of lowered lashes.

As Alice turned to hide her smile against Jay, he tipped his forehead to hers. "Crush?" The question fluttered in his softest whisper.

"Oh yeah." Mmm. The responses Henry inspired with voice alone. This poor young woman would never hear him direct those tones at her.

"Caitlyn." Henry maintained a pleasant, cordial distance. "My apologies. You have an Alice and a Jay on your list?"

"Yes, sir. You're dropping them off?" Caitlyn raised her chin. "Dominants aren't allowed upstairs until after six today."

"A wise decision." Warmth flowed into Henry's voice. The restriction had been Emma's, presumably.

The girl tapped a keyboard, studied Alice and Jay for a long moment, and nodded. "Any electronic devices to check?"

Jay dug his phone from his pocket and laid it in Henry's open palm. She swiped hers from her purse.

"Place them in my box, please, Caitlyn."

He'd had them leave their phones at home last time. The club's rules forbade camera-enabled gadgets beyond the lobby. Henry wouldn't have forgotten.

"Yes, sir. Access?"

"Both of them, at any time, for any reason."

"Yes, sir." Behind the counter, Caitlyn locked the phones into Henry's numbered box. Seventeen. "They're all set. Tea will be served in the second-floor salon."

"Thank you, Caitlyn. They know the way."

Henry escorted them to the grand staircase, where the twisting climb loomed beyond an ornate banister. "Look after each other, please." Rumbling and intimate, he quieted her distraction. "Be assured you are perfectly safe." He kissed Jay's cheek. "But if you need me, either of you, whether merely to hear my voice or to ask me to return early, simply come to the desk and ask for your phones." He kissed her with equal gentleness. "You may call at any time." Tight lines bracketed his eyes as he stepped back. "Otherwise, I'll retrieve you when the gathering has concluded." He waved toward the stairs. "Go on. Best not to be late."

She clasped Jay's hand. The faster they moved, the less time nerves would have to take up residence. "Hop to, loverboy. We can't let everyone else eat all the fancy little cakes."

She won a chuckle from Jay and what she resolved to call an amused grunt from Henry.

The stairs welcomed her first, but Jay followed with minimal tugging. If a benevolent god existed, tea would go perfectly, they'd make connections, and Jay would have a wonderful time.

Three-quarters of the way up, peeking over her shoulder, she warmed at Henry shadowing them with his protective gaze. The buzz of voices below heralded more arrivals. Hitting the second floor, she turned right and entered the salon.

She'd eyeballed the dimensions on her first tour. Almost forty feet square. Respectable, if not massive. The room could've accommodated seventy-five people for a sit-down meal. About twenty milled around now. All women.

"Alice." Dragging her name out, Jay bounced from foot to foot.

"I know." Goddamnit. She rubbed circles on his hand. "No worries." Five tables set for six dotted the room's left side. A lounging area with seating in a rough circle lay to the right. "Women love you. *I* love you."

"Women love me for five minutes because I flirt." Strong shoulders sinking, he curled into a compact shell. "I can't flirt with these women."

If Jay played the charmer at a safe, no-pressure gathering, he'd come off like an unscrupulous letch.

"Be yourself, sweetheart. We can handle this." Most of the attendees clustered in twos and threes, chatting near the tables. "Look around. We're perfectly dressed."

His laugh topped an uncomfortable undertone. She'd have followed up with a tease about getting *un*dressed later, but he'd have died if he ended up noticeably aroused in a room full of women he intended to befriend.

Across the room, Emma emerged as the sole familiar face. Laughing, she left her conversation partners and strode toward them in a modestly cut sheath dress in cornflower blue.

"Alice. Jay. I'm pleased to see you both." Greeting them with handclasps, Emma lingered on Jay. "I do apologize. I'd hoped to have more of the young men attending. We had a late cancellation, unfortunately."

Alice pasted on a bright smile. In five minutes, her hopes for Jay had gone to hell.

"We'll sit down to tea in a few moments. We're shy a few guests yet." Emma gestured toward the clusters of chatty submissive socialites. "But this is an excellent opportunity to mingle."

"We're happy to help any way we can." Mingle made for a nerve-wrackingly vague instruction. She analyzed and Jay socialized, but he relied on his charm to lead. This tea party cried out for design specs. "Are there specific people we should talk to, or lines of conversation—"

"I expect certain things will arise naturally." Emma brushed her arm below the shoulder. "You'll find us a talkative bunch. Henry mentioned once that you're an engineer?"

"Mechanical. Design for now, not implementation. Metals and plastics, mostly." Someone needed a tray of fancy little cakes to cram in her mouth before she babbled to death.

"Alice is science smart." In one solid, lanky press, Jay stoppered her discomfort. "Henry calls her his brilliant problem-solver. He's so proud of the way she figures stuff out."

Henry called her his what? Why didn't she know that?

Jay quirked his lips. Surprising her made him damn happy and less hoppy. Either she'd calmed him or Emma had.

She shared his smile. "Thanks, Jay."

"Then teatime is just another design challenge, Alice." Pouring out brisk warmth, Emma brought her hands together in a done-deal clap. "Start with questions."

"You sound like Henry." Two pages of questions in her contract proposal. A four-hour interrogation afterward. "He always starts with questions." Asked them in the middle and after, too. An art, the way Henry operated, but not an unscientific one. She'd ferret out the most suitable conversational curves so the guests delivered meaningful data without prodding.

Emma chuckled. "That's all him. Victor and I had nothing to do with it. He was already determined to tease every drop of information from his playmates when we met."

The difference between pride, bragging, or attempted reassurance eluded her. Emma kept her crunching limited data sets, scrounging for any return.

Gazing past them, Emma waved. "But here, let me introduce you to someone."

She handed them off to a brunette in a lavender sundress, prompting the conversation by asking about the woman's new job. When Emma left to circulate, Alice took over the questioning. Another woman joined their knot, and then another. The chatter encompassed work, summer vacation wishes, and obnoxious rent increases—and not at all the club or the activities they engaged in here.

Hovering at her shoulder, Jay kept his head bowed and his tongue mute. She edged closer, brushing his chest, and he gradually joined the conversation until Emma's voice rose over the crowd. Tight knots broke up in search of seats.

Jay's name filled a place card at the second table they circled. Alice's did not.

"We're not together?" Leg twitching, Jay zoned out beside the table of unfamiliar names. Not Emma's. Not the women they'd met so far. Jay and five strangers.

Alice swallowed a curse. "Help me find my spot?"

Two tables away, her name rested alongside five more unknowns. She studied angles. "I'll be facing you, and you'll be facing me." Henry wouldn't have asked Emma to split them up. The placements had to be her idea. "So if we need something...."

"Tip of the head and a dash out the door?" As women took seats nearby, Jay raised his comedic defenses. "I can toss you over my shoulder."

"Try it and you'll be apologizing all night, goof." Her soft elbow in his ribs produced a teasing *oof.*

"You know a threat's supposed to be something I don't want, right?" With a charming smile, he erased the tension in his face.

"I'd never threaten you, sweetheart." She graced his cheek with a friend-kiss and injected cheer in her whispered undertone. "I don't think Emma meant to make us feel threatened, either. I'd rather have you at my side, but this makes logistical sense." Her table started filling up. "We'll interact more, make more friends."

"Right." Scanning the room with murky brown eyes, he lost his smile. "Women friends."

The women here presumably preferred dominant men in their lives. But they'd banned dominance today, and Jay stood out as a curious anomaly. "Henry's proud of you for trying. You heard him say so."

Pulling out her chair, he touched his lips to her head. "Thanks, Alice." He hustled to his table without waiting for another of her lackluster pep talks.

She sat across from a woman of Emma's generation, poised and polished. Women somewhere in-between—younger than Emma, but older than Alice—occupied three seats. A younger girl dashed into the last.

As Emma stood at the neighboring table, the room quieted.

"Thank you all for joining me." Her light tone carried through the sunny space. "It's been a long while since our social sphere has held a regular gathering for submissive partners." Clenching her chair back, Emma surveyed the attendees in a slow turn. "We're going to correct this regrettable lapse. We are none of us alone, ladies and gentleman. We are each other's support system."

Around the room, women nodded, including four of the five others at Alice's table. The shy girl beside her kept her gaze trained on her plate.

Her youth and demeanor stuck out among the smiling women in their mid-thirties or so, the ones comfortable in their skins.

"Those of you with masters may have your own rules to follow, but let me remind all of you that tea is our chance to share and learn without strict supervision—no prying eyes or twitching ears." Emma delivered her message in crisp, distinct syllables, the measured voice of a teacher or frequent lecturer. "Speak freely, and know everyone here is a friend eager to understand and willing to advise on any difficulties, whether accepting our own newfound desires, adjusting to a new dom's methods, or hoping to return a spark to a longstanding relationship."

Women traded smiles and glances as Emma raised her name card. "Some of your dominants requested the opportunity for you to practice poise and service, so if your place card displays a teapot"—she tapped the one beside her own name—"please come with me now. You'll be responsible for serving your tablemates."

Shy Girl sucked in a breath and scurried toward Emma. The teapot design tagged her as Leah. Others rose and followed. Jay lodged himself at the back of the pack, his athletic grace hobbled with short steps and hesitance.

Silence reigned across the tables. A feather falling would've constituted a ruckus.

"You know why a gathering of subs is so quiet, don't you?" Joan, by the name on her place card, had been in Emma's sphere earlier. Slim, stern, and matronly, she likely matched Emma in age. Despite her dry tone, her mouth twitched.

"No one's given them permission to talk." The short-haired brunette to Joan's left jumped in with a teasing singsong. Kelly, by her place card. "We all know that one, Joanie."

"Wrong." Julie. Another brunette, much longer and a shade darker than Kelly. Hanging on to half these women's names would be a feat. "It's because bound hands can't reach the straps on ball gags."

Kelly and Julie laughed like old friends, and the last unknown joined them. Giggling once, Alice locked amusement down as guilt hit. A submissive tied up and vulnerable hadn't been a laughing matter for Jay.

Crow's feet lengthening, Joan smiled straight at her. "This is all new for you, isn't it?"

"A bit, yeah. I mean, yes." She resisted the unladylike urge to shrug. "Did Emma tell you?"

"She did, but that's not how I know." Joan shook out her napkin and laid it across her lap in time for Leah's return with a two-tiered round platter of fancy little cakes.

"Oh?" Catching Jay's eye, she tossed him a smile over Joan's shoulder as he carried a tray to his table. Henry might've suggested having submissives act as servers. Tasks calmed Jay like nothing else. "Then how?"

"The lifestyle seems intense and serious when you're starting out. You weren't sure if laughter was acceptable." Joan lifted a cake from the platter. A diamond-studded wedding band gleamed on her ring finger. "When you're new, you don't know what to say. How to act. What's proper and what's taboo."

Raw exposure grated. The rest of the women at the table knew each other. Tea gave them a chance to reestablish existing friendships. Every judgment Alice made about Leah's naïve youth, these women thought about *her*.

"You watch what everyone else does, and you tell yourself you're your own woman and what they're doing doesn't matter, but the truth is it does, and that bothers you." With admirable precision, Joan centered her cake on her plate. "I'm not so old I don't remember."

"Yeah, but you've been with Leo forever." Kelly nudged the older woman with a friendly shoulder-bump. "You've never jumped from dom to dom learning new rules every time." The chair thumped and dragged as Kelly shuffled forward and glanced around the towering centerpiece of cakes. "How long have you been playing, umm, Alice?"

"Just under a year." August might win favorite month for the rest of her life.

Julie whistled. "You're practically a baby."

"I'm an adult." Hell yes she was. Not like Leah, who poured tea at Alice's elbow with a trembling hand. "Being new doesn't make me infantile."

"Still sensitive about dependency and belonging." Pursed lips failed to hide Joan's smile. "It's all right."

Alice bit back a snippy response and thanked Leah for her service.

Coloring in a pale pink blush, Leah moved on.

"She'll get over that soon enough." Kelly held out her teacup. "Alice, Julie didn't mean to sound gauche. This place attracts an established crowd. You must have had a submissive friend? Or met a great guy and discovered his unusual hobbies?"

Henry expected her to make friends. Emma'd probably chosen the seating arrangements for a purpose she didn't comprehend.

"I met——" Henry was hers. Hers and Jay's, and no one else's. Their love occupied a new space in her life. "Um." Describing what they meant to her, talking about their relationship with strangers, roiled her stomach. Hell, she hadn't fully explained things to her sister. "It was——"

"We're being unfair, piling on Alice when she doesn't know a thing about us." Joan thanked Leah for pouring her tea and received a hesitant head bob in return. "We'll come back to you, Alice. We've more than enough to chatter about. I have my Leo—twenty-nine years—but Kelly and Julie have yet to settle down, isn't that so?" She talked right over their nods. "And Shannon——it's been too long. Are you still with Bryan?"

"I am. He and Marissa are expecting a baby." Hands flying, Shannon gestured as if every word required a push for sustenance. "I thought we'd have to cut back, but with the stress he's been wanting a more frequent outlet."

"Your lover's having a baby with someone else?" Fuck. Self-censorship would be a great skill to practice. "Sorry——"

Shannon waved her off. "No need. Bryan and I aren't lovers. He's my dom. Marissa's his wife."

A flurry of questions turned the conversation lively and unstoppable. The more the others talked about their relationships, current and former, the less her nerves jangled. She even managed, without naming Henry, to admit that her current dominant was her first, and he'd introduced her to the club, and the level of attention and control he offered suited her perfectly.

Attempts to draw Leah into conversation failed, as she blushed every time Alice spoke to her. Leah's dominant must yank the leash awfully hard. And she looked young, from Alice's oh-so-high perch of twenty-eight.

Might've been Leah's French braid. Or her baby pink shirt with the knee-length pink-and-black plaid skirt. Or the white socks with the folded-over cuffs. If Leah's dom had picked her clothes the way Henry had chosen hers and Jay's, the man's schoolgirl fetish clanged loud as a fire alarm. Henry's choices suggested the two of them formed a matched set of capable adults. Maybe Leah's dominant dressed her in schoolgirl chic because he'd sent her to learn. Alice refrained from asking.

The women surrounding Jay wore neutral masks and plodded through inconsequential talk, nothing driving a visible reaction. He'd looked happy—well, not unhappy—serving tea. But she'd lost track of him when the conversation took off, and now he sat head bowed, shoulders hunched, and plate untouched.

Perching in his lap would go too far, but dragging her chair over? Or flat-out taking him by the hand and leaving. She'd disappoint Henry and piss off Emma, but Jay in distress trumped both.

Emma stood, and the chatter evaporated. "If you've finished your tea, please find a seat on the far side of the salon." In a sweeping gesture, she encompassed the collection of chairs and short couches. "Those of you who've attended before undoubtedly remember our open-floor discussions of yesteryear."

Chuckles sounded around the room, including from most of Alice's tablemates. Awkward, stony silence marked the women at Jay's table.

"For those who haven't, the guiding principle is merely this: All topics are open for thoughtful conversation and assistance, so long as participants treat each other with respect."

First at her table to stand, Alice still launched herself too slowly to catch Jay. Her table was near the windows, the sunlight filtering in through the sheers. His was nearest the door, and he zipped into the hall as if he had his bike beneath him.

Nervous as he'd been, he might've downed a boatload of tea and needed the bathroom. Chasing him down and embarrassing him wouldn't win her points.

But the stairs waited that way, too. Their phones. Henry's voice. If he'd dashed downstairs, she'd fucked up her partner duties bigtime. Narrowly propped, the door blocked her view. Resolving to give him five minutes before she went looking, she snagged a two-seater couch angled toward the door. The seconds ticked by.

Most of the women had migrated to the lounge area. Emma introduced one. Molly. Holly. Something like that. Molly, or Holly, or whoever, wanted suggestions to make her negotiations with dominants generate more fulfilling scenes.

No brilliant strategies presented themselves. She'd picked a smart-as-hell dominant and let him interrogate her for hours. And fallen in love. Some of the two dozen others handled the advice giving. Good stuff, maybe, but she'd hit four minutes on her count. Four oh one. Four oh two.

A woman sat in the space on her right. Jay's spot.

"Hi, Alice." Skittish-eyed Leah strung two whole words together. A whisper, but a complete sentence. "May I——" Her blush deepened. "I don't know anyone else here."

She almost reminded Leah she didn't know *her*, either, because Leah hadn't said a word during tea. "Sure." Taking her irritation and worry out on the kid would've been cruel. Leah had spoken without being asked, even if her objective was Jay's seat. Scaring her would be counterproductive. "Sure, that's——"

Jay shuffled in the door and stopped. Shifting his weight, he scanned the room.

Fuck it.

Standing, she beckoned to him with a firm *come here*. No silly waving, tentative gestures, or curling fingers. A mimic of Henry at his most commanding, she formed a solid wall and curt demand.

Jay hustled to her side.

Reeling him in tight with one arm, she whispered, "You talk to Henry? You wanna leave?"

He shook his head, but he clung to her. Always pushing himself.

Leah's seat poaching suddenly seemed a gift and a half. Jay needed her strength. Cupping his face, she aimed to match Henry's gentle murmur. "Waiting pose. Relaxed, please." Heart thumping, she sat.

He sank, his shoulders and neck relaxing. Warm and heavy, he curled against her calves and laid his head on her knee.

She brushed his hair back and settled her hand above his ear. Only then did the silence and the stares register.

"You have a sub?" A pinch-faced woman packed into a too-tight blouse glared across the circle. "Dominants aren't supposed to be here."

"I'm not—"

"Obviously he's the junior." The tall brunette who'd sat beside Jay at tea nailed condescending snob from the get-go. "She's training the boy for her master. Or he's a dom learning how the other half lives. You should've warned us, Emma. Inviting a pretender—"

"He's not pretending anything!" She choked back the urge to swing a teapot at the queen bee's head. Anyone who'd thought him a dom eavesdropping should've fucking asked. "If you'd bothered to talk to him, you'd know that."

"Ladies. We've an excellent point for discussion here." As Emma cut through the cross-talk, she projected calm pleasantry. Navigating outbursts and flaring tempers fell under her usual job description. "The purpose for our tea has been to get to know each other better. We mean to offer support and understanding."

Alice soothed herself in Jay, in the softness of his thick hair and the wash of his breath. Even if tea had gotten as fucked up as her first night at the club, Jay at least took comfort from her presence. He wanted so damn bad to help warn players about Cal and make Henry proud.

Palm up, Emma gestured toward Ms. Queen Bee. "Wendy, the seating assignments weren't random. You might have benefited from asking Jay about his living situation."

The tall, bitchy brunette stared at Alice and Jay.

Clicking her tongue, Emma dropped her arm. "The relative silence from your table likely means you also missed the opportunity to speak with Claudia. Both could have suggested new ways of looking at your current difficulties."

"You're cubs? Long-term?" The slim, muscled woman in the jewel-green shirt had been sitting on the brunette's other side during tea. "Co-submissives, sorry. We shortened it at our house. Long story. I'm Claudia." With one jaunty wave at Jay, she raised her status from Team Ostracizing Bitch to potential ally. "My Charlie couldn't get the day off work. He was so disappointed."

Perking up, Jay delivered a hesitant return wave.

"Our master almost had to discipline him for moping. Charlie's so overdramatic." Beneath a cap of strawberry blond hair, Claudia wore a fond smile. "If you're allowed, we should get together sometime. Shoot hoops."

Imploring Alice with his eyes, Jay tumbled into the give and take of their weekly bedroom inspection. Waiting on permission unlined his face and quieted his fidgeting.

Her basketball skills hovered south of abysmal, but she'd toss up a million air balls if Jay got to hang out with another submissive guy. She nodded.

"We'll ask Henry." Jay, at full volume and vibrating, would for certain launch his campaign tonight. Or in the car. Hell, on the way to the car. "He's flexible about free time."

"I thought I recognized you two." Far down the circle, an older woman in a tangerine dress bent forward and offered a wide smile. "Your show last month was fantastic."

"Our show?" A phantom swat struck Alice's ass. Meet-the-abuser night. Their reason for being here. Emma mentioning witnesses' confusion in passing paled beside a stranger praising her for something she hadn't done and wouldn't have chosen.

"I saw it, too." Voice rising as she bobbed her head, Leah flushed bright pink. "That's how I knew who you were today. And then I got to sit right next to you."

Emma must've known about Leah's fascination when she put them side by side.

"Your show was so—" Sighing, Leah laced her fingers and tucked her thumbs inside. "I begged Master to spank me afterward, and it was amazing. He'd been wanting me to be ready, but I was too scared. And then I saw your performance." A dreamy haze filled her pale brown eyes. "I wanted to thank you."

Holy shit. Thank God for Jay steadying her while she fumbled for words. "But I was sobbing." She'd lacked control over her reaction. She hadn't been able to think her way out. "Frightened." Scattered emotions had magnified her fears. "Childish."

"That's how I thought I'd be." Rocking in the seat, Leah matched Jay at his squirmiest. "That it would hurt, and I'd disappoint Master. We'd watched so many scenes, and all the perfect subs wanted more spanking. What if I didn't?" Lips pressed together, she curled her arms to her chest. "I got too afraid to try. But your master was so tender with you, and he"——she waved baby-pink fingernails at Jay——"was so protective. That's what Master wanted me to understand. That he'd be loving, no matter how I reacted. That I could trust him to find my limits."

"I'm"——astonished the girl had strung so many words together——"happy for you, Leah." Everyone called confession good for the soul. They never mentioned the aerobic exercise slamming her chest. "But I wasn't acting. My punishment wasn't some show we were putting on."

"Anyone who's spent ten minutes talking to Calvin Gardner would know he'd never play in a scene Henry created." Across the circle, Julie draped her arm around Kelly. "Especially not as the villain. His ego's too big."

They both knew whom she belonged to, then. Letting her share at her own pace had been simple kindness.

"The mean one?" Wide-eyed, Leah turned toward her. "His part wasn't scripted?"

Words failed. Alice shook her head.

Fiddling with the tail of her braid, Leah pushed into the corner of their seat. "He really tried to poach you from your master?"

"Cal's dangerous." If the bastard tried touching Jay again, he'd lose a hand. As Jay stroked the top of her foot alongside her sandal straps, she scratched the base of his scalp, willing love and security by osmosis. "I sure as hell wouldn't trust him with my safety."

From some of the horrified expressions around the circle, a hug-your-neighbor break would've gotten a slew of yes votes. Whispering women shifted in their seats, adjusted skirts, and brushed invisible crumbs from blouses.

"Smart." Julie cleaved the buzzing gossip with a bitter laugh. "He's a user. He plays nice to establish trust, and then he fucks you over so he can watch you break."

"Get over it." Two seats down, a pencil-skirted thirty-something with a pointed pageboy dropped her head back and huffed at the ceiling. "Sadists get an unfair stigma. If you don't like their style, don't play with them."

"Sadists. I like," Julie shot back. "Responsible ones. He isn't. He's all about his own mastery. No aftercare for the broken, no praise for taking what he dished out, just kick-your-welted-ass-out contempt."

"He doesn't respect safewords." Jay held fast, bunching her dress in his fingers. "He wants to make you scream it, not 'cause he cares about testing boundaries, but so he can gorge himself on that moment after."

As she glanced up, she met Emma's gaze.

Emma winced and closed her eyes.

Slowing, Jay curled his shoulders inward. "The one when you realize he's not stopping." His hair slipped sideways, exposing the back of his neck. "When you know you aren't anything." Hollowed and dull, his voice dwindled like a fading song. "You were never anything."

So fucking wrong. Channeling Henry's patient courage, she swallowed her protests and reassurances. He'd worked hard to give Jay this chance to grow. Before their return visit, Jay would've been horrified and ashamed to share even with his lovers. Now his truths streamed out in front of strangers he hoped to help. Pride shouldn't hurt so much.

Pixie-haired Kelly tugged at her white Capri pants and clasped her hands in her lap. "I played with him. About seven years ago."

Before Jay. She aborted her instinctive reach for him. Whatever Kelly meant to tell would be difficult for him to hear. Hard for everyone in the room, even the skeptics, because no one wanted to imagine themselves in a nightmare.

"He hadn't learned to hide himself yet." Biting her lip, Kelly traded a glance with Julie. The two women looked at Jay, at her, and at Emma.

"I think it's time." Emma, her gentle voice at odds with her pin-straight posture, crossed her ankles and smoothed her dress. "If you're both ready."

Jesus. Not only the seating arrangements but the whole guest list had been deliberate. Handpicked for specific criteria—knowledge of Cal, social standing in the club, ability to spread gossip. Factors Emma would've accounted for, invisible to the club at large but familiar and intimate for the woman who handled the secrets and tidied the messes.

Rocking forward, Kelly raised her heels and tapped her knees together. "I wanted more pain than I'd been getting, and he had a reputation for delivering. We negotiated limits and went straight into the scene."

Jay sucked in a deep, slow breath.

Henry had to have known. Since Cal had gone after them in May, Emma wouldn't have made this move without running her strategy past Henry. Their phones formed Plan B. Plan A—keeping Jay in the salon, his comfort zone, and showing him Cal's pattern of victimization. Hard as hell when her body shouted at her to drag Jay to safety and her head compiled a list of reasons he meant everything.

"And it was good—the man does know how to handle a whip." Running her hand through her hair. Kelly shook out the short tips. "But it was also more name-calling and snide remarks than I wanted. Contemptuous, like Julie said. You know."

Several women nodded, and murmurs rolled through the room. Alice's couch was an island of silence. Newcomers, her and Leah, with no experience to offer. Jay, harboring experience he didn't altogether want to share.

Having met Cal made believing dominants defaulted to contempt easy. But Henry and Santa William stood as evidence in opposition. She'd been lucky, falling in with the right crowd. Hard to say which was more common.

"He stayed within the negotiated limits, barely." Lips twisting, Kelly rolled her shoulders.

Julie rubbed her back.

Kelly shakily exhaled. "I might have played with him again except for his attitude."

Bobbing, Jay wrapped his hand around her calf and dug in. He'd lived that exact moment. But by then, Cal had become a more experienced, more cunning predator.

"He released the scene, with no aftercare——"

"Red flag." Julie muttered, and a dozen women mm-hmmed.

Kelly, nodding, smacked her foot on the floor. "And he had the nerve to say my 'babyish limits' curtailed his fun. My ass had beautiful bruises that lasted weeks. To tell me I needed to open myself to pain——after one play session?"

Her tightlipped headshake repeated around the circle.

Cal'd probably been a controlling, arrogant ass from birth. If only Jay hadn't run afoul of him. If only he'd met Henry first. If only, if only, if only.

Eyes hard and jaw tight, Kelly scanned the room. "I was noncommittal to get out, but I've never gone near him again. He'll do anything he thinks he can get away with." As she landed on Julie, her gaze softened. "The charm's a front."

"I fell for the charm." Julie fumbled for her seatmate and locked fingers. "About six years back."

Again before Jay. The jackass had honed his skills, treating the club as his hunting ground.

Staring across the circle at Jay, Julie slipped her hand beneath her long hair and held the back of her neck. "Did he leave you scarred, too?"

Jay flinched, and she echoed him. The hush in the room could've been battering ram or blanket.

"He w—" Jay's voice cracked. "He would've, I think, but someone stopped him."

He'd gotten out physically unscarred, but he hadn't escaped unharmed. Her flaring anger at the women who'd gone before and said nothing fizzled out. Somewhere, maybe not in this room, but somewhere, existed men and women who had encountered Cal after Jay.

"I didn't have anyone around to stop him." Julie smacked her forehead with the heel of her hand. "Stupid. Basic rule. Hindsight, right?"

Slinging her free arm around Julie, Kelly whispered words too low to carry.

Julie shook her head and clasped Kelly's hand. "Three good sessions here, and I thought I knew him well enough to meet him somewhere else."

Jay trembled. Cal might've issued him the same invitation.

Henry never would've found him.

"I thought I had a good long-term prospect with him. Great skills, lots of charm." Rolling her eyes, Julie huffed and smacked her fist on the couch. "I had submissive honeymoon euphoria. I went to a private dungeon I didn't know, and I found out he liked caning as much as he liked whipping, and I found out both leave scars when the wielder wants them to."

Alice lurched, instinct, like throwing an arm in front of her sister when the truck stopped short.

Issuing a gentle Henry-size smile, Jay kissed the crook of her elbow.

She pried her fingers from his shoulder and ruffled his hair. Hell, she might write herself a prescription. Touching him calmed her as much as it did him, and Henry would absorb the unrest from both of them when he arrived. Every person present deserved the same loving, reciprocal partnership, whatever their tastes.

Head bent, Julie crossed her arms over her stomach. "I should've said something. If enough of us had, word would've gotten around."

Hard-earned regret etched half a dozen faces.

Jay folded into a formal waiting pose, one Henry would be proud of. "I was lucky enough to meet someone who insisted I take proper care of myself."

Henry would never disrespect Jay. Love him, guide him, command and coddle him, yeah, every damn day. Thank God for that.

"Back then I——" He rubbed his palms down his thighs and gripped his knees. "I think I wanted to be scarred, like I'd look at the marks and know I deserved them." Raising his head, he scanned the room and stopped on

Emma. "But he——Master Henry wouldn't let me think that way. I wanted to please him so badly that I learned to say *no* for him."

Emma smiled, brilliant and encouraging, every inch the guide Henry had promised.

"I'm glad I did. That was five years ago, and I——" Jay swayed and steadied himself. "I've only recently started being willing to deal with what happened."

As the sunlight dimmed, silent stares cast a heavy, dark shroud around the circle.

"Don't play with Cal. You'll get hurt. The bad kind of hurt." Jay shifted again, all pent-up energy in coltish legs. "That's all I wanted to say."

At home, she'd have invented a task to get him moving. Pouring out his discomfort in physical ways relieved his stress like nothing else. Here, he'd been forced to find another way. To choose to speak for himself.

Standing, Emma drew off the focused attention of two dozen women. "We all may make a difference in the attitudes and behaviors in this club by showing the honesty and courage Jay, Julie, and Kelly have shared."

Jay sagged.

"I love you," she whispered, and kissed his cheek under the pretext of straightening his tie. "You are everything to Henry and to me, you hear me? He's gonna be so damn proud of his good boy."

He burrowed into her hair and pulled a deep breath. "Best part of my life came outta the worst. Henry changed my world."

He had. Still was. The whole afternoon, orchestrated from start to finish. He knew Emma well enough to trust she'd provide prods. He believed in Jay's readiness to take this step. He trusted Alice to analyze on the spot and choose the right course for Jay however the tea played out.

Hands clasped singer-style, Emma performed as a soloist on stage. "The board is moving toward updating the club's policies. Expanding into non-play hours for introductory and ethics classes. Training more monitors to respond to situations with the potential to escalate. Enforcing behavior guidelines more strictly for full voting members."

Those points belonged to Henry's agenda. Maybe Emma had taken proposals to the board while he worked behind the scenes.

"Speaking up will make a difference."

"It'll give subbies a reputation for being difficult, you mean." The pencil-skirted woman who'd snapped at Julie over sadism offered Emma the same scorn. "Report, and everybody knows your business. The whispers go around, you get labeled a tattletale, told you're blaming players unfairly, and suddenly nobody invites you to scene."

Jay might've feared those things. Uncertain of the right move, unwilling to lose what he thought he had. She'd spent far too long stuck in the same silence trap, tiptoeing around him and Henry.

"I know, Iris." Emma closed her eyes. "I know, and I'm sorry." Her face hardened into stern lines. "We're putting an end to it." She scanned the circle, each woman—and man—briefly subject to her full attention. "Please come to me privately with concerns you feel didn't warrant stopping a scene and reporting. I'll increase supervision on members when I have multiple, independent accounts of line-crossing."

Among the women, glances traveled and shoulders straightened. Even shy Leah uncurled from her tight ball.

"As submissives, we have the strength to protect each other. We have the duty to be mindful and maintain a safe space for all members." Emma raised her voice to a rich, teacup-rattling roar. "When that isn't the case, we will take steps no matter how well-respected or longstanding the member." Muscles corded and angry, she seethed with tension through her neck and arms. "My husband cofounded this club. I will not tolerate abuse under this roof."

The room ebbed and ticked over like an assembly line shifting from break time to high-speed output. Stories tumbled into the circle. Not just Cal stories, and not just bad ones. Women exchanged recommendations, warnings, and promises to take more care for each other.

Christ. If Emma had been that forceful a speaker on Jay's behalf five years ago, the voices she'd been up against must've rated on a seismic scale. What side had her husband been on?

* * * *

With the last attendee departing down the grand staircase, Alice blew out a breath and sagged on her feet. "That was as emotionally exhausting as a good scene."

Solid at her back, Jay draped his arms around her waist.

She wrapped her arms overtop. "Too bad it didn't come with the euphoric buzz."

He nodded, rubbing his cheek in her hair.

"We used to host two a month." Emma said.

Whoops. Not quiet enough. She'd meant her comments for Jay.

"First Wednesday and third Saturday." On her way toward them, Emma patted chair backs and straightened pillows. "Of course, Victor handled operations then, and I had more time to schedule a social calendar for submissives." She carried herself with the same hostess poise she'd possessed at the start of tea, not a mahogany hair out of place. "The lifestyle can be isolating. Judging a dangerous situation grows difficult when the master's commands define the new normal."

"I had Jay's example." She gave silent thanks for his unwavering support. "And Henry never pushed me for anything I wasn't willing to give."

She'd clung to independence as a shield, thinking when the relationship sputtered out like every other, she'd decide the moment. Trying to end things the first night she'd safeworded, she'd staggered beneath pain and loss.

Emma shot her a sly smile. "Well, he only wanted everything from you."

Telling her a month ago he loved her, Henry'd spoken as if he'd always known. Unquestionable. The foundational design element of his creation.

"And it only took months to get." Sighing, Jay rattled her side to side. "You're so stubborn."

Henry hadn't pressured her because he'd seen the string of quick breakups in her history. She'd been clinging to a failed model. A snort escaped her as she raised her hand to muffle it.

"Not stubborn." She hadn't understood what the new model could look like. Now she did. "Clueless. I had no idea what I was doing."

As she leaned into Jay, he held her up without question.

"Victor used to take on novices to train." Emma rubbed the ever-present pearls at her throat. "Years ago, before—" Closing her eyes, she canted her head and grimaced. "We invited them into our home. Usually one, sometimes two, living with us full-time."

"You were okay with that?" Unfathomable. First Santa William stayed with a wife who despised his appetites, and now Emma had indulged her late husband's desires for more conquests by bringing them home. Accepting Henry could, and did, love her and Jay with equal depth and ferocity had been hard enough—and she'd been the other woman. If she'd been Jay, only not Jay, because jealousy washed through him like water in a sieve, but if she'd been Jay and he'd been her, she'd sure as hell have felt slighted. "Your husband being with other people?"

"Oh, no, not at all." Settling in a high-backed chair, Emma gestured them toward the facing couch. "The training relationships were nonsexual."

She sat, and Jay flopped beside her. Reaching over the back, he snagged a tray of cookies from the console table. His discomfort must've fled with the departing crowd.

"The girls weren't my co-submissives the way you and Jay are with each other." Emma smiled at them and crossed her ankles. "When Henry first told me he'd taken on a new sub, I thought he meant like Victor and I used to do."

"Like how?" Leaning back, she fought the desire to curl her feet up under her dress.

"Young women visiting the club in hopes of finding a long-term master often lack experience and refinement. We helped them understand what they wanted and taught them how to approach dominants and negotiate for those things."

Munching, Jay snuggled into her side. More outings would be good for him. Reinforce his self-worth. She'd have to mention his courage to Henry.

"Victor commanded their obedience, and I provided a role model." Eyes distant, Emma swayed from her plumb perch. Her face lit with soft curves. "When they were ready, we expanded their comfort zone with dominants whose integrity was beyond reproach. Many of the girls keep in touch with me."

"Dominants with integrity, huh?" Giving in to Jay's tray-waggling, Alice snatched a macaroon. "Bet I can name one."

"Two, actually." Emma laughed, light and graceful. "Victor helped Henry and William polish their skills. We had quite the happy household then."

"They *lived* with you?" Jamming the cookie into her mouth rescued them both—her from a verbal faux-pas and the cookie from certain crumbling between her clenched fingers.

"No, no. Will had his harpy, poor boy, and Henry was a sought-after bachelor."

Emma must've gotten Henry's permission to talk openly. She'd handed out valuable lessons about Henry and his cultural circles. Even Emma's handling of tea had been a lesson in how to conduct herself as a submissive.

"But they dined with us weekly, and Victor often oversaw their scenes. No matter how many girls stayed with us, I never went wanting for attention." Joy melting into weighty lines, Emma plucked at her dress. "The house is quiet now."

The couch cushion itched. Or the tag in her dress was the culprit. Easing prickly emotions had never been her strong suit. She always fumbled the words.

Jay laid the cookie tray aside. "Your husband did a good job. Henry's amazing at figuring out what we need when we need it." Bouncing against her in his casual puppy sprawl, he matter-of-factly waded into the emotional whirlpool. "Too bad Master William doesn't get to use his training as often. I met his wife once. She hated me, and I wasn't even trying to get in her husband's pants."

Sugar-rush filled, he launched to his feet. He gestured wildly, hunching his shoulders and raising his voice to a shrill, nasal tone as he imitated Santa's wife ranting over dinner while Henry tried to converse with his friend.

Laughter pinked Emma's cheeks.

"——commented on her unusual placement choice for the floral arrangement. He was extra-polite." Dropping to the sofa, Jay jostled her seat. "I got to pick flower petals out of his hair when we got home."

Alice mimed plucking petals from his hair. "Beautifully done," she whispered. "He'll be so proud of you."

With his honesty, Jay had made excellent inroads with the other subs, and Emma had professed certainty word would spread. And easing Emma's loneliness? No way she could've managed, not like Henry's joyful comedian.

"Is this a closed party, or is anyone welcome?"

Henry.

She whipped around as Jay hopped to his feet. Trained until desire became instinct, flowers opening to the sun or hounds running to his whistle, Jay danced in place, waiting for a command.

"Henry." Standing with substantially more calm, Emma beckoned him in. "You're always welcome."

He greeted Emma with a light kiss on her cheek and a half-embrace.

For the first time, shadows of inadequacy left Alice undisturbed. She didn't have to compete for Henry's affection.

"I've come to collect my lovelies." Stepping back, Henry glanced at the two of them.

She idly wished he'd turn. With his dress shirt tucked in, missing the tailored drape of his slacks over his ass constituted a crime.

"Be proud, Henry. They did well." Emma cast a broad smile at Jay, but he only had eyes for Henry. "Though I'm sure they'll be happy to get home. They've had a big day."

Henry smiled and Alice chortled, recalling Jay's preferred definition of a big day. Henry's cock definitely qualified.

"I wish I'd been having a big day," Jay teased under his breath.

"Come here, my dear boy."

Jay plastered himself to Henry and burrowed against his neck.

Wrapping him up, Henry whispered something that made Jay squirm. He stretched out his other arm. "Alice, did you enjoy the tea?"

"I think it was a success." The mental inventory scrolled. They had so many things to tell him.

Tucking her by his side, he kissed her with unhurried tenderness. "But I'll take your kisses over tea any day."

Chapter 2

Six fifty-five on Friday night. Lounging with Jay on the couch, she studied the clock with annoying regularity. What were theoretical physicists doing if not developing ways to control time? She'd build the damn mechanism herself—six fifty-six—if they'd tell her what materials would make haste possible.

"Nervous?"

"He kicked us out of the bedroom." Half an hour ago. No subs in the bedroom until Henry commanded them. He'd disappeared inside, and now it was four—no, three—minutes to seven. "What do you think he's doing in there?"

Jay shrugged and reached for her feet.

She yanked her legs back from the tickling threat.

He launched from the other end of the couch and sprawled atop her. Heavy and warm, in his thin T-shirt and soft sweats, he exuded the woodsy freshness of his post-work shower. "Something that'll make us very happy?"

"An excellent guess." As the clock hit seven, Henry emerged from the hall. "Certainly one in line with my intent."

Jay scrambled off her, and the two of them sat in near-synchronicity. Backs straight. Shoulders squared. Postures begging Henry to look and not find them wanting as he ran through their safeword ritual. Paradox, how the simple exchange persuaded waves of calm and excitement to coexist. Calming nerves, exciting arousal. Their nights created the safest, most thrilling space in her life.

"Alice, do you recall the night you first wore the Velcro cuffs?"

"Of course." As if she'd forget.

"Seeing how they worked beforehand helped, did it not?" A stern and forbidding master standing over them, he raised a single eyebrow.

"Not only for your sense of safety, but for your curiosity—your desire to understand the how and why of the physical mechanism."

"Yes, Henry." Restraints on the menu? Rolling her wrist against the couch cushion, she replayed the sense memory of soft interior padding and the frisson of excitement from the exterior scratching the sheets.

Beside her, his posture stiff, Jay rubbed his pinky and ring fingers against his pant leg. His confidence needed rebuilding, and restraints could trigger a setback. His reaction—

Henry cleared his throat.

His time. He'd take Jay's needs into account without her overanalyzing.

"It's less distracting when you comprehend the purpose and the mechanics, isn't that right? Less time spent categorizing the how and more spent enjoying the act."

True. She loved him for shutting off her mind, suspending her in a moment without making her anxious or somehow lesser for needing the freedom he provided.

He pierced her with his sincere green gaze. "I've been deficient in my approach to anal sex with you, Alice, and for that I apologize."

Wrong. Beyond patient, he'd waited months for her to request more than the barest touch. And then he'd been tender and understanding of her failure.

"I've focused on encouraging your curiosity, engaging your adventurous and competitive desires. But your difficulty last week showed me my error."

Henry, make a mistake. She scoffed in silence. A dominant partner who apologized and admitted his errors without hesitation had to be uncommon if not rare. Logic insisted others enjoyed similar relationships, but emotion declared only Henry—and emotion beat in time with her heart.

These moments quelled her doubts and wondering over how the hell she'd ended up granting a man so much control. He never assumed his every action was correct because he'd been the one to do it. Following his own ethical code, he listened to her and to Jay, and he made things right when he believed he'd missed a step.

"I haven't let you see enough." Lifting her hands, he delivered a comforting squeeze. "Your observable data is limited to a single successful example, one in which your role was minimal."

Valentine's Day. Until then, her window on her lovers' relationship had offered a view confined to how she fit into it. And in the month since the club disaster, since she'd moved in, Henry had restricted his games with Jay to hands and mouths. No intercourse.

Of course. He'd orchestrated distance for Jay. Granting him time to expel the pain and anger at the source, in the room where he'd been assaulted, had opened him to greater acceptance of himself and Henry's love.

"We'll correct the oversight tonight. For that, we'll need an experienced volunteer to demonstrate." With one incremental turn she hastily copied, he put a sunny smile on Jay's face. "You'll receive the lion's share of attention tonight, my boy." Henry all but purred his promise. "Do you feel up to the challenge?"

"Yes, Henry. Thank you." Control lay beyond Jay, his voice vibrating as he bobbed his agreement. "I'll be a good boy for you and Alice."

For her. Not merely for Henry. Jay wanted her approval, to be her beloved pet and sit at her feet as he'd done after tea. His easy acceptance allowed their roles to shift fluidly. Henry held absolute control, but her power, and Jay's, depended on intuition. In sensing each other's needs, they stepped forward or fell back to maintain harmonic balance.

"I'm certain you will. No intestinal issues that might interfere with playtime?" Even-toned, Henry made the question routine. Only he could turn *you won't shit the bed, will you?* into a loving, tender inquiry.

One she worried about. Unlikely, but not impossible—and God, what a humiliating nightmare. The possibility clenched her ass shut.

Smirking, Jay shook his head. "Clean as a whistle. No fullness, no discomfort, and you know I showered when I got home, so no bike sweat, either."

She'd have to learn his lack of embarrassment if she intended to be as open and naturally submissive. Nothing Henry asked meant to humiliate them, only to benefit them. And they'd given him a perfect right to the answers.

"Come along to the bedroom, then, my dears." He pulled her to her feet as Jay bounced to his. "We have a full agenda."

* * * *

A vast expanse of emptiness, the bed lay bare down to the fitted sheet. The velvet wall bench stood near the foot, pressed into service as a sideboard. The appetizers—toys small and large, metal and glass, in shapes way more complex than her all-but-retired bullet vibe—sure as hell looked filling. A half-dozen, lined up to Henry's exacting standards, shared space with condoms, lube, and the assorted contents of his nightstand.

"Did you set this up like a lab space to"—mmm, Henry'd stripped Jay while she'd taken inventory—"make me more comfortable?"

"Certainly." He patted Jay's ass. "Up on the bed."

Jay scrambled up, all long limbs and tanned skin. One sexy fucking addition to her design kit. With his sweet smile and toned muscles, he'd distract her from her what-the-hell-am-I-doing nerves.

"Anything worth doing is worth doing properly, is it not? Your education is worth doing." Strong and unyielding, Henry uncovered her inch by inch. "And our delightful demonstration model——"

Sprawled on his side, Jay waved in a quasi-salute.

"——is worth more than simply doing."

"Worth loving." Naked, she stood in the circle of Henry's arms.

"That he is." He blessed her lips with a kiss. "Go and join him, please. We'll want him on his back for your first lesson." With her hands clasped between his, he kissed the tips. "Map your model."

Wriggly and glowing, Jay rubbed the sheets. "Yeah, come check me out. I'm mappable."

She crawled up the bed and nudged him onto his back. Kneeling over him on all fours, she traced the peaceful, rounded slopes of his shoulders and masculine, blunt-cornered planes of his chest.

Heat bumped her thigh. In lifting his hips—ah, at some silent request from Henry, who slipped a towel beneath—he rubbed his cock against her. Bare skin flashed in the gap between them. Nude Henry.

She feathered Jay with kisses from his forehead to his jaw. "Thank you, sweetheart." Submitting to her fumbling went above and beyond. "I'll do my best to learn fast."

Lips clamped, he muffled a chortle.

"What's——"

Henry swept in around her waist and reeled her backward. "You'll do your best to learn *slow.*"

She bounced on her ass, in an awkward pile in his lap. Christ, her heart drummed through her chest. With one playful, commanding, unexpected move, Henry had her begging for him.

"You and Jay are familiar enough with fast." Chuckling, he nestled her between his thighs. "So eager to explore new places." His cock needled her back as he settled her how he wanted her. "To conquer new challenges."

He tapped Jay's knees, and their lover bent his legs. Pushing inward, Henry took her along for the ride. "You've a lovely mind for mechanics, Alice."

They formed a narrow V, legs outstretched, with Jay snuggling his feet under their calves. Reinforced cross braces, they'd cushion his squirming, god-that's-fucking-fantastic tension.

"Let's put it to use." Henry massaged her fingers from base to tip. "We'll begin with these."

Toes curling, Jay wiggled his hips.

From the bench behind them, Henry produced the lube bottle, a condom, and cotton balls. The cotton went inside the unrolled condom. If this lesson included an art project, the grading had better be pass/fail. Folding her fingers, Henry left only the middle extended and promptly sheathed her in latex.

What the hell? Condoms as a birth control backup, sure, hopefully not for much longer, but not for this, not when Henry didn't. Jay might believe she didn't want to touch him.

"I'm not squeamish." She deserved to be an equal, dammit. She shared the same intimate connection with Jay. "I want—"

"It's not about what you want, Alice." Holding her motionless, Henry deepened his voice to a professorial growl. "You'll obey me, or you won't play this game." The lube bottle hung suspended in his other hand, ready to coat her jury-rigged raincoat. "Choose."

The fire in her blood cooled. No rushing. No forcing. Not a competition. When Henry slapped a dominant card on the table, his reasons never involved denying her or Jay intimacy or bonding. Swallowing her objections, she flexed her finger. "I'll obey, Henry."

"Good girl." He nuzzled her cheek. "Thank you."

Despite Henry's care, stray drops fell to the towel and his fingers grew shiny as he slicked lube over her condom and Jay's curves. When he guided her between Jay's cheeks, she alone stayed dry and disconnected.

Shivering, Jay wriggled farther under her calves.

Henry brushed her face with his knuckles. "Play." With faint grazes and slow circles, he made her breath stutter. "Like this."

Slipping and skipping, the condom gave her no feedback from Jay. Her clumsy hand blocked her view. Jesus Christ, she didn't come close to copying Henry's fluttering. She'd never shift Jay's encouraging smile into overwhelming pleasure.

Henry, drawing his knuckles up her cheekbone and teasing her ear, managed to give her tingling joy with no trouble. "How do you feel?"

"Like I'm inching down icy back-roads during a blizzard in a rear-wheel drive coupe." Fuck. She owed Jay a massive apology. Henry might as well banish her from the damned bedroom.

Thundering like an avalanche, Jay unleashed a torrent of chuckles. "Sorry," he gasped between fits, clutching his stomach. "Sorry, Henry." He snorted. "I've always wanted to shoot snowflakes."

Yeah, wanted it so bad the firmness had run screaming from his cock.

"All's well. No need for apologies." Henry strong-armed her around the waist. "Nor from you, my frustrated doubter."

"But I'm failing." She flailed her useless floppy-sack finger. "My fumbling is boring Jay to death."

"Are you kidding?" Propping himself on his forearms, Jay dug his feet back under her. "You've got all your attention focused on me." He launched his melty chocolate puppy-dog stare. "Nothing better. Do it again?"

"You aren't failing, Alice. You're learning." Leading her back to Jay, Henry kissed her shoulder, his lips soft and warm. "You've encountered a difficulty." He nipped, quick and sharp, and soothed her with his tongue. "You have tools and knowledge to ease the way. This is your opportunity to ask."

His brilliant problem-solver. Mystified, more like. "I can't judge how much pressure I'm stroking with." Maybe sharing their experience was the point. "Is sex really this foggy with one of these on?"

Shrugging, Jay showed off his sexy abs. "I've never tried one on my finger. Or stuffed with cotton. Sounds itchy."

Unfairly singled out. Great. "Then how come I have to?"

"You're allowing frustration to distract you." Nudging her head to head, Henry cracked the icy, paralyzing confusion encasing her. "You believe this"—he squeezed her finger—"is a punishment."

"No, you have a reason. I know that." But with her attitude, she'd treated him like a petty man who'd punish her for months of condoms. Unattractive, unkind, self-centered Alice. Ugh. "An important one, because you made the game contingent on accepting the condition."

"Two, actually, but a reasonable deduction." Henry spread their hands wide on Jay's thighs. "What do your fingers have that mine lack, sweet girl?"

Henry's fingers surpassed hers in every measure—longer, thicker, better manicured—"My nails." Hers extended past her fingers. "They're too long and sharp."

"Two lovely pets are reason enough for me to tend mine with care." Humming, Henry interlinked their fingers. "The cotton and covering owe nothing to squeamishness or hygiene. They are, as you surmise, a safety measure."

As he dragged her fingers down Jay's thigh, pale pink lines erupted on the creamy skin hidden by his bike shorts all day.

Sighing, Jay pushed closer.

"Despite his well-muscled, enticing exterior, our Jay is delicate inside." Henry cupped their hands around Jay's balls. "We don't wish to risk a scratch."

Jay's soft skin and fuzzy hair tickled her palm. Cocks twitched above her fingers and against her back.

Jay waggled his ass. "Hear that? Muscled and enticing, Alice." Sexy and cute, too, with a devastating grin. "I'm worth bundled-up cotton-finger."

"You are, but I could cut my nails." She wouldn't miss them. They'd grow back. Or she could adopt Henry's regimen. "Now."

Henry tsked. "Ah, but you'd still have to wear protection for the second reason."

Tipping back, she found solid support on his shoulder. "Which is?"

"Practice." He kissed her forehead. "Toys are neither a finger nor a cock, and we've several of Jay's favorites to try in your hands tonight. When you wield one, will you feel sensation at the tip? Will you know how rough, how fast, how hard?"

"No." Not without wireless hookups, pressure sensors, and software. She'd gain knowledge through experience, the way Henry—of course. Henry had mapped her pleasure centers, her likes and dislikes, and taught her and Jay to play in tune. "Only Jay can tell me what he needs."

"Exquisite." Henry captured her mouth. Delving inside, twining their tongues, he stroked her breathless. "Tell him what you're doing, Alice. Talk to him."

Craft a scene the way Henry did, hold Jay spellbound with her voice and bring him to climax. Easy. Right.

In dark eyes and expectant brows, Jay offered a wealth of trust. He cocked his head, and a stray lock of hair tumbled across his forehead.

Oh God. All of his faith, aimed at her. She buried her face in Henry's neck. "What if I can't? What if I say the wrong thing?"

"What will help you most in this moment?" Henry matched her plaintive whispers with a strong rumble. "What do you want?"

"I want to"—*feel in control, but how*—"see what I'm doing." Not hurt Jay or disappoint Henry. "Run a simulation." A hundred.

"Good. Identifying your desire and locating the proper tool will bring the fulfillment you seek." He placed his finger at her lips in a silent shush. With his opposite hand, and hers, he massaged Jay's ass. "Such tight beauty, round and firm, deserves appreciation."

Legs bending almost double, Jay rocked into their caress.

"Yet it obstructs my view of another beauty. One I would claim with fullness and depth." Henry skated his fingers through the lube coating Jay. "Would you enjoy that, Jay?"

"Yes, please." Ending on a whimper, Jay unfolded his elbows and dropped to the sheets.

"Then you'll hold yourself open for us." Deep notes transformed Henry from coaxing questioner to demanding dominant. "Present yourself. Show Alice where you most want her touch."

Jay slapped his hands to his ass and spread his cheeks. Lube laid a shining path for her. He flexed, flashing pink.

Henry doused the tip of her swaddled finger. At this rate, she'd use the whole lube bottle before she got up her courage. She traced Jay with steady pressure, circling his faint thrusts. Pushing toward her, that's how he created his rhythm. An anti-Kegel. "Is this my invitation?"

Exhaling, he stuttered. "Uh-huh." His cock twitched, well on the road to hard again. "Ready when you are."

She'd hurt Jay with her incompetence. She wouldn't like it. She wouldn't be able to get him off this way. She'd——

"Small steps." Henry steadied her shaking hand. "The finished design will show itself in time. Push when he does." As the tip slipped inside, Henry guided her in a slow thrust. "Jay understands your need to study each component. You please him with your care and attention."

Jay squeezed her in the vise of his body. Just to the middle of her finger, the second knuckle, but solid. Throbbing. Her heartbeat or his, drawing her deeper.

"You are not being judged," Henry whispered. "Shall I forbid you to judge yourself?"

The pressure popped. She tumbled forward to the last knuckle, her loose fist sliding on excess lube slicking his skin.

Groaning, cock waving flaglike over his abs, Jay gripped his ass.

Her heart thundered. "Am I hurting you?"

"Not hurting." Jay laughed. He clamped down with powerful muscles. Jesus. As he pushed and pulled, she bobbed in the current.

"You're in control." Startling, a revision of her mental map. She wouldn't be powerless and in pain, either. Henry would never use her that way, but stray fears clung like cobwebs.

"When I wanna be. Told you it doesn't hurt." As he relaxed, he freed her to move. "But you gotta want to let someone in. You choose to surrender."

"Well said." Pumping Jay's cock, Henry wrung loose a happy whine. "That trust cannot be rushed, and it does not arise from the head." He settled his hand on hers. "For now, explore."

At each Jay-wiggle, she grew bolder, testing every masturbatory trick she used herself.

Jay, laughing, invented his own hot and cold rating scale. "Neighbor. Friend. Friendlier. Partner. Friend."

"Is thrusting better?" She drew back. Jay liked Henry's power. She'd have to deliver despite having less mass.

Henry encircled her wrist before she could pull free. "Stay within the place you've made for yourself." He nudged her into a slow spin, drilling forward. "You see how he surges toward you?"

"Thrusting's good. I like thrusting." Rocking, Jay set the bed in motion and moaned with her moves.

Hell yes better. She developed a clockwise twist deeper, a counterclockwise twist shallower. Eyeing the tightening in his balls, she picked up her pace.

"More." Jay flexed his hips and drove himself against her. "Please."

Grinding accomplished nothing. Her finger didn't reach farther. Faster, she could do. *More* stymied her.

"So eager he is to seek pleasure." Tugging her backward, Henry rolled the condom down. His quick work snuggled her index and middle fingers together, double-sizing her makeshift cock. "So eager to be the center of your understanding."

"Gonna give you two, stud." Share what she was doing, check. Ask for what she needed—"Push for me. Show me you want me inside."

His effort overcame cotton and latex, the pressure more familiar, her awareness better attuned. She slipped in with patient ease. Double-fucking-tight.

Bouncing his ass in rhythm, Jay gripped her on every pullback. He curled his toes into the mattress. His cock swelled. "Please," he chanted, his begging mixed with vibrato breaths and tenor whimpers. "Please, Alice."

"Do you hear the changing tones of his need?" In the shadow of Jay's thigh, Henry extended two fingers, mimed turning his hand palm up, and gestured in a come-hither motion. "Listen to the roughening timbre. The wild swing in pitch."

She copied the slow swivel and stroked upward. A smooth bump rolled under her touch.

Cock jerking, Jay jammed himself toward her.

Henry caressed her arms, an infusion of strength and confidence. "Take his pleasure as your tuning fork."

Fingers firm, she rubbed the gentle curve with persistent repetition. Memorized the placement. The spot where guy-magic happened.

"I need, fuck, I need to come." Jay arched off the bed, his thighs straining. "Can't wait. Please. Please."

"Come, Jay." This storm surged at her direction. In two fingers, she held the power to command him. "Come for *me*."

He shuddered and groaned. His cock leapt. A white arc surged over his chest and spattered his neck. A second splashed his sternum. The third pooled above his navel. He lay painted with his climax and gasping for breath, all because of her.

No blizzard-blind fumbling. She'd built a fucking hydroelectric dam connecting her to Jay with high-voltage wires, and the controls lived inside her. She'd even short-circuited the bedroom lights. Dim, with new fuzzy halos.

"*Breathe.*"

Her chest heaved at Henry's command. Her lungs rejoiced. Fuck, no wonder she'd gotten lightheaded. Shivering, she giggled. "I did it." She'd put the stunned grin on Jay's face and the triumphant streaks on his chest and belly. "I did it."

"Hell yeah you did." Propped on his elbows, Jay scanned himself to her buried fingers and blew her a kiss. "You fucked me good."

Cock thumping her back, Henry clenched her thighs with surprising force. His low growl vibrated through his chest and pushed into her. "Magnificent."

A violent surge of desire overloaded her. With the raw strength of his ownership, he cut her imagination loose sure as if he'd toppled her and fucked her across Jay's chest.

"You've pleased me, both of you, with your patience and courage." Henry lifted his hands, and the color rushed back under her skin.

He kept encouraging her in this powerful direction. Nothing matched the thrill and the sober responsibility of cradling Jay's trust and happiness in her hands—or the exhilaration of choosing the right route.

"Yoo-hoo, Alice. You aced the lesson." Stretching with puppyish abandon, Jay levered his feet and waggled her legs. "Good thing. Not surprising."

The lesson went beyond cutting loose her subconscious fears about anal sex. Jay's pleasures weren't the only ones exposed to her here.

Head shaking, Jay laughed. "She's got subspace face. Dom-space face?"

Henry had given her a firsthand, guided tour through his emotions as their dominant. This brilliant flash of heat and accomplishment, this slow-burning contentment flowing in after, he'd shown her in the only way she'd appreciate.

"Success can be surprising when our girl underestimates her readiness for deeper understanding." Henry kissed the back of her head as he helped ease her fingers free. "You're her first, and firsts are a breeding ground for creativity, invention, and revision."

Settling down, Jay cupped his hands behind his head with ostentatious flair. "I'm a great first."

She graduated to washcloth duty, bathing her Jay-slate clean from shoulders to balls. "You were fantastic."

"You're having fun, right?" Jay cradled her in a loose hug, tapping her back with excess energy. "I want this to be good for you. Whatever's got you worried or weirded out up here"——he nudged her forehead——"when you're trying to receive down here"——and squeezed her ass——"you can ask or test."

"I'm good now." In a lazy sweep, she wiped a nonexistent splash of ejaculate from his jaw. "I like this game." She invaded his mouth, her kiss weighted and dragging and molasses-sweet. He tasted of submission and satisfaction. God, Henry must love that flavor on them. "A lot."

Jay's low whine chased her. Eyes closed, he grew a teeth-baring grin. "And I love putting that sexy fucking smirk on your face."

His eyes widened, and he wriggled taller, pressing his shoulders back. "I'm your stunt double."

Henry corralled her and hauled her into his lap. "Let's find you both another pleasurable challenge."

At Henry's direction, Jay rolled onto his stomach and hugged a stack of towel-draped pillows. The height propped his ass and bent his legs.

Henry passed her a clear glass toy from the bench. The weighty cone shape resembled a Christmas tree on a stand.

Measured against her fingers, the toy came out on top by less than an inch. More girth, yeah, but nowhere near what her lovers carried around in their shorts. "Kind of stubby, isn't it?"

Jay snorted.

"You wound me." Henry pressed their gathered hands to her heart. "Have I ever failed to satisfy?"

Hell no. "You're a lot bigger than this is."

He tickled her ribs, chasing her as she squirmed away. "You'll appreciate small in due time."

"I'd appreciate small." Drumming his feet on her, Jay wiggled his ass. "I'm super appreciative."

"We'll have you hard again soon enough." With a heavy massage, Henry pushed him into the pillows. "I've plans for you."

Jay stopped grinding. "Thank you, Henry."

"Starting small is a retraining exercise." Henry poured lube over the glass toy and her cupped palm. "A reminder of how pleasure builds and grows."

"We're gonna run out of lube." Especially if he meant to use every item on the bench.

"Should the two of you empty a bottle a night in play, I would judge it well spent." He slicked her fingers and the toy's tip. "You will never upset me by using more than needed."

Practicing what he'd taught her, she eased forward. Tingles traveled to her toes gripping the bedsheet. Jay's reward for his patience with her playtime might include Henry as the main event. "This is a warm-up."

Jay pressed back, taking the full depth with a low sigh.

"Mm-hmm." Outlining the wide circle base, Henry teased Jay where curved glass met soft skin. "Stretching is beneficial—and enjoyable. Isn't that so?"

The plug dipped and jumped. Jay worked fantastic fucking muscles, pumping divots in the sides of his ass and flexing against his lovers. "I'm an exercise fiend. I love this workout."

Too tempting. She elevator-button-pressed the toy's base.

Groaning, Jay dug his knees in and lifted toward her.

In doggy-style, that'd be her plea for Henry to fuck her harder. "You want thrusting?"

"God yeah." Jay dropped his head. "I want it, please."

"Not with this toy." Henry stayed her hand. "Jay, you've a wonderful opportunity to help educate your playmate." Twisting, he fluttered his fingers over the remaining toys on the bench. "List three activities you enjoy while wearing your plug."

"Only three?" Jay shot a sexy smirk over his shoulder. "Doing chores. This baby's how Henry convinced me dusting was a necessity."

Henry set a slender steel dildo and the lube between her legs. Taking over her massage, he stroked Jay from knee hollows to ass curves.

"All that bending and reaching?" Jay sighed with heavy appreciation. "Dust needs to happen faster."

She got hands-on lubing the toy, a heavy sphere below an elongated ellipsoid shaft. An exclamation point, held straight up by the ball end.

"We'll find more uses for your bending and reaching talents." Henry clamped down on Jay's perfect cheeks. "I do so enjoy supervising. A second?"

Pushing toward Henry, Jay whimpered. "Waiting—you haven't loved waiting pose until you've done it with the weight of a plug in your ass."

"One more, please."

As Henry wiggled the glass handle, Jay tightened his feet into iron bands across the tops of her thighs. "Having this in your ass and Henry in your throat is amazing, especially when he won't let you touch yourself."

A glimpse of her future, watching and partaking. Slippery rivers of lube flowed into a friction-reducing cushion to protect Jay from the metal warming in her hands. Ready for her training and his pleasure.

"My dick's in stiff-breeze mode then. You could breathe from across the room and I'd come."

"Well done." Humming, Henry freed the plug. "Your enthusiasm fills our Alice as easily as your toys fill you." Glass toy deposited on the bench, Henry adjusted her grip on its steel cousin. "You'll have the thrusting you desire as your reward."

They slipped the toy home together. Wrapped around her, Henry controlled the speed and power of their thrusts—slow and easy.

With a feline arch in his back and a whine in his throat, Jay dragged his face along the sheet. Tensing and relaxing in turn, he formed ripples in his long muscles as if he'd slam toward them given the chance.

Heavy-handed, Henry petted one flexing thigh. "With words, if you can. Will you speak up for Alice? You've quite enthralled her."

"Me?" Jay shimmied, speeding their thrusts and whimpering as they dug their knuckles into his cheeks. "I, yeah, I want her——" He shuddered. "Fuck, deep and short, please." He sucked in a hard breath. "I want her to feel all of this."

"You look amazing." Best damn sales pitch ever. Guided by Henry, she traded long strokes for short ones. Staying deep, she upped her pace. Metal gleamed, the lube lending a colored sheen.

"Define the *this* you wish her to feel." Henry slipped under her and rolled Jay's balls against the stacked pillows.

Shaking, Jay groaned. "Intense. Intensity. Perfect gear, muscles fluid, lungs burning, gonna be so fucking good to summit——"

"Lift up and show me your cock."

Jay jolted his hips in the air.

Her thrusting ceased. "God, he's gorgeous."

He hung stiff and bobbing, gravity coaxing a bead of pre-come into a dangling thread. The thick ridge running up his underside made a tempting target.

"He is. An exquisite muse." Intercepting her as she reached for Jay without conscious control, Henry rubbed his thumb in her palm. "One more toy tonight, but you'll have to share."

A toy for her. Small suddenly sounded delightful.

Jay uttered a light fuck-me-now whimper. "I love sharing."

Easing the steel free left Jay exposing a wider ring of deep pink, open and flexing. The final toy curved in a shallow arc with five glass spheres of increasing diameter above a looping handle. Henry shoved the pillows aside. Cock swinging like a compass seeking north, Jay accepted each globe with a low sigh and stretch.

Henry pressed a condom into her palm. An extra two fingers alongside the toy would be more than a stretch. Cupping between her legs, he tugged her folds. "Open."

Fuck yes. The condom slipped. She clamped the packet at the last second. With shaking hands, she tore the foil.

"Turn over."

Her?

No—Jay flopped on his back, arms and legs spread, cock proud and straining over his stomach. The toy's looping handle grazed his balls.

"Wrap him up, sweet girl." Kissing her throat, shrouding her in his hot breath, Henry thumbed her clit. "He comes with his own toy attached. One you have a fondness for, if I'm not mistaken."

"Not mistaken." She planted her hand alongside Jay. Wrapping his cock had one reason—putting him inside her. "I'd call fond an understatement."

Jay thumped his stomach. No hands. She'd primed him for maximum pleasure. Adorable wrinkles gone, he'd turned plum dark and ripe.

"You've both accomplished a great deal." Henry parted her with slow sweeps. "To help you retain your newfound knowledge, we'd best let the material"—he drove his finger into her—"sink in."

Aching need registered in a flash of heat. As she'd focused on Jay, on learning and comparing, hoping she'd unlock the secrets of fantastic anal sex, her body had grown restless. Rivers of lube had nothing on her readiness.

Unrelenting, Henry pumped and rubbed, slicking her clit.

She hung her head, hair dangling and flowing over Jay. He rippled his abs beneath her. Beyond Jay's covered cock and lean thighs, Henry fucked her on his fingers.

Fucking beautiful hands he had, swift and sure, attached to a brilliant, intuitive man who loved her. Tension compressed her into a ball, the collapsing star driving toward one energetic burst.

Henry swept free and left her hugging the edge.

"Please." Grappling with hunger for Jay, she developed a rattling voice. "Please, Henry."

"Up on your knees. Straddle Jay. Face me."

The room spun as she scrambled. Jay's earthy-eyed lust and worship burned like an afterimage in tandem with Henry's stern, heavy stare.

Squeezing Jay's base, Henry tilted him upright. "Claim him, Alice."

She sank, shaking and sliding, taking ownership of Jay as she swallowed his hard flesh.

Whimpering, he dug into the mattress. No wonder, if he'd gotten as close as she had. Strung tight with need, they waited on Henry's permission.

"Your patience and enthusiasm have been a delight, my boy. I'm so pleased with you." Flattening one hand to her belly, Henry hovered at her clit. "You needn't hold back. Touch our girl all you like."

In a jackrabbit leap, Jay launched them together. Fondling his way up her ribs, he cupped her breasts.

Henry dropped pressure on her clit, his thumb an insistent demand. "Ride."

She rode hard and Jay matched her, his balls swaying across the glass handle. He defined perpetual motion, mapping her skin with his fidgety impulses. Cracks let starlight through where he touched her, where Henry touched her.

"Need——" She gulped for air. No oxygen, not here in deep space. "Gonna——" Just elemental forces goading her to——

"Come."

Her star exploded. One low demand shattered her and radiated shock waves.

Henry grabbed her chin and tilted her head. "Watch." He pulled the handle between Jay's legs.

Groaning, Jay bucked like a goddamn bronco as each bead emerged.

She clung to him with bent legs, struggling for purchase, slapping her hands on his sides behind her.

Jay thrust wild. Gluing his hands to her hips, he hauled her down to meet him.

A command performance. The hard, fast fucking she sometimes begged Henry for. God, what a reward. The scattered debris field of her exploding star reassembled and shook loose again with Jay's final thrusts. She sagged, panting and spent.

Henry pushed her backward, and Jay caught her. Their labored breathing filled the room. Praising them with reassuring caresses, Henry existed everywhere at once, spreading the excited electrons of dominance. He rolled them on their sides, straightened her cramping legs, and cradled her as Jay pulled out. He stripped and discarded the condom. He peeled them apart, finally, as breathing came easier and her heart rate slowed. Sweat and silicone lube made them all damp and slick.

"On your back." Planting kisses, Henry drew a line down Jay's throat. "Knees up."

As Jay followed directions, Henry rocked back on his heels. He stroked his cock in a loose-fingered grip. He'd hardened watching them. As solid as the toys, but longer. Thicker. The spreading lube brightened his erection.

Jay hip-bumped her, eagerness writ in his broad smile despite his sleeping cock.

Nodding toward the toy bench, Henry positioned himself at Jay's entrance. "All of that beauty is in service to this beauty. Relaxation, stretching, and comfort to permit this pleasure."

He slid into Jay, slow but unceasing. Inevitable for Jay to sheathe him. Inevitable the green sea, dark and intense, deepening his stare. Inevitable the whimpering submission in return, Jay beautiful with his slack jaw and bared neck.

Toys enhanced playtime, but neither metal nor glass nor leather matched their boundless love. For that, they needed only each other. Sated and content, she snuggled beside Jay.

Henry took Jay with unhurried, serene strokes. "You remember this part, don't you, my loves?"

Valentine's.

Curling his arm around her, Jay kissed her forehead. "I'm glad you stayed. Glad you're still staying."

"Me too." Hypnotic, the slide of Henry into Jay and the tender, unguarded gaze he pinned on them both. The doubts of four months ago rang like echoes of another life. "I was so frightened of my own happiness. Now I can't imagine being unhappy here."

She traced Jay along the sexy fucking vee cutting a line through his abdomen. She'd kept her distance that night. Believed these intimacies off-limits. Look but don't touch.

But fuck, the two of them in motion. Kneeling with his knees spread wide, Henry supported Jay in between, lifting his ass off the bed. He hugged Jay's upthrust legs and stroked his thighs. He pumped with life, love, and the promise of forever.

Even Jay's cock, pulsing with definite interest but sluggish response, understood that truth. He'd come hard with her, but three times on a play night was his norm. Maybe he'd like help. On Valentine's, she'd shoved the idle fantasy aside.

Henry laid his hand on hers, the two of them covering Jay's hip. "You sound as though you want something."

Breathy moans flowed beneath his deep calm. Her breathy moans. She snapped her mouth shut. Damn, now she'd denied him the pleasure of her enjoyment. Gathering courage, she licked her lips. "What I wanted in February but was too nervous to ask for."

"Oh?" Henry turned the full force of his expectant gaze on her.

Ask, and it shall be given you. Whatever creed Henry lived by, that rule slotted near the top of the hierarchy.

"I want Jay in my mouth while you're making love to him."

As Jay gasped, Henry's smooth rhythm stuttered. "Washcloth first." He resumed thrusting at a slower pace. "A fresh palate deserves a fresh palette."

Her cotton massage carried away traces of latex and spermicide. Nothing but Jay-skin and Jay-musk for her. Extending her tongue, she descended.

He arched his back, straining toward her. His intermittent whimpers fluttered in his abs beneath her cheek.

Lying on his stomach, she lapped at his cock. Good God, the view.

Jay twitched and grew, his cock filling out his soft skin. His balls swayed in time with Henry's rhythm. Inches away, Henry sank and emerged, over and over, veins like fractal patterns squiggling under his surface. Beautiful.

She slipped her mouth around Jay. He'd gotten too long for lapping, unless she intended to move back. Fuck no.

Henry's quickening thrusts pushed Jay into her. Not a blowjob—Henry making love to both of them. He lacked Jay's muscle definition, but his abs showed now, rolling and flexing to drive him deeper. Rocking with Henry's power, Jay became an unstable platform. Her hair tumbled into her eyes.

Henry swept the strands back in his fist. "So lovely." Strain deepened his baritone into growling bass. "The both of you." He leaned over them, his thrusts rapid and abbreviated, a jolting rhythm. "Together. Exquisite. *Mine.*"

His bellow vibrated in her bones. Three hard thrusts, and on the third Jay joined him. Almost nothing left to give, but he pulsed and jerked all the same, eager to deliver in the midst of Henry's climax. She swallowed with primal satisfaction.

Chapter 3

When the three of them arrived at the club Saturday morning, Henry charmed Caitlyn into sending them back without an announcement. Knocking, he pushed the ornate paneled door from ajar to open. "Bedeviled by the torment of a thousand paper cuts, I see."

Tiny amid the dark, heavy furniture, Emma sat behind a wide desk stacked with papers.

"What flurry of wood pulp has landed on your desk this morning?" Henry strode inside. His presence lightened the shadows collecting along the high ceiling and deep corners. "This is the glamorous work you would have had me take on?"

Deferring with a teasing bow, Jay let Alice enter first. The oversized office cried out for a poker game at the round conference table, the sort that went all night with suit coats slung over seatbacks and women in tight-laced corsets serving whiskey, neat, from silver trays.

"Hardly, Henry." Emma carried on writing as she cast a swift glance at him. "Penning lines is my specialty."

Chuckling, Henry waved his partners into the seats before the glass-topped desk.

The leather supported more than cushioned. Spine straight, Alice perched at the edge with her knees clamped together. The massive furniture, the broad desk, imbued Emma with the power to decide fates with a penstroke. Assessing her suitability for Henry, Emma could find her wanting.

"Truly, I hoped for something similar to what you're doing." Emma signed her missive in an elegant hand. "I thought you might teach an ethics and safety class for dominants."

The heaped papers appeared all of a kind, possibly a form letter for the membership. The individual words stayed stubbornly indiscernible from this side of the desk.

"And I thought we might teach submissives together——a mandatory class in their first thirty days on safe negotiation." With swift grace, Emma folded the letter into thirds and slipped it into an envelope. "Recognizing abuse. Setting limits. Seeking help." As she licked the flap, she raised her eyebrows at Henry. "Things worked out superbly from my perspective."

No kidding. They'd dragged their asses to the club on a Saturday morning for Henry's first class for submissives. Next week, they'd take on dominants.

"Victor always admired your cunning. He got more than he bargained for when he taught you to play." Heavy-handed and welcome, Henry kneaded Alice's shoulders. "I've been blessed to discover that joy twice over."

Not blessing but—"Skill."

"Talent," Emma said, their words overlapping.

As they traded a stare, her flicker of irritation disappeared in the other woman's subtle smile.

"Blessed is good. I'm blessed, too. And I'll let Henry pick his own words." Flashing his tongue at her, Jay drummed the arms of his chair. "We ready to rock this?"

"Certainly." Emma wrote a name across the envelope. *Master* something. "I'll leave this with Caitlyn and walk up with you."

With the letter slotted into a numbered box behind the reception desk, they climbed the grand staircase. Emma, in her flowing white dress with its floral silhouettes in navy, led their troupe. Her low heels matched the blue, naturally. "I've put you on the third floor. The classroom setting seemed appropriate."

The green-ribboned staffer at the second-floor bag check nodded as they passed.

"I appreciate your commitment, Henry." Making the climb, Emma spoke without turning back. "I know you've other calls on your time and skills."

"I wouldn't have done this if I didn't find it valuable and rewarding, Em." Henry rapped his knuckles on the banister. "My time is my own. I choose to spend it in this endeavor."

"Still. Your assistance is a godsend. Things have been sliding." At the top, Emma waited with her back stiff and her face pinched. "Too many things, for too long."

Henry planted his feet beside her and dipped his head. "You might've asked for help earlier, *sverchok*."

The falling tone of Emma's hum suggested otherwise. "Stress does strange things." She pushed a tiny laugh through a strained smile.

"You've seen nervous and confused novices strangling themselves in knots. Grateful for what's given and afraid to be labeled a burden."

Like a woman so afraid of throwing a wrench in the gears she'd segregate herself from her lovers for months while they all silently wished for more togetherness. Alice banged her toes reaching for the next step.

"You haven't been a novice in a long while, Em." Frowning, Henry touched her shoulder. "And you've never been a burden. Either I've been a poor friend, or you've been a skilled liar."

"Or I thought I might handle a few things myself." Arms folded, Emma hugged her elbows. "And discovered a problem larger than I could manage."

"I did, too." Shit, she came off the stairs and tumbled into their conversation with the subtlety of a rodeo clown. "Wanted to handle everything myself at first." No way Emma needed a distraction or a rescue, and she sure as hell wasn't the woman to offer one. And yet, "I got all turned around and panicked."

Rocking back a step, Henry pressed his hand to the middle button of his jacket. He glanced from her to Emma and back again. "I specifically told you—multiple times—to come to me, Alice."

"I didn't realize then how tiny things mattered so much. How they piled up." Did they ever. Festering wounds and unanswered questions were the worst. "I thought I'd only bother you for big stuff. But big-small is a slippery emotional slope. I couldn't calculate the difference."

"You didn't accept that those decisions belonged in my hands." Cupping her cheek, Henry rolled his thumb across her lips. "You harbored a nascent, unformed concept of submission."

She did still. Her whole system came together patchwork quilt-style. Complex systems like sex and love deserved the certainty of Euclidean geometry or Newtonian mechanics, not all this quantum Heisenberg shit. What she wouldn't give for a fucking manual.

"I was nascenter than Alice." Hands in his pockets, Jay teetered heel-toe. "I didn't ask questions I should've or protect myself. Giving away all the decisions? Two words: thrill ride."

"You, my dear boy—" Henry tugged him forward by his shirt and slapped a kiss on his mouth. "You had been steered down the wrong road."

"I like your map better." With his spreading grin, Jay proclaimed *like* an understatement. "Even if the trails are all named 'Trust' this and 'Safety' that. I memorized them so I can recite 'em in my sleep."

"I wanted you safe even if you chose another dominant." Henry smoothed the wrinkles from Jay's shirt.

"That's why this class will succeed." Her steps brisk, Emma waved them past the first three doors. "You're an exceptionally ethical man, and your pets come from either end of the trust spectrum. Look at their balance now."

Exposure rankled. Jay, sure, he'd been hard-wired with an inability to withhold trust. And, yeah, she'd gone into this unwilling to trust people with her emotions. Extending trust to Henry and Jay had been slow and scary. Adding Emma—knowledgeable, overly insightful Emma—she'd get there. When she had more data.

Emma opened a door and flipped on the lights. Illuminating her face, they captured porcelain translucence. A thin surface of delicate perfection rested on a wistful hollow beneath. "They'll make excellent assistants."

Not the same, though. Had Emma's husband been alive, five'd getcha ten the two of them would take on prized pupils for further study. Handing the job to Henry smacked of passing the torch. So long as Emma refused to grapple with the problem, no one supplanted Victor. But once she'd gotten up the courage to ask, Henry's initial rejection must've stung.

What the hell. Some premenstrual surging hormonal solidarity shit had to be causing her uncomfortable sympathizing. Worse than cramps.

"Well?" Emma ushered them into the space, her gaze on Henry. "Will this do?"

The setup mimicked a high-school classroom, right down to the old-fashioned, one-armed desks. Jay swung into a front-row seat, slouched low, and raised his hand insistently.

Unbuttoning his coat, Henry leaned his ass against the teacher's desk. His crossed arms tightened his dress shirt. Gravity turned his pants into showpieces outlining his extended legs.

Fucking delicious.

"You have a question?" Henry smoldered, his gaze low and intense as coals waiting for the prod to stir him into flames. "Speak."

Arching his hips, Jay almost managed to pull off casual resettling. Gave himself away wetting his parted lips. "I wanna show how well I perform in this subject." His impish undertone disappeared under Henry's unbroken stare. "Do you allow oral presentations for extra credit, sir?"

Their heat throbbed in her chest and rooted her to the floor. In her imagination, Henry lowered his zipper, stood his cock upright, and ordered Jay to his knees. Her lovers sang with muffled whimpers and low-toned growls.

"See me after class." Stern-voiced, Henry lifted his chin. "Be prepared to show your work."

In a full-body shudder, Jay dropped his head back. "Oh yeah. This room works for me."

"Show-off." She teased through her laughter. In the contest for her favorite Jay, happy, sexy, confident Jay won hands-down. He'd challenged some insecurities Wednesday at tea. Henry's presence today made boundary-pushing safer. Still, he surprised the hell out of her, giving his playfulness a sexual charge in front of their hostess.

"The room ought to do fine, Emma, thank you." Henry patted the teacher's desk and left it behind, striding down the aisle with a disciplinarian's focus. "The atmosphere might encourage our pupils to be attentive."

The blackboard at the front held chalk in the tray. She battled the perverse urge to write *Master Henry* in elegant script and claim the seat beside Jay. Not their purpose today. Maybe another time. Leaving the chalk, she wiped dust from her fingers.

"I can have the staff bring in a whiteboard setup if you'd prefer." As Henry measured the space, Emma tracked him with a subtle swivel. "Though the old-school blackboard seems more your speed."

Jay chortled. Henry barked a laugh. Emma smiled with a touch of pink in her cheeks.

Alice pasted on a grin. Henry's aversion to technology and appreciation for the personal touch wasn't a secret, but Emma's familiarity nudged the border of flirtation.

"No board necessary, Em. A static presentation wouldn't suit our purpose." Finishing his circuit, Henry laid his hand on Jay. "I've no intention of dictating to our guests. I am not their master. Encouraging and modeling discussion and interaction they take home to their partners or practice as they seek new ones matters far more than a list of rules on any board."

With a graceful nod, Emma conceded. "I'll leave you to it. I'm certain your able helpers will keep your hunger for power in check."

Distinguishing friendly teasing from patronizing condescension on Emma's lips proved impossible. Or she needed to get her ears examined. Insecurity wouldn't show up in a routine physical, though.

Jay dug his shoulder into Henry's hip. "We'll keep him focused. If he's lean and hungry all morning, he'll make a meal of us—I mean, of power—tonight."

Laughing, Emma bid them farewell.

* * * *

Four arrivals, and every one a man.

At Henry's command, Jay hopped to on greeter duty. The room swelled with a mix of masculine swagger and self-conscious laughter. At least the smell didn't mimic a locker room.

Standing with Henry behind the teacher's desk, she stayed in his orbit. They'd run through the class twice Thursday at home, a great non-sex distraction but also preparation for what Henry would expect of his assistants. Making everyone comfortable enough to listen and participate topped the list. Bro-wattage bursting the meter, Jay locked that shit down.

A fifth prospective student hovered in the hall. Yet another twentysomething male, this one in jeans and a logo t-shirt.

Stepping out, Jay extended his hand. "Hey, I'm Jay. You here for class? My dom's coaching. Handing out tips for offense, defense, special teams—any position you're looking to play, this class is gonna up your game."

The student's response faded beneath the others' chatter.

With an equally quiet reply, Jay jerked his thumb over his shoulder.

Leaning around him, the baby-faced new guy stared through the open door at her and Henry. "Dude, no way."

Jay rocked on his heels. "All mine, man. I'm serious—you work on the approach and knowing what you wanna offer, and it's starting line every night."

"Fuck, it's third-string out here. You hustle hard and you're lucky you get three minutes of playing time all season."

"I remember. Once that desperation gets in your head, the game's over. The only offers come from teams you gotta say no to, but you won't, because who the hell else is bidding, right? Warps your skills. You gotta say no. You got to."

"This the shit your class is gonna teach?"

"Hell yeah."

Student number five sauntered inside.

For a man who hated carnivals, Jay made a top-notch barker. He roped in a sixth and a seventh, the noise level rising with each addition.

Henry stayed out of the fray, assessing his troops from the bunker behind Desk Hill.

Turning her back to the room, Alice relaxed against the desk. Nice ass-height. Comfy resting spot. "Are they what you expected?"

"More or less." He matched her quiet tone. "Perhaps not what you imagined?"

"I thought there'd be fewer guys." Or none, or ones less rowdy and more—submissive. "The tea only had Jay."

"Early afternoon, midweek, with talk and sharing as the stated objective, favors a different crowd than the weekend lure of actionable information to assist in acquiring a partner." Hands clasped behind his back, Henry bent to her ear. "More than a few men enjoy being ruled by a powerful woman. The poster image for the scene, as it were—the whip-wielding, leather-clad woman in spiked heels with a male pet—is a classic for a reason."

Intoxication. Submissives drank in dominance like a cocktail fusing with their cells, pushing arousal toward the critical line between heightened awareness and subspace. "You think they're all looking for one?"

"Possibly." He surveyed the milling students. "Professional dominatrices do good business, but pay-for-play isn't allowed here, and sex is rarely included in a professional session." As his eyes narrowed, he gained a bristling undertone in his voice. "Expert amateurs are less common, and these men might welcome any edge to attract one."

A couple of the guys had abandoned the pretense of conversation in favor of watching her. She added her stare to Henry's.

The tall, wide-eyed blond bumped a desk in his retreat. The stocky crewcut bowed his head and gazed up at her, his grin slow and spreading.

Holy shit. "They think I'm—"

Henry hauled her along the desk. As he boxed her in and dipped her backward, she caught herself on his chest. The smooth underside of his jaw where he'd shaved this morning invited her tongue.

Sighing, she tipped her head. Behind her, the submissive had traded his smile for a pouty sulk. She bit back a laugh. "Guess they don't see me in charge anymore."

"*They* don't need to." Alpha posturing satisfied, Henry resettled her upright. "Jay delights in your control."

"But leather and heels? A whip?" Not in a million years.

"Jay likes pain for the sake of pain no more than you do." Henry kissed her temple. "But he'd enjoy playing your pet for a day." Green eyes flashed.

Shivering, she fingered his shirt. A thinking Henry was a creative one, and a creative Henry showed his love in panty-drenching performances.

"A consideration for a later date." Glancing away, he smiled. "We have other obligations."

On approach, Jay waggled his eyebrows. "In a compromising position with the teacher, Alice? Afraid you're getting an A-minus, wanna boost that grade?"

"Says the student who begged for a shot at extra credit."

"You can earn yours now." Reaching under Henry's arm, he tugged her wrist. "Collect a student for me. Your fan stalker's hanging out in the hall."

"Her what?" Henry took a half-step toward the door.

"Tease." Hopping off the desk, she smacked the back of her hand against Jay's chest. "I think he means the church mouse from tea."

"Hey, she took my seat and made big eyes at you." Hands spread wide, Jay poured on the arched-brow, pouty-lipped puppy stare. "Total stalker move. I can't be letting other subs think you're not taken."

Men. First Henry, now Jay.

"You're adorably possessive." Kissing Jay's cheek, she checked in with Henry. "Mind if I—" She nodded at the door.

"Please."

She popped outside. Fifteen feet down the hall, Leah took deep breaths and studied the floor. Or her shoes, pale yellow sandals matching her sundress. Operation good cheer, act one: The greeting. "Hi, Leah."

Leah jumped.

"It's nice to see you again." Pretending she hadn't witnessed the reaction, she covered the ground between them and stuck out her hand. "I didn't know you were coming."

"Hi, Alice." Leah fiddled with the closed top button of her thin cardigan. The shade about matched her blush. "I didn't know, either."

"You decided at the last minute?" Handshake maneuver sputtering out, she went for the girl version, linking elbows. Smooth as a machine-tumbled stone. "I bet you know all this stuff already. You have a master, right?"

"Master dropped me off downstairs. He said this class would be good for me." Leah rubbed one foot against the back of her other leg. "Master says I have to develop my confidence. Do you think he'd be disappointed in me for not going right in?"

"I think we can walk in together, and class will be fantastic." Estimating what Leah's dominant would make of her behavior would be looking into a data black hole. "Do you always call him 'Master'?"

"As much as I can." Strolling at her side, Leah kept her head down, but the tightness in her body unwound. "Always at his home and inside this club. I have to get special permission anywhere else."

"Sounds like a deep commitment." Asking whether her devotion to the man or the lifestyle had come first would be too personal. Leah forming complete sentences counted as a victory. "Have you been together long?"

"Since last semester. Master's a professor. Not my professor." Tightening her grip on Alice's arm, Leah shot her a hasty glance. "He's not like that."

"A man with ethical standards." Her pair stood chatting beside the blackboard. "I know a few. Good guys to hang on to." She steered Leah to the front. At least Jay would be a familiar face for her to start socializing.

"Sweetheart, look who I found."

"Miss Leah. I remembered you being taller." Delivering an over-the-top bow, Jay produced his gentlest charm smile. "I suppose that'll happen when I spend all my time on the floor. I like to curl up there when I'm nervous, though."

Blush in full flame, Leah offered a quiet, "me, too."

Getting better. An encouraging nudge ought to help. "Leah, I'd like to introduce you to my master, Henry. He's teaching the class."

Head bowed, Leah stood silent.

"Good morning, Leah." Henry rolled out his smooth baritone. "Did your master select your outfit for you?"

Studying the floor, Leah nodded.

"He chose well. He must care for you very much. Are you his pampered pet, submissive Leah?" He added stern emphasis on her title.

"He calls me kitten, sir." Leah whispered. "He brushes my hair. I like that."

"As you should. A well-behaved pet is her master's joy." Formal and polite, Henry kept his distance. "Please extend my regards to yours."

Leah glanced up, her smile brief but sweet. "Thank you, sir, I will."

Behind Leah's back, Alice pointed two fingers toward the front row.

Henry issued a subtle nod. "Alice, perhaps you'd care to sit with your friend? Up front, please, where I may keep an eye on you."

"Thank you, sir." Infusing the teasing title with warmth, she kissed his cheek. Love lived in moments when their intellectual gears turned in synchronized motion. Made the tune-ups worth the work.

While she coaxed Leah into shedding some shyness, Jay ushered in a trio of women and a handful of stragglers.

Checking his watch, Henry called to Jay. "That's time. The door, please."

They'd drawn a crowd of eleven men and six women. Not bad for a first class with a limited publicity window. Taking the seat behind her, Jay dragged his desk closer.

Henry tugged his shirt cuffs into neat alignment. "Those of you concerned about the potential for sexual acts today may relax. I expect this class will prove to be the most people and the least action this room has hosted in its long history."

Laughter emerged from a dozen students.

"Those of you hopeful about the potential for sexual acts today"——Henry delivered a stern frown at Crewcut Boy who'd eyed her up——"I'm sorry to say you'll be disappointed."

Sitting sideways in her front-row corner seat, she oscillated between his casual command and the attendees' intense concentration. Talk of the club's formal reporting policy for harassment and line-crossing caused dropped gazes and strained faces.

"No one desires to have their consensual kinks become fodder for the court system. That's understandable." Ignoring the furtive nods, Henry removed his suit coat, folded it neatly, and laid it across the desk. "All the more reason we must take special care to police ourselves."

"Report somebody, right." The tall blond who'd retreated under her scrutiny hunched over his crossed arms. "Like the response won't be. 'You're a sub, you were asking for it.'"

Worming his hands around her chair back, Jay found sanctuary beneath her arm. She twined their thumbs together.

"You all met Emma when you arrived?" Henry waited for a nod, mumble, or respectful *yes, sir* from the entire class. "Trust her discretion. If you wish to privately alert the club to a troublesome member, ask for her downstairs. If not for yourself, then for the safety of future players." Sighing, he settled against the front of the desk. "But after the fact isn't ideal, is it? The hurt has been dealt. The pain gnaws with little rat teeth, a dull ache and a sharp pinch you cannot shake. Shame. Self-doubt."

Five bewildered faces floated in a sea of seventeen. The rest followed the current with the tight shoulders, thin lips, and knowing eyes Jay shared.

"If you find yourself beyond your limits and wish to stop mid-scene, the club's current policy requires the recognition of universal safewords—green for go, yellow for caution, red for stop." Henry enunciated each with crisp care. "A shout of 'red' will draw the attention of monitors or other players to assist."

If she'd understood safewords worked outside scenes and been able to get the word out, her first visit would've gone a hell of a lot differently.

"Our hoped-for outcome is to avoid that situation." Somber and intent, Henry projected fear-easing confidence with his wide stance and steady voice. "Though the goal isn't always possible, knowledge and skills bring it closer."

Standing in front of Cal, her throat tight and her heart racing, she'd thought only of protecting Jay. Her cry for help borrowed more from a dominant challenge than a submissive surrender.

Squeezing her hand, Jay puppy-tilted his head.

She squeezed back, her headshake a subtle *it's nothing*. Not now, anyway. She'd talk about their encounter later, if any attendees raised a related question and Henry called on her to elaborate.

"Just as we educate our dominant members to respect limits, we encourage our submissive members to set limits."

The wave of reactions spanned tart nods and slouched shoulders, eager smiles and skeptical stares. In his slow scan, Henry no doubt assessed and catalogued each.

"As saying 'no' can be difficult, we will practice, today, the art of bargaining—saying no and saying no without saying no." He clapped once. "Lecture over."

Reassigning seats, he set off a flurry of movement. Like snowflakes, the class drifted into position.

"Rows one and four, you'll stay in these places. You're dominants in this exercise. You command the space."

She held back a laugh at the straightening backs and stern expressions of trying-on-dominance rippling down the outer rim.

"Two and three, you'll rotate clockwise." Finger twirling, Henry demonstrated the speed-dating style exercise. "With each topic, you'll start from scratch, negotiating with a new dominant. Submissives, your answer is always *no*. I want to see a robust defense."

Wide eyes and deep breaths spread like a contagion. By the end of class, they ought to see more confident determination. Hoped to, at least.

"Dominants, first round: Convince your potential partner he or she is exceptionally special to you despite your ten-minute acquaintance and that you know a private, intimate place the two of you ought to go." Slipping into the last open seat, Henry evened out the pairings. "Begin."

Alice mimicked a guy-lean and touched the desk across from her. "I'm feeling this great long-term energy between us, but I want you comfortable enough to be honest. The crowd's got you rattled. All these people judging you. How about I take you somewhere private and we talk about making your fantasies real. Would you like that?"

Leah blushed. "You sound like a nice dominant."

This could take a while.

Chapter 4

Henry might hate a mid-afternoon surprise. He might strip her, tie her to the bed, and leave her until he deemed the hour a fitting time for play.

As Alice walked the four blocks between the subway platform and home, the eighty-three percent of her not nervous about his reaction to her new implant eagerly anticipated his arousal. In her favorite scenario, she barely got the words out before he yanked her pants down and fucked her against the door.

He wouldn't. Part of her wanted him to want to, begged him to lose control the way she did when he touched her. That split fell closer to sixty-forty. She depended on him to stay in control of her safety so she didn't have to.

Maybe he'd bend her over the table for sentimental reasons.

She unlocked the apartment door, and—nothing. Sex god Henry might be, but he wasn't omniscient. Laughing at herself, she dropped her things on the side table. As she toed off her shoes, their soft thud formed the sole sound in empty rooms.

Even the master bedroom revealed no master. Either he'd gone out, maybe to meet a client or his agent, or he was painting behind the lone closed door. She'd never interrupted his work. Her desire didn't qualify as an emergency.

Damn. She'd allowed spontaneous, urgent need to overrule her. But in the excited rush of accomplishment, only sharing with him would do. Gnawing indecision tasted of bile.

Henry exited his studio, shutting the door behind himself. "Alice?"

As he had when he'd made their breakfast, he stood in bare feet. White cotton pants, dabbed with colorful finger-smears, flowed loose around his legs. Drawstrings dangled and teased.

"I thought I heard someone come home."

A seeming concession to formality, his button-down, too, wrapped him in a thin layer of relaxation. Untucked and short-sleeved, the pale blue-green sea beckoned her to break the surface.

"It's not quite two."

Her heart dropped a beat between her legs. Fuck, she loved him casual as much as she loved him formal.

"Is something the matter? Are you ill?" Frowning, he beckoned her over. "You're distinctly pale."

Not all of her. Rushing blood made her plenty rosy elsewhere.

"No, no." She fumbled for command of her tongue. God forbid she give him the wrong impression. "I'm not sick." She stopped beyond arm's reach, iffy on controlling herself any closer. Bands of steel compressed her chest. "But I did see a doctor. And then I came home to you."

Green eyes widened before they narrowed. Henry tipped his head. Nostrils flaring, he stepped toward her.

She battled the urge to bolt. Not to escape, no. To make him stake his claim.

"You say nothing's wrong, yet you've come seeking me in the middle of the day." Circling left, he stalked her, his voice deep, his words slow. "I can't help but think something is right, then." Idly dragging her shirt up her back, he sent tingles across her skin. "Do you wish to share with me? Something you want to be mine, sweet girl?"

Mouth dry, she nodded.

"Tell me about your doctor's appointment." His steps brought him around in front, maintaining the distance she'd originally imposed.

He was going commando. His thin pants draped over his hardening cock, a sculpture waiting to be unveiled. She'd find the shape with her tongue, and he'd fit—

His amused hum startled her from her stare.

"I—you said to think about it, and I did. I talked over the options with my ob/gyn." She raised her left arm. "So, here I am."

Stiff and silent, he watched her with darkening eyes. God, why wasn't he saying anything?

"It's good for three years. An easy swap with my pill." Her shirt hid the tiny insertion site. Duh. She dropped her arm. "It started working, uh, immediately."

"Immediately." Inhaling through his teeth, he stepped nearer. "You've arranged this"—another step—"to come home to me early"—a third, their chests almost touching—"and offer this gift?"

Infinite distance yawned in the sliver between them. The momentary pinch in her upper arm faded beneath the anticipation she'd nurtured since she'd known today she might finally feel him flesh to flesh. "Please."

"My sweet Alice." He gripped her waist, lifting her even as his lips completed the circuit with her own. He navigated the hall with her clinging to his hips. "This is the secret you've been keeping from me for nearly three weeks."

"You knew the whole time?" She'd called the day after Memorial Day. Their talk on the deck at Santa's cabin had started her down this road.

"I suspected. You forget—understanding your inner workings is my responsibility." Lips soft against her ear, he kneaded her ass in both hands. "As with a great many things about you, it's a pleasurable privilege indeed."

"So this is another example"—she nibbled his neck—"of you waiting"— tasted the strong slope of his shoulder—"for me to come to you?"

Henry jammed her back to the wall beside the bedroom door. Thrusting, he drove her clothes between wet lips eager to part for him.

She bucked and moaned for more.

Solid and all-encompassing, he leaned in. "I can be an exceptionally patient man, Alice."

Her body tried to flex, an involuntary shudder, but his weight pinned her.

"Perhaps we ought to see how patient *you* can be."

"Today?" Her voice came out an octave too high. He could make a game of testing her. She might've teased her way into not getting him inside her.

"Mmm." He swayed and nudged as he inhaled along her jaw. "No, not today." His sucking kisses throbbed below her ear. "Even my patience will meet its limits today."

"Even yours?" Her chest pushed forward as his retreated in equal measure. If his patience had limits, she'd caused them. Pleased him by switching to long-term birth control and coming home to him. Pleased him by wanting him inside without barriers.

"You've never entrusted this privilege to another." He rumbled in low tones thick as polymer resin, sealing out other sounds. "Being your first is quite stimulating." He lifted her from the wall. "But not so much so I can't manage better than the hallway."

Her thrumming body dubbed the hallway perfectly reasonable, but then she'd thought of little else for hours. As he sat on the bed with her gathered in his lap, he left her at a loss. He hadn't issued a command. She curled her fingers in thin cotton linen. His shirt buttons rolled like river stones under her thumbs.

"It's all right, Alice." Leisurely kissing her mouth, her throat, the upper slopes of her breasts, he slipped off her blouse with unhurried attention. "Undress me if the urge takes you."

Permission blanketed her with comforting weight. She pushed his shirt wide, baring his chest, long before he finished unbuttoning hers.

Stroking his solid flesh and crinkling hair, she shoved aside the mental voice demanding to know when she'd grown accustomed to waiting for permission. The pre-Henry Alice would've clung to control, and now she craved his.

Her blouse slid to the floor, bra following after. Supporting her back in spread hands, Henry bent over her and claimed her breast.

With his heated mouth, he set her squirming against his cock. The moment sparked with strange intimacy, as if she'd never done this. Absurd. She'd lost count of their sexual escapades, and the last time had been less than two days ago.

He rolled, sprawling her on her back, the comforter soft and floaty beneath. Knowing for weeks, he might have something special waiting. The dresser between the windows——

"No games, my beautiful girl." Hand warm on her cheek, he turned her to face him and kissed her forehead. "Some things deserve to be appreciated on their own."

Her eyes stung. Regardless of the trappings, their love was special. To Henry, she was special. Her voice failed.

"I love you, Alice," he whispered. "I think you know, but as I thoroughly enjoy saying the words, I'm afraid you'll have to put up with my utterances."

He skimmed her with deft hands, gathering her remaining clothes with the unhurried precision he'd used on her blouse. Standing silent at the foot of the bed, he roamed her nudity with his gaze alone. He folded his pants over his arm once and again, digging into rebellious fabric refusing to take a crease.

With the jerk of his cock, belated understanding jolted her. His imposed distance and deliberate movements guarded against ending their pleasure too quickly.

She breathed deep, a failed attempt at calm. He might be able to control himself, but she couldn't equal the feat. Anticipation made her clench, kept her lips wet and plump, set her clit jumping.

"An experience to be savored." Pushing her up the bed, he spread her knees. "I want all of your attention." With a finger-stroke, he sent her hips upward, chasing a firmer touch. "You know the feel of my fingers?"

Her answer straddled the line between a moan and a "yes."

He parted her lips and teased her entrance. Her muscles contracted.

"You feel me circling? How slick you are, how your body yearns to pull me in?" He thrust.

She ground against the heel of his hand.

"Focus. When I do this——"

Unf, fuck, a miniquake rippled down her fault lines.

"——you feel my knuckles shift and bend, don't you? Curving and bumping tight walls."

Every inch. Rocking, she met his strokes.

"Your exquisite flesh grips no matter how I move." He brought her close but never edged far enough to send her over. "Your body strives to lock us together, to surround and hold me."

If she held him locked to her, inside her, he equaled her strength with his unceasing gaze.

"Squeeze for me, Alice. Make me feel you."

She poured her tremors into one focused clench.

Eyelids fluttering, he sucked in a gratifyingly shaky breath and exhaled a hum. "Exactly so."

His voice had sunk deep and low. Hearing him demanded concentration, faded all else to nothing. The bedrock of his voice and the slide of his fingers consumed her.

"Give me your hand." He guided her to his cock and controlled her movement, a wisp over his heat, over soft skin and firm pressure beneath. "Nothing between us. Not ever again."

In his grasp, she traced the underside of his cock. Taut and thick, he possessed infinitesimal ridges and furrows outlined for her.

"From now on you'll feel me just as you feel my fingers inside you."

She circled the curved flare below the head, the smoother, tighter skin. For her, please God. Please Henry.

"A snug fit, flesh to flesh, nothing to hide texture and heat from us both." He teased her to the edge and slipped free as she whimpered. Tongue wide and flat, he lapped her from his fingers and sucked them clean. "Nothing to diminish our pleasure in each other." He lowered himself over her.

Arching, she welcomed the prickling softness of his chest hair brushing her nipples. She burned where they touched, yet she craved the inferno. His cock grazed her inner thigh, and she raised her knees.

"Soon." He parted her lips with his cock, rubbing up and across her clit.

Panting, focused on a single point of contact, she abandoned attempts at control and writhed unashamed.

"Squeeze for me." Green depths commanded obedience. "Again."

Her motion might have been voluntary or the conditioned response of her body to his authority. Clenching her muscles, she smothered aching emptiness. Her whimper turned pleading. "Now?"

"Now."

His deep thrust carried confirmation, swift and hard and unlike any time before. Because this moment *was* different or because he'd made it seem so, she didn't know. They were utterly naked to each other, a feast for an unrealized hunger swarming her. He overwhelmed her senses with his groaning pleasure, and she quaked in orgasm with him buried deep.

Vision blurred, ears buzzing, she blinked to awareness as her hips slowed their uncontrolled dance. Her fingers and toes tingled. Her scalp, too, where he'd curled his hand in her hair. His breath gusted hot and harsh against her neck. She ducked her chin, and he entwined their tongues.

He held his cock motionless until their mouths broke apart. No, not entirely. He hadn't thrust, but he twitched. The way his cock jumped when she palmed him just right. She contracted.

Henry hissed a curse between clenched teeth. "You're determined to make me come quickly, my little minx."

"S'only fair." She floated, lighter than air and so powerful. As if she could control him as effortlessly as he controlled her, with a single word, a single movement. "You made me come with one thrust." As she pecked his cheek, her giggles spilled out. "New record."

"A record I'm pleased to have you hold." Nuzzling, he dotted her face with seemingly random kisses. "Not one I'd care to emulate."

"But I want to feel you," she whispered, gripping tight to hear his response, a low rumble on the cusp of breaking. "All that power dammed up behind your self-restraint, pouring into me." With the right incentive, shaping truth like he did, she might find his release valve. "I want to feel you the way I do when you're in my mouth, when nothing's between us and your cock swells against my tongue and the warm rush——"

His groan drowned her out. He bucked in short thrusts, hard and pounding. With her need sated, nothing distracted her from his passion, fucking beautiful and powerful, each sensation as intense as the first. She hadn't imagined the intimacy. No trick of words or anticipation had created this hyperawareness.

Never cresting, her wave of pleasure shook her all the same. She urged him on as they crashed in a tangle of greedy hands and needy moans.

Driving forward, he pinned her to the mattress under his full weight, his cock buried. A scalding pulse of heat sent tremors cascading to the ends of her world. As her head fell back, he closed his mouth over her throat. His growl vibrated against her skin.

They lay entangled, breathing in the quiet, the air rich with the tang of sweat and sex. He rubbed circles on her hip. When he raised his head, she fought a throaty whine and tensing muscles. Cleanup and cuddling appealed, but the moment of loss when he left her body always stung.

Cradling her tight, he rolled onto his side without pulling out. "We've no need to rush, my sweet girl." He hummed a light melody and caressed her lower back. "Nothing to fret over, to check and discard. Only the two of us, our bodies joined."

She burrowed into the curve of his neck and relaxed. So focused on getting him inside, naked, she'd neglected to consider the aftereffects. No condom meant no hasty departure.

"I like it." Lying in his arms, she embraced the novelty of his cock softening inside her. His satisfaction and his body's slow retreat were her accomplishment. "I like feeling you. I like not rushing to separate."

He nipped her ear. "I'm rather fond of it myself."

Biology eventually conquered them. His cock slipped free, and her sigh followed. He nudged her to turn over. Resettling her in the shelter of his body, he draped an arm over her hip.

"You've many lovely qualities inside and out." Stroking her breasts and belly, he tweaked her nipple. "But my favorite may be your forthright honesty."

An honest woman would've included Henry in her deliberation. "But I kept a secret—okay, tried to keep one—from you for weeks."

Chuckling, he tickled her ear. "You investigated the matter, I'm certain. Consulted expert information to determine the efficacy, safety, reliability and so forth of the options."

"Of course." Important decisions deserved a methodical approach.

He kissed her shoulder blade. "As did I, before I made the suggestion."

The faulty light bulb in her head flickered on. He wouldn't have recommended anything he thought would be unsafe for her. He applied care when introducing anything new to their bed.

"You took what time you needed to complete your investigation"—he transferred his kisses to her neck—"and evaluate your findings."

"I, well——" The gulf between artist and engineer narrowed. Different reasons and perspectives, but she and Henry operated with the same thoroughness and clarity of purpose. "Yes."

"When you grew confident in your understanding, you made your decision." He swept low, combing her short curls, and lower still, cupping her sex. "Did you call for an appointment then, Alice?"

"Yeah." The heel of his hand formed a perfect pressure point for rocking. Her lazy post-orgasm contentment shifted toward renewed arousal.

"And booked the first opening your schedule accommodated." He traced the seam of her lips, sticky and slow to part.

"Uh-huh." Were they having a conversation? She'd lost track, and the blame lay squarely on him and his probing fingers.

"And that was today."

"Mm-hmm." The excitement of coming home. The nightstand clock swore less than sixty minutes had passed since she'd slipped off her shoes.

"After which, you came straight to me. Direct in your desire, telling me what you'd done and what you needed from me, unable to wait for the end of your workday or to hold your tongue until suppertime. Tell me, dearest"—calm, reasonable conversation descended into seductive tones—"wherein lies the dishonesty?"

His thrust superseded her answer. Curling his fingers inside her, he drew out a moan.

She shuddered into amused certainty. "You don't want a washcloth?"

"Cleanup would be premature." He used his hold to push their bodies together. "Seeing as how I intend to feel you around me at least once more this afternoon." His growing interest in another round prodded her backside. "I don't expect a cloth will prove adequate."

Their initial urgency dissolved, he toyed with her, teasing angles and positions in a long, slow fuck. Demanding she describe the experience each time he entered, he let her grip the head before he withdrew, rubbing and bumping all over again.

She tumbled onto her back, her ankles hooked over his shoulders. With his broad chest, he wedged her thighs to her stomach. Her knees bounced above her breasts as his thrusts tipped her pelvis and drove her across the bed. The headboard braced her shaky arms. Keeping her pinned and helpless, he woke shivering delights in synapses that only fired in his presence. Lungs heaving and muscles burning, she burst into orgasm with him at his low command.

Forceful, overpowering dominant Henry evaporated in the aftermath, the tender, thoughtful lover coming to the fore with a flicker of green eyes. He rolled her on top and insisted she stretch her legs. Held her with steady, calming hands. Tucked her hair behind her ears as he kissed her cheeks, her forehead, her lips.

"All right, my sweet girl?" He brushed her left bicep above the thin line where her birth control implant had gone in. "Not too sore?"

"Just-right sore." Nuzzling his ear, she basked in his closeness and cataloged the softening of his cock. *Protective* best described the emotion, his vulnerability measured in her emptiness. "I love you, Henry."

He kissed her with patient passion, a simple declaration of affection. They lay sated and sleepy for most of an hour before he carried her to the shower. As they soaped each other, the warm sweep of their hands renewed his erection.

She stood under falling water, one leg over his hip as he supported her thigh and cupped her ass. He thrust with slow, gentle strokes. Orgasm gleamed far in the distance, forgotten. Enjoying each other's bodies mattered more than chasing fireflies. Before Henry, she'd never considered sex might be just this, too—closeness, affection, and love.

By the time they'd dried off and redressed, six o'clock loomed. Jay would arrive any minute, ready to help with dinner, possibly horny and eager to play. "Henry?"

His answering hum echoed as he pulled steaks, vegetables, and a hunk of blue cheese in wax paper from the refrigerator.

"What about Jay?" She wouldn't leave him out, but her mind seemed bent on reliving the afternoon, affixing better understanding to everything else she associated with the name *Henry.* Cuddling would be enough for her tonight.

"I've a few thoughts about that." Dinner fixings deposited on the kitchen island, Henry tugged her toward him. "Something special."

He talked. She listened. They settled on a course of action with time to spare, in full agreement. When their beloved ball of energy came home, bubbling over with stories about his day, neither interrupted to spoil the surprise. *Happy early birthday, Jay. You're going to have a fabulous Friday night.*

Chapter 5

While Jay set the table for Friday dinner, Alice struggled to act business-as-usual. Henry intended to crank the best night of the week to eleven for Jay's thirtieth birthday surprises. For the first time, she knew how he intended the night to go from first kiss to climactic finale.

In blissful ignorance, Jay shared a story about the dog walker he'd encountered in a cramped elevator. Calm and encouraging, Henry asked all the natural questions.

Breathe. Relax. Laugh at the punch line. Review instructions for a fucking awesome night. Review instructions in case Jay panicked. Had he been ten thousand kinds of nervous with Henry's instructions on repeat before their nights together?

"...think Alice's day went as good as mine." Dishes in place, Jay abandoned the table and swept her up in a hug. "She's got faraway eyes."

Henry skirted the island and wrapped his arms around them both. Laying his head on Jay's shoulder, he tipped his forehead against hers. "Our girl often has much on her mind." In one confident gaze, he clipped her concern. If all went well, they'd share this position horizontally by the night's end. "Not all bad. Perhaps anticipation carries her eyes ahead of the clock."

"I do look forward to Friday nights." Pursing her lips, she planted a barely-there kiss on Jay. "The new experiences are top-notch."

Tonight they'd be doubly so. Jay hadn't been inside her Wednesday or yesterday, either, because making him wear a condom when he didn't have to was dishonest and unfair, and letting him go bare would've spoiled the surprise.

"If we wish to keep Alice in the here and now, we ought to offer her an enticing view." Henry scraped his teeth along Jay's neck.

Wriggly and whimpering, Jay rocked between them.

"Run along to your room and shed your clothes, please." With a growl for Jay, Henry released them. "You'll dine au naturel."

Jay scurried around the corner.

Leaning back, she tracked him down the hall and into the bedroom. "You're clear."

"For but a moment." Henry rounded the island and opened the low cabinet. "He'll be quick." A pot lid chimed. "Then we shall see what we shall see." Reaching across the counter, he placed a sacred trust in her hands. "If you'll do the honor?"

She babied the cuffs as if handling the world's official kilogram prototype, a rare and delicate treasure. Centered on Jay's place setting, they rested in reverent offering. Her exhalation shuddered through her.

Henry caught her up before she'd registered him. Hands overlapping on her abdomen, he nudged her with his chin. "Merely a starter set," he whispered. As she leaned back, he held her steady. "If he isn't ready, the night will be equally lovely without them."

"I know." Her hands looked small over the top of his. Slim. Pale. Fragile. "I just worry."

"You seek the results before you've performed the experiment." Comforting and safe, he swayed with her. "Our boy will give all he's able. As will you." With a head-top kiss, he warmed her. "Your confidence will help him. Can you find it for me, sweet girl?" Henry pep talk. His low rumble soothed as much as his truth. "Trust your capabilities. Trust I know the extent of them. Trust our love will help him stretch his boundaries and rebuild the strength to love himself."

"I can. I will." Bare feet slapped against hardwood in the hall. "Showtime. You have mine?"

He tickled her stomach. "Hidden up my sleeve."

Her squirming flight pressed them closer. "So that's how the magic happens."

"Magic?" Jay skidded to a stop and swung in a circle, arms flung wide. "One naked me, at your service. Izzat better, Alice?" As he whirled, his cock bobbed against his thigh. "I'm a fabulous view."

Fuck yeah he was. A spire of lean muscle, slim and solid, narrowing at his waist—but most beautiful of all, his flashing smile.

"Woo. Dizzy." Wobbling to a halt, he planted his hand on the table. Strong, tanned fingers lined up alongside his fork. He jerked and froze.

Henry, tightening his arms around her, kept her heart in her chest.

Jay traced the cuff.

Her fingers tingled with the memory of soft edges and rougher Velcro flaps. The pull. the restraint. had jumpstarted her clit like live wires. Jay had given her an incredible night. She wouldn't do less for him.

"What's this?" Jay whispered. His fingertips stayed on the cuff.

"Welcome to your birthday dinner." Henry matched Jay's soft tone, minus the slight tremble. "The birthday boy deserves a party favor."

Jay squirmed in a naked dance of bowed-head, lip-chewing fidgets. "My birthday's not until next weekend."

"Your gifts are ready now." Henry ran his hands up her arms and squeezed her shoulders.

Chin lifting, Jay tracked the movement.

"And we wouldn't wish to punish their eagerness, would we?"

In a hurried headshake, Jay scattered hair across his forehead. "You always say eagerness is a joy, with—" Staring at his party favors, he dropped two fingers down one cuff's inner lining.

"With what, my brave boy?" Henry would smother Jay's fears as he had hers. with tones low and gentle. His chest rose and fell in steady rhythm at her back.

"With the proper restraint applied," Jay whispered. Muscles drawing tight across his abdomen. he held his breath. Remembering the flick of a sadist's whip?

"And so it is. A great joy." Henry, in his bedrock-firm voice, left no room for doubt. Their eagerness, his control—perfect equilibrium. "My rules are a restraint you embrace, are they not?"

"They keep me safe." Wide-eyed faith and bent knees promised his submission.

Goddamn, she'd pay to keep his sweet, open beauty like this forever. He'd agreed, whether he realized the truth yet or not. And she'd read his cues the way Henry did.

Humming, Henry nodded. "Tell me why I keep you safe. Jay."

Jay flashed a brilliant grin. "Because you love me."

"I do love you. You're my good boy." Henry's declaration wriggled through Jay from the tilt of his head to the twitch of his cock. "My strong boy. Strong enough to allow yourself to be vulnerable, to give your whole heart to me and to Alice." He cocooned her in a tight band across her chest, his warmth and pressure inducing a contrary shiver of pleasure. "We take good care of your heart. do we not?"

"You do." Jay bounced heel-toe. "So good." As he idly tipped the cuffs, a steel D-ring clinked against the plate. "I don't—I've never— you're amazing. Spectacular."

Heart soaring, she wrestled the urge to shout hallelujah. Did he realize——

"As are you." Henry squeezed. If he didn't want to call Jay's attention to the cuff Jay tumbled over and over, she wouldn't, either. "Tell me your safeword, please."

Let Jay arrive at his own speed. Slower than his default setting, but so important.

"Tilt-A-Whirl."

"When will you use it?"

His choice, not Henry's command. No force, no coercion, no tempting him or distracting him with hands and mouths while restraints slipped around his wrists.

"When I have to stop." Jay clutched a cuff in each hand. "When I'm not ready."

"Good boy." Palms up, empty, and open. Henry reached past her for him. "If you're ready to extend the trust with your body that you do with your heart, bring me your gift, Jay."

Neoprene rustling, Jay stared as if magic had placed the cuffs in his grasp. After three steps, he sank to his knees and extended his arms above his head. "I'm ready." His clear tenor promise, at first wondrous and thin, gained strength. "I'm ready, Henry."

Henry laid a hand on Jay's bowed head. "I'm proud of you, brave boy." Smoothing Jay's hair, he nudged her forward.

She took over the calming strokes, pressing Jay to her. As she cradled him, his breath warmed her belly. His trust warmed the rest of her.

Accepting the greater responsibility, Henry worked around her and removed the cuff from Jay's left hand. Velcro scratched beside her ear. Leaning across her, he took hold of Jay's hand and kissed the pulse point in his wrist.

"A gift for my Jay, who works so hard at his lessons." Fingers steady and sure, he closed the first cuff. "Good boys deserve special rewards."

Repeating the ritual on the right, Henry branded her through their clothes with the heat of his erection. Good girls deserved special rewards, too.

Forearms resting on her shoulders, he squeezed Jay's fingers. "But how to best honor a man who lives to serve?"

"Let him serve." In her half-embrace, Jay nodded and shuffled his knees.

"Indeed." Henry tugged Jay up. "On your feet."

Catlike, Jay rubbed his face against her belly and stood. Naked but for the black cuffs with their gleaming metal rings, he sported an almost solid erection. Henry's praise puffed him up in all the right ways. He made no move to cover himself, to hunch or hide his excitement for greater submission. Brave Jay, proud of himself and of his role.

"Ladies first." Henry stirred her to action. No missing cues, not tonight. Cupping Jay's face in both hands, she toured the softness of his lips.

He gazed at her with sleepy-eyed adoration. In choosing to accept Henry's control, he made the only decision he ever needed to make and gained peaceful contentment in return.

She kissed him with lingering passion. He had no idea what awaited him. For once, she out-eagered him. Waiting to share herself with him tested her patience. But making the night special gave the occasion well-deserved reverence.

Henry chased her kiss with his own, pressing her tight between masculine angles. Pulling away, he nodded toward the table. "Clear the place settings, please, my boy. It seems we won't need them, not when we have a beautiful server available to us."

As Henry complimented Jay's streamlined athleticism, Jay stacked plates and cleared without complaint. Different demands for different desires. She'd have questioned. Resented the busywork. Instead, she fetched their light meal from the fridge, lining dessert-sized dishes on the island. Their final resting place had yet to be created.

With the chairs against the wall and the table empty of all but the linen tablecloth, Henry patted the top. "Well done. Up you go."

Jay hoisted himself up, his swinging legs flexing in oh-so-tempting ways. "I'm serving from the table?"

"Lie back." Henry guided Jay with a hand on the center of his chest. "You're serving *as* the table."

The wood spanned just long enough to accommodate Jay's lanky frame as he wriggled into place. Curving chest. Muscled abdomen. Sloping arrow toward his stiffening cock. Powerful hips and thighs made for pumping.

"It's only fair." Leaning back, she gripped the island. "I got my turn spread across the table." Solid, cool granite would keep her hands off Jay until called for. "Time for Jay to return the favor."

"He makes a lovely platter." Henry dragged a line from the hollow at Jay's throat to his increasingly interested cock. "And I've a mind to feast." With a lone finger sliding up Jay's shaft, he drew forth a whimper. "Dessert is always so enticing."

She groped for the dishtowel. Granite, granite, cloth. Henry lifted Jay's head, and she slipped the rolled towel behind his neck for cushioned comfort. Fingers dallying on his throat, she bobbed with him as he swallowed. Mirroring Henry's hold at the pulse point behind his ear, she encountered a horse at full gallop thundering beneath.

"So difficult," Henry murmured. "How hard he works to stay still for his master." He swooped in and kissed Jay with a force powerful as gravity, as if he'd push him through the table with lips alone.

Her dampening panties clung to her. Caution. Slippery when wet.

Jay, singing a chorus of moans, lay otherwise immobile.

"Magnificent. I know my boy will remain in position because I ask it of him." Henry stroked Jay bicep to wrist and fingered the wide cuff. "He needn't be tied to respect the rules and restraints I give him. Such a delightful pet."

In his smooth face and dark eyes, Jay radiated sheer bliss with perfect stillness.

Copying Henry, she traced the cuff on her side. "He's well-trained, but it's more than that."

"Yes, he reveals his true heart here, where he is safe and loved." With slow reverence, Henry kissed his cheeks. "Would you like Alice to feel as secure in my service as you do, my boy?"

Jay aborted his nod and curling fingers, blips and ripples testing his obedience. "Yes, please."

"We might find her something decorative so she may share in your bravery. To feel my claim on her as you do."

As Henry extended his arms in silent request, she grabbed the leather forearm sleeves secreted in the dishtowel drawer. Tonight they'd be a symbol, not buckled together as she'd worn them in January. Her steady pace horse to Jay's fractious colt. If he grew worried as the night progressed, he'd have her example and she'd have the glory of restraint and the weight of responsibility clasping her tight.

Precise and careful, Henry centered her wrists a foot above Jay's face. Her playmate would have an excellent view of her joining him in bondage. Henry repeated his steps. Confirming her safeword. Kissing her pulse points with open-mouthed gentleness. Buckling the sleeves. No quick-release Velcro for her. No need.

Their faces cradled in his hands, Henry rubbed their cheeks. "Now both of my beautiful pets are ready for dinner."

A long, slender, rectangular platter waited atop the island. Plastic clung to the cut fruit and continued below, a thin protector to keep juice from making Jay too sugar-sticky to play with. A barrier like the ones they'd abandon later. God, the moment couldn't arrive soon enough. As she helped position dinner atop Jay, he gave the tiniest flinch at the lingering chill and inhaled the sweet aroma.

The feast of pineapple fingers and pear cubes, apricot slices, whole strawberries, and pitted cherries spread from collarbone to navel. Miniature bowls of honey, nuts, and whipped Greek yogurt topping covered his sternum. Cool delights for a warm summer's night. Fuel, not food. Bites of sugar and protein to keep them wide awake and wanting.

Henry swirled pineapple in the topping and carried both to Jay's lips. "My taste tester must sample everything." Swiping the treat sideways, he left a speck of white behind. "Try some of my cream."

Slow and teasing, Jay licked his lips. Henry pressed closer. Jay sucked the topping clean and nibbled the pineapple. Only when Henry gave permission did he snatch the whole treat and swallow.

Service and love. Jay excelled at merging the two. She savored each bite to share with her lovers in a communal sensory feast. The fruit and its toppings, soft, fluid, and tart-sweet. The man beneath, firm, supple, and salted. Obedient to their commands.

She held an apricot slice between her teeth, dipped it in honey, and brought it to Jay. Rubbing and bumping noses, arousal flaring, they nuzzled their way through the bite. How he kept his chest so still she'd never understand.

His urge to please Henry went far beyond her own. His need didn't stop at fulfilling a function or ask for reasons. The freedom to follow Henry's commands without fear drove him. In the right hands, in Henry's hands, his trust reaped rewards.

"What an exquisite table I've found." Henry fed Jay on alternating bites and kisses. "A grand centerpiece worthy of my home."

Drugged bliss flowed in Jay's eyes, melted cocoa pools. He tracked Henry, gaze following as he would in body given permission.

"Strong, rounded corners." Starting at Jay's shoulders, Henry traveled along his collarbone. "A sturdy frame that warms to the touch."

Henry stroked the notch at the base of Jay's throat, and his tension thrummed beneath her hands on his ribs and thigh. Did Jay ache, holding back the desire to tip his head and bare his throat to the man he worshiped? God knew she did when Henry touched her there.

"Intricate details that invite closer inspection." Bending, Henry sucked Jay's throat. "A master craftsman poured love into this creation."

Jay's breath caught, but he held his position. In the wrong hands, his marrow-deep desire to please for whatever reason and in whatever way his master decided made his willingness to use his safeword paramount.

If he'd hesitated, been less confident in his promise, Henry would've run an alternate plan. The cuffs on Jay would've snuggled her instead, and the beautiful leather sleeves would've gone unused.

With a delicate kiss, Jay accepted a strawberry from her lips.

"But the crafting creates nothing not already present. The creator merely reveals the true form hidden within the rough surface." A dark forest of thought, vast and impenetrable, stood behind Henry's eyes. He toured Jay with a sculptor's touch. "The shape of greatness begging for release."

Far from disappointing her, Henry pulling back the curtain impressed her more. He'd prepared for whatever level of involvement Jay was ready to accept. If Jay's soft eyes and complete unconcern for his bonds hadn't convinced her of the certainty of Henry's judgment, the magnitude of Jay's erection would've quelled any doubt.

"An undeniably masculine masterpiece." Swaying low, Henry inhaled. Aromatic fruit, ostensibly. The musk of Jay's arousal inches from his lips and twitching closer, more likely. "Adonis himself would weep."

Although fruit juice trickled down the plastic film coating Jay, he lay in compliant stillness. Hard and straining, his cock hung above the spillover pool at his navel. Pre-come drizzled in a line to his stomach.

She pulsed with hunger, and not for the handful of bites remaining. Jay had journeyed long past ready and deep into subspace. She arched her brow. When Henry granted permission in a nod, she shifted the bowls to the island.

With a firm hold around Jay's wrist, a reminder of restraint, he curled Jay's fingers tight. All but the pointer, which he swiped through the puddle. He brought Jay's finger to his mouth and sucked while Jay moaned.

"Mmm, a dessert fountain." She sponged sweet syrup with the last apricot slice. Jay-flavor added salty tang, a culinary complement. Empty plastic wrap joined the bowls on the counter.

"Perhaps we ought to feast from the source." Guiding Jay, Henry squeezed the base of Jay's cock, turning him vertical. Balls tightening, Jay twitched his hips. In their joined hands, Henry and Jay held back a real fountain. Henry adored driving them to the edge and making them wait.

Lapping at Jay, she cleaned his stomach with open-mouthed kisses. "Be a shame to waste so much richness." She'd get her fill, but not until Henry took his. Jay trembled under her tongue. Her retreat left shiny but unsticky skin behind.

"A shame indeed." Henry sighed. Pre-come beaded at the tip of Jay's cock. "We mustn't squander a drop."

The surface tension held. Grew. Stretched.

The bead broke free, slipping down the flared head.

Henry engulfed Jay to the root.

Jesus God, cram her fingers in her panties and call it a day. Orgasm hovered a hairsbreadth away. For Jay, too, if his guttural exhalation came from as deep as it sounded.

In a leisurely, tugging withdrawal, Henry breathed *I own this* all along Jay's length. The chorus of whimpers confirmed his claim.

"Taste from the source, Alice." Henry's low command settled on her shoulders. "My boy's beautiful cock is yours for the night, sweet girl."

God yes. All night, every climax hers while Henry held the reins.

"Make it dance."

She replaced his grip, holding Jay nice and tall so he'd see the climax of his first gift. Closing her eyes, she relished the sweep of Henry's hand as he pushed her hair back and angled her to optimize their view. She rolled her tongue around Jay at his tip, dividing her attention between her appreciation for him and for their leader.

Henry removed himself to the head of the table. The bulge in his slacks lined up behind Jay's sweet face as he watched her blow him. A vision of beauty on both sides. On a future night, Henry'd promised, he'd unzip and feed Jay his cock. But for now he'd let the birthday boy watch his own enjoyment while he reinforced the cuffs' safety and comfort.

"Tonight we give pleasure to the man who pleases us with exquisite skill throughout the year." Grasping Jay by the hands, he held him captive against his chest. Black cuffs stood in stark contrast to Henry's white dress shirt. "His beautiful surrender, his love and trust."

He nuzzled the backs of Jay's hands. She did the same along Jay's cock, long bobs and hard pulls. A team, Henry's voice and her lips.

"He brings me more joy than ever I hoped for." Henry stroked lazy figure eights, infinity bridging Jay's cuffs and the sensitive heels of his hands. "I cannot imagine life without my Jay."

With the low hum of a perfectly tuned engine, Jay vibrated. Cupping his balls in her free hand, she matched the other to the sweep of her mouth on his shaft.

"I suppose I'll have to keep him with me forever." Light musing turned possessive as Henry lowered his voice. "My good boy, bound to my service."

With Henry squeezing his wrists, Jay teetered on the edge. His balls pulsed. Ejaculatory inevitability. He'd come in a—

"Come for me, my boy. Share the salt of your submission with our girl."

He washed over her tongue, and she drank him down. His heat caressed her like a sip of Henry's port. The good stuff. Stoking her own fire even as Jay's cooled. He lay slack, motionless now by stunned afterglow rather than Henry's command.

"Well done." With reverent care, Henry lowered Jay's arms to the table. He brushed the back of his hand over Jay's forehead, cheek, and neck in a tender, flowing path. In his crinkled eyes, he held a smile for her as she bathed Jay's cock with equally patient attention. "Where have you gone, dearest boy? Hmm?" Henry's fond, teasing tone seemed no more than Jay deserved. "What glorious vision has glazed your eyes and stolen your quick tongue?"

A quiet, contented Jay. Such a rare sight, not to be missed. With a light kiss and a gentle pat, she left his softening cock to its rest. She'd recall him to action soon enough.

Standing straight twanged the crick in her back. Too much enthusiasm spent bending over her table.

Henry swept out his arm, and she scurried in for snuggling. Kneading her back with a pressure-laden fist, he kissed her cheek. "Played to perfection. Our poor Jay is spellbound."

Dazed satisfaction shone in brown-saucer eyes and a lazy smile. In wearing him out, they'd muted his natural smirk.

"We could wake him with a kiss." She pushed a wayward strand off his forehead. Henry had glued his fingers to Jay's pulse. She wouldn't panic unless he did. "Works in fairy tales."

"So it does."

They did the honors together, a kiss for Jay at each corner of his mouth. Henry paused beside his ear. "Wake and move, my boy."

Shuddering and blinking, Jay sucked in an endless breath. "Henry?"

"Yes, dear one?"

"I love my birthday present. Especially the people who gave it to me."

Chuckling, Henry rubbed Jay's chest in a flurry. "Alice and I gathered as much."

"We love you too, stud." She dropped her voice. "And your birthday's not over. You haven't unwrapped all of your presents."

If he tried any harder to stare at the outline of Henry's cock and her boobs simultaneously, he'd get whiplash. Classic Jay. Rounding the table toward his feet, she caught herself in a near-stumble. Classic Jay *wearing handcuffs*.

Not a single sign of interest in removing them. They'd cleared the first hurdle, accustomed him to the gripping weight without distressing him. No more than a new thing Henry'd asked of him.

Sliding her hands under his legs, she massaged his calves while Henry chafed his hands.

Jay flashed a goofy grin. "Whazzat?"

"Improving blood flow." Henry returned Jay's smile. "You sent so much into your beautifully hard cock it's a wonder you've any left to circulate."

"I could do it again." Wiggling, Jay flexed his feet against her stomach. "I know I could."

Lowering Jay's hands, Henry nudged his shoulders. "Up you go. I expect Alice is eager for that very miracle."

"Oh yeah." She tugged his ankles, the tablecloth coming along for the ride as Jay slid to the end. Standing between his knees, she splayed her hands across his chest. Warm and angled, with his lungs a bellows beneath the surface. "I've got just the place to enshrine him."

Clinging to her with his arms slung around her neck, he breathed honey and pineapple in the thin space between. Neoprene and Velcro rasped against her shirt. "I'm a good boy. I won't let you down."

"You're a good boy." Only an idiot or an ass would tell perfect, giving, trusting Jay different. "The only way you'd ever let me down is if you kept going when you needed to stop." The response Henry would offer rolled off her tongue. "You remember your safeword?"

Nodding, Jay squeezed her between his knees and released. Squeezed and released. "Tilt-A-Whirl."

"You remember when to use it?" Slipping through her fingers, the silky hairs at the base of his neck tickled.

"When I'm not ready." He shifted his weight and sat taller. "When *I* decide. Because it's my right to have a safeword and to use it."

"Got it in one." Pressing the back of his neck triggered an immediate bow. "And it's my responsibility to respect your safeword." She laid her lips against his forehead. "It's the most important thing I'll ever do in my life."

Beyond Jay, at the opposite end of the table, Henry emanated lust in blazing green eyes and fingers grinding white against the tabletop. Approval emerged in his restrained nod. He'd fuck them both into the floor, the wall, or the nearest handy anything if he hadn't planned the night to the finest detail.

Pride in them, in their behavior, growth, and love—in those moments Henry came closest to the edge. When he tortured himself with delayed gratification. The touch of masochism in the master's need for self-control.

Stepping back, she let Jay's arms bump across her shoulders and snatched his hands as they dropped. "Let's go, stud."

He hopped off the table, linen falling in a heap behind him. "Oops."

"Leave it." She swung their linked hands. "You have places to be." Walking backward, she pulled him along in a hip-swaying saunter. "Gifts to unwrap."

This one, though, belonged to Henry. Obedient, naked, bound Jay following her down the hall, his strong, unscarred back on full display. The greatness Henry had uncovered and refined with years of painstaking patience. The man who knew his worth and took pride in his service. Nothing would take that away from him.

* * * *

Dark green silk gleamed under the bedside lamps as Jay helped her peel back the comforter.

"Top sheet too, my lovelies." Henry opened the button at his throat. With long, graceful fingers, he traced his shirt placket. "We want a level playing field for this exercise."

Jay swung toward Henry. "Exercise?"

"Mm-hmm."

Unnecessary, the sheet joined the comforter on the floor. In Henry's bed, they bared themselves in heart, soul, and body with nothing to hide beneath.

Henry beckoned Jay to his side. Closing his hands around the cuffs, he raised Jay's arms between their bodies.

Go time. If they'd planned well, Jay would gain so much confidence. If not—contingencies. More love, more trust, more time.

"Do you recall the night our girl wore these for you?" Rasping his thumbs across the cuffs, little more than a whisper, Henry shouted in the silence. "The trust, courage, and joy she demonstrated?"

Jay rocked on the balls of his feet. "I remember." Up. Down. "Alice is fearless."

"Is she, now?" Henry turned a skeptical brow on her. "Alice, is this true? Are you fearless?"

"Not even close." She gentled her denial for Jay's tender edges, the open wounds they sought to seal. "Sometimes I conquer my fear." The silk rippled under her sliding fingers. "But sometimes, when I'm in a safe place, I embrace it."

Humming, Henry prompted Jay for his safeword and got the standard answer. "Tell me again when you will use it."

"When..." Jay studied his cuffed wrists. The hands holding them.
Henry, and her, too. His rocking diminished until he stood firm. "When
the fear is more than the fun. When I can't embrace it."

"Exquisite." Claiming a fierce kiss, Henry led a dance of two strong,
masculine jaws in a rhythm directing her heartbeat.

Toes curling, Jay whimpered as they parted.

"Go ahead, Alice." Henry must've judged Jay relaxed enough
for the advanced game. She'd prodded him with incessant questions
Wednesday. Plan and plan again to make every step right for Jay. In
memory, Henry whispered.

*"My hands loosed his bonds once we'd snapped the locks. What he
wants and what he's ready to handle are not always in harmony."*

The under-bed strap yielded to her questing fingers. Warm from its
slumber beneath the mattress, sturdy nylon slipped free. A simple-latch
carabiner dangled at the end. No locks.

"Pull the safety tab." As Henry guided Jay through using the cuffs'
quick-release, Velcro scratched the air.

She rounded the bed as an unobtrusive servant. Not a role to which
she'd ever aspired.

"If his body responds with fear, he will feel he has failed."

But as she readied their safe haven for Jay's submission, service
dumped a cocktail of contentment and anticipation into her bloodstream.

"Allow me, my good boy." Henry refastened the cuffs. The more trial
runs, the better. On and off, the blanket across the colt's back without
added weight.

She rested the second strap atop the fitted sheet. Jay blew out a breath.

"We will provide as different an experience as possible."

Only the wrist straps. No ankle straps, no ankle cuffs. The lightest
of restrictions, repetition morphing into routine. She and Henry had an
advantage mustang breakers lacked.

Jay wanted to be tamed.

"Shall we prepare our girl for playtime?" Laying his hand to Jay's cheek,
Henry turned him toward her. "She appears shockingly overdressed."

Jay pranced in place, his hips wiggling and his ass tightening.

"His partner naked, symbolically bound, as equal in vulnerability as he."

At Henry's direction, she approached and bent her head. Taking his
sweet time sliding the tiny button at the back of her neck free, he woke
shuddering pleasure.

"Untuck Alice's blouse, please."

As Henry fingered her neckline. Jay gripped her waist. Hands pressed to her sides, he raised the camisole out of her pants.

"Lovely."

Their cooperative conspiracy left her naked but for the leather encasing her forearms. Rounded edges, tight stitching, swirling scrollwork. The wind's leaping joy etched onto the dark, steady earth. Hmph. Spending so much time listening to Henry had leached his artistic whimsy into her engineered order.

"My best boy is in your hands now, dearest." Henry kissed her palms and stepped away. "Mind you feed him well."

A feast of familiar flavors but unknown sensations. To start, a reinforcement of their success in the dining room.

"His back protected, safe from pain and exposure."

With her Henry-kissed palm over Jay's heart, she walked him backward to the bed. "Sit, sweetheart."

In silence, with trusting eyes rich and dark, he obeyed. Not innocence but wisdom. Faith that this time would be different. Faith enough to make her legs wobble if she let it.

"Slide back." She projected nothing but confidence. Certainty.

Weight on his hands, he followed her command.

"I want every inch of your beautiful body on this bed." Weeks of practice in their shared room naturally framed praise as the output of her desires. "Henry's generous to give us so much freedom to play."

She straddled his extended legs and knee-walked closer. The sway of her breasts drew his gaze as she pushed him prone. With gentle sweeps, she splayed his arms wide. Moment of truth.

"Feminine hands."

The snap of the carabiner closing shot through her. Jay's shiver called for comfort. Nuzzling his hand, she tugged his index finger into her mouth. Swirls teasing on her tongue, the soft pattern of his fingerprint tingled. Uniquely Jay and all but invisible to her senses.

Whimpering, he shifted the bed with his rocking beneath her. Comfort and arousal. Stretched across him, she snapped the second strap in place. Ready to ride. Her rodeo, at least for now.

"A feminine voice."

Gripping him between her legs, she rested at the low end of his ribs. "Are you comfortable?" Under her kneading hands, he lay warm and firm-chested. "Are you eager to please me?"

Lifting his hips, Jay grimaced. "I'm sorry, Alice." He turned his face away. "I'll try harder."

She stuffed down a twitch of panic. "Try harder?"

His cock. Not hard yet, because he'd barely had time to recover.

"Oh, sweetheart." With deliberate unconcern, she shook her head, reached behind her, and delivered a reassuring squeeze. "We've got time for that later. You told me once you have two hands and a mouth." Arms spread, she rose on her knees. "I've already put your hands to work for me. You're such a good boy to accept my bonds."

As Jay's eyes widened, he licked his lips. Bingo, baby.

"But now I have a job for your mouth. For your quick, clever tongue." Slow moves forward. Building anticipation like Henry'd taught her. She'd make him proud. "I swallowed your joy. Will you swallow mine?"

Opening his mouth, Jay strained toward her.

"An exceedingly clear demonstration of your femininity."

She descended on him with the deep notes of her arousal thickening the air. Henry held his silence. If Jay didn't safeword, they'd add Henry back into the mix. When the straps had become nothing to fear, a meal paired with the wine of her climax.

"A negative outcome would be worse than denying him the attempt outright."

Jay's tentative probing demanded encouragement. "The first night you did this for me, you gave me so many orgasms I thought I'd die in Henry's lap."

He deepened his strokes, flicking his tongue inside, and she clenched down. Flood his senses with feminine heat and musk, slick lips and a slippery, trembling clit, and they just might lick this.

Lick it. Giggles floating in her abdomen, she set off more contractions.

"He wants so badly to submit. A setback would devastate him."

As she gripped the headboard, the leather sleeves rippled with her forearms. Tension built between her legs, fueled by Jay working his hot breath and strong, flexing tongue.

"I tried to match the feeling. Vibrator fizzled out. Shower sprayer beating water right against my pussy failed. Only you and your mouth got the job done right."

Moaning, Jay shot into overdrive, delivering heat and speed and pressure. She poured every gram of concentration into not smothering him between her thighs. Jesus God, Henry'd taught him well.

"But a success, a success filling our bound boy with confidence and pleasure? That would be a joy I've waited years to witness."

She lifted an inch and he chased her, extending his neck to keep his tongue between her lips. Tension lining his arms, Jay formed fists.

Rustling behind her revealed his feet sliding on the sheets as he raised his legs. Mmm. Cock revival underway.

Beyond, Henry stood with his shirt untucked and unbuttoned. He fingered his belt buckle, erection distending the fly beneath.

Lost in shudders, she sagged. Jay latched on and sucked her clit hard. Their giddy boy of pure enjoyment. In treasuring this night forever, Henry would immortalize them on canvas.

She rode a swell of pride and power to orgasm.

* * * *

Uncurling her fingers from the headboard, she harbored the certainty she'd have the chance again tonight.

"You're an artist, Jay." If her mental checklist hadn't highlighted the game waiting, his long, flat strokes would've kept her in place for another round. "Your tongue is your brush." A mechanic with great torque. Leave the percussive maintenance to Henry, though. He knew how and where to strike. "You're such a good boy to study with a master painter."

"Henry," he whispered. With a happy Jay-whimper, he vibrated her clit.

"Henry." Aftershock rippled through her belly. Better move before she got too attached to staying right here. She hefted herself backward and straddled him. Time to remind Jay how much he loved Henry's voice. He hadn't flinched at Henry's name or the word "master." She had a green light. "I bet he's so proud of you."

"He is?" Arching his chest under her, irresistibly cute and catlike, Jay licked his shining lips.

"I am." Using his deep tones, Henry soothed like nothing else. "You created a portrait of pleasure I won't soon forget." With his voice, he lubricated moving parts, reduced friction, optimized every element for top performance. "You've earned the reward our girl yearns to deliver."

Busted. Rubbing herself along Jay's abdomen, she'd given away her excitement.

"I get a reward?" In full-on fidget mode, Jay delivered a ride better than rubbing. His grin showed his teeth. "Nobody mentioned a reward."

As Henry rounded the bed, he nodded to her. "A bonus gift."

She skirted the erection Jay'd been so worried about not having. Settling on his thighs, she stroked his hard shaft. "I said I'd have a use for this later, didn't I?"

Jay whipped his head sideways and scanned the nightstand. He was gonna fucking love this. Love the fucking, too. The soft cuff hampered his reach for the drawer, but he didn't flinch from the pull. "Henry? May I please have a condom?"

Henry ran his finger along the nightstand. She matched him on Jay's cock. Poor Jay didn't know where to look.

"Alice wants to give you a first time as you did for her." Shirtless, bending across the bed, Henry rested his face beside Jay's. "I might be tempted to name it fairness—equality for my beautiful pets," he whispered. "But we both know how competitive our girl is, don't we?"

Henry winked, and Jay nodded in rapid, repeated agreement. Damn teases. God how she loved them.

"I expect you'll enjoy letting her win this one." He treated Jay—a bound Jay welcoming his master's touch without panic—to a slow kiss.

She flash-froze the image in her head.

"Happy birthday, my boy." In pulling back, Henry granted her room to work.

With a swift stroke up Jay's cock, she recaptured his focus.

"Henry says you've always been responsible about wrapping this up." A month of fantasizing and more than forty-eight hours she'd been ready for this exact moment. A lifetime for Jay, since the first time his cock stood up and he knew what to do with it. "You don't have to tonight." She added a purr to her voice. "Not with me. Not anymore."

Jay jerked in her hand. "For good?"

Powerful desire coated her lips, and she shared the slickness, sliding his cock along her sex.

He caught his breath. "You mean it?"

"Mm-hmm." He had a beautiful cock. Firm and purpling between her legs. Perfect ridges for grinding her clit. Her lubrication prepared them both. No substitutes, no barriers.

"But Henry should—"

"Be first," they finished together.

She bent and kissed his brow. "Don't worry, sweetheart. He was."

"Alice gives us a lovely gift." Henry spoke, and she acted. A harmony if ever she'd found one. "One in which I've partaken this week."

Three times Wednesday. Not once Thursday. A long day of emptiness to raise her expectations and her eagerness for Jay.

"Her choice shows us how much she values our love, hmm?"

Value indefinable. The variable becoming a constant, neither subject to the rules governing all others.

"How committed she is to loving us."

Damn straight. Not a man before them had shared this nudity with her. And now she got to be Jay's first. Maybe his only. Her clench tightened her whole body, curling her toes and clamping her jaw. No wonder Henry got off on commitment and control.

"Her decision opens the doors for much more spontaneity in our life together."

Spontaneity. Her cue. Gripping Jay at his base, she raised up and swallowed his flared head. Not quite inside, but rubbing. Close enough for him to whimper every time she tugged. She fingered her clit with her free hand.

Dancing in her other hand, Jay flexed his thighs between hers. Clever, eager man. Too big an outward nudge and she'd slide right down.

They'd agreed Jay would be quick, even after coming at the table. No way he wouldn't be with this enticement. Avoiding any whiff of failure on his part meant priming her to climax almost as soon as he filled her.

"Our girl's slick, smooth heat surrounded me with nothing between us. She'll brand you, my boy." Henry sent his deep, low promise shivering along her skin. "Here is your home." His hum quieted Jay. "Our home."

Burying him, she throbbed on the edge. Jay groaned and bucked deeper. She slapped her hands to his sides and went for a speedy ride.

"Magnificent creatures," Henry murmured. "The beauty of powerful thighs. The thumping of racing hearts."

Oh God. Desire surged. Jay's chest heaved with his breaths.

"Naked but for my gifts. Both bound to me. Mine."

She shook with pressure beyond her capacity to contain. "Please," she mouthed, and Jay mirrored her. "Please."

"Come for me, my dear ones."

Jay pulsed, bathing her with heat. She collapsed on him in a shaking heap, their hips joined.

* * * *

Snuggled closer than a blanket, she breathed in rich, musky Jay-scent. "How ya doin', stud?" Snaking her fingers through his hair, she waggled his head.

Grinning, he bumped her nose. "Best first time ever."

"You feel amazing. I'm gonna keep you right here." With her squeeze, she drew a thrusting reply raising her up. Shame to make the bedsheet the lone witness to his tight, muscled ass bench-pressing her weight. "Mm-hmm. My new Jay-accessory. Goes with all of my outfits."

Her running patter and praise gave Henry time to unsnap the straps from Jay's cuffs. Letting him keep the snug wristbands would be victory enough. Henry refused to tie him down with a masculine presence at his back. No argument from her.

As Jay pressed up, she ground down. Inevitable she'd lose him eventually, but for now a controlled clench kept him inside.

He swung an arm toward her waist and halted an inch away. "Wha…"

"Startle yourself?" Freedom always came as a surprise to her, too. She kissed him with soothing persistence. "It's okay. You can touch me now. Ask Henry."

"Henry?" Any wider, and Jay's eyes'd be fit to burst. "I—I did it." With shuddering breaths, he vibrated his whole body and a good bit of hers. "I didn't have to stop." Tipping his chin, he just missed clocking her as he stared between them. "I'm—everything's—safe."

"Completely safe, my brave boy." Pants discarded, Henry sat with his hip near their heads. "And such a delicious conduit of pleasure for Alice."

Naked Henry. Yum. The power dynamics of a dressed Henry in the bedroom sent her soaring, but he'd decided to remove as many reminders of trauma as possible. No contest. Crafting the best experience for Jay remained paramount.

Squeezing him settled bittersweet heaviness in her chest. Too soft to hold soon, no matter how she ached to grip him forever.

Jay laughed and squirmed. His cuffs dragged on her thighs. Mmm. Her turn next.

"Share what's delighted you so, my comedian." With rapt attention, Henry traced Jay from ear tip to jawline.

"Alice is tickling my balls."

"Say what?" She tapped his shoulders. "Doing no such thing, goof."

"Yeah-huh." Pulling up his legs, he cradled her ass with his thighs. His smirk signaled he'd converted to post-orgasmic euphoric scamp mode. "You're all slippery and wet and warm. Like caramel sauce on a sundae."

Henry laughed. Hard, not a polite chuckle but a full-out head-back shoulder-shaking laugh. Beautiful and deep.

"Newsflash, buster," she whispered. "That sauce tickling your sundae comes courtesy of you, too, you know. We're swirled like the gooey-melty spoonfuls at the bottom of the bowl."

Moaning, Jay licked his lips. Oh God. She'd unleashed the dessert fiend.

"Convenient, as I've a use for your bounteous supply." Henry unfolded his hand and raised a green circle between his thumb and index finger. Jay's cock ring.

Mouth hanging open, Jay convulsed in a rolling shudder. Oh yeah. Thought he'd finished for the night, the gifts unwrapped, the toys put away. Nope. More pleasure to give and receive.

"You got my presents." She swallowed her sigh and let him slip free. Nudging his thighs apart, she knelt between. "But Henry saved the best for last."

"Better than everything so far?" Jay zeroed in on the ring with single-minded attention. Bondage he craved. "Gonna hafta be incredible."

Flaccid and gleaming, Jay displayed adorable wrinkles. Henry cupped the whole package with possessive strength. "My boy knows who owns him."

Abdominals tensing, Jay bobbed his head with spring-loaded repetition. Not tied down, but sure as hell bound. Anticipation remained an aphrodisiac with qualities she'd only begun to catalog.

"He takes pride in his service, as he should." Circling the flared ridge below the head of Jay's cock, Henry molded Jay to his thumb. "He will rise to the occasion when the time comes."

With his smooth push, Jay's balls descended through the basic band of darkest jade. The polished stone's inner surface bore an inscription there and gone, Henry too quick and the engraving too distant. Jay's cock squeezed through last, malleable and slick with their climax.

"Good boy." As Henry patted Jay's cock, glowy-eyed Jay stretched and preened. "How easily my ownership slides over you when you've been prepared with careful thoroughness." Leaning across Jay, Henry kissed her cheek. "Our boy is properly attired for his final gift of the night, and you've earned a reward for excellent performance."

Her heart leapt. Advance knowledge didn't make the confirmation any less exciting. If anything, knowing increased her anticipation and made her wet with waiting. "Thank you, Henry."

He tugged the bright stainless steel rings dangling from her forearm sleeves. "Jay." His soft call roused instant attention from their basking boy. "Atop the dresser lies a short tie Alice would very much like to have. Fetch it for her, please."

No need to specify which dresser. The best goodies came from the bureau between the windows. Jay trotted over with a wiggle in his ass. Taking advantage of the cock ring's added weight to play. She would. No cock, though.

"You're entertaining naughty thoughts." Henry enwrapped her and twirled like a dancer dipping his partner. "The darling puckering of your breasts tells me so." He laid her into warmth, Jay's heat clinging to the sheet. "What has captured your imagination?"

Nestled in proof of Jay's bravery, sheltered beneath Henry, she tasted the idea on her tongue. "Clamps."

His possessive growl shuddered through her and stopped Jay in his tracks. Bending close, Henry breathed against her neck. "A bold adventurer is an unceasing delight." He nipped her earlobe, his sharp pinch soothed by his tongue. "The dangling weight appeals?"

"Mm-hmm." Trust him to read her mind. Or her inability to resist peeking at Jay as he bounced toward the bed.

"Here?" Henry tweaked her nipple, swirled down her stomach, and tugged her labia. "Or here?"

"Either." She squirmed under his fingering. "Both." As he flicked her clit, her hips jumped without permission. "Ahh——I don't know."

"Then we'll find out together some night, shall we?" He sealed her *yes* with a kiss. Sitting up, he beckoned Jay closer.

Jay bounded onto the bed, rocking the mattress but landing in a controlled knee-slide inches from her side. Perfect waiting pose, the requested toy lying across his open hands.

She had to laugh. "You're such a fucking beautiful show-off."

Head bowed, Jay shot her a smirktastic grin below dancing eyes.

Henry cupped Jay's chin. "Exuberance pours from you as a mighty waterfall, splashing us all with your joy. I hardly knew what a desert I inhabited before your lush waters brought new life." In his silky smooth baritone, Henry carried a gruff undertone. "I'm so very pleased with you. You nurture my soul, dearest boy."

Jay sucked in his breath.

Rapid blinks held her sympathetic tears at bay but did nothing to stem the flood of love.

"Th-thank you, Henry." Wide-eyed and trembling, his voice shaking, Jay clutched the leather. "I brought you this." He thrust his arms forward. "For Alice."

"So you did." With his soft smile, Henry promised he'd recognized Jay's emotional overload. "If you give that to me——" He coaxed open Jay's clenched fingers and retrieved the tie. "You may lie beside our girl and snuggle. Her lovely breasts look to need warming."

He swooped in and captured Jay. Angled jaws and rounded lips merged. Beauty in motion, Henry taught a master class in fluid dynamics with his mouth. Jay's tremors shook themselves out, yielding to Henry's persistent calm.

"Yes, you're more than up to the task." Grazing Jay's hip with a long-fingered slide, he nodded. "Go on."

Jay curled at her side with catlike grace. Mild headbutting nudged her arm from his path. Clasping his shoulders, she played with the wispy hair at the nape of his neck. These moments. Jay, calm and cuddly. Henry, powerful and confident. Give her these moments, and every care fell away.

Kneeling beside her, Henry stretched the strap taut. Eight inches long, and no give in the dark leather. Take away the metal lobster snaps at each end, and the strap could've been pulled from her flogger.

"Raise your arms for me. Alice." He vibrated his voice at her frequency, a tuning fork for her arousal.

Clit fluttering, she stroked the knobby headboard spindles. In her tipped-back view, he worked upside down. His growing erection hung over her chest. If Jay peeled himself from her breasts and swiveled, he'd have Henry in his mouth in a hot second.

"You're licking your lips," Henry murmured. "Always thinking."

Her shoulders dug into the mattress as she lifted her head. Jay's weight held her down. God, if only Henry'd lean in a smidge.

"Always chasing"—*snap-snap* went the lobster hooks, and a devilish curve took hold of Henry's lips—"the thing just out of reach."

Leather looped the headboard and attached to her sleeve rings. He'd limited her grasp to the thick wood, the smooth leather, and the slippery fitted sheet curving around the mattress. The strap's stitched edges offered rough contrast under her thumbs.

Henry laid his hands overtop. "Wiggle for me."

She full-body shimmied on the sheet.

"Competitive minx." Smiling, he squeezed her fingers. "Wanting to play the comedian with Jay's fine example."

Moaning, Jay abandoned one breast for the other. After the heat of his mouth, the cooler air stung wet flesh. In sprawling, he pinned her and pressed his twitching cock to her thigh. Good to go three times a night. Henry never missed on a prediction about Jay's responses. Hell, he intended the ring less as an erection aid and more as a claim and a method to keep Jay from blowing his stack the second he realized what a lucky man he'd be.

"You caught me." Aiming for sultry, she succeeded, by the flicker in Henry's eyes. "Always wanting to go farther." She wiggled her fingers in his grip. "Always safe in your hands."

As Henry led her through the safeword ritual, she kept her answers short and sweet, confident and excited for Jay. Latched at her breast, he'd take her responses to heart. Freedom and responsibility shared a bed with her. Each a unique delight.

Henry sealed the ritual with a kiss. Gentle graze growing possessive, he gripped her hair in one hand while with his tongue he promised pleasure her body begged for.

She succumbed. Ceased pushing and accepted what he chose to give. Released the moan building in her throat. Spread her legs and rocked against Jay's muscled thigh.

"Good girl." Henry nuzzled her cheeks. "We want our Alice eager to be filled." He sat back on his haunches beside her, his cock hard and the tip shining. "As eager as my good boy often is."

Tugging, Jay stretched her nipple until she popped free in a rush.

Henry laid his hand on Jay's back. "The birthday boy deserves to be the center of attention at his party, don't you think?"

"Yes, please." Eyes gleaming, Jay thrust his hardening cock against her. Either every pulse stiffening him burned her, or she'd developed a sympathetic reaction throb. "Please, Henry. I waited like a good boy."

"You've been patient a very long time, waiting for the woman who loves us both to enter our lives. The one you are safe enough to be your true self with." Squeezing his ass, Henry prompted another thrust.

In mid-whimper, Jay glanced her way.

She waved, leather pulling her wrists. Nothing to fear or be ashamed of. If not for her, not for him, either. "Love you, stud."

"Alice and I want to share you between us." As Jay beat an eager-footed tattoo on the mattress, Henry liberated a bottle of lube from the nightstand drawer. "A fantasy you entrusted to me long ago."

An unfulfilled one, in Henry's telling. Their lovemaking beside her on Valentine's had been more meaningful than she'd known.

"I haven't forgotten, my boy. Not a single one."

The first time Jay'd relaxed enough to let Henry penetrate him in front of someone else. The first time he hadn't frozen or gone limp at the attempt, fear or shame dragging him down.

"I know you'd never forget," Jay whispered. "You've always told me the truth. That I could have what I wanted when I was ready for it."

Henry thought him ready, or she wouldn't have gotten the bullet points Wednesday. The reasoning behind his just-in-case alternatives.

"That you'd help me get there. That you love me." Jay blinked and swallowed. His cock thumped her thigh. "I love you, Henry. I love you, Alice."

Reassurances in words and kisses spilled from them both, escalating to hot, trembling need. Henry maneuvered Jay between her legs and aligned their bodies. Jay, the cock ring weighing him down, dragged his balls across her with every rock and thrust. Pre-come speckled her belly with warmth.

Henry slipped his hand between them. Jesus, fuck, two fingers inside and she jerked. The bonds held her fast. Jay sucked at her throat.

"Let Alice feel your depth." Retreating, Henry spread her wide. "Enjoy her."

As Jay arched away, his cock dipped and rapped her clit. Jolted, she brought delightful tugging down on her wrists. More restraint, the leather *shirr*ing along the wood.

Henry guided him to her. "Watch the pleasure you give her."

Groaning, Jay pressed ahead with aching slowness. Blunt head flaring, the sweet curved ridge beneath popped deep. Christ, he filled her more than he'd ever done. Lack of condom, addition of cock ring, thrill of fantasy—analysis tumbled through her and out again, lost in a haze of fullness and Jay's intense gaze.

"Do you see her thoughts zip and bounce?"

Inches from her face, he'd see nothing but her satisfaction rattling from her fingers to her toes with every tug against the headboard.

Tender and soft, Jay kissed her. "Dunno how much thinking she's doing."

"Precisely as little as we'd like her to, hmm?" Henry's hand between them disappeared.

Hand. Hands. Hardness under her hands. Headboard spindles. Thank God she'd started trimming her nails shorter or she'd leave half-moons behind.

"She's all trembly and doe-eyed." As Jay settled deep, his smooth cock ring bumped—*yeah, fuck, right there, Jay.*

No movement. Shared breath. A happy whimper, Henry must've—

Grinding, oh God, grinding to meet Jay's lunge and his kisses, fucking fantastic—

"—loses herself as you do, dear boy. Thoughts spinning, pleasure building, using the tethers I've given her to set her free and call her back to us safely."

"I see her, Henry." With his steep nose and criminally full lips, Jay boasted the most beautiful smile. "I see her letting go."

As she lifted to nuzzle him, the leather pulled her back.

"It's fine to join her. Letting go needn't be frightening." Rising beyond Jay, Henry commanded attention with his broad shoulders and sloping chest. "You've only one thing to remember." Jay blocked her view of the goodies beneath. Pout-worthy. "Alice." Serious, growly-man Henry. "Tell me your safeword."

"Pistachio." She rocked on waves, Jay buried inside and setting a slow rhythm. "Gotta listen for pistachio and Tilt-A-Whirl."

"That I do. Very carefully." Smiling, Henry bowed his head. "Forever and always."

"'Stachio." Snickering, Jay tickled her nose with a kiss. "Tillawhirl." Caresses graced her upper arms. Jay of the warm palms. "Nope, no thinking in there."

Henry, rumbling, settled a low fog of satisfaction around them. "We'll send you after her."

Groaning, Jay arched back, cock sliding and teasing.

"Easy, dear boy. Patience. A moment more and you'll have me."

Stretched and lubricated so he'd enjoy his present to the fullest measure. Henry's fullest measure was a damn good size. With long fingers, Henry pressed a gentle command at her ankle, and she *whoosh*ed her feet up the sheet. Knees high, pelvis tilted, not a bad angle for—

Fuck me.

A heartbeat. A slow, driving pulse, a double pump or a shockwave or—*oh God*—defying comparison. Gasping, Jay dropped his forehead to hers.

"My perfect instrument." In thrusting, Henry created a chain reaction through Jay and into her. "My beautiful Jay delivers pleasure in both directions." Fingers wrapped around Jay's flanks, Henry brushed her stomach. Steady strokes betrayed his fascination. "Has your reality matched your fantasy?"

"Better than fantasy." Jay, moaning, held them captive. He mesmerized Henry with the flexing muscles in his back and her with his dark eyes and curving biceps. "Best gift."

"Not so." A deeper thrust accompanied Henry's gentle denial. One-two, Henry's powerful motion and Jay's bobbing answer. "The birthday is yours, but the best gift is you."

Jay surged with driving hips and bounced her feet off the bed.

Snatching her ankles, Henry pressed her to his sides. "This intimacy we share is a gift." As he ran his hands up her legs, she kneaded his waist with her feet. "A meaningful communion."

Kissing and nipping, Jay buried his face in her neck. Hot breath accompanied urgent shudders. The earlier orgasms, the cock ring, and Henry's slow pace gave him more time to enjoy his fantasy. But he'd waited so long and—*fuck, yes, do that again*—the overwhelming pleasure had to be doubled in the middle. She wouldn't last long herself.

"Boundless love surrounds and strengthens us." Leaving her clinging to his hips, Henry increased the pace. "And at the very heart is our Jay, giving all, devoting himself to his lovers' pleasure."

Immersed in his own, too. Theirs fed his to overflowing. Streaming moans from his open mouth, Jay rolled his shoulders above her. Henry hadn't blanketed him the way he did her when he took her on all fours. Chancy mixed with bondage, but nagging instinct insisted Jay wanted the same full-bodied ownership.

She nuzzled his ear. "Ask." Off-script, but Henry wouldn't take what both men needed without a sign from Jay. "What you want." She tugged Henry with her toes. Fuck the extra weight. The orgasmic plateau beckoned, and she'd damn well hold up both of her men with it. "Give him the words, sweetheart."

Cuffs dragging, Jay crawled up her arms. He curled his fingers around hers, their hands locked together by choice, their bonds worn by choice, their service granted by choice.

"More." Jay kissed her cheek. "Please, Henry." Wriggling his ass up, he came dangerously close to leaving her empty. "Let me feel you at my back. Make me yours."

Her men grew heavier. Jay, sinking. And Henry. Finally claiming his right to rest the weight of his needs on them.

"I'm so grateful." Henry met her gaze over the curve of Jay's shoulder. "For my sweet loves." Ducking, he kissed Jay at the back of his neck. "For their courage."

A featherstroke from climax, Jay quaked and ground against her.

"Their inspiration." Henry gained power and momentum, deepening his thrusts. "Their hearts and bodies freely given."

Her heels skidded across Henry's back. Her lovers buoyed her through a slow, pulsing orgasm.

Thank-yous falling from his lips, gentle and trembling, Jay filled her with warmth. Henry followed with a low growl, his hands planted beside them and his arms strained and flexing.

As Henry sheltered them beneath his body, she cradled her men for as long as he allowed. Kisses and praise sealed them together.

"Sit up, my boy." Henry whispered, when Jay had grown too soft to hold. Wrapping Jay in a breath-stealing chest hug, he kissed him hard in the sweet spot below his ear. "Time to free our girl and sleep."

Few words and uncountable touches passed between them as they tidied up and readied for bed. Lined up at the sink, toothbrushes in hand, they bore matching hazy gazes and contented smiles. Sliding into fresh sheets, she shivered at the phantom brush of restraints. Jay's victory meant more nights like this lay ahead. Greater spontaneity, a wider selection of toys, and the power of Henry's ownership. *Fucking awesome birthday, sweetheart.*

Chapter 6

Henry's unbeatable clock-sense got the three of them to the club on time Saturday morning, even after he'd let them fool around and feed each other breakfast in bed.

Stopping in the salon on their way upstairs, they greeted Emma and her early arrivers. Introductions and the understated confidence in Henry's welcoming speech dialed down Alice's nerves during the quick run-through. Who didn't want to spend the morning in a Henry-led game?

The early birds rearranged the third-floor classroom into a pillow minefield. Seventeen cushions scattered on the floor. Every student desk pushed to the wall.

"Incoming." On hall monitor duty, Jay eased off his doorway slouch. His squinting lean gave way to a smile. "Daniel's on his way."

Their Emma-assigned play monitor sported bulky shoulders and a placid face. Throw on a set of horns and he'd make a credible buffalo—and jump on trouble just as fast. Since the dom class would have a flow different from the sub class, Emma and Henry had worked out arrangements.

Claiming the post by the door, Henry spoke to Daniel in low tones while she and Jay mingled. Doms in everything from formal suits to cutoff jeans swaggered in with ready handshakes. Attendees sported color-coded nametags, blue for regular members and orange for guests.

She and Jay made a full circuit, talking to every player. Henry's ostensible disinterest created the illusion of an aloof presenter reviewing last-minute details, but his attention lay like his hand on her neck. Combining the attendees' interactions with his submissives and information Emma relayed from the front desk via Daniel's headset, he'd have a complete picture of each participant before he greeted the class.

She had her eye on a few, though they all came up wanting beside Henry's easy control. This one too nervous. That one too overbearing. One creepy blond leveled a dead-eyed shark gaze at Jay the whole time they talked. The mix of ages, from those who'd get carded to those with gray temples, came as a surprise. Never too late to take up a new hobby, apparently.

Jay leaned beside her, hip to hip against the teacher's desk. "Time for the show."

Sure enough, Henry was making his way to the front, and the noise level dropped accordingly. He stopped before them, his back to the crowd.

Jay settled into his at-ease pose, hands clasped behind his back, and she copied him.

Approval written in his soft eyes and slight smile, Henry nodded. "Are you ready, my dears?" His gaze lingered on Jay.

"Ready and waiting." Jay bounced on his toes.

She cracked a smile. "For you? Always."

"An enticement if ever I heard one." He winked. In a quick pivot, he faced the assembled crowd and thanked them for attending. Thirty in all, a full house.

"For those who do not know me, I'm Henry. I'll be your instructor today, along with my partners, Jay and Alice." As he gestured, they stepped to either side and nodded in greeting. "Although we'll keep this class relatively informal, I'm sure you'll all understand when I ask you not touch them without my express permission."

"If we can't touch yours, are we meeting slaves or what?" Voice ringing out in challenge, shark-boy clapped his fist in his palm. "I came here to get my hands on new flesh."

A few chuckles drifted out, but most of the men and women wore blandly disapproving expressions.

"Ten minutes of mingling, and you haven't determined the answer for yourself?" With his pitying tone and slow headshake, Henry made his unmet expectations plain. "Perhaps you require assistance in being a good judge of character. An observant player." He cleared his throat.

Expectant air flooded her lungs. She bowed her head. The cushion at her feet came as close to Henry-green as the pile of options had allowed.

"Waiting pose, please."

Half the class knelt, with near-perfect precision. She silently congratulated herself on almost matching Jay's smooth style.

Henry laid a hand on Jay's head. "What makes you believe your temporary submissives aren't here already?"

Fifteen of Emma's friends had agreed to play along under Henry's supervision. With unobtrusive pillow-nudging as they mingled, each early bird had staked out a class partner and now knelt at his or her side.

Rueful grins and teasing murmurs spread through the fifteen standing. A baby-faced man in a too-tight collar glanced at the woman by his side and delivered a cheerful salute to Henry.

"We'll begin with a brief policy overview, after which we'll play a game, and we'll end with a broader discussion of what being a dominant in this club entails."

Sour-faced, the shark crossed his arms over his chest. His own partner apparently unworthy of his time, he stared at Jay.

Head bowed in a properly submissive position, Jay remained oblivious.

Henry launched into a short speech like the one he'd given last week. Aside from shark-boy's disdainful sniffs, the crowd stayed attentive.

She stared back. Fuck this guy and his attitude. Semi-subservient respect for Henry's friends like Santa Will, she could manage. Enjoy, in the right context. But this rude guest needed to check his intense interest in her pro—Henry's—property.

Henry, strolling a circuit as he delivered his address, passed in front of Jay.

Stare swimming her way, the shark bared his teeth in a silent laugh.

Suppressing the urge to charge him linebacker-style, she scrunched her nose and shot him her best *whatever* glare. Job done, Jay undisturbed, she bowed her head.

Henry smoothed her hair in passing. Behind her. He hadn't crossed her staring contest, though he could've easily. In his intro, he emphasized responsibility and awareness, the rise and fall of his voice lulling her like the tender comfort of story time. If they hadn't been demonstrating obedience, she'd have curled around his legs and tugged Jay along with her. Or, more likely, met a Jay who'd had the same thought in the middle.

"—to learn three things about your submissive and successfully ask them to perform one task for you." Henry spread his arms wide and gestured toward the walls. "Have them fetch you a seat from the edge of the room. Submissive partners, on your feet, please."

Unfolding, she stretched on her tiptoes. One of these days she'd master the loose-limbed zen of waiting pose. Though more than a few of Emma's friends sneaked in a casual stretch. Maybe the trick lay not in the perfection but the pursuit.

"Today's safeword?"

"Reset." The word reverberated off the chalkboard and the wood-slat blinds in a single, determined voice of seventeen layers, though she had ears only for Jay's rich tenor.

"Well done." Henry clasped Jay by the shoulder. "Dominants, you will respect 'reset' as a safeword. If your attitude would receive a polite dismissal of interest on a play night, your submissive will say, 'reset,' and you'll need to begin again."

"First thing I'd do"—shark-boy drawled with cool indifference—"is slap that word straight out of its head."

The woman beside him teetered back a step. Craning their necks, the pair in front shuffled aside.

"You intend to strike a potential partner as your opening statement?" On a curving arc, Henry approached the gap in the front row. "You do realize identifying as submissive does not make them your property."

Choice did. An offer, an acceptance, and a more explicit set of relationship rights and responsibilities than she'd ever considered, let alone written in a contract. Surprisingly, pleasingly efficient. Henry didn't mouth platitudes. When he promised to meet her needs and address her concerns, he meant every word.

"Does to me." Shark-boy shrugged. "Open strong, and it won't get any wrong ideas about what it's good for." He laughed, low and ugly. "Which had better be deep-throating my dick, or the first slap won't be the last."

Among his classmates, headshakes traveled like an airborne contagion. Rolling her eyes, a blue-tagged female dominant in the first row mouthed, "asshole."

About right, except an asshole held a ton more appeal.

"If you gratify yourself without meeting your partners' needs, you'll quickly find yourself with a dwindling supply of players for your games." Despite Henry's nonthreatening posture, his clipped censure came through in his tone. "If you truly desire to master someone else, you must first master yourself."

"If I truly"—shark-boy sneered—"desired to master someone else, I'd pick up a whip and show them their place."

With a clenched fist, Jay tapped his thigh. Jaw tense, he leveled his gaze.

She drifted closer, narrowing the distance between them to inches.

Shark-boy feinted with quintessential bully swagger, the eye-widening, shoulder-twitching provocation that always ended with *and two for flinching.*

"I see." In one casual sidestep, Henry blocked the man's line of sight to Jay. "And when they object? When their safeword rings in your ears?"

Silence draped the classroom. Not a rustle of clothing, not the squeak of a shoe interrupted. If echoes sounded, Henry and Jay had them locked behind steel facades.

"Safewords are for pussies." Shark-boy dripped, thick and oily, his disdain so much sludge tracked in on his fancy shoes. "Pathetic sluts who can't please a real master."

She slipped her hand over Jay's knuckles. Unfurling tense fingers, he entwined them with hers.

"Safewords are required. They form the first rule of safety." As Henry tucked his hands behind his back, his finger-wiggle greeting put a smile on Jay's face and a heel-toe rock in his stance. "This club's rules are based on the safe, sane, consensual ethos as both a moral imperative and a liability issue."

The club banned extreme forms of play— unpredictable games likely to lead to injury, like breath play, and dangerous risks to the property, like fire play. Attending the sub class and listening to Henry and Emma had taught her that along with the rules against professional—paid—sessions since the club structured itself as a nonprofit social group. Like the way her dad belonged to the Elks lodge. Except with sex.

"My slaves' first rule is no safewording." Shark-boy kicked a cushion aside and rested his hands on his hips, elbows out. "I'm done when I say I'm done."

"You won't be moved from that belief?" Neutral, deceptive calm meant Henry had already determined this conversation's end, and a punk attempt at intimidation sure as hell would lose.

"From the only real fun?" The moron laughed like he'd won a prize. "I make them scared and begging for it, until they don't know what's coming and can't stop it."

A sea of expectant faces looked to their master. Smiling for Jay, she nudged his head. He kissed her temple, the brush of his hair little-boy sweet and the strength of his clasp grown-man strong. They didn't need to wonder what Henry would say.

"This class is not for you. Nor is this club." Henry extended his arm toward the door. "You're free to go."

"You can't throw—"

"The color of your name tag tells me you're a guest. A probationary member sponsored by another, perhaps? You have no privileges. You admit you would not abide by the club's code of conduct, and you have disrespected your instructor and your fellow students."

A slight head tilt from Henry morphed Daniel from placid doorpost to buffalo scenting a threat to the herd. "Let's go, buddy. Master Henry says you're out, then you're out."

"Your name and photo will be marked in the club's database. I recommend you don't attempt to return."

"No, wait." The shark turned guppy, fending off Daniel with a wild swipe. "I was promised a full membership."

"Were you?" Eyes lighting with curious satisfaction, Henry almost smiled. "That won't be happening. Be certain to give your"—frost coated his voice—"benefactor—"

Red heat swept from the guppy's blond hairline to his bobbing Adam's apple.

"—my regards. It's a shame you learned nothing, but I suppose your head is stuffed too full of his diatribes to admit any knowledge."

Not a random shark—a friend of Cal's stirring up trouble. Trying to intimidate Jay, maybe, but Jay had eyes only for Henry just now.

Daniel marched the malcontent out with a solid grip on his upper arm.

Turning his back, Henry zeroed in on his submissives. His low hum rumbled as he neared them and nuzzled her cheek. "Your trust gives me all the power I need." For Jay, he delivered a bruising kiss, fast but rough. "And all of the exquisite service I could ever desire."

He swiveled in place before a crowd filled with nodding heads and envious smiles. "As we've disposed of the unpleasantness, let's consider a more enticing thought. How might we deliver a session that satisfies our desires and encourages our partners to return again and again—and to tell all of their friends?"

* * * *

As Jay scooped up their gear after class, she reached for a bag. "You want a hand?"

"Naw, I got them." Duffels dangling over each shoulder, he pecked her cheek. "I'll load the car so we're ready when Henry's done with the just-one-more-question-sir crowd." He trotted for the door.

"A moment, please, my boy." Henry, his voice carrying across the salon, stood in a knot of class attendees. "You and Alice may take those to a changing room. I'll be along to instruct you shortly."

As Henry resumed his conversation with the three stragglers, Jay bounced on his toes and nodded toward the hall.

She scurried over. If Henry had booked club playtime for Jay's birthday, he hadn't said a word to her. "You know what that's about?"

"Not a clue." He snaked through clusters of doms and subs making tentative overtures near the second-floor reception desk. "But good things come in threes. Like you, me, and Henry." Smirking, he ducked into the first open changing room and slung the bags on a padded bench. "Last night scored a hundred out of ten on the best-fantasies-ever chart, and class with Commander Henry stoked the fire, so the universe owes us a third." He crossed his fingers in a crazy configuration. "I'm pulling for sucking Henry's cock all afternoon."

Gaze straying to the duffels, she nodded. "Good choice." Henry hadn't opened the black one with the purple stripe during class. "Don't need toys for that." Cool and metallic, the zipper glinted against her finger. "So what's in the extra bag?"

"An excellent question." Henry shut the door behind him.

She twirled in guilty fascination. Wasn't touching. Nope, not her.

"If the two of you will strip down to your undergarments, we'll find out." He closed in on Jay and tugged him with fingers slipped between his buttonholes. "Let me help you with these."

Kicking off her shoes, Alice shucked her sundress with a swift yank.

"Folded, please." Henry roamed Jay's chest under the guise of unbuttoning his shirt. With firm strokes, he cued up Jay's whimpers like a needle hitting vinyl.

She halved the dress three times and laid the neat square beside the bags. Henry had worked Jay's shirt partway down his back, bunching cloth at the elbows.

"Arms straight." Long fingers curled with strength over tight muscle, Henry squeezed Jay's biceps.

Desire pulsed between her legs.

"You must let your shirt go if Alice is to fold it for you."

Shirt. Right. Take Jay's shirt. Sneak a deep breath of mingled maleness, except Henry noticed because he always noticed. He met her gaze with a slight smile and soft eyes, a sweet bed of deep green moss.

Squirming between them, Jay moaned. The rasp-and-tick of his belt opening followed. She drew his shirt clear and stepped back to fold.

"You are every inch my beautiful boy today, Jay." Henry slipped the belt free and let the pants *flump* to the floor. "What a lovely pair you and Alice made for our class." He splayed one hand in the small of Jay's back and eliminated the gap between them. With the other, he gripped the fine hairs at Jay's nape in a white-knuckled hold. "I'm proud to claim you for my own." Growling and demanding, he conquered Jay with a harsh, nipping kiss.

Boneless in surrender, Jay issued muffled whimpers hurtling her into their sexual currents. The changing rooms weren't for playing. Clanging knowledge couldn't erase her desire to witness an infraction. A tiny breach. Except nothing on Henry or Jay met the definition of tiny.

Henry pulled free.

Jay, gasping, dropped to his knees and pressed his face to Henry's distended dress slacks. "Please." Eyes closed, mouth open, he dragged his cheek along Henry's erection. "Please, Henry."

"My good, good boy. Do you understand how exquisite you are on your knees? What a delicious temptation?" With hypnotic repetition, Henry combed through Jay's messy black hair. "When we arrive home, I'll allow you to show me. Not before."

Jay shuddered. "Thank you, Henry."

Home. Upstairs might not be in their future. But why the undressing—

"Your fingers are twitching, Alice." Henry tipped his head toward the bench. "Go on and open the bag. We've a schedule to keep."

The zipper flew with a satisfying zing. Inside—casual shorts, t-shirts and sneakers. Athletic-style gear. Sets for her and Jay, and even dress-down khakis and a short-sleeve polo for Henry. "Are we—"

"Save your questions, please." Henry beckoned her over and kissed her. "We haven't finished celebrating someone's birthday."

Something sporty and designed for Jay-fun. Biking? Hiking? Climbing? Kayaking?

Henry let them dress themselves, chivvied them downstairs, and retrieved their phones from the desk. Instead of pocketing his as usual, he listened while Jay hauled the duffels. More astonishing, he placed a call while Jay loaded the trunk.

"Yes, thank you for checking. They can run long." Henry stood tall and blank-faced, offering no clues. "Quite well, I think. Time will tell." The polo shirt gave him a rakish, informal air. "We're still on for one?" He opened the back door and gestured them into the car. "Lovely. We'll see you there."

The door latched. Henry approached the driver's door. She and Jay paused in mid-seat-belt pull.

"Biking tour on the Emerald Necklace."

"Sailing cruise in Boston Harbor."

"Sailing? But you like biking."

"Henry likes sailing." How Jay to imagine Henry's likes before his own, even for his birthday surprise. "And he put on boat shoes."

The door opened, and speculation ceased. Seat belts clicked. Boat shoes. Damn. When had Jay become the more observant one?

Henry guided the car through crawling Saturday traffic in the Back Bay and slipped into a rare empty parking space. "Wait here. I'll be a moment."

She peeked down the block of brownstones converted into small shops. "Restaurant."

"Lunch for on the boat."

"Or to stow on a bike's gear rack."

"Boat." Bouncing his knee against the door, Jay stuck his tongue out. "When I'm right, you're gonna be mad you didn't guess it first."

"Bike." She bumped his leg. "When I'm right, you'll crown me queen of the guesses." Eyes trained on the front stoop five doors down, she crowed at Henry's reappearance. "It's a cooler." Too big for a bike rack. "Maybe you're right about the boat."

Jay shrugged, affected nonchalance in his too-cool-for-school smirk. "I've got the birthday magic."

Cooler deposited in the trunk, Henry drove across the Charles with smooth, silent precision. Not heading toward the harbor, but in the wrong direction for the fenway, too. Where the hell was he taking them?

* * * *

They left the car in a lot edging toward capacity at a park spilling over with Saturday-in-June enthusiasm. Shouts, laughter, and barking dogs flowed from soccer fields and baseball diamonds.

With the cooler in his arms and a bag over his shoulder, Jay swung toward the sights like a puppy sniffing out a new home. Henry led them past napping babies, cranky toddlers, and children running full-tilt. Teens using sports as cover for flirting and adults using sports for foreplay. The whole place vibrated at Jay's frequency.

They'd passed half a hundred decent patches of grass for a picnic, but Henry kept to the blacktopped path cutting through it all. Trees arched above them. Beyond the tunnel of shade, a woman leapt from red-hued asphalt. The *smack* of a bouncing ball sounded as she came down, curls bobbing in a close-cut cap around her face.

Last week's tea. Claudia. A day out with other submissives.

"Basketball." Her murmur and Jay's shout hit the air as one.

"Just so." Stepping off the path, Henry angled toward a man reclining under a tree. "Tell me, did either of you successfully guess?"

Jay's hair flew as he shook his head. "Not even close." Damn happy about being wrong, though, with his boyish grin and messy mop.

"Does 'starts with B' count as matching the category?" She shot Henry an inquiring eyebrow and a sly smile. "Because I said biking."

"And if it does?" He swerved, intercepting her and leaning in. "What prize does my sweet girl hope to receive?"

"Not just me." If prizes were forthcoming, she'd go halfsies without complaint. "Jay said boating." Sailing, but close enough. "That's a 'b' word, too."

"Is that so?" Losing his flirty undertone, Henry extended his arm. "Would you like a prize, Jay?"

"Man, would I." Jay hoisted the cooler higher. "Place to set these down would be fan-tas-tic."

No joking innuendo about a prize?

"Set up under the tree, please. The duffel contains a blanket." Henry carried on without missing a beat. "I'll content myself with the shade while you run yourselves ragged."

Jay outpaced them. Not hard, since incomprehension rooted her to the ground. Alpha bro attitude from the submissive begging to suck Henry off less than an hour ago.

Linking his arm in hers, Henry kissed her forehead. "Come along, dearest. We've introductions to make."

She walked out of self-preservation. He'd never let her faceplant, but he strode with purpose, and her choices were match him or stumble.

Jay dropped the gear courtside and snapped out their picnic blanket.

More bags rested on a blanket a few feet away, where the stranger climbed to his feet. "Henry." He walked past the crouching Jay without a glance. "I've never seen you so casual."

"A gentleman dresses for the occasion, Stephen." Henry tweaked his collar. "Within reason. You won't lure me onto the court, I'm afraid."

Laughing, Stephen thrust out his hand. "Didn't expect to."

The men shook with arms extended, gazes locked, and short nods exchanged. A bouncing ball and thudding feet beat a background rhythm unchanged by their arrival. As the alphas brushed territorial boundaries, Henry left one arm clasped around her.

"If your boy can keep up with Charlie, that'll be gift enough." Stephen boasted kind eyes, towering height, and the t-shirt and shorts motif everyone but Henry bore. "I'm glad you called. Claudia says your girl has spine, and she's a hard one to impress."

Henry swept up said spine. "Stiff and supple by turns, and always with exquisite timing. Stephen, this is my Alice."

His Alice. Warmed by the certainty of Henry's claim, she stuck out her arm. "Hi. It's an unexpected pleasure."

"Nice to meet you, too, Alice." Glancing at Henry, Stephen waited for his nod before shaking her hand. Navigating boundaries got tricky when players followed different rules. "My pets have been looking forward to this."

"We would've, too, if we'd known." She laid her head on Henry's shoulder. Him and his surprise gestures of love. "But I like this way better."

"I'm pleased." Nuzzling, Henry dipped his nose into her hair. "Your playmates for the day are warming up. You ought to join them." A nudge of command colored his voice. "Jay," he called. "Thank you for setting up. It's a fine job. Go on and play."

Ahh. Dom time. She edged onto the court. The last time—gym class? Tenth grade. Hoo boy. The things she did for Jay.

Claudia, basketball on her hip, sauntered over. "Alice. Cool." She tossed a nod at Jay. "Charlie's been insufferable all week waiting to meet you guys."

"Not true." The guy shooting imaginary baskets from the half-circle topping the painted rectangle stopped jumping. "I've been in suffer*ing*."

Beside her, Jay laughed and ruffled his hair. "At least you knew. I'd've gotten some practice in if I'd known."

"Hi, Charlie here—you're Jay, right?" The skinny blond zipped to his target like a magnetic lock. "So great to meet you." He pumped Jay's hand. "Claud said you two had a good vibe. I was so disappointed about the lunch thing. Like work was sooo important I couldn't skip out." His full-body droop swung stringy hair past his shoulders. "You know how work is. Or not. Do you work? I do, but socializing with the guys is tough. Master S gets all territorial." He jerked toward the quiet mountain standing on the sideline. "Don't tell, but I love when he pulls that shit."

Face blank as a porch-sitter in a twister, Jay mirrored Charlie's nod.

"Master S says work comes first and playtime is a reward for after. Like eating vegetables, right?" Charlie patted his stomach beneath the words *finish him* on his t-shirt, where a gape-mouthed Pac-Man approached a blue ghost. "What the big man says goes. You know."

Hovering within inches of slack-jawed yokel, her chatterbox stared without answering. Charlie hadn't said anything Jay wouldn't—at home. Or in the club. But he'd donned his guy-armor out here. Understanding why Charlie hadn't seemed beyond him.

"Claud came back with all these lunch stories and I was way jealous." Charlie scowled at his girlfriend with exaggerated drama. "She's not big on details, so when Master S pulls more out of her than, 'it was nice,' I know it was wicked crazy."

Her silent urging didn't drive Henry from his dom-talk or propel him to Jay's side for comforting support. They'd pulled the separate mingling act before, at Henry's gallery show. She'd played the bridge between them, the lover two friends shared. But why bother with subterfuge here?

"I was so jealous I whined my way into corner time, and that sucked." Cheeks puffed, Charlie blew out like a deflating balloon. "It lasted forever. I mean, for-ev-er."

In mid ball-bounce, Claudia flashed her hands up, palms out and fingers spread. *Ten minutes,* she mouthed.

Unwanted, intrusive awareness swamped her. Jay wouldn't appreciate the comfort. Henry hadn't called Jay to him or hurried out because he knew better than to try. The months before she'd been invited in, the times she'd wavered between fantasizing Henry and Jay were a couple and thinking them just roommates. Because they never got touchy-feely in public.

"I hate corner time. But Master S let me crawl over and apologize for acting bratty, and that rocked."

Talk about no boundaries. Jay babbled in private, but Charlie took the cake.

"I give awesome blowjobs."

Two cakes.

"Five-star-restaurant blowjobs."

Pizza parlor birthday sheet-sized cakes.

"Oh man, did Claudia tell you——"

"Enough, little frog." Stephen wrapped massive arms around Charlie and knocked their heads together. The blond went limp, closing his eyes and sagging into his master's embrace. "You get all afternoon with our new friends."

Henry slipped alongside her. She almost—almost—copied Charlie's move. But Jay wouldn't join in. Distance didn't belong between them. Not after the communion they'd shared last night. Not after they'd spent the morning in sub-mode while Henry gave lessons in dominance.

"Don't eat up every minute with chatter," Stephen warned. "I want to see your ball-handling skills put to use on the court, Charlie."

Jay swiped the ball from Claudia and danced toward the basket. The wider the world, the smaller Henry's hold over them. Wrongness itched at her, a nagging center beyond her reach.

As Charlie rattled off locations where he'd displayed his skills, Henry scratched between her shoulder blades. Trust him to find the perfect spot without a map. "Have a good game, my dear. I'll be watching."

Jay sank his shot. Claudia recovered the ball while Stephen whispered in Charlie's ear.

"You sure you won't play?" Knowing the answer, she selfishly hoped for a different one.

"Today is for our boy. I enjoy seeing him unburdened at play." He inhaled, sharp and deep, his nose buried in her hair. "This court is not mine."

But I am. Jay is.

Henry had held court like a king this morning. His retreat to the picnic blanket, though poised and graceful, tore at her.

Grabbing the hem of Charlie's t-shirt, Stephen exposed his submissive's chest. "Give me this. You can start shirts versus skins. Since we're in public, you and Jay will be skins."

"Yeah, girls on guys!" Charlie whooped. "Your dom's awesome for setting this up, Jay."

Jay stumbled, and Claudia dribbled past him for the basket.

Charlie laughed. "Claud kind of kicks my ass at hoops, but I can't say I hate it when she slams into me and goes up for a shot, you know?"

"Yeah, I—" Grinning, Jay swung around and spotted her. "Alice, you okay with those teams?"

"It's your birthday." Adorable the way he checked in, though. Like she got first dibs on him. She did, didn't she? After Henry. "I'll play however you like."

Charlie whistled. "Dayum. I gotta have more birthdays. Claud, you think—"

"Hell no." Laughing, Claudia grabbed her rebound. "I know how you like to play, and it involves me doing all the work."

"Maybe the both of you boys can give Claudia a challenge." Stephen sluiced the shirt over Charlie's head and draped it on his own shoulder. "No offense intended, Alice. I don't know you well enough to judge your contribution."

"My goal is to avoid hindering Claudia's inevitable victory."

Stephen stood rubbing Charlie's bare chest—hairier and not so firm as Jay's—in the middle of the park. Bent and bit his neck, for chrissake.

"Me and basketball have a passing acquaintance." Words fell out of her mouth on autopilot. Henry would never pull those moves on Jay in public. "In that I usually passed on playing." Worming her fingers under Jay's shirt, touching his hips, she lowered her voice. "I bet Henry would hold this for you." If he wouldn't listen to Henry here, he'd damn well listen to her. "Shirts versus skins is traditional. You know how he likes to uphold traditions."

Jay jogged to their courtside blanket. Liminal space in the big oak's shade. Not center court, where the pressure to be a man trumped all. Where Charlie's easygoing approach to manhood locked him in stunned silence. He exchanged quiet words with Henry before yanking his shirt over his head.

"Don't worry, Alice." Claudia dribbled and shot from behind the wide arc painted on the asphalt.

Accepting Jay's shirt, Henry maintained middle-school-dance distance, all the way. Appearances.

"Swish." Charlie whistled. "Nice one, Claud."

As the ball bounced into the grass, Stephen smacked Charlie's ass. "Hop to, little frog. Play a good game and you'll earn a treat. I expect a dazzling display of athletic exertion."

Dazzling? She'd be outclassed before the first play. Thank God Henry wouldn't expect the same from her. Face intent, mouth moving, he stood inches from a bare-chested Jay. Time to invest in lip-reading classes.

With kisses for Charlie and Claudia, Stephen retreated to the blankets. Two dominants, sitting around discussing who knew what while their submissives entertained them.

"Seriously, don't sweat it." Claudia squeezed her shoulder and let go. Maybe she lived a testosterone-soaked life, too. Years without a female friend to hang with. "We'll have you shooting like a pro before the food hits the blanket. Enough to score off Charlie, at least."

"Whoa, hold up, I am a major impediment to any drive for the basket." Charlie hopped and hooked his shot up and off the backboard. The ball bounced along the rim and out. "Shit."

Claudia rolled her eyes. "You're a major impediment to any drive for your team, you mean."

"That didn't count." Charlie snatched the ball. "Practice jitters."

Bearing a wide grin, Jay jogged back. "Shirtless." As he slung his arms around her, his woodsy scent enveloped her. "You like?"

"My stud." Not Henry's, though, not in public. "This is supposed to be your birthday game, but here you are giving me a present." Allowing Henry to act like a boyfriend in public would be a better one. He didn't have to voice disappointment or crack the dominant façade. Down to her bones, she knew Jay's public distance pained him. "I love when you and Henry get all naked and sweaty."

Charlie dribbled to Claudia and faked a pass. "Or you put girl cooties on the gear. Did you lick this ball?"

With a well-timed reach, Claudia swiped the ball from Charlie. "What, you think because I licked your balls before breakfast that I snuck out to the garage…"

The teasing bickering carried through the first game. Light trash talk. Wagers won and lost. She lasted two half-court games to fifteen points and dragged her ass in a third before her body begged for a reprieve. Bent over, she gripped her knees with trembling knuckles and sucked in lungfuls of air.

"Jay, bring your playmate here." Henry waved them over. "You've quite worn her out."

A heat sink of sweet male musk, Jay hoisted her to his bare chest. Three games hadn't winded him. He dripped more sweat on his daily routes. "One Alice, coming in for a landing." Crouching, he laid her beside Henry with the delicacy of a researcher sliding a prize into the balance pan for weighing.

"Thank you, my boy." Henry kept his voice low. "I'll keep our girl with me, but you're free to continue your game. Are you having fun?"

"Tons of fun. Thank you, Henry." As the men reached for the same strand of hair stuck to her forehead, Jay grazed Henry's fingers. "I'm glad you played, Alice." With his goofy grin and shining eyes, he more than recompensed her for her aching lungs and tight calves. "I'll make it up to you with games you like better later. Promise." He plastered her face with tiny kisses and loped back to the game.

Stephen jogged out to take her place, congratulating Charlie with a massive hug and a deep, delving kiss. Claudia got the same treatment billed as consolation for her unprecedented loss.

Fumbling for water, Alice came up with an empty bottle. Must've swigged the final drops during their last drink-and-dash.

"Try this." Henry held a glass to her lips. Orange juice-ish, but with a sweeter kick. "Better?"

"Definitely." She swished her second sip before swallowing. "Honey?"

"Maple syrup." He dug in the cooler and presented her with trail mix. "Have some raisins, please." Nuzzling her hairline, feeding her bite by bite, he kissed her temple. "At least I'll get something healthy in you before the birthday cupcake feast."

"Anything you wanna put in me is healthy in my book." As she waggled her eyebrows, he rewarded her with a laugh and a growl.

On the court, Jay drove to the basket and dropped one in over Charlie's block. She hooted while Henry clapped.

"You know it's adorable that you set up a playdate for his birthday, right?" A picnic at the park totally nailed normal family. "It's baby-panda levels of cute."

"He's an active man." Kneading her leg across his lap, Henry drained her aching weariness. "He needs stimulation."

A pent-up Jay bounced like a big dog denied a daily walk. Different from how his energy flowed at home, though. Or even this morning at the club. He didn't seek Henry's approval here. He passed out high-fives and kissed her with abandon, but he didn't display the ease with Henry that Charlie did with his master.

Stephen touched his subs as if the world beyond didn't exist. All the time. Henry limited himself to touching Jay in guy-approved ways. Maybe Jay gravitated toward Henry in private to soak up attention he refused to request in public.

Henry switched to her other calf, and sadness washed through her as her muscles unknotted. Anyone paying attention for five seconds would see Claudia and Charlie were two people in love with Stephen and each other. But anyone looking at Henry and Jay? They'd see two men in love with the same woman.

"You're fretting, my dear."

"He needs to see he can be proud of himself for being yours outside the apartment." Maybe Charlie would be a good example.

Staring out at the court, Henry paused his massage. "Yes, that too."

She downed her drink, he finished the massage, and they settled in to watch the game. Jay and Claudia had pulled ahead. Stephen and Charlie huddled and hustled to catch up.

Lying on his side, Henry propped his head on one hand. The other lay on her bare stomach, her shirt nudged aside as he sketched sweeping arcs with his thumb. Lavishing on her all the possessiveness Jay shied from on a day out.

"I'm sorry, Henry." She couldn't leave it lie.

"Sorry for what?" Brow raised, he drew back.

"That you can't touch Jay like this." She waved toward the runners and Frisbee-tossers, the dog walkers and kid-wranglers. "Out here, I mean."

"Ah." He glanced at the court. "He isn't ready for that."

Jay missed a block, his jump a fraction of a second too early to stop Charlie's shot.

"For now, it's enough for him to know he has my rules to guide his behavior. He takes comfort in that."

Stephen walloped Charlie with a hug and a kiss on his head. "Great shooting. Nice hop, little frog."

Alice held back a sigh. "But you want more."

"I always want more." Henry claimed her mouth as a conqueror reveling in his spoils. "To own every last inch of you both." His smile carried a distinct wolfish pleasure. "Lucky for me, I'm a patient man."

* * * *

At dinner Thursday night, music blared. Jay hopped from his chair, froze, and turned toward Henry. "It's Peggy's ringtone."

The name rang a dim bell.

"It's all right. Go on and take your call, my boy."

Jay raced to the hall table and snatched his phone.

Was Henry sick? No calls at dinner was practically a rule. Hell, it might be in Jay's contract. The time belonged to the three of them to unwind and talk without interruptions.

"Exceptions to every rule," Henry murmured.

Jay tilted sideways, almost perpendicular at his waist. "But you said Saturday lunch." Palm flat and fingers spread, he tapped his thigh. "No, I know." Rocking foot to foot, he fiddled with the charger cord. "I didn't—I'm sorry, Peggy." His head dropped until his chin grazed his chest. "I know you're doing a bunch of work just for me. I don't mean to be ungrateful."

Jay, ungrateful?

Henry shared her frown.

"Who's Peggy?" Aside from some liar who thought she had the right to make Jay feel guilty.

"Eldest sister. Something of a second mother." Matching her whisper, Henry rapped the table twice. "He'll lose this argument, I'm certain."

"No, it's not that—I can, but—no." Mouth twisted, Jay glanced at the dining room. "Okay. I won't. See you then." He lined up the phone on the charging pad with Henry-level precision and dragged his feet on his return. "I'm sorry, Henry. I didn't mean to interrupt dinner."

"The phone interrupted dinner, my dear boy. You waited for permission, as you should." Picking up his fork, Henry acted as if dinner would simply resume its normal course. "Have your weekend plans changed?"

Jay slumped into his seat. "Peggy says I need to show up earlier."

"To what?" She hadn't gotten an inkling of special plans, but Henry must've approved them already.

"Jay's family is hosting a birthday celebration at their farm." Henry laid his fork down with a slight *clink*. "I'd intended for us to discuss this after dinner."

"We're going out of town?" Last-minute trip surprises would take getting used to. Maybe Henry meant to test her trust, reinforce his control over the household. The cabin weekend had been amazing despite the lack of warning. Fantastic shower, lovely deck—fuck, no sexy thoughts when meeting Jay's parents. "How early? I can't cut out of work. We're…"

Face reddening, Jay stared at his plate. Corner creases grew around Henry's eyes and mouth.

Shit. She'd stepped in it this time. "I'm not going, am I." Good enough
for the fucking but not for the family. As cream sauce dripped from her
fork tines, she forced a nod. "Okay."

Her flat tone missed *okay* by a mile. Stupid and unfair, because no way
did Jay think of her as a part-time fuckbuddy. If he'd suggested taking her
home for Christmas six months ago, she'd have freaked. So what if the
guys left her home? New puppies needed constant looking after. Not her.

"You'll have plenty to keep you entertained, Alice." With his low rumble,
Henry coated her in soothing balm. "I don't expect I'll be going, either."

Hold. The. Phone.

"Jay, when does your sister demand your presence?" If Jay leaving him
behind upset Henry, he concealed his hurt behind a neutral front.

"In time for dinner." Not a speck of birthday excitement infused Jay's
mumble. "Friday dinner."

He'd miss Henry's time with them. Excellent reason to pout like a kid
denied dessert.

"Did you express to her that you'll have to abbreviate your workday to
arrive in time?" No, obviously. Henry had heard every word of his side of
the conversation, same as she had.

Jay shook his head. "No, Henry."

"Because you didn't wish to inconvenience her?"

"She's doing all the work—the cake and everything." His tenor earnest
and naïve, Jay shrugged. "I shouldn't make things harder for her."

Baking a cake. So much fucking work. Alice bit her lip.

"Are the inconveniences arriving early poses for you less important
than those a Saturday lunch poses for your sister?" Henry hooked Jay on
the sharp point beneath gentle inquiry.

Jay didn't want to be away from them Friday night. He just hadn't been
able to put himself first, say "no," and disappoint his sister.

"It's all weekend." He toyed with his napkin. "I'll be back
Sunday afternoon."

Way to dodge the question. "And we're not welcome."

"I'm sorry, Alice." Apologizing, Jay left lightspeed in the dust. "I've
never brought anyone home before."

The fuck? He'd taken Henry to meet his family. They'd been together
for years.

"Not, you know"—Jay fumbled toward Henry—"someone special."

Either Jay had stopped making sense, or her misfiring brain had ceased
rational thought.

"I mean, not overnight." Jay babbled under her stare. "Not with anybody knowing. I don't talk about"——his crumpled napkin disappeared into his fist—"it."

It.

His love life. His preferences. His lovers.

She struggled to breathe. Before Christmas, Henry'd said Jay's family knew them as roommates. His meaning had bounced off her then. Jay made the truth real tonight. To his family, Henry wasn't someone special in Jay's life. She was likely nonexistent. An it.

But would she bring Henry and Jay home to South Dakota? God no. Not because her men made her ashamed, but because she'd end up ashamed of her parents. Dad would call her a whore, and Mom would pretend everything was fine.

"It's okay, Jay. I was just..." Hurt. Angry. She refused to guilt him the way his sister had. "Surprised."

Celebrating Jay's birthday last weekend hadn't been about the timing working out better for her or getting ahead of their sweetly impatient birthday boy. Henry had expected Jay's family would take priority this weekend.

"Surprised, yes. Alice is correct. We'll miss you, but your desire to visit family is understandable." With years of experience cushioning the blow, Henry managed to sound unaffected. "I'll be certain to assign homework to occupy you while you're away, my dear boy. I'd hate for you to fall behind."

"I'll keep up, Henry." Eager and smiling, Jay loosened his death-grip on his napkin and sat up straight. "I promise."

She returned his smile to reassure him, but her twitchy nerves lingered. Territorial—clingy—had never described her in a relationship, and uncertainty pricked like a hedge of sticker bushes. If a right way to feel existed, what was it?

The bastard thorns insisted on staying the night. She slipped under the covers without even a mock squabble with Jay over who'd sleep in the middle. As he flopped beside her, her muscles tensed.

Playfully wrestling with him, Henry delivered a good-night kiss that ended in a smooth switch. Henry claimed the center, and Jay curled on his left.

She lay on her back, inches of distance a yawning chasm, eyes adjusting to the darkness. Henry's silence weighed as if the ceiling cranked downward. Normally she'd welcome his keen insights and prods to share. But wanting to avoid hurting Jay left her with nothing to say.

Murmuring good night and nothing else, Henry blanketed her in relief. Right now, she needed to process. Alone.

She could leave. Take the bedroom they never treated as one. If being in this relationship hadn't changed her beyond recognition, she'd sleep fine alone.

Long way to go to prove a point to herself.

Back to her lovers, she hugged the edge of the bed and lay awake as night passed into morning.

* * * *

Jay's empty seat at the dinner table Friday drew Alice's eyes more often than it should. By the time she'd finished work, he'd already gone. She should be enjoying her time with Henry. In the eleven months since she'd started seeing—fucking—her men, she'd spent only two nights alone with him.

On those nights, she hadn't felt abandoned. Unwanted. What the hell was wrong with her? Jay was with his family, not cruising to meet other women. Knowing her attitude wronged him made her feel worse. Ashamed.

"Alice." Watching her for the last hour, Henry hadn't challenged her silence. "It's after seven o'clock. Have you finished your supper?"

She'd choked down four bites. Five, maybe. Didn't matter. "Yes, Henry."

"Then tell me your safeword, please."

"Pistachio." The ritual lacked Jay's infectious excitement, their doubled anticipation, the conspiratorial glee of sharing Henry's attention.

"When will you use your safeword, my dear?"

"When I want to stop," she whispered. She and Jay heightened and reinforced each other's arousal. Being without him made her incomplete.

"For any reason."

Why didn't they have a word that stopped important things? If they had, Jay wouldn't have submitted to his sister's demands and left them.

"Do you promise to use your safeword if that time comes, Alice? Lift your head and look at me when you answer, please." Face unreadable, Henry stared at her with those perceptive green eyes.

Her breath caught in her chest. "I promise, Henry."

"Thank you." Surveying the table, Henry stopped on her plate.

He'd require her to eat more, have her clear, and—

"Go to the bedroom and undress." His tenderness disappeared under pure command. "Lie on your stomach on the bed and wait for me."

Fumbling, she pushed the chair back and stood. "You're sure you don't want—"

"I'm certain I've told you what I want from you, sweet girl."

After a quick detour to the bathroom, she stripped off her clothes, lay on the bed, and steeped in her own nudity. Air wafted across her back. Cool silk sheets cradled her breasts, her stomach, her thighs. The linens retained the faint scent of Henry—and Jay. Breathing deep, she chased the tenuous connection.

Loneliness answered her, the bed empty and her with it.

Henry filled the door frame.

Her heart thudded for his broad shoulders and narrower hips, for his forbidding stare and his strong hands.

He entered in silence and passed behind her. His clothes rustled, faint clues to his movements. The shirt, button by button. The belt with its buckle. Pants. Socks. Underwear.

The mattress sank in slow waves rolling up from her toes. He added his weight to hers, their bodies electrical fields rubbing edges and generating heat. Settling astride her hips, he rested atop her ass. His hands landed on her shoulders.

She sparked hot as a live wire. Christ, how had she functioned all day with shoulders so tight? No wonder sore and empty formed the sum total of her emotional battery.

Henry balanced his palms inches from her head. "You're upset with Jay, sweet girl."

Not sweet. An utter bitch pissed at her lover because what, he couldn't tell his sister no? Worried about them meeting his family? A selfish, immature bitch. "That obvious, huh?"

Warm and tender, Henry blanketed her back. "You're making yourself tense. Tell me what you feel. Say the words aloud."

"I'm—" The sheets offered a comforting hollow for her face.

"Alice. Don't hide from me or yourself."

"Rejected." The word burned and scratched her throat. "Like he doesn't love us." Her eyes itched. "I know I'm stupid to think that, and he loves us, and I'm being a bitch." A chill rattled deep in her chest, beyond his reach. "I'm sorry. I'm sorry, Henry."

Lips pressed to the nape of her neck, he hummed a low, soothing melody while he warmed her with his breath. Minutes slipped by as she inhaled in deep gulps.

"This isn't something you've allowed yourself to feel before, is it, dearest?" Henry rumbled, his voice as much vibrating against her back as in her ear. "You've avoided deep emotional ties with your sexual partners. You hoped, perhaps, you might avoid this moment—this pain when you feel one has wronged you."

"I know Jay didn't wrong me, Henry. I get it." Christ, if he'd let her put the whole damn attitude behind her, she could focus on trying to enjoy the night without Jay.

"Nonsense. You know no such thing."

"I kn——what?" Where was Henry's vigorous defense of Jay? His chiding for her unkindness and distance?

Forearm flexing, Henry levered himself up. "What you know is that you are here, and he is not." Seated across her thighs, he massaged her back and sides, his kneading heavy and deep. "And what you feel, perhaps, is that you are a shameful secret."

His prodding drove a sob from her. In her only other long-term relationship, she'd actively avoided chances to meet her boyfriend's parents. *Hi, I'm Alice, and I'm using your son for mediocre sex. Is that what marriage is like?* Today, her heart starved because Jay hadn't taken her home for the weekend. So fucking juvenile.

"Your feeling is magnified now, both because you love him, and thus your soul finds perfection where it is not, and because you've never allowed yourself to feel such pain before." As he dug into her shoulders, knotted muscles rolled and shifted at his command. "Every slight, intentional and unintentional, has pooled in a reservoir of pain."

Wrong. Her brief flings hadn't touched the real Alice. No exposure, no hurt. Lovers hadn't been worth more of her time or attention. *And I wasn't worth theirs.*

"You've kept a distance, believing it insulated you from the risk. The electrical current could not reach you, could not shock you, could not burn you."

In his splayed hands, Henry covered her shoulder blades. She couldn't help but let his warmth touch her. He delivered more than a physical sensation. A comfort. A love.

"But when that painful current reaches you now, it electrifies the entire pool. It's not the lack of insulation, sweet girl. And the answer is not to add layers. You cannot keep out what is already within."

Was he right? Embracing maturity, she'd constructed her self-image as a fun, flirty, sex-positive woman who didn't need a man——or another woman, for that matter. Independence was her emotional fulfillment.

But she liked her men's touch. Not the physical touch alone but the emotional one. Losing the amazing flutter in her chest when Henry gazed at her or Jay curled himself around her like vacuum-formed plastic would break her. Strong, solid Henry wouldn't let anything hurt her if he could prevent it. Not even herself.

"This is merely another kind of confrontation, my brave Alice."
Resuming his massage, Henry used force enough to carve her into the
mattress. "Allow the tears to flow. Do not berate yourself for feeling as you
do. Acknowledge and accept your pain as valid." With every declaration,
he smoothed a wave from the slope of her ass where his weight rested to
her shoulders. Pushing up and out. "Whether Jay intended to cause pain
is irrelevant. All that matters is that you feel. Only then can you dislodge
the resentment that will form if you refuse."

She'd never resent Jay. He was so open and trusting——and he'd left
them. How could he claim to be Henry's boy with blazing pride and act so
damn ashamed? A scream built in her chest. A demand he explain himself
to her, right now, goddamnit. Her breath blew hot in her face, clinging to
the sheets and her cheeks.

Wide brown eyes wavered in the heat mirage. Jay, with downturned
lips as he swallowed her scolding rage and believed he deserved no less.
He'd take whatever punishment she dealt, fair or unfair, and apologize
until long after her pleasure coated his tongue and his jaw ached.

"I can't. I can't." She blinked until his sweet face faded. "He'd never
defend himself."

Tightening his hold on her, Henry growled. Not happy-sexy growl.
"You must accept your feelings before you empathize with his. Jay is not
here to be harmed. You've no need to minimize your pain in front of me."

Of course he'd recognized the brave face she'd worn for Jay. But
things too big for her to process could be shared during Henry's time. Tell
him everything. Tell him or use her safeword.

Someday she might need to safeword, but not as an excuse to run from
her feelings again. She might make new mistakes. She wouldn't make the
same one.

"I thought we were a family." Jay'd called the three of them a family
so many times. "He said, Aren't we good enough to meet his real family?"
Sharp and raw, she scratched the stillness with her whispers. "Why would
he go and leave us behind?"

Sheltering her beneath himself, Henry braced her with his firm chest
and enclosed her in his steady arms. "That's right, my sweet Alice. Let
yourself feel without blame."

He comforted her with weight and warmth as her tears came, bringing
a few guttural sobs she stopped trying to hold back. His gentle humming
told her he understood. That he'd help her fix her confusion and pain, find
a stopper at the bottom and drain her supposed reservoir. Henry would
bail out her pain a bucket at a time if he had to—and he'd never stop.

"You're in new territory, dearest. The terrain of love is unfamiliar to you, and Jay has helped guide you here. It's natural to feel abandoned when your steps carry you farther than he has gone, in a direction he is not yet able to travel." With his nose buried in her hair, Henry released a soft sigh. Maybe he, too, still pinched in pain's vise. He wanted Jay here with them, safe and happy, able to tell his sister "no."

"You'll each try to take that burden on yourselves. For Jay, the sense he has failed you and must take those steps to please us. For you, the sense your pain must be suppressed or ignored because it was unintended." Henry dabbed her neck and shoulders with tiny kisses. "Alice. My sweet, sweet girl. That Jay did not intend to harm you does not make you less harmed, nor does it make your feelings worthless, stupid, or, heaven forbid, *bitchy*."

Her sob hiccupped into a giggle. Henry cursed with such disdain for it. He swore rarely, and with purpose.

"Aha—progress. Music from your lips." Taking his time, he traced the curving outline of her ear with his tongue. As he reached the sensitive lower lobe, he triggered shivers in her. "Tell me what you've learned. Tell me your feelings at this exact moment."

"I made errors in my premises. I was angry at Jay because his behavior didn't fit." Ideas she'd chewed on all night and carried to work this morning. "But then I thought about what I would've done differently, and I—"

The reservoir might be deep. Henry encouraged her to think things through her own way, but he wanted her to have all of the information— as she and Jay had wanted for him in wrestling with returning to the club. His breath lapped like waves on her skin.

"I was being hypocritical. I feel guilty. Ashamed. People aren't as easy as plastics and metals." Materials behaved according to natural laws, no response unquantifiable. "I don't know where their fracture points are. I don't—" She plunged into chilly, deep waters. "I don't want to break Jay."

"And yourself? Will you break yourself, then, to avoid hurting him?" Driving his fingers between hers, Henry pressed his warmth into her. "You must know I can't allow that. I will never make one of you whole at the other's expense."

Closing her fist, she squeezed back. "I know. I'm—I feel—safe knowing that. But sometimes I see Jay hurting, and I need—I feel like I need…" Remove sex from the equation, and the same need drove her to make life line up perfectly for her sister. "I need him to be happy."

"He will be. This challenge isn't one he can conquer overnight. But with our understanding——and the properly leveraged application of pressure?" Henry clenched his bent legs around her hips.

Arousal swamping her, she gasped for breath. Her body, waiting for her mind to catch up, held all she needed for the thrill she'd tried earlier to force into existence.

"He'll learn better awareness of his emotional needs." Forehead resting on her temple, Henry sharpened his tone. "Realize his first impulse may not be what's best for him."

She flushed. "Like I'm learning? Not to hide or minimize what hurts me, even if that's my first instinct. To revise flawed premises."

"My brilliant girl." As he rolled his hips, he branded her with sudden heat.

The expression of emotion. Not their nudity or position, but her sharing and growing understanding——those things aroused Henry. Her willingness to be open and vulnerable to him, to let him guide her, triggered him. And those traits were ones she and Jay shared.

Nestling against the upper curve of her ass, he flexed his cock. "Tell me about these flawed premises of yours."

Now? Her mind had jumped to a new track, one she hoped led to destination fucking-Henry-town. "A false dichotomy." Drain unstoppered, her words spilled in a rush. "I thought love wasn't real because it couldn't be perfect. Everywhere I looked, people were fucking it up. That couldn't be love. And then I felt it. And it was perfect."

"Until Jay put someone else first." Henry murmured.

She nodded, the prick of tears less acute, acceptance a heated towel after her cold swim. "Love doesn't make every problem disappear." She'd stumbled in equating love with perfection, assuming imperfection as evidence of nonexistence. "It's not an either-or——either we're in love and perfect or things aren't perfect and love is an illusion. Imperfect love. I can't quantify it, but I feel it."

"And at this moment? What feelings accompany your love?" His questions came quick, in baritone approval thickening with arousal.

Breathing deep, she took stock. Henry deserved the whole truth—— and so did she. "Unhappiness. Hurt. Anger. At Jay for going, and you for letting him go, and myself for being so selfish. And—arousal." Less shameful, because Henry had already revealed his own. "Need."

"So much swirling within you, yearning to be released." Embracing her like a second skin, he rocked them. "Will you trust me to do that for you tonight, Alice? To find the proper release?"

"Always." Her voice didn't wobble, though she waggled her hips. "The evidence stacks up solidly in your corner."

Chuckling, he patted her ass. "I'm pleased to know you've been checking out my solid stack." He sat up as she giggled. "Wait here." He left the bed entirely. "Eyes closed, please."

Anticipation, flowing into hollows where hurt and anger lingered, diluted the mixture. She shifted focus to his light footfalls, to smooth sheets and her lovers' scent clinging to them—their fragrance no longer a stinging reminder of absence but a promise of return.

"We haven't done this in a while." Henry spoke over the rolling glide of a drawer. "But perhaps it will prove precisely what you need tonight, dearest."

The drawer closed with a quiet but solid *thunk*. More sliding, closer, from the nightstand. No need for condoms, but lube, maybe, and her ass was rather accessible. He wouldn't introduce a new toy tonight, would he? Unless he thought a distraction would help her.

He grasped her ankles and slid her feet apart. "Tell me your safeword, Alice."

"Pistachio." Uttering her safeword, she unlocked the woman who reveled in surrender. The woman shivering for his control as he knelt between her spread legs.

"I believe you're ready for this. I believe you need it. But if you disagree, you need only say your safeword and I'll stop. Do you understand?"

"I understand, Henry."

With softness, he brushed her left shoulder and descended to her ass. Teasing flickers—her suede flogger.

"Jay's absence tonight is fortuitous." Henry caressed her with his voice as much as with flowing suede. He hadn't spanked her since the night at the club. He hadn't flogged her for longer than that. "He may not yet be ready to watch pain, however fleeting, displace your pleasure. You, too, must be granted the chance to recall your enjoyment without undue pressure to perform."

In a light slap, he created a waterfall of suede tails tickling her shoulder.

Back twitching, she pushed her breasts into the sheets. Her tingling fingers, at the end of arms splayed wide, curled and relaxed.

"Good girl." A second slap, to her opposite shoulder, fell as gentle as the last. "Let yourself go with the feeling. Raw emotion, open and vulnerable." The flogger swished in a teasing zigzag. "Thinking has no place here and now, not for you."

Thwack!

Moan escaping, she squirmed and danced from the pattern change, the unexpected burn on her ass cheek. Her cry mingled with the snappy echo, the sound of *please, sir, may I have another.*

Though she hadn't spoken, Henry obliged in his slow, steady rhythm. Flogging her more with heavy drag and thudding fall than stinging tails, he wielded her suede as an extension of his hands. Nothing to fear or fight existed in such a natural evolution of his deep massage. This touch—his touch—was love.

Nothing had been ruined. The night at the club hadn't left a permanent mark. That night, like last night, had been a single, discrete imperfection. Her responses to pleasurable pain remained her own. Her truth.

Spilling joyful tears and uncontrolled giggles, she soared with goddamn effervescence. Shook up and fizzing, she tingled to the tips of her fingers and toes. She would follow Henry's lead, and she'd offer Jay her hand to help him farther down the path. Imperfect love was real. And they could reach perfection together.

As Henry brushed her outer thigh, her oversensitive skin goosebumped. "Are you with me, Alice?"

"Always with you." Throat dry, body humming, she nodded and struggled to produce words. "Happy. Harder. More?"

A growl. Happy-sexy growl.

She cascaded in instinctive, shivering reaction. Henry growling from across the room—over the phone, across the continent, even—would clench her muscles in the hope of squeezing his cock.

"You'll have your more, my little temptress." Suede tails rained over her shoulders in quick succession. "And I'll have mine."

Her giggling euphoria deepened into a moan as he delivered. Her body throbbed, a growing chorus of pleasure-pain, each nerve ending raising in harmony and all praising Henry in every *thud* against her skin. With his voice he became the low rumble of the timpani, a vibration she registered not in her eardrums but in the pulse of her sex.

White bliss erupted behind her eyelids. Her loud cries marked an affirmation, a promise—a wordless challenge urging Jay to come with her from his lonely bed in northern New Hampshire. Floating in lazy-daze land, where time never intruded and all places converged, reaching Jay became reasonable. Rational.

"Jay came, too," she mumbled. Henry ought to know, in case her overeager desire had fouled his plans for the night. "S'okay?"

A chuckle dotted his groan as he kissed the notches of her spine. "That's fine, my sweet. No doubt he did. You're superb at sharing with each other."

The bed rippled. Her flogger lay fanned out beside her.

Tugging, Henry lifted her backward. Her body followed with agreeable unconcern. Everything about her grew soft and pliant in lazy-daze land. Nudging between her legs, parting her lips, Henry demonstrated everything about him stayed firm and demanding.

With his welcome invasion, he unbalanced her. Bracing for his thrusts would've required controlling her own body, and just now more than slumping and sighing taxed her skills. But Henry didn't require her help.

"My beautiful girl." Hands splayed over her ass, he caressed where the flogger had landed. Reddened her skin, certainly. Blossoming into bruising reminders, possibly. "Such an exquisite peak."

Pumping with growing force, he rocked her forward. Neat trick, how he'd gotten her knees to hold her up.

"It's left you so open for me." In constant motion, he skimmed her thighs, her hips, her ass. "This delightful laxity in your muscles. All of your tension has drained away, hasn't it?"

Tension existed no more than time or thinking did. "Mm-hmm. All gone."

"Good girl." Steadying her with a deep thrust, he rubbed slick fingers above their joining and pushed one inside.

Her ass tightened, but not to shove him out. Wrapped around him, twice-filled, she clenched in newfound pleasure.

"That's it, my lovely Alice." Stiff and unmoving, he hummed approval. "It's easier without distracting thoughts, isn't it?"

She scraped together focus for a tentative backward push. "Easy," she echoed, as he met her thrust. "Smooth." She giggled. Awkward attempts had raised her suspicion she'd never catch up to Jay and his beautiful acceptance, his effortless taking of not just Henry's finger but toys of varying sizes and Henry's cock. Her frustration had held her back. But now when Henry retreated, she pulled him in, eager to seek out fullness again. As she rolled her hips, her muscles stretched to accept him.

"Good girl," he repeated. "Beautiful instincts." Voice low and strained, he clamped her hip in his other hand. "But not so quick." Following the curve of her pelvis down and under, he cupped her sex. "Not without you."

He grazed her clitoris.

Swollen and sensitive, she shuddered and buried her whine in the sheets. Pushing back, she demanded more.

"Easy, my sweet." He crooned in his soft baritone. Touch firming, he thrust his cock deep and fingered her ass in a steady rhythm.

She tumbled beyond the ability to separate sensations, to identify and quantify. Only Henry remained, and he was everywhere. Everything.

With his deft hands and hard cock, he brought heat, motion, and a blur of pleasure. As they sprinted to the finish, his heavy breaths overtook her own, his grunting exhalations more than a match for her high-pitched moans. Shoving her across the line first, Henry followed in the same second. Thunder from the timpani. His rolling growl filled the room.

Rippling with aftershocks, she held him fast as he handled cleanup. The cooling drag of a baby wipe swept away excess lube once he'd cleaned his hand. He stretched over her, and the trash can liner rustled.

At her command, her mouth moved with sluggish obedience. "Two points?"

Lying down, he rolled them onto their sides. "Two spectacular points, driving up the inside lane and encountering no defenders." Behind her, still connected, he wiggled gently. "Practically a free throw."

"Helps to be on the same team," she teased. Either he actually understood basketball, or he'd picked up the lingo watching Jay. A birthday surprise Jay had enjoyed almost as much as the night before it. "Don't wanna keep you from scoring."

Turning her in his arms, he caused her whimper with his departing cock. He nuzzled their noses. "Open your eyes, Alice."

Obedience automatic, she blinked and cleared her vision.

Loving green eyes waited on her. "Every player wins on my court." He kissed her with unhurried thoroughness. With love.

She yawned afterward, unable to stop herself.

Henry chuckled. "Take your well-deserved rest. I'll wake you as needed." Rolling her once more, he ordered her to stay on her stomach. Cool, arnica-coated fingers soon canvassed her back.

She dozed through aftercare, following his directions with half-lidded eyes, drinking juice at his patient insistence. She snuggled close when finally he pulled the sheet over them both. Adrift in contentment, she wandered through stray thoughts—a tender mental goodnight to Jay first among them—until sleep took her.

* * * *

Alice's nagging bladder urged her out of Henry's embrace Saturday morning. His chest hair tickled her cheek. Cocooned in the covers, the lingering scents of sex and sleep swept into her lungs as she pushed free and rolled to the mattress's edge.

Henry snatched her wrist. "Straight back to bed afterward." With heavy, suckling kisses, he teased her palm. "I've plans for our morning." Fingers trailing, he let her slip away. The arousal of anticipation promised she'd make her escape brief.

Tender but not sore, her ass smarted less than the absence of Jay's toothbrush in the filigreed holder. She followed Henry's advice, breathing deep and accepting her disappointment without judgment. Feel and release. Better the momentary sting than the unreachable, incurable ache.

As she rubbed her ass, her reflection smirked. Sure, the emotional philosophy contradicted her physical desire for the flogger's bone-deep *thud* over the crop's sharp *thwip*. Didn't mean the strategy wouldn't work for her. Henry's idea-presentation techniques raised her capacity for adapting to most anything.

Like the towel-draped pillow greeting her from the center of the otherwise empty bed when she returned. For weeks, the pillow had belonged to Jay. A soft platform for her demonstration model as Henry guided her and their submissive lover reveled in the attention.

Toes curling, she plucked at the soft fiber rug. "Jay's not here."

"No, he isn't, is he?" Henry, standing nude beside the special dresser, closed a drawer with a near-silent bump. "But you are." He turned, and metal glinted through his fingers. "And class is in session."

Test day, more like. But he'd thrilled her with his touch last night. Relaxed her, filled her, and showed her pleasures only he delivered. "For me?"

"Jay has homework to keep him in the proper mindset this weekend." He nodded toward the bare sheet and its waiting centerpiece. His thickening cock nodded, too. "Did you imagine your tutoring would be less thorough and demanding than his?"

Not for a moment.

Stepping to the bed, touching the warm nest where they'd lain, rattled her with an intoxicating mix of excitement and trepidation. The solid rock of his authority settled in her mental sweet spot, his anchored calm freeing her to float weightless. "May I, Henry?"

He scanned her in stillness, motion limited to the steady downward drift of his gaze and the slow upward curve of his lips. "On your stomach, please."

As she crawled into position with shuffling knees and swaying breasts, she envisioned herself an instrument to bring them both pleasure, a tool molded for his grip.

"Hips centered on your pedestal." He rolled out his beautiful baritone lush and low, vibrating against aroused flesh. "I've something I wish to admire."

Settling on her stomach propped her ass in the air and brought shivering awareness of her nudity. She lay open, exposed. Behind her, Henry admired and assessed with mossy green eyes and a keen mind that missed nothing. Her constant and variable both, unexpected joys delivered with steady hands.

"Such tempting sights you present." Gripping her by the ankles, he drew her legs straight and together. "In uncounted positions." The bed dipped with his weight. "And because you've been such a good girl at your lessons"——solid and strong, he straddled her legs——"we'll soon have many more positions to try, won't we?"

The shudder started in her shoulders and coursed to her toes. "Yes, Henry. Please."

With one hand creating a gap, he slipped something cool and hard between her thighs. A bottle. Lube.

"Hold tight, sweet girl. Keep this warm." Pushing her legs together by flexing his own, he sent energy flowing like a pulse between them. As he leaned down, he tickled her with the heat of his body and the hair on his chest. "I'll have use for it later."

Stretching, she arched into him. "Promise?"

He kissed her cheek. "Hold out your hand, Alice."

She offered up her palm. Kisses or cuffs, she'd love whatever he gave.

Gleaming silver landed with a hefty smack. A plug like some of Jay's but smaller, a smooth metal bulb at one end and an elliptical handle at the other.

"I promise." He traced the sleek, curving slope. "You won't be permitted to play with your new toy without it."

"All mine?" As she stroked her toy, she sank into thick, wet desire.

"All yours." Clenching his hand, he wrapped hers around the metal. "Feel the shape of pleasures to come."

God, when he put it that way, the echo reshaped the thumping muscles between her legs.

"Share your warmth as you are with the lubrication." Henry slid back on his knees and kneaded her shoulders. "Temperature play is a game for another day."

Delicious Henry-promises. She'd call them teases, except they never were. He delivered every goddamn time.

She caressed her toy with the same thorough attention Henry gave her. Memorizing the angles and curves, she mapped her expectations on steel he'd chosen for her alone.

With his broad hands, he spanned the dip in her spine and crested the slope of her ass. "Your cheeks are delightfully pink." Breath flowing over the object of his praise, he chased the whisper with his lips. The gentle pressure sparked the pleasure-pain of awareness where her suede had left an impression. "A hint of color. Increased blood flow."

Wet warmth—oh God, he tongued her slow and firm around the underside of her ass, along the crease at the top of her thigh. As her mouth fell open, her moan pushed forward to urge him on.

"Not overmuch for my sweet girl, though, hmm?" He scraped his teeth, light and teasing.

"No, Henry." Shivering and nuzzling the silk sheet under her head, she rocked into the rougher nap of the towel beneath her hips. Delicious contrast. "Just right. You're always"—amazing, sensational, powerful enough to be worth her surrender—"just right."

"Such gentle, flowing curves you have." Cupping her ass, squeezing faintly, he joined his promise of safety and self-restraint with the surety of his complete control. "Round and full as a woman ought to be."

Praise tickled as he woke her base instinct to be pleasing to this man, to have her femininity recognized and appreciated.

He traced the cleft between her cheeks and parted her, ghosting across muscles she struggled to relax for him. Not as easy as last night, when she'd been spaced out from her flogging.

Skirting her outer lips, he rubbed on either side. "Here, too. Full and heavy." As he tugged her lips, he swept between. "Rich with passion. Guarding sweet treasures."

Demanding as a cat, she pushed up for more petting.

He pinched.

She jerked.

"Easy, dearest." He drummed the back of her thigh. "You'll dislodge the bottle you're warming with your lovely flesh." Kissing, he followed the line his fingers had set out. "Such an infraction would delay our game. You wouldn't want that, would you?"

Never. His waiting games were hard enough without her adding to the anticipation. "No, Henry. I want your claim on me. In me."

Humming, he nuzzled up her spine to the back of her neck. "And you'll have it. You are always mine, Alice." He rocked against her, his cock hot as iron tipped into a mold and hard as the finished piece tipped out. "However I choose to claim you."

With energy crackling beneath her skin, she shuddered and danced in his grasp. An aching pleasure, belonging. Long desired, finally and fully obtained, hers without question.

Arm extended, he curled her hand in his. The hair on his forearms darkened him against her paleness, both vivid against the navy blue sheet and missing only Jay's deep summer tan alongside. Henry stroked her fingers. "Open for me."

His low murmur shot straight from her ears to her wet center. Somehow she'd traded her pussy for a muscle car's engine, all power, vibration, and revving need. As she unclenched her fist, the metal weighed heavy in her palm.

"Good girl." He plucked the plug from her as if grasping a feather. "Wearing this will remind you to always be so—open and available for my pleasure." Slipping away, he dragged the metal over her back. "We'll train your body to awareness of its responsibilities."

Awareness, hell. She purred and fluttered with more than simple awareness. She'd attuned to him on a molecular level, as if their atoms comingled, electrons flying between them without regard for boundaries of the flesh.

The metal handle sank between the top of her cheeks, the bulb a weight resting at the base of her spine. Part of her nervous system waiting to be plugged in. Rolling her hips brought tremors, tiny shifts of the curving metal wobbling in place.

Henry growled. "Your curiosity is an incessant delight." Sliding past her opening, he stroked deeper down her legs. "And how do you find your toy, Alice?"

"Weighty. Thick." Making her hungry and desperate to have her fill. Not merely the toy, but him. The fullness of his cock.

In a slow spiral, he twisted the lube bottle free of her thighs.

"Round. Blunt." Saliva deserted her, left her parched and licking to call it back. "I want to feel it, Henry. Please."

Wet heat drizzled against her ass. Lube, trickling down, set her shivering. Her skin heightened every contact as if he'd flogged her this morning, too, as if she hung in the infinite moment between one strike and the next. The kiss of lightning.

Oh God, he swept the streams with his fingertips and redirected them to his desires. Back and forth he went, crossing and recrossing the place she no longer feared he'd tread. Hoped for, yes. Begged for.

Sheets rustled, the scratch of his legs against her smooth ones faint beneath her harsh breaths and his humming pleasure. She ached to spread herself and offer him a wider view, more room to maneuver, anything to urge him to sate the never-ending need building and pushing at her.

"What lovely eagerness, flashing an exquisite, hidden beauty." Voice soft, he clamped his legs around her with punishing pressure.

Her leaping joy nearly dislodged her new toy.

"But we want to stretch your pretty holes gently, not tempt me to bury myself."

Christ, he'd fucking kill her. Torture her with waiting. "I like when you bury yourself." *Please. Please-please-please.*

"You like me here." He sank his thumb into her pussy.

"Yesss." Her moan filled the room.

"A proper introduction will have you begging for me here as well." Ending his circling tease, his finger slick and stiff, he entered her ass.

She offered no resistance, only surrender and acceptance—and mute astonishment as his knuckle bumped her with the pressure and pleasure behind his steady thrust. Jesus, *fuck.*

He'd buried himself all right, his thumb in her pussy and his finger in her ass, his hand stuffed between her clenching cheeks.

Thrusting blindly, she scrabbled for purchase on the sheet to leverage herself deeper on him.

He chuckled, gruff and throaty. "You feel magnificent to me, dearest." As he squeezed, her rhythmic contractions rolled in from all sides. "But tell me how *you* feel."

"Owned." Like a stress ball he commanded and shaped. Utterly his to play with as he would. "Naughty." Filled and dying for more, she blazed with the illicit thrill. "In all the best ways."

"Good girl." Digging his free hand into her ass cheek, he growled. "My sweet Alice. Unsurpassed perfection, fucking yourself on my hand."

Fuck, she was. She'd started tilting up and down, experimenting with the depth of his hold from either side. And her new toy waited. She'd take more soon, play with bigger toys and graduate to the fullness Jay savored, Henry prodding them to accept him inside.

"Stretch your arms over your head." As he pumped one-handed, he spread her ass in the other. Watching her, maybe. Anticipating as she did. "Wrap your hands around the headboard."

Shuddering, she gripped the spindles. Solid wood in her palms and soft silk under her cheek.

He stretched, too, sliding his thumb free.

She whined at the loss.

"You want to come for me, don't you, Alice?" He pulled his finger back. "To show me you enjoy this game?"

"I do." Pulse racing, she hovered on the cusp. "I want to."

Drops of lube fell, scattered, and she trembled. Thicker pressure, but not her toy, not yet, because that sleek weight rested at the base of her spine.

Henry, humming appreciation, sank two fingers in her ass and thumbed her clit. "Every inch of you is mine, Alice. Inside and out. You have the leverage you need, your strong grip on the headboard." He thrust his fingers deep. "Your strong grip on me."

Buzzing in her ears and tingling in her toes threatened to split every atom in her body.

"That's it, good girl. Show me."

Fucking herself on him, she jolted with each swipe against her clit. Dug her hands into the rails and shoved back harder.

"Take your climax and show me how much choosing this excites you. Show me you want it again, and again, and I'll put your new toy where it belongs."

Lightning sizzled. The room went white. In her clamping release, she found emptiness on one side and fullness opposite. As she shook, he nudged her thighs apart and drove her knees wide, holding her open with his legs. The weight on her spine disappeared.

A magic trick. Her new toy rested where his fingers had with no more than gentle pressure in the midst of explosive pleasure. Drawing the metal deeper, she mapped its shape inside her as she had in her hand.

"Wondrous." Henry murmured. Her toy began slipping away. "Shall we play tug-o-war?"

Fuck no, he wouldn't steal her plug that fast. In one fast, tight pull, she regained smooth control.

Chuckling, he tugged again. He'd promised her this toy, and now he kept trying—

"Training." As she flexed and grasped, the plug made sensations real, gave her a focus better than any imagining. "This game is practice."

The plug waggled up and down, sending vibrations inside her and plucking her clit. A nod in her lover's hands.

"Such a quick mind and a competitive spirit you have." With bumping knuckles, he brushed her cheeks on either side of the slender handle. "We might add another layer of difficulty. A bonus round." He wedged the blunt head of his cock between her labia.

Oh fuck yes. Seeking his thick heat, she wiggled backward.

With teasing swipes, he coated her in her own slickness. Wielding his cock with confidence, brisk and slow, rubbing and flicking, he remained always out of reach. He jostled her toy. "This is a mere placeholder. An invitation readying you for my possession."

M.Q. Barber

She whined her impatience, dropping her head and pulling on the headboard. He hadn't given her permission to move her hands. Hair shrouding her face, she closed her eyes. Nothing to see but the dark sheet in any case, and she had better senses in her arsenal.

Her nose, buried in the sheet, brought her their mingled scents, citrus and leather and fainter traces of Jay's sweet, woody musk. Her ears captured Henry's purring growl. Her skin sang with input. The roughness of his legs, spreading her wide. The probing tip of his cock, firm but gentle. The squeeze of one broad hand on her ass. The warm weight inside her revealing its shape with her every contraction. Shivering, sensitized need rose, humming through her veins.

"What say you, Alice?" Holding her toy in place, he plunged and claimed the rest of her with his cock. "Will you tug doubly hard for me?"

Stuffed. Fuller in front than behind, but oh so deliciously owned. The heat overwhelmed, as if she sweated out a fever. Her body contracted without consultation.

Henry, groaning, pumped deeper. "Do that again, mischievous minx."

Controlling the motion fell beyond her ability. But obeying him on instinct—her body never failed her in that goal. The flickers in her belly drove flames low and spreading, a leaping wildfire determined to win this tug-o-war. A single pull for a double reward, her lover and her toy buried, her body molding to their intractable demand.

"Do you know yet why I've chosen this toy for you, dearest?" His voice held the rough burr of strain.

Sized for a beginner. Easy to clean. The lessons he'd taught as she'd played with Jay unrolled in her head. The shape, though—strawberryish in three dimensions. A spade in two. And he'd always called their fun a game. "A spade." But he'd choose for deeper reasons. Aesthetics. Meaning. "I don't——" Fuck, his thrust knocked her mind off course. "I don't know why."

"The ace of spades." He drew back. "The highest card in the deck. Extremely valuable."

Shoving hard and squeezing, she pulled him in. Maybe she'd manage not to lose her grip before he lost his.

He drove her harder, hips slamming, his swaying balls slapping her center. "But it's a matter of perspective, isn't it?"

"Per-perspective?" Fuck, she'd lost. Or won. Whatever outcome the shaking in her thighs portended as heat blazed a path to her curling toes and clenching fingers.

"Just so." Harsh breaths split his words. "Those wide, curving lobes and sleek pointed tip." Groaning, he gave two sharp thrusts. "Viewed from the opposite side, a spade is—"

"A heart." Snaking under her skin, the bonfire exploded in a supernova with two brilliant centers. They burned together, atomized in endless white-hot pleasure.

* * * *

"Let go." With heavy strokes, Henry rubbed her knuckles. "Come back to Earth with me, sweet girl."

*Mmph*ing agreement, she jerked her hands open. The headboard spindle's imprint decorated her flesh. Death grip, Christ.

Bent over her like armor shaped for her alone, he *tsk*ed. "You played well this morning. Well and hard." With soft lips swift and dancing on her red-lined palms, he soothed her aches. "You threw yourself into our game with ease and excitement and much less fear."

"My fears seem silly now. This was—is—amazing." Though he'd slipped free while pleasure locked her in a feedback loop, her toy rested snug inside her, a constant reminder of his plans for her.

"Not silly. A necessary step in your growth." Folding their arms around her, he brushed her forehead with a kiss. "Your progression is a gift, Alice. One I am privileged to watch and to guide." With nudges and rolls, he righted her beneath him.

Her ass hit the fitted sheet. *Holy fuck*. The plug handle bounced against the mattress, shifting the metal inside her and dear God in heaven when she squirmed just right——

Henry broke out a Jay-sized grin. "You ought to see your eyes, dearest. Widen them any farther, and I'm terribly afraid they'll wander off somewhere." Nipping her bottom lip, he ended on a sharp tug. "Though I'm quite fond of your open-mouthed joy in discovery. Very enticing."

"God, Henry." She lacked the romantic words for this experiment, but he'd interpret. "Equal and opposite reaction, I can't even—I don't want the ripples to stop."

"Had I begun with this game last summer, your fears would have cast the experience in an unpleasant light." He dropped a kiss on her jaw. Warm and supple, his lips. Thoughtful and generous, his mind. "You might have come to see this pleasure as a chore to be dreaded. An obligation rather than an act of love. But now…" Falling silent, he raised his head and stared at her, his eyes a deep pine forest of adventure and rapture.

"Now I'll ask for it. For"—his cock—"greater pleasures."

"Exactly right." With one intense kiss, he bathed her in longing fulfilled and the promise of more. "Off to the shower. It's time we begin our day."

Every ass-bouncing step stretched her. Squeezing kept her post-orgasmic flood—and Henry's release, God, holding a piece of him after sex ended hadn't lost its thrill—from soaking her, but squeezing tightened her ass around the outline of rippling metal, too. Like the sex hadn't stopped. Addicting.

Lazing in heavy-headed subspace beneath the heated spray, she twisted and bent at his direction without worry. He'd never let her slip. Safest place in the world, his hands.

Until he grasped the ring nestled between her ass cheeks. "Time for a break."

"But it's my toy." Burying her face in his neck, she mewled in protest. "I'm not done playing."

"You may fight with me now, and lose this argument, or you may submit and enjoy the rewards good behavior brings." Firm, growly-voiced Henry wrapped one hand around her hair.

"Submit," she whispered. Draping herself on him almost made up for the loss of her new toy. The water droplets on his collarbone begged to be licked off. "Experiment over."

He tugged her hair, tipping her head back, and delivered a commanding kiss, all hard lips and pushy tongue. "Now I know you're missing your playmate." He kissed her forehead. "You've stolen his pout. All but the pleading eyes."

He'd know better than her how best to adapt her body for this. But going slow grated when Jay made these games look so beautiful. Still, she helped push the plug free—easier out than in—and washed the metal with soap and hot water.

"Well done." Henry toweled her dry. "You're my good girl. Even when you aren't quite certain you want to be."

His gentle handling and praise lasted through their morning routine. Attentive and tactile, he dressed her in loose-fitting Saturday-at-home clothes. No underthings.

A teasing shiver rippled through her. Leaving the decision to him, giving him unfettered—and sometimes delightfully fettered—access to her anytime he liked, soaked her in pride-laced naughtiness.

He rubbed her ass through her thin cotton pants and delivered a light spank.

Enough to wake tingles. Not enough to hurt. She arched her back and wiggled.

Chuckling, he gave her a push. "Beautiful instincts. Now go and put your toy away, please."

A drawstring pouch waited on the special dresser. Fingering the bag against the nap, she discovered rough pleasure. "No velvet?"

Henry wrapped her in a crushing embrace. "My Alice is a strong woman. Suede is her velvet."

Damn straight. Her suede rested in a drawer, wiped down and laid away with care after last night's flogging.

"Prickly when pushed. Soft when stroked." As he eased open the strings and flipped the top, he exposed a green satin lining. "And so welcoming within."

Forcing herself to let go, she nestled the plug in its home. No, its home away from home, because its true home sat empty and wanting it back. But Henry said to wait, and she'd wait. Experimenting on her own and skipping steps might have unforeseeable consequences.

"Lovely, thank you." He pulled the strings, closing the bag, and squeezed her shoulders. "Off to the kitchen with you."

He rattled off instructions and sent her ahead. By the time he emerged, clean-shaven and dressed, she had the table set and the omelet ingredients chopped and lined up beside the stove. Within minutes, he turned out a made-to-order feast. Fluffy eggs. Flavorful ham and veggies. Thick slices of toast slathered in butter and jam.

Quiet settled while they ate, good for musing but also for missing. Halfway through her omelet, she hadn't fended off a creeping fork or a teasing plea for a bite. Messy dark hair and a bright smile and deep, liquid eyes whose owner's sweet tenor—*Share with me?*—echoed Henry's frequent refrain with different intent.

Warmth engulfed her, Henry covering her hand perfectly with his long fingers. His eyes softened to tiny black centers on mossy green discs. "I expect we'll have waffles next Saturday."

Swept along in his understanding smile, she needn't worry he'd read ingratitude or ambivalence into her behavior. They both knew the sex had been fantastic and the omelets delicious. Her tense funk flowed out in a sigh. "You think he's having birthday waffles?"

Henry shook his head. "I expect he's eating whatever has been put in front of him, without complaint." As a frown flashed across his lips, he waved a dismissal. "A discussion for another day. Today, we have an evening out for which to prepare."

"We're going out?" With a puzzle in the offing, she swam clear of the satiation of sleep, sex, and a full stomach. "Do I get to know where, or is this one of the great Henry mysteries?"

"No mystery." He cut his omelet, leaving a crisp diagonal behind. "It's time." Assessing her with a piercing stare, he chewed and swallowed. "As our dear boy has given us this opportunity, we mustn't waste it."

"We're going to the club." Certainty struck deep as a well-seated support post, straightening her spine. "On a play night."

"On a party night. They've a Fourth of July soiree, an annual event."

"Clever." As they mingled with the contacts they'd made at tea and in class, they'd expand their anti-Cal reach among the membership. Twisting her fork over, she prodded the omelet. "Guess I'd better get all of my rebellion out at home."

He hummed a discordant note. "You ought to be you, dearest. Whatever else our agenda holds, do you believe my primary concern would ever be other than your comfort and safety?"

"No." Outfoxing Cal would please him, sure, as much as crushing the jackass's balls beneath her heel would her, but Henry always had higher goals. "This is for me." Since the night of her spanking, she'd only entered the club during off-peak hours. Morning classes, afternoon tea, and Jay's painful, necessary breakdown. "Testing phase." Without Jay at her side. "Isolate the variables for total focus."

She'd ace this exam. Be the best goddamn sub in the place, Henry's perfect companion.

"A monochromatic work, but lovely all the same." He smiled his teasing grin, the one with the hint of white teeth behind kissable lips. "My bold adventurer is ever anxious to scale new heights."

"Will you take Jay by himself——" No. The permutations had a best order, and that wasn't it. "It's not just that he isn't here——you would've taken me alone first anyway."

"Yes." Eyes narrowing, he tilted his head. "Tell me why, Alice."

"If I do well, you'll have my support when Jay's ready. Double the protection for him. Enough safety to satisfy you and let him have fun showing off his submissive side the way he wouldn't do at basketball." Better for Jay to have them reinforcing their pride and love for his true self the next time he attended the club during playtime. "And if I flop, he won't bear witness. My faltering confidence won't infect him with extra fear or shame." The conclusion fit, though she lacked visual confirmation of the evidence chains. "Either way, you won't let him play until I've proven I can handle a night out first."

"Exquisite." He folded his napkin and laid the rose linen beside his plate. "I yearn to capture the movements of your mind in color on canvas. Such a beautiful, rolling sea."

No less than she ached to map his. With love and comfort, he coddled her when she needed and pushed her to grow in the times between.

"Alice." A wolfish smile lurked in the corners of his mouth and his eyes. "Stand up and step to your right, please."

Fuck yes.

Heart racing, legs trembling, she pushed back from the table. He'd delivered those words in her dreams since the night in August when he'd made her fantasies real. If she prayed before bed the way she had as a child, knees on the floor, elbows on the bedspread, hands pressed together in front of her face, she'd thank God every night for that moment.

Hands clasped behind her back, she waited for his next command. Close enough to prayer. He answered hers in uncounted ways.

As he stood, he displayed the best sort of surprise, his hardening cock rippling under his pants. He delved in his pockets and pulled out——

"My toy."

He held the pouch on his palm.

She flexed with stubborn impatience, a rush of heat. "But I put it away like you said."

"You did." In his other hand, the black cap of the lube bottle peeked over the side as he rounded the table. "And I promised you would reap the rewards of your good behavior."

The choice between staring at the bulge in his pants or the one in his hand proved impossible.

"I know you ache to progress with speed. But in this you've set aside your competitive desire for victory and your insatiable craving for comprehensive knowledge." Boxing her in, he laid the pouch and lube on the table. "And why have you done that?"

"Because I respect you." For so many reasons. He'd given her proof after proof. "I trust your judgment."

"And because you've shown your willingness to follow my direction"—— he gripped her hips, and thin cotton slid south——"I'm inclined to grant you latitude."

"I get to wear it again?" Halle-fucking-lujah.

"For a short time." Stooping, he swept her pants off. "We'll increase the time—and your comfort level—incrementally."

The idea felt pretty damn comfortable now.

He skimmed the backs of her legs and kissed her ass cheeks. "Practicing your lessons ought to be pleasurable." One-handed, he continued upward, beneath her shirt, and bent her forward. "Lean on your elbows for me. Back arched, please."

She shoved her ass in the air and wiggled.

The suede pouch gave up its treasure to his slender, penetrating fingers. Swish and flip, the lube opened. Heavy breaths sounded behind her, deep and focused. A man blowing to start a fire. Or to warm metal in his cupped hand.

As he pressed the tip of her toy between her cheeks, lube flowed in a steady stream from above. With slow rotations, he stirred anticipation in sensitive flesh while the plug gained a protective coating, slick against her skin. Her shiver owed nothing to the modest chill.

"Good girl," Henry murmured. "Be aware of your movement and the feelings, both physical and emotional, wearing your toy inspires."

Sliding deeper, growing wider, the toy burned, but oh God, what a beautiful burn. "S'good. Makes me want it all." She stretched in welcome, her muscles beginning a satisfying workout. The slick suction and gentle *pop* of full depth came with familiarity, the thrill without the fear. "Giddy and expectant."

"Proud of yourself, are you?" He returned the lube to the table. Massaging her ass, he made her toy shift and bump. "You should be."

"Are you going to fuck me now?" God, she hoped so. He'd gotten her wet and clenching without a single brush of her pussy or clit, and the far side of the table beckoned in memory. "Is that part of my reward, too?"

"No, Alice." Growling, he spun her by her elbows and hoisted her onto the tablecloth.

Her thudding ass rattled the plates. Rocking into weighted fullness, she moaned.

He silenced her with a hard kiss. "Your reward is firmly lodged in place. This?" As he spread her knees wide, he dragged her to the edge. "This dessert is *my* reward." Sinking to the rug, he buried his face between her legs and inhaled. "Shall we see if I might make you come for me as many times as I denied myself the pleasure of taking your ass these last eleven months?"

Chapter 7

The salon bustled with party-lured players eager to see and be seen. Not Alice yet, not until Henry commanded her. Moving through the crowd at his side, greeting a handful of familiar faces, she eased her fast-flowing currents of anxiety. No sign of jackass Cal, though she scanned for him in a relentless visual sweep. Henry wouldn't let anything happen to her. But her first night had ended in disaster anyway. Not this time.

Men who'd taken Henry's intro dominance class—"How Not to Be a Dick," as she and Jay dubbed it—sauntered over and said hello as Henry circulated with consummate skill.

Henry acknowledged each with stern paternalism, an approving nod and a solid handshake. For those who kept their greeting to her brief and respectful, he made quiet, individual recommendations—"The lovely yellow-ribboned brunette in the floral stockings, do you see her near the rose settee? You ought to speak with her. Her play style would pair well with your own." Those who stared too hard or ignored her presence had no such luck.

His no-hurry pace set her unstoppable adrenaline on a collision course with his immovable calm. She'd die—in comfortable shoes, at least—before they left the salon. Nearly an hour, and they hadn't gone upstairs. Hadn't flashed anything more alluring than her calves. Jay had better ones anyway. Muscular. Vivid and defined in their motion, a living machine with a deep tan, so fucking gorgeous walking naked to the shower—

"Ah, there we are." Steeped in satisfaction, Henry ended their wandering.

"What?" She eased up on her toes, but nothing popped in the crowd. "Where we are?" A knot of corseted Amazons on ungodly heels parted, revealing a blond-bearded gentleman in a fine suit. "Santa!"

Heads turned, because *fuck*, she'd clamored as loud as a kid on Christmas morning. Her cheeks flamed.

Rolling out a belly laugh, Will snatched the attention. "Now that's the eager welcome a man longs to hear."

He strolled straight to them and exchanged a half-hug with Henry. They shared the brand of affectionate masculinity proclaiming the two brothers in arms if not in blood. Confident in their territory, unconcerned with power plays and posturing, enjoying each other's companionship.

"Will, you remember Alice, I'm certain." Touch firm and steady, Henry stroked her back.

Her embarrassment faded in the shadow of their comfort. If she'd done wrong, Henry would've corrected her. Or covered for her and saved his corrections for at home. In private.

"With fondness." Santa Will inclined his head toward her. "She's lovelier each time I see her. Radiant with good health." His gaze lingered on the canary yellow ribbon draped around her neck. "Are you well cared for, Alice?"

"More than I thought possible." Every day, she woke astonished and grateful for her men—even when one went missing. Henry had more than made up for Jay's weekend defection. That man kissed and tongue-fucked like nobody's business. She'd lost count of the orgasms, her world narrowed to his mouth and fingers and the rippling pleasure with every clench of her ass. Long after she ceased begging him to stop—but not with her safeword, because what if he'd actually stopped?—he'd gathered her and carried her to bed. She'd napped the afternoon away until he'd fucked her awake to shower, dress, and discuss how the night would go.

"Henry has you all buttoned up." Waving upward, Santa Will left a generous handspan between his gesture and her body. "Such a pity."

Her navy outer dress mimicked a long jacket, boxy and lined from neck to knee-length hem with half-dome silver buttons.

"Appearances, Will." As he'd done while twisting her hair up before dressing her, Henry kissed her neck and breathed across her earlobe.

The temperature rose ten degrees. Maybe fifteen. No one else in the salon took note, though Santa wore a broad smile.

Henry smoothed her dress across her collarbone, wrapping her in his embrace from behind. "Tell me your safeword, sweet girl."

"Pistachio." Her heart trotted into a faster rhythm.

"And if you need others' assistance?"

"Red." The solution she hadn't thought of in time to protect Jay or herself. Henry had reinforced club-wide safewords in class, and Emma had reviewed guidelines with everyone on staff. "I'll shout *red* until a play monitor helps me, sir."

"Excellent." Kissing her cheek, he filled her with his scent. Dark, commanding leather and crisp, cordial citrus snaked into her lungs.

"She's learned well." Santa winked at her with one merry blue eye beneath a fuzzy blond brow. "You must be proud."

"I am. And delighted to show her off." Henry fingered her top button and pushed her dress open. "Unwrap yourself, Alice." Slipping away, he claimed a post beside Will.

Each button a new tease and thrill, she worked slowly while nearby players turned and watched. She held a captivated audience for her obedience. Shrugging free, she revealed her underdress.

Santa sucked in a whistling breath.

Henry held out his arm.

She folded the overdress and laid it across his forearm. He'd chosen the play outfit beneath, too. No confining corset tonight. "The rest, sir?"

"My pocket is empty and waiting."

Mmmf. His arch fucking tone and expectant eyes got her wet every damn time. Bending forward, pulses fluttering in her thighs and belly, she reached beneath the sides of her dress and pulled down the panties. Over the garters, over the hose, over her thin-soled shoes and off. Navy silk dangled from her fingers.

"Inside my jacket, dearest." Clasping her wrist, Henry raised her outstretched arm to his face and inhaled. "Against my heart."

She stepped into his orbit. Pressed to him full-length, with his fine suit and masculine breadth, she drew strength from his heat. Her own exothermic battery. Tucking her panties into his inner breast pocket earned her a forehead kiss.

"You're stunning," Henry murmured. "Give us the full effect."

Her underdress swayed with her as she retreated, at once hidden and revealed to the crowded salon with its low-voiced chatter. Even in her shimmering curtain of sheer fabric and no undergarments, she qualified as fully dressed relative to dozens of others. Wide, opaque stripes of shadowed evergreen swathed her hips and breasts, and the whole of the dress floated slip-like around her on spaghetti straps.

"Marvelous." Santa scanned her, chignon to slippers. "Might I steal a kiss from this vision of beauty, old friend?"

"A choice she may make herself this evening." Yellow ribbon coaxed from her neck, Henry affixed it to her dress in a floralesque knot. "But mind your manners, Will."

Her second test. She'd passed the exposure level without flinching.

"In your company, Henry? Always." Santa's flourishing bow to her came off with handsome grace despite the rotund body his suit didn't entirely mask. "What say you, lady?"

Jay would've presented the same extravagant playfulness at home to make her giggle and make Henry growl and claim him. The night Santa'd visited them provided inspiration. Curtseying to her admirer, she shot him a saucy smile. "An elbow kiss, Santa?"

He guffawed, sending their nearest neighbors back a step. "Bested by my own words. Yes, then, an elbow kiss." He rose to his full height, a good eight inches on her. "Your sweet is a delight, Henry."

As Henry hummed, she extended her arm.

Santa Will lifted her upturned wrist with two fingers, ran his nose along her inner forearm, inhaled, and pecked her elbow with a beard-bushy kiss.

No tingles, but fondness all the same. Her body didn't consider him a threat. Interaction accomplished. Alice two, fears zip.

"This isn't the same little Alice who waited on me last month." Backing off, he released her wrist as he stood tall. "That girl carried nerves in her eyes." He nodded to her with new respect. "You've brought a woman with you, Henry. A breathtaking one at that. With a yellow ribbon? Brave man."

"Would you care to help me keep the jackals at bay, Will?" Henry smoothed the dress draped over his arm, but his gaze followed the line of her body instead. "I thought Alice and I might take in the sights. She has a lovely appetite for novel adventures."

"No boy this evening?" Frowning, Will looked over their heads at the crowd in both directions. "Is he well?"

"Quite well. A family matter."

"Ah. Distasteful things."

Santa's home life beat out Jay's for complications. Rejection left simmering too long in Resentment Reservoir. Though she had Henry to purify her emotional wells, Santa went without.

"If you'd care to make it a foursome"—Henry floated a light, careless tone—"perhaps we might tempt Em away from hostessing for a spell."

"I've tried, Henry." Will exhaled with gusto. "She's a stubborn one."

"Stubborn can be managed." Cupping her chin, Henry caressed her cheek. "With the proper incentives and care."

She nuzzled into him. "Dominant can be managed." Her smile peeked through without permission. "With the right incentives and care."

Both men laughed, Henry flashing white teeth and Will's red cheeks rounding.

Joining in, she snuggled beside Henry not out of a need for protection but because she wanted to. He'd been right about the body chemistry. She craved him like a drug. No—like a vitamin or mineral. Salt. Necessary for her survival and damn tasty.

Henry squeezed her ass. "Will, have you——"

Fuck, he kept his massage going, strong and possessive. If he'd let her wear the toy tonight, she'd be halfway to Climaxville. Focusing beyond her rolling arousal took effort.

"——Jacob's seat?"

"If I can make myself appear respectable enough." Squaring his shoulders, Santa almost managed an imposing presence. His wry smile softened the effect. "Em gave me the sharp side of her tongue for fighting."

His friendly tone suggested admiration, and his blue eyes sparkled. He ought to——damn. Harpy wife.

"She also says you've been wrangling wannabes on Saturdays." Will nodded, decisive and firm. "Those young ruffians could use a smack from the decorum stick."

"Young ruffians and good girls." With teasing gentleness, Henry smacked her ass.

As he propelled her forward, her laughter spilled out, loud and unexpected. Dropping a fancy dress over her head didn't magically give her polite dom-sub society manners. The quiet obedience even Jay-the-comedian excelled at eluded her. Ribs heaving with suppressed chuckles, she slammed her lips together.

"Henry, your lovely little one is having a veritable attack." Will's false concern upped the difficulty level on regaining control. "Don't you let the poor dear laugh?" Ducking his head level with hers, he mimed a severe frown. "So dour you are. It's no wonder she needs Santa's jolliness to brighten her day."

Henry snorted. "My girl has a fine playmate to give her plenty of jollies." He stroked her hair as she quieted. "But she's trying exceptionally hard tonight to be a model of submission."

"Head of the class?" Clapping Henry on the shoulder, Will rocked them both. "I'd say she has the teacher's pet position all sewn up."

By default. Her favorite competitor had conceded the field, leaving her to play for both of them tonight. If she lost her shit in front of Henry's best friend, Jay'd never get his chance.

"It's not only me she wishes to impress." Confidence filled Henry's declaration, though she hadn't told him her intention. He knew her well enough without asking. "My Alice has a kind heart, and you've rather found a place in it after your valiant defense."

"An easy decision. The man's a jackass, and your Alice is—" Sighing, Will stared past her, somewhere over Henry's shoulder. "A lively, spirited darling, and an innocent in the scene before she met you, I'd say. Her first explorations, finding her legs and taking those tentative steps? It's lovely to watch. If we can't protect that, we may as well go out fighting." He stiffened. "And we may yet tonight." Leaning closer, he dropped into a deep whisper. "He's here, watching you."

Cal. As her heart tripped into overdrive and her throat tightened, a phantom hand slipped into her own. Jay. Hot and trembling and gone when she tried to squeeze back.

Will smirked. "He seems more irked than usual."

No walls or corners waited to trap her, just people and fancy furnishings. She sidled away from the chairs grouped around a low table.

"The classes and Em's outreach are making waves." Henry, curling his arm around her, pulled her in front of him. "Perhaps he's having trouble finding a partner."

Widening his stance beside them, Will flexed his hand. "Coming this way."

She hadn't caught sight of Jay's tormenter, and her protective escorts had likely cut off any line he had on her without a word.

Henry transferred the overdress to her arms. "If you want to avoid this, sweet girl, simply tell me."

Temptation tasted like fear, thick and chalky.

He rubbed warmth into her hands. "He'll skirt the line. Give offense but stop short of a threat I can point to as such. Deliberate unpleasantness is his stock-in-trade."

"He'll be prodding to see if he can hurt me." Because tears and pain aroused Cal, and he didn't care about obtaining consent.

"Precisely."

His moral shortcomings made him unsafe. Not the pain, the games, or the toys—the person wielding them who didn't respect limits but pretended to long enough to steal trust. Jay's trust.

"It's fine, sir." She emphasized the title Henry earned with his caring leadership, the one the pompous ass demanded like a defiant child. "Every word out of his mouth is worthless bullshit." She blew out a breath. Her blood sought vengeance for Jay beyond the campaign to cut off Calvin Gardner's supply of naïve novices and not-my-problem dominants. "I'm ready for this."

"Yes, you are." Forceful, possessive, Henry growled low and claimed her mouth.

As her tension flowed out, she turned pliant and submissive in his arms. A moment worth living in forever. Pure freedom from everything but pleasure.

Will gave a slight cough.

"I see the cuddler-in-chief"—the fucking sneer Cal embedded in his voice tensed her right back to fight status—"has returned with his crying cunt. No little bitch tonight?"

Ignoring the intrusion, Henry gentled his kiss to a slow devouring as he cradled her.

His unconcern restored her to reason. Satisfying as kneeing Cal in the balls would be, she'd only set back their cause. And Jay wouldn't get to enjoy the sight anyway.

"Funny, I could've sworn I just saw a whiny little bitch," Will mused. "Wherever did he go? Oh, Cal, I didn't see you there."

Inarticulate scoffing served as a reply. Weeks of rejections might've knocked Cal off his game.

Henry kissed her forehead. Leaving one arm around her, he faced the jackass. "Cal."

"Henry." Cal dragged out his name. "You're one short tonight, aren't you?"

"The whereabouts of my subs are no concern of yours." Offering a close-mouthed smile, Henry lacked the warmth that permeated his voice when she or Jay pleased him. "Though I'm certain it eases your mind to know they are well cared for."

Cal's perfectly tweezed and arched eyebrows shot together. "Too frightened to show his face? I always preferred to see the back of him." He oozed glee in a conspiratorial whisper. "He only sobbed for the whip. Cram his mouth full of cock and he'd beg for more."

She scrunched the dress, resisting the urge to rend and tear. At her back, Henry dug in with curling fingers.

"Beg?" Will snorted. "Sounds like his mouth wasn't full if he had the breath to beg for more." Thick fingers flying, he waved a dismissal.

Cal flinched.

Glorious. God, let Santa keep going.

"His partner at the time must not have been big enough to keep him satisfied." In his mellow bass, Will goaded with an oh-so-cheerful fuck-you singsong. "I've never heard him begging with Henry's cock in his throat."

Choking on a laugh, she lowered her chin to smother the sound. She'd have laid money on him never watching Jay blow Henry, but he hadn't lied. If he hadn't witnessed the blowjob, he would've missed the theoretical pleading.

"Your pet is dangerously close to mockery, Henry." Arctic chill in his eyes, Cal glared at her. Unlike their first meeting, the hair-gelled hedgehog sported a shirt tonight. He'd hauled out a netted, nipple-chafing monstrosity belonging on a raver two sizes smaller.

Her chuckles came harder. He'd lost the ability to unsettle her and thrust her back to the wall. This pathetic man clung to shreds of power she refused to grant.

"I don't expect you to control the lumbering ape." Cal waved at Will. "But these ludicrous classes should be teaching cocksluts civility."

Will eyed the fingers flapping inches from his chest and raised his stare to meet Cal's.

Hand plummeting to his side, Cal rounded on Henry. "You're brainwashing them into baby games and disrespect."

She sucked in air between giggles. Fuck it. She was no church mouse, and she had a yellow ribbon. She'd damn well enjoy herself.

"I find her laughter pleasing." Tickling her in his gentleness, Henry traced her collarbone with a lone finger. "Whether it pleases you is irrelevant. My desires are the only ones she needs to sate."

Obedient as a compass needle chasing magnetic north, she swayed toward him. "Your desires are mine, sir." He'd calmed her with no more than a touch, and the softening line of his lips suggested she'd pleased him. Reciprocity. "I'm privileged to belong to a man who knows how to wield his power to motivate his lovers."

Eyes darkening, Henry slipped his hand behind her neck. Santa had better be on guard for them, because the world stopped existing beyond their heated stare. Stroking, teasing, Henry twined wisps of her hair in his fingers and tugged.

Christ, that pull. She tipped her head, a motion inexplicably tied to breasts and belly, a tingling ache he roused and soothed daily. She burned with competitive fever to outdo their morning, to take his cock where she'd only taken her toy. To show the room how her gently commanding lover mastered her. "Will I get more sizeable rewards for good behavior, sir?"

Tightening his fingers, he dropped his gaze to her throat. "I've gifts aplenty for my good girl." In his stare, he promised bruising kisses she'd need a midsummer turtleneck to hide.

Intrusive Cal huffed. His slacks rustled. "If your bitch wants to open her mouth, she should be on her knees. At least then she'd offer something worthwhile with her noise. Does she squeal as loud as the slave boy?"

Clenching her fists beneath her overdress, she almost swung at the bastard's jaw. Self-control edged out of reach.

Henry held her captive with firm fingers and steady eyes. "Prodding." He breathed for them both, slow and untroubled, and even her lungs obeyed his tempo. "My girl has no wounds to infect." With his intimate tone, he salved verbal grazes and slights. "No weakness to exploit."

Henry and Jay had seen to that. Sealed the three of them together with an amalgam of love and pain and growth. Cal's barbs offended without significant injury. Inconsequential, like the man himself. "None, sir."

Fuck, the things she'd do to earn his smile. Approval in upturned lips. Delight in smoldering eyes.

Alice three, fears zip.

"Be easy, Cal." Will's thunderous clap silenced nearby chatter. Maybe he imagined crushing Cal's skull between his hands. "I'm certain the girl didn't mean for her laughter to imply anything about the size—or lack thereof—of the bulge in your pants." Pinching his fingers, Will shook his head in teasing concern. He'd pitched his voice loud, his rumbling bass gathering attention and snickers. "She's a giggly little one by nature, and she likely has her eyes on bigger prizes." With a satisfied lip-smack, he leaned in as if confiding a secret. "The things she does in a man's lap—Calvin, you can't imagine the pleasure."

True, if misleading. Cal couldn't begin to understand the joy Will took in non-sexual cuddling.

"Why, the evening she spent in mine?" Sighing like a bellows, Will tweaked her chin and winked. "The best I've had in ages."

As Henry cradled her close, he tickled her neck. "You still blush beautifully, dearest."

"Any of these whores"—Cal flung his arm wide toward the crowd—"can be taught to adequately suck a cock."

A disapproving murmur raced through their nearest neighbors.

"I don't see any whores here, Cal." Mild though it was, Henry's voice carried in the following quiet. "To whom were you referring?"

"Sounds like sour grapes to me." Gaze on her, Will brushed his knuckles along her cheek.

She tipped into his touch. Nuzzling as performance art. He meant to goad Cal, and Henry was letting him. So long as she only participated indirectly, the club's rules would survive.

Will tsked. "Poor Calvin calls them whores and cries when they won't play with him."

"Whores play when I tell them to play." Cal thrust forward.

Forearms clashed in a cross beside her head. Will left an echo on her cheek, so fast he reacted. With a beefy block, he shoved Cal back a step.

Henry stood motionless as he did before a sublime work of art. "Lay hands on her and I'll have you ejected." Voice cool, light, and measured, he projected complete unconcern. "Has your dullness dimmed your eyes as well?"

"Yellow ribbon, Callie-boy. Touch by invitation only." Arm still raised, Will cracked his knuckles. "If you need a refresher on the house rules, Henry could kindly school you on Saturdays with those hoping to better themselves."

"A lovely thought, Will." Henry wrapped her, settling the weight of his palm above her ass. "Some novices have delightful minds. The quick-witted and strong-willed few." Bending his head, he trailed his lips across her jaw. "Others, however"—he pulled back, leaving her heart racing—"claim expert titles while neglecting the comportment and refinement implied by such things."

Flushing, Cal cradled his arm to his chest. Under her stare, he let it fall. His eyes gleamed with pale blue flame. Oh, he hated her. If he hadn't hated her before, he sure as hell did now.

She tossed him a wide fuck-you-very-much smile. The quick rhythms in Henry and Will's responses teased her imagination. Ten years gone, fifteen maybe, the two of them might've prowled the club with pleasurable intentions, stalking submissives and trading off control between them. Now she and Jay played those roles in turns, the stalking partner and the double-teamed submissive. Jay'd gotten his. She'd have her turn soon.

Cal lifted his chin. "You've wasted enough of my time, Henry. Play your word games and pretend they're powerful. Hide behind your ape, parade your sluts—"

"I hope I'm not interrupting." Slipping from the crowd, a slender man in formalwear cast an assessing glance at their standoff. "I wanted to thank the woman whose honesty inspired my kitten."

Leah popped her head around the man's arm and waved with childish enthusiasm.

The stranger extended his hand. "Andrew. If I may, miss?"

Henry brushed the makeshift yellow ribbon corsage on her chest. Her choice tonight. And what a sweet fuck-you.

"I'm always happy to meet a gentleman." Accepting the newcomer's handshake, she smiled for Leah. "Your girl served with distinction at tea. She has excellent attention to detail. Let me introduce you to these gentlemen—this is my master, Henry, and our good friend Master William."

Cal slunk away without a word.

* * * *

The crush on the third floor beat out the salon. Snug between Henry and Will, with her overdress left at the second-floor desk, she thanked genetics for giving them broad shoulders. They funneled traffic the way a proper roofline shed water.

Hand-lettered signs swarmed near the ceiling. *Prepare to be shocked. We've got the key to satisfaction. Please hold applause until the performance is finished.*

The first two rooms—electrical stimulation and chastity play—they bypassed. At the third, Henry checked his watch against the schedule. Inside, a modest audience attended a concert. Unclothed, the woman at the piano and her string players delivered a frenetic melody, judging from the fast bowing and the hints of sound escaping.

Will shadowed Alice. "Stopping for Clara's Quintet?"

"Perhaps later." Henry resettled his cuffs over his watchband. "My dear girl would hardly see the sights if I ensconced her in the music room."

"That, and you'd hardly be seen yourself." Will created a gap in the crowd, and they returned to the flow. "The low profile you love can only do so much in stirring up support. A leader has to be visible."

"How odd." Clasping her hand as he led them, Henry swirled his thumb in her palm. "I would have sworn my good friend Will was speaking, yet I hear Emma's words in his mouth."

Will chuckled. "Caught." Turning, he nodded respectfully to a woman in full body paint with rippling tiger stripes as she passed. "But when she's right, she's right."

A *thwack* resounded from the next room. *Get benched and drenched* graced the sign.

Henry shuffled her in front of the viewing window. A half-dozen spanking benches in different materials and configurations sat spaced around the room. Black-ribboned attendants demonstrated positioning and restraints on volunteers from the crowd.

The furniture saved the spankers' knees, maybe. Put submissives in more vulnerable postures. Like being bent across a table and left to wonder what her dominant would do with her. As she shifted her weight, her bare thighs rubbed together. Without underwear, she was one slip-raise and a zipper pull away from taking him inside her.

Breathing across her neck, Henry sent a shudder coursing to her toes. "The more pleasurable sort of spankings you enjoy, are they not?"

Even the tear-streaked players wore smiles as they massaged reddened cheeks. Pressing into his embrace, she nudged. A gratifying bulge thumped her ass. "You too, sir."

Nibbling her neckline, he hummed around his teeth. "I take pleasure in every activity guaranteed to make my sweet girl wet and ready for me." With his hands at her hips, he teased her dress up an inch while she squirmed. "Tonight offers an excellent showcase of this club's potential to do so. Most of the interest groups have practitioners giving demonstrations."

"It's not a party." The room signs with attitude. The excess of play monitors. The enormous crowd and its surging sea of seduction with an educational bent. "It's a career fair."

Henry chuckled in her ear.

Beside them, Will joined in. "Another woman who knows when she's right. Will you be putting her words in your mouth?"

"Something like that." Henry enveloped her in a full-body press. "If my girl sees a vocation that arouses her interest"—his twitching cock exposed his own—"I'm certain I'll have a position to offer her."

She sweltered in thin silk chiffon. Any and every position. If he invented new positions, she'd grab with both hands.

Will leaned on the glass. "A man could feast on her moans."

Oh God. Had she lost control of her throat? She snapped her lips together.

"Delicious." He kissed his fingertips and spread his hand in a starburst. "Is that how you spent your day?"

Nudging her to his shoulder, Henry nuzzled. "We played a game of spades this morning."

Pride spurred her to playfulness. "I thought we were playing hearts, sir."

"So we were, my sweet girl." He tapped his thumbs against the top of her ass. "So we were."

Eyeing them, Will laughed. "I bet both of you won that game."

"Always," Henry murmured.

The men escorted her at her pace, pausing when she paused. Henry quick with questions and encouragement, Will with supportive but unobtrusive interest.

At the flogging demonstration, wielders asked rapid-fire questions of everyone seeking a session. Soft slaps crossed palms as the supplicants chose materials. Agreement on both sides, and a wielder went to work.

Flexing muscles, he flowed controlled power as an extension of his arms to a chorus of yelps and moans. A series of brief snaps grew into a gorgeous rhythm until he swung in a continuous figure eight.

Echoes of last night caressed her back. Fucking amazing. Did Henry wear this determined, focused face when he flogged her? With godlike power and precision coursing through him? She'd never know, not unless Jay wanted to experience the thudding sting.

"Henry, tell me you've invested in a mirrored wall." A growling edge sharpened Will's voice. "She's shaking with the need to watch."

As her slip dress swished at her thighs, a current of air tickled the flesh beneath.

"My Alice has an exquisite eye for beauty." Henry wrapped his arm tight across her chest. "Inner workings arouse her interest." He pinched.

Fuck, the pleasure-pain in her nipple replicated in her clit with his squeeze. "Please."

Prompted by her hoarse whisper or his own pleasure, he delved between her legs. "She delights in the function underlying the form. The rhythm of a runner's steps." Her dress, draping across his wrist, shrouded his actions. "The arms pumping in counterpoint. The lungs filling to capacity." With thudding strikes, he churned a two-fingered footrace propelling her toward the finish line. "As each element's purpose is fulfilled, so she is as well."

She ground against his hand, thick and solid and forcing her focus inward.

He drove his fingers inside her, stroking hard. "Show us what victory looks like, Alice."

Breathing deep, she arched forward. The tape broke across her breasts. Her feet slapped the far side of the line with an adrenal rush courtesy of generous, commanding Henry. In an indistinguishable wave of noise, the hall buzzed as blackness stole her vision. She sagged on wobbly legs.

Henry held her secure, one arm a band of iron around her chest and other terminating between her legs.

She caught her breath in slow gulps. "Thank you, sir."

He kissed the back of her neck like he meant to brand her. As he eased his fingers free, he left her dress cascading down her thighs.

Shivering from the ticklish touch and the loss of him, she opened her eyes.

"Welcome back." One shoulder resting against the glass, Will greeted her soft and low, with uncharacteristic seriousness in his eyes. "A woman unbound, unashamed, and undone is a beautiful sight."

"A joy beyond measure." Henry sampled her on his fingers and claimed her mouth after.

Unashamed. The word lingered as she recovered her balance. Greedy and tender, Henry stole her soul and gave it back in a stronger frame with unexpected flourishes. The heat in her cheeks grew out of excitement and pleasure. Embarrassment no longer registered, not in his arms. Whoever she became, whatever she needed, Henry would never disparage her for being herself.

She wriggled and twisted, breaking his hold only to throw her arms around his neck and hang on tight. "I love you, Henry." Breaching protocol, but she'd whispered, and aftercare came in all forms. Including the scent of him, his solid base and floaty zest, steady and whimsical and so strong when she buried her face at his throat.

"My love for you is boundless, dearest." He spoke as if they stood alone, not near elbow to elbow with strangers. The polite bubble they'd gained while mini-sceneing in the hall had popped. "You surprise, delight, and challenge me daily. What is a life well-lived if not that?"

In the last year, she'd approached well-lived. The last two months redefined life with a blueprint unlike any she'd drawn in girlish fantasies. Somehow, the future promised even better.

"Lovebirds. Can't take you anywhere." Loosing an explosive sigh, Will patted her head and Henry's cheek. "We haven't covered half the circuit yet, and you've mired your feet in canoodling." With his broad back, Will acted as a boulder in a stream, sending passing players to either side. "You promised the girl adventure, Henry."

"So I did." Chuckling, he pulled her into the flow of traffic. "And I keep my promises."

They passed nurses with medical implements, police with handcuffs, and a demonstration of gags from cute and squishy to metallic and alien. One boisterous group governed a game with a spinning wheel of so-called punishments. The latest victim played catcher for the ring toss, a fake cock strapped on like a miner's headlamp. Either he had terrible depth perception, or the crowd had awful aim. Or they liked watching him bend over and retrieve dropped rings. Decent ass. Not so cute as Jay's or sexy as Henry's.

"Master Henry, isn't it?" A woman interrupted the teasing as Henry and Will debated the merits of various games for a dinner party. "I was hoping I'd run in to you."

Swiveling, Alice stumbled back a step. The woman had dogs.

Henry caught her with his arm around her back. "I don't believe we've met, Mistress…"

Not dog-dogs, but men in tight-laced hoods with ears and snouts. Two nearly nude men wearing black leather shorts, harnesses, and collars.

"Summer." The woman's hand emerged from flowing dress folds of lush grass green. Foot-long leashes dangled from shiny D-rings at her dogs' necks.

"William." Blowing in like a blond snowdrift eager to mix the seasons, Santa Will stole the handshake heading Henry's way.

One of the dog-men growled, and Summer thunked the leash's solid handle against his chest. "Castor, heel. You, too, Pol."

The men dropped to padded knees and planted their hands in front. Not hands, not really. They wore booties like miniature black boxing gloves. The growler held his head high and his back at a stiff slant while the other man nuzzled his mistress' skirts.

"Sorry about that." As Summer dropped her hand between the growler's pointed ears, he quieted. "Castor's overprotective."

"Understandable." Henry nodded rather than offer his hand. His right hand, where her scent and taste had dried. No wonder Will had nabbed the handshake. Given the growling, Henry's refusal wouldn't look like a snub. "A good dog minds his mistress' safety in all situations until told otherwise."

Her possessiveness no longer struck her as wrong. Henry belonged to her as much as she did him. As a master claimed obedience and service, a pet had as much right to claim protection and attention. A one-sided claim was no claim at all.

"I'm no threat. I'm downright jolly." Will backed off a step. "But you said you've been looking for Henry?"

"I wanted to thank him." Summer turned toward Henry. "Thank you, I mean, for starting up those classes. The opening's been great for niche groups. Emma confirmed for me tonight that she swayed the board into a monthly munch and intro class for pup play."

Okay, an intro class probably taught them how to get those booties and masks on. Did a munch teach them how to eat Scooby snacks in them?

Henry squeezed her hip. "A munch like Emma's recent tea or something more casual?"

Christ, he knew her inside and out. Knew she'd stand here puzzling until she understood every rotating gear in the conversation.

"We'll do a Super Bowl chow spread. Most of the pups are guys. But it'll be open to novices and curious onlookers. Does your pet like puppies, Henry?"

Alice wrenched her uninvited stare from the dog-men. Too late to play it cool.

"My Alice has something of a puppy at home." Soft-lipped, he kissed her cheek. "But he's away for the weekend."

"Oh, poor thing." Summer made a sympathetic face, all drooping lips and pinched brows. "Would she like to pet Pol?" She patted the dog-man rubbing his face against her leg. "He's a good boy, and socialization is always helpful."

Stepping forward on a goodwill mission, Alice held out her hand, palm flat. Dad's lessons had stuck. His brother'd been bit by a neighbor's dog. She and Ollie'd heard the speech a hundred times.

"So you'll be socializing them in the classes, then?" Will raised his voice over laughter leaking from the game room. "Stellar notion. Start everyone off on the same page."

As the dog-man sniffed her fingers, he nudged with his sleek leather nose.

"Mm-hmm." Skirt swishing, Summer rocked on sandaled feet. "We'll go over safety with props and positioning, basic commands, that sort of thing. We'll have a playroom for the pups. No marking or mounting, but some fun romping."

The leather hood ran up and over the man's head and laced down the back to his neck. Supple but gleaming, the mask lacked the tingly softness of her suede. She settled for scratching a shoulder blade, human and familiar. Summer's puppy leaned in, tilting his head and whining in a pitch lower than Jay's.

"Too undignified for my Castor." Summer rubbed the back of his hood. "But Pollux will play hard enough for both of them."

Not as hard as Jay. Or as sweetly as Jay. She pulled her hand back. In a puppy hood, he'd lose his beautiful smile and his steep, slender nose. These stand-ins couldn't compare to irreplaceable Jay. A stealthy twist let her capture Henry, curling their hands together. She'd missed Will's remark. Something about costuming.

"If you want colorful, hit the far end." Tossing her head back, Summer nodded down the hall. "The pony players have outdone themselves with elaborate getups."

They shared a round of farewells before Summer patted her play partners between their leather ears. "Up, boys."

The dog-men, back on two feet, flanked their mistress as she left. Something wagged between their legs with each step.

"They have tails," Alice whispered. They had to sway somehow. Servos? "Are they sewn into the shorts?"

Grinning, Will shook his head.

"Some are." Henry glanced over his shoulder. "More likely those are attached to a toy and inserted." He patted her ass.

His touch tapped a live wire. Wearing a toy for hours. Added weight tugging at her and slapping her thighs.

"For a fuller experience," Will deadpanned.

Strange and silly as the rest seemed, she clenched her ass in respect for overlapping desire. Complementary kinks. She just wanted her toy bigger and attached to a green-eyed man with a commanding baritone. "I know what filling I'd prefer."

As Santa laughed, Henry gripped her face in both hands and planted a kiss on her. His stiff-tongued invasion came with a side order of hardening cock at her hip.

She pushed into the pressure. Twice now she'd come at the club, once from Jay's incomparable oral fixation and tonight from Henry's magnificent fingers. One of these nights, she'd return the damn favor already.

Henry dragged their lips apart. "Come along, my dear."

But not tonight. The possibility of Cal wandering the halls tinged the mood. Henry and Will had a habit, conscious or not, of covering angles and watching each other's backs. They spoke a language of low-toned phrases and subtle nods.

Dozens of colorful signs speckled a viewing window ahead. A yellow-ribboned man wearing train-covered footie pajamas dashed into the hall. A pigtailed woman in denim overalls chased him, her own yellow ribbon flapping around her arm.

The signs—no, closer inspection turned up kindergarten-quality crayon drawings. The lone sign read *Littles Coloring Contest*. Trees, horses, and houses competed with stick figures holding hands for most-popular subject. The unskilled art probably assaulted Henry's eyes.

"Who are the Littles?" Maybe they sponsored a contest every year. Coloring was an odd pick.

"You are, sometimes, little one." Will winked.

Henry gestured toward the door. "Did you have a mind to enter?"

"A coloring contest?" Christ no. "What am I, five?"

Raising his eyebrows, he held her gaze.

Club civility, right. Check the sarcasm at the door with the camera phones. "I mean, no, thank you, sir."

He steered her nearer, putting them at an angle clear of traffic. "I'd make a fair wager your tea-serving admirer spends time here."

"Leah?" Inside, adults colored and played. Stuffed animals, cheery totems, crowded the low tables' centers. "Why?"

"Little is a state of mind." Wrapping his arms around her, Henry clasped one wrist in his opposite hand above her navel. "For the ageplayers, this is a role-play performance, one they don with their clothes and props."

In the far corner, a crowd sprawled on a rug while a woman read aloud. No Leah and her master, but other couples cuddled as they listened.

"But for the littles, expressing their inner innocence and need are necessities." Fondness lightening his tone, he stroked her stomach with his habitual thumb sweep. "When they feel safest, they are free to reveal true selves the outer world will never see."

He'd brought Jay here. Or brought this idea, this comfort, home for Jay. Henry cultivated caregiving and unconditional love in his fields of expertise. A full-grown man with a child's heart, Jay would never carry a stuffed animal or run around in footie pajamas. "He wants the security of childhood without the childish things."

"A lovely deduction." Henry kissed her cheek. "Our Jay needs that security emotionally. Mentally, he has outgrown the trappings and rejects them."

"Except story time." She'd gotten him an origami book and folding papers for his birthday. Not far off the mark from a coloring contest, minus the kiddie stigma and with the added bonus of keeping his mind and hands busy. Chess instead of Candyland.

"Private joys." Henry murmured. "I give him the things he needs but for which he might be ashamed to ask."

Part of the joy of loving Jay, but part of Henry's responsibility as a dominant, too. Making Jay not the lone beneficiary. She spun and stared into bottomless rings of pine green. "What do you give me that I'd be ashamed to ask for?"

Not the sex for damn sure. Even the kinky stuff. Being ashamed of her arousal triggers would be pointless and unsatisfying.

"Shelter," he whispered.

A chill shivered through her and left tingling goose bumps behind.

"A place in which you and your happiness are valued. A place in which you may be dependent and needy without fearing consequences."

Not something she'd ever ask for. Or so she'd have argued just three months ago. She tried to drop her gaze.

He clutched her tighter, his eyes narrowing and nostrils flaring. "A place that will not fail you."

She couldn't look away. He'd given her that place before she'd known how to ask. His heart, where she knelt side by side with Jay.

"I—you—" As her throat closed, her mouth moved without sound. *I know you won't fail me.*

Through his intense scrutiny, he understood her in ways she didn't herself. His love overwhelmed her. But what she'd imagined as a current trapping her beneath the waves instead gave her buoyancy to surface.

A shadow fell over them, the hall lights bowing to Will's broad back.

Henry rubbed his nose against hers. "A bit much to think about here, dearest."

With words delivered low and intimate, he came close to freeing her tears.

Humming, he swiped his thumbs beneath her eyes. "And, of course, I provide the opportunity for one stubborn bastion of independence to recognize a person's strength is not lessened merely because she has the good sense to take shelter in a rainstorm."

The hiccup clogging her throat broke through with a giggle attached. "Are you calling me stubborn, sir?"

"Does that seem to you a statement I would make about my ever-obedient Alice?"

His feigned amazement coaxed out her second giggle. The teary pressure along the bottom of her eyes retreated. "Ever obedient, huh?"

A smile peeked through Henry's solemn demeanor.

This lifestyle he'd introduced her to, sex didn't cover the half of it. Like Leah with her master, or the dog-men with their mistress, or the grown-ups attending story time in the room behind her. An arousal trigger for some functioned as an instruction manual to life for others. "It's not all whipping and blowjobs."

Will's cough carried a suspicious undertone.

Henry laughed without subterfuge. "No. Although light whipping is likely at the pony showcase."

"Yes, yes, everyone loves to see the ponies." Rotating like a wide-bellied top, faux-grumpy Santa pushed out a pouty lower lip. "Will no one think of the rope players?"

"There's a rope demonstration?" Purple lines on mocha skin. The beautiful honeycomb design had crisscrossed the stranger on stage on her first night. Before the threats and the spanking. "Like the one we watched?"

"There is." Head tilted, Henry studied her.

"More advanced," Will added. "The main hall's open platform isn't optimal for suspensions."

"Suspensions?" Decorative rope paled beside the possibility of functional rope, its strength put to use. What elegant architectural routes did creative minds devise to cradle living, breathing sculptures?

Henry clasped her wrist. "Is rope play something you'd like to see, Alice?"

Her affirmative answer sent them striding through an area crowded by more dog-people in harnesses and the pony-people with tack as colorful as promised. She took in a fraction of the whole, grasping but the fringes of the games they passed.

The leather gave way to cotton and nylon. Players swished by in short skirts with rope leggings or paraded on rope leashes by their bound wrists. Time slowed to a crawl as Will exchanged greetings and complimented ties. Not a person passed without comment. The room ahead bore *We swing a little knotty* on its sign.

"William, dude!" A shirtless man in threadbare jeans and sandals hustled through the hall. "I'm about to take over in the demo room." He slipped his hand through the short brown curls on his head. "Thought I'd missed you. Surprised you haven't sniffed out a couple of rope bunnies and headed upstairs."

"The night's young, Justin. I've had the pleasure of spending time with my best friend and his delightful pet." Will gestured to them in a wide sweep. "Henry, Alice, meet Justin, one of our up-and-coming riggers."

Henry, asking the chicken-scrawny guy about his planned scene, jumpstarted the conversation.

Justin's explanation came with a spate of arm flailing and head ducking. "It makes more sense in the air, I guess." He unbent and shook out his limbs. "You gonna watch the demo?"

Behind him, a woman sauntered out of the room in nothing but coils of rope. The fiber twisted around and over itself, a knotted puzzle mapped to flesh. The rope sketched in hints of clothing, a corset around the midsection, a slanted skirt to the knee, a top with a peek-a-boo window between the breasts.

Tracking the paths and imagining the reverse, Alice grew dizzy. "That's incredible."

"You like?" Justin waved to the woman. "Van's one of my best."

"You made that?"

"Took him an hour to wrap." As the woman strolled closer with short, pencil-skirt steps, the coils shifted around her thighs. "All that delicious standing still while the rope tightens." She extended a manicured hand. "Vanessa."

"Alice." Forcing herself to stop staring at the knots, she greeted her with a proper handshake. "Love your dress."

Vanessa ran a visual sweep bottom to top. "Love yours. The hint of what they're missing sells it. Justin, Amie's raring to go and the room's about full."

"Ah. My cue to be masterful." Justin pressed his hands in prayer and bowed. "Great to meet you. I hope you'll stay. Van'll find you spots." He jogged off, sandals slapping at his heels.

"Well, Henry?" Will offered his arm to Vanessa, and she accepted. "Are we parting ways, or will you and your little one sit for a spell?"

She crossed her fingers. *Stay?*

Henry traced her hairline and smiled. "We'll sit in, Will. I expect I'll need that refresher on knots and wraps soon."

Victory danced in her blood, heated and jumping. God, Jay should be here to toss her across his shoulders and spin until they collapsed and dragged Henry down with them.

Vanessa found them seats, though Henry declined one on her behalf and settled her in his lap instead. His warm thighs made for a better perch than the wooden folding chair. Curling around him, she tucked her fingers under his lapel.

As Will took the seat beside them, Vanessa bent and whispered in his ear. The knots on her back matched the front for beautiful tension and strength.

"Is it the symmetry or the asymmetry that entrances you so, sweet girl?" Henry pitched his voice low. "Or are the coursing lines so many gears turning in your mind?"

"Gears, sir." Locked together, they rotated as one piece in fluid motion. The linen of Henry's dress shirt teased her fingers. Her scant knowledge of rope play didn't answer the hundred questions on her tongue. The stretch and strength of the materials. Their roughness or softness as they snaked around her. "Too many."

Vanessa paraded up the aisle, ropes slow-dancing across her hips and shoulder blades.

Tap tap tap went Henry's fingers on her spine. "Save your questions for after, and any the young man fails to answer in his demonstration, Will will gladly field for you."

"What's this I'm being volunteered for?" Santa patted her knee. "If it involves tying this one up and watching your boy please her, I can clear my schedule."

"In time, perhaps." Thick currents played in Henry's tone. "You've always been a marvelous rigger."

His darkening, distant eyes rolled a storm under her skin. Cloud lightning flashed in her muscles, setting her shivering.

Henry engulfed her in a tight squeeze, but he said no more as Justin called everyone's attention to the front. The presentation proceeded step by step, each function explained, every choice identified and qualified.

Eye bolts dotted the massive exposed wood joists in the ceiling. Justin zipped from laid-back chill dude to serious instructor as he covered hard points and drop lines and checked in with "rope bunny" Amie for tingling, numbness, and fatigue.

By the time he'd finished, she hung from the ceiling in a meditative lotus. Ropes girded her hips and crossed in a Celtic knot above her breasts. Serene and still, she seemed a statue. Some ancient deity enshrined in artwork Henry'd be able to name.

"Normally about now I'd fetch Amie's favorite bunny ears vibe"— Justin slipped his hand between his partner's thighs, drawing a low sigh—"and torture her awhile, but my time's up."

Will launched to his feet and clapped with gusto. The crowd followed. Henry displaced her gently, steadying her before he stood.

"Well?" Cheeks round and cheery, Santa Will peered at her with bright blue eyes. "Do we have you on the ropes, sweet Alice?"

"I haven't heard the details of your pitch," she teased. "Length, thickness—a girl needs to know these things."

He laughed, and they were off. The questions she'd held poured out like an upended box of nuts and bolts. Santa's workshop held the tools to fashion them into answers. Her steam ran dry in the mathematical details of millimeter counts and better-safe-than-sorry weight tolerances for ropes supporting vigorous, swinging bodies.

Henry, the constant support post at her back, massaged her temples. "I do hate to pull you away from the physics of proper weight distribution when such talk makes your eyes shine and your stomach flutter, but we've put in enough of an appearance. You have a reward waiting at home. A round of hearts before bed?"

Fuck yes. The flutters in her stomach gained seismic ratings. "Yes, please, sir."

"Will." Henry extended his arm, and the men clasped forearms. "We'll talk soon. I trust we haven't disrupted your plans too terribly much."

"Not even an inch, and don't you dare hesitate to ask again. Alice, if I may?" At her nod, he pecked her cheek with fuzzy exuberance. "Enjoy your games, pet, and give that boy of yours an extra squeeze when he gets home for all the fun he's missed."

Gazing back through the window as they left, she nudged Henry in the ribs. "I think Santa's getting lucky with Ms. Rope Dress tonight."

The woman approached and laid a hand on Santa's chest, a hand he covered with his own and raised for a kiss.

"Will has a talent for knots." A smile crossed Henry's lips. "If we should happen to need a rigger in the future, he'd be my first—and only—choice."

The demo rigger'd put his hands all over his model's body. Henry sure as hell wouldn't let just anyone touch her or Jay so intimately.

"At home?" They'd have to get creative with the furniture to make room. And inviting someone into the bedroom, even Santa, wriggled like creepy-crawlies climbing her arms and legs. Henry's bedroom was their refuge.

"No, I haven't suitable hardware. Jay supported your weight the last time your legs left the floor. The bedroom hook is enough for anchoring floor play, but I wouldn't trust it for full suspension unless I'd bought the apartment above and made a modification or two." He glanced sideways at her. "Yes, I know you'd hate being the cause of such expense."

"It'd be awfully extravagant, sir."

As they slipped from the hall into the main room, Henry halted and squeezed her hand. "Extravagance is not the concern for me it is for you, but your feelings, and Jay's, are. Our bedroom will remain for private joys, a place in which you may approach me without shame, sweet girl."

A promise. A commandment, the way Henry spoke. She returned his squeeze. "Here, then?"

Hard to imagine being so exposed. Henry'd taken baby steps with her compared to how some folks behaved around them. Rows of seats filled with watchers and faces lining the window didn't trip her trigger. Not for arousal, anyway, even if being part of the crowd was fun.

"Upstairs." He led her around knots of people. "Nothing so open as this."

Not—— "The fourth floor?" Reclaiming the space might help Jay, but he'd be uncomfortable, too, and Henry wouldn't push such nervous territory with bondage. Not when he'd been so careful about testing the cuffs in a safe space.

"No." Flat and unyielding, he drew her beside him. "The fifth. Will maintains a private room." He brushed her cheek in a kiss. "He hasn't the luxury of sharing his joys at home." Sidestepping, he curled her into his embrace. A pair of pony players passed them, manes braided and tails bobbing. "On a night like tonight, the fourth floor will busy indeed."

Bigger crowd plus fewer open rooms equaled—a big headache for Emma. She had to be getting slammed at the desk. "All the space on this floor is eaten up with demos."

"Precisely." Unwinding her, he started them forward. The stairs waited down the shorter hall near the far end. "And all of those inspired by the ideas raised here will be begging for a place on the fourth."

"Natural outcome of a career fair, sir." She swiveled, tip-toeing backward in front of him. Mmmf. Him. That suit. Her man knew how to dress. "Interns taking on new positions."

"Or assuming familiar ones." Eyeing her, he smoothed his tie down to his suit and fingered the edge. "We'll see what positions we might find for you to fill at home."

"Master Henry." A gray-haired man in a fancy suit with a full vest approached them—no, just Henry. He didn't so much as glance at her. "My apologies for the intrusion, but I must speak with you."

"Master Laurence." Henry inclined his head. "The night seems a success. The board must be pleased with the turnout." He tugged her to his side. "May I present the distaff pride of my collection?"

"The woman you boys have been squabbling over?" Flicking his gaze across her, Master Laurence scowled. "A fine pet, I'm sure, better seen than heard."

What. The. Fuck.

"An exquisite flower in bloom." As his teasing tone vanished, Henry settled into his neutral dom voice. "A traditionalist such as yourself would naturally prune with more vigor, but I anticipate her full growth with great pleasure." Shoulders squared, he rested his hand on the back of her neck. Weighted, but not gripping. He rubbed his thumb beneath her ear. "Have you heard squabbling? I fail to see a reason for it. The woman is mine, without question."

His possession. So socially inappropriate. So sexually thrilling.

"I'm told Masters Calvin and William nearly came to blows over her in the salon. *Again.*" The old man's puckered lips matched the rest of his wrinkled face. "No official complaints, but we can't have you boys feuding. They've both been steady members over the years. I'd hate to see either ejected."

Jolly Santa and that fucking jackass merited the same regard from this dick. If a feud existed, Cal fed it with his predatory behavior and constant needling. Like a scorned kid who kept trying to prove himself better than them.

"No feuding, of course. A rift dividing the membership could throw the club into chaos." Henry swept his hand down her back. "Perhaps cause a loss of confidence in the board's ability to manage affairs."

Maybe Emma had the right idea, and the board would stick and grind without a fresh mechanic to grease the gears. This guy looked like he'd trained his first sub before Henry's birth.

Master Laurence grunted. "These classes of yours best help train them to know their places. Master William ought to know better than to raise his fist to a fellow master."

"This evening? An exchange of words, nothing more." Henry looped her ribbon around his finger. "Cal forgot himself and attempted to touch my pet. Will reminded him of the rules for yellow ribbons. Prevented him from breaking a core rule, in truth, and perhaps saved him a sanction. My dear girl would have been obligated to report such a deep infraction."

"Oh?" The old man squinted at her. "I'm told she invited the attention, and that Master William had his hands all over her."

Fucking Cal. He'd gone crying to a sympathetic ear with half-truths. No one else would've done it for him.

"Alice?" Clasping her chin, Henry leveled a green stare at her. "Tell Master Laurence what happened, please."

Time to shine. Henry was counting on her.

"I gave Master William permission to greet me, Master Laurence." She tucked her irritation behind a docile tone. "He touched my arm and my face. As he is my master's friend, I knew he'd behave with impeccable manners. I did not grant Master Calvin"—allowing him a title coated her tongue with filth—"the same permission, nor did he ask. He assumed, and Master William shielded me from an unwanted intrusion."

The old master must've crammed lemons in his mouth. No possible way could anyone twist a face so sour otherwise. "Well. That would put you in a more respectable light, young miss." Like a kid worrying a loose tooth, he pushed out a papery cheek. "You'll vouch for the girl's honesty, Master Henry?"

"I would stake my reputation on it." Henry spoke like he'd sunk footers into the earth three stories down. "As it happens, I needn't today. I witnessed the exchange. Her account is accurate."

Master Laurence quizzed Henry on the nuances. Her thoughts likely rated as high as a dog's. Not even a dog-man's. Just a dog's. Unless her ribbon rather than her sex predetermined his attitude. He sure acted like he figured himself a pillar of proper behavior.

Scanning the crowd, she tried floating on their happiness. She'd explained her side. Henry would handle the rest. Best case, Cal would receive a black mark in his record. Santa wouldn't, and she and Henry would go home for playtime.

Spiky hair and a skintight shirt flashed in a gap.

Could've been any jackass with an overabundance of hair gel. They hadn't run into Cal for hours. He might've left after tattling to the old man.

A laughing woman in lace plunged her fingers through a ring in a nude man's collar and tugged him down. In the space beyond, Cal gloated. Gaze fixed below him, he walked a slow circle. The same fucking stalking move he'd pulled on her. On Jay.

As the collared man stepped forward, he exposed a low padded chaise holding a brown-haired woman with her head bowed. Red ribbon flickering on her arm, she hugged herself. Her curls hid her face, but those pink bows—

Cal slid onto the seat.

You miserable fucking ass.

She plowed through the crowd, muttering *sorry* in a perpetual feedback loop.

Cal sat knee to knee with his trembling prey.

"Leah!" She shouted. She had to. Reaching her would take too long. "There you are."

Cal froze.

Leah lifted her head. Christ, she had eyes near brown as Jay's, wide and tear-filled. She opened her mouth. "*Red.*"

The noise level dropped. Players turned as Cal scooted away and stood.

"Red, red." Sobbing, Leah jumped to her feet and flung herself forward. "Red."

One slippered foot sliding, Alice caught the shaking girl. "It's okay. You're okay. I've got you."

Leah, her breath heaving, blasted her neck with heat.

Three black-ribboned monitors pushed through the onlookers.

"Leah, honey, where's your master?" Surely he'd run to his sub's rescue if he'd heard her call.

"I don't know." Sniffling, Leah clutched the back of her dress. "He said sit here like a good kitten and he'd reserve us time upstairs."

Stuck in line, if the desk was as busy as predicted.

"Excuse me." She focused on the nearest play monitor, a brawny guy in a white shirt. "Can you find her master? Master Andrew. About your height, slim build, brown hair, brown eyes, wearing—" Shit, what color—

"A navy suit with a powder blue tie." Henry stepped up beside her. "Try the desk first, and please ask Emma to page him if necessary. We'll remain with the girl."

"I was supposed to stay on the bench." Mascara smudged Leah's cheeks. "Do you think he'll be mad?"

"Not at you." She tugged a springy curl dangling from the girl's hair bows. "Look how well you remembered what to do. Better than I did. He'll be extra proud of his kitten."

"Calvin?" The old man must've followed Henry. "I thought we'd found you a partner for the night."

"Master Laurence, I'm glad you're here to witness this affront." Puffing up his chest, Cal glared at her. "You see how Henry's whor— horribly trained submissive stalks me. She's interfering in my enjoyment. How many years have I belonged here? How many years did you and my father serve on the board together? Her behavior is shockingly uncivil. I can't understand how she's allowed to roam unchecked."

Henry *tsk*ed through his teeth. "Odd, how often these disturbances involve Master Calvin of late."

Cal sneered. "Odd, how often these disturbances involve your pets."

"Indeed. One might say you've been targeting them." Tipping his head, Henry eyed Leah. No longer shaking, she still hadn't eased up on her hug. "And now their friends."

"Enough, the pair of you." Master Laurence waved between the men and snagged Cal's forearm. "Calvin. Let's us go and chat in Emma's office."

"I didn't touch the brat." The whine in his voice grated.

"*Master* Calvin." The old man sighed. "Would you rather we have this talk in the boardroom? These escalating outbursts can't continue."

"I sat to rest my legs, and she started shouting. And now my night is interrupted once again. How is that fair?"

"He said Master loaned me to him." Leah shook her head, curls swaying. "But he'd never. I know he'd never."

Master Laurence closed his eyes. His face sagged. If disappointment could bring on a heart attack, the play monitors had better be ready with CPR. "We'll sort things out downstairs." He snapped his fingers and gestured to the monitors. "Help Master Calvin find his way, please."

"I know the way." Cal stalked off with two men in his wake. "My father would be appalled by what this club has become."

"Master Henry, I trust you'll inform the girl's master of the procedure in the event he wishes to lodge an official complaint?"

"Of course." Henry bowed his head. "My Alice and I will wait with her and explain the situation."

Master Laurence faced her.

She hastily copied Henry's head-bob.

"I may have misjudged you, miss." Eyes narrowed and lips twitching, Master Lawrence coughed into his fist. "Pardon. You remind me of another opinionated young woman who acts as she sees the need." He parted his lips in a fine smile, the first time he'd looked other than sour. "And now I'll have to go and steal her office for a bit."

As she waited for rankling resentment at being compared to Emma to creep in, her growling jealousy remained surprisingly silent. She'd never manage the hero-worship levels of fixation Leah lavished on her, but a cautious admiration for and a growing friendship with Emma seemed almost manageable.

The master nodded to Henry. "If there's to be a report, I'll want the both of your statements as well."

"Certainly, Master Laurence."

The old man strode off.

Henry seated her on the chaise, and Leah cuddled at her side until her master arrived. Whether Leah's tears or Henry's phrasing persuaded him, Master Andrew insisted on holding Cal accountable.

The clock in Emma's office struck four before they'd finished giving statements. The board had a week to deliberate and assign reprimands or punishment, if any.

She dozed on the way home, warm and buttoned up in her navy overdress. When they reached the bedroom, Henry peeled her clothes off and tucked her against him beneath the sheet.

"Reward?" The question emerged in a yawn. She stretched her limbs, rubbing their legs together. If he needed release, she'd force herself awake. "You want?"

"When you wake." Nestling close, he kissed her shoulder. "Sleep, my love. I'm pleased with you beyond passion tonight."

* * * *

Henry let her sleep in after their late night, and between rewards and brunch and showering, the morning disappeared with unexpected speed. A text from her little sister rattled her phone just after one on Sunday afternoon.

Vid chat now?

She shot back a *yes*, booted up the battered laptop she'd gotten through her employer's buying plan, and claimed her chair at the dining room table. With schedules at odds for weeks, they hadn't exchanged more than texts in—God, two months. Not since Henry's gallery opening. Lots to tell. "Remember those guys I was fucking? Yeah, so I kind of moved in with them, and it's mostly fantastic." Just like that.

Texting and social networks kept her updated on the graphically detailed medical procedures she didn't want to hear about and Olivia's near-daily pleas for more sleep. But neither matched talking to Ollie face to face in real time.

She had the apartment practically to herself for explaining. Henry had holed up in his studio for the afternoon, and Jay would be on his way back from his parents' place. Unless his family suddenly needed him more than they did.

Ugh. Unkind. Letting the territorial resentment sail through, she clutched the important emotion, the anticipation of Jay's return by dinnertime.

"You look like you're having a good time." Spoon dangling, Ollie waved as the connection clicked through. "Gonna fill me in?"

"Why are you always eating cereal when we talk?" The guy thing would be an ease-into-it discussion.

"Uhh, because it's breakfast time in California, duh. And since I am awake—mostly—and functioning—mostly—at breakfast, and—most importantly—I am not working at breakfast, it's about the only time we can gab." Ollie slurped mushy colored marshmallows. Her garbled words following might have been, "and I like cereal."

"I'm over cereal. Pancakes for me." Especially the light, fluffy crepes Henry topped with fresh fruit and whipped cream. God, he spoiled them. Last time anyone had made breakfast for her every morning—fifteen years gone.

"Pancakes take too much time."

"And obviously they don't contain enough sugar for you."

"Don't knock the Charms, Allie. You used to pour me a bowl every morning."

All those weeks of Mom rushing to work or the hospital to see Dad while Alice took charge of getting Ollie and herself off to school.

"I should apologize." She kept her tone dryly amused. Ollie didn't need to know about the sugar cabinet she shared with Jay, where a half-eaten box of Charms lived alongside the mountain of sugary goodness Henry eschewed. "I've scarred your taste buds for life."

Ollie pointed her spoon at the screen. "What's that behind you?"

"Like I'm falling for that."

"Seriously. Pan your cam. That's so not your apartment. Did you get a bigger place and not tell me?"

"No." Shit. She'd intended to work up to this part. "Not exactly."

"Oh my God. You're there." The spoon slipped from her fingers. "On Sunday? Holy shit. Is it a sex thing?" Ollie ducked, brown hair flying as she dug for her spoon. "It's a sex thing and I'm interrupting. Jesus, Allie,

I know we haven't talked in forever, but tell me you didn't check your messages in the middle of a sex thing."

"I did not check my messages in the middle of a sex thing." She nailed the blank-faced, deadpan delivery.

"Like I'm gonna believe you now." Ollie waved her recovered spoon around. "You probably have a guy's head between your legs."

"Ollie!" Dropping her face into her hands, Alice knocked her elbows on the table. "Ouch. You want me to stand up to prove I don't?"

"No, don't ruin the moment. It's good to have goals." Crunching her cereal, Ollie delivered a Jay-worthy grin. "I can be happy you're having a fulfilling-but-loveless sex life, even if I'm in Droughtsville, population: me."

"I'm playing the world's smallest violin for you."

"I call bullshit. The world hasn't invented a musical instrument you can play."

"Funny, smartass." Also true, but little sisters didn't get to win sniping contests.

"If it's not a sex thing, why are you at their place on Sunday?"

"Well—it's not—" just their apartment or loveless anymore. "I kinda moved in."

"No fucking way. With smoldering art guy and flirty bike boy? Ms. I Have a Plan for Everything and You Are Not on My List?"

"Smoldering?"

Oh God.

"Is that him? Can your boy-toys see me?" Ollie flailed with maniacal-toddler energy. "Hi, boy-toys! I want you to know that yes, these are my best pajamas, because obviously I knew we'd meet today, and no, it's not uncool for a twenty-five-year-old med student to wear magic ponies to bed. Also, it's unfair of Allie to keep your hotness to herself. If you're there, I demand evidence."

Standing beside the door to his studio, lips twitching, Henry raised one eyebrow.

"Thanks, Ollie." God knew what torments he'd devise with a prompt like *smoldering*. "I'm so gonna pay for that."

"What'd I say?"

"Nevermind." Ah well. She'd enjoy whatever he did. "No, he can't see you."

"Did you really move in?" Wide eyes filling the screen, Ollie dropped to a whisper. "Did I get you in trouble?" Her teasing tone fled with the color in her face. "Will he hit you because of what I said?"

"Christ, no. I told you, it's not like that."

Henry stood remote and still as a lonely mountain peak. Fuck. He'd finally flogged her again, and two days later baby sister jammed her foot in her mouth.

"Henry, I'm sorry, it's not—she didn't mean—"

"You're babbling, dearest," he murmured. He approached the table and stopped just beyond the webcam's range. "If I may?"

Vacating the chair, she waved. "Be my guest. Ollie, meet Henry, my smoldering art guy. Henry, meet Olivia, my nosy sister."

Henry pushed the chair back and sat. "Good afternoon, Olivia. It's a pleasure to meet you. Alice has mentioned you with fondness many times."

"I hope not. If my name's been coming up while you're fucking my sister—"

"Ollie, cut it out." She leaned in. Henry smelled of freshly cleaned floor, orange and woody. Murphy's Oil Soap. He avoided using turpentine or mineral spirits to clean brushes in a closed room. Taking a deeper whiff, she resisted the urge to nuzzle. "I was trying to tell you I'm living with Henry and Jay. We have a relationship. A serious thing."

"Like"—Ollie squinted—"a long-term thing? With"—who knew what her hand-waving represented—"both of them?"

"A very long-term thing, I hope." Henry answered before Alice knew how to explain. "I'm deeply in love with your sister, Olivia, and I would like for us to be cordial at the least. Friends, preferably. Family, if you'll extend the definition."

"Mr. Sign on the Dotted Line for Sex is in love with my sister." Flat disbelief emanated from Ollie in eyes and voice.

"I am, yes." Henry ignored the disdain, as if Ollie were a truculent teenager and rudeness to be expected.

"Do you still hit her?"

"Ollie." Mortification walloped her ass harder than Henry ever did.

Laying his hand on hers, he tilted his head. "Alice herself has firmly corrected me on the semantics involved, Olivia. No. I do not hit your sister. I occasionally, with her consent and for her pleasure, flog her. Spank her. Tie her down and fuck her." He spoke with calm precision, thoughtful truths leaping shamelessly from his tongue. "I also, it should be said, embrace her frequently. Kiss her softly. Make love to her tenderly. If you wish for more explicit descriptions of our activities, you would be better served to ask her—and to listen more closely to her answers."

Mouth hanging open, Olivia sat utterly silent.

Henry pushed himself up and cupped Alice's face. Rubbing her cheekbone, he kissed her opposite cheek. "Talk to your sister, dearest. I'm pleased you haven't felt a need to hide our relationship." As he drew back, he trailed his fingers down her neck. "I'll just be smoldering in the kitchen." Alice giggled.

Henry tapped her nose with his index finger and headed around the table.

"Wait." The shout came through the laptop speakers loud and squawky. "Wait, Henry, please."

He halted.

Alice reclaimed her chair. "Stop bugging him, Ollie."

"No, that's not—" Ollie winced. "I want to tell him I'm sorry. Henry?" She scanned back and forth. "I'm sorry for being so—me. For thinking you were hurting Allie. I can see she's happy."

Eyelids fluttering, Henry drew a deep breath. "You speak the truth as you see it, and you're quite protective of your sister, Olivia." He stood beyond the camera's sight, his voice light and crisp with an amused tang. "For which do you mean to apologize? Shall I apologize for the same? We'll let it go, hmm? I believe we each understand the other's concern properly now."

Ollie hung her head. "Thanks, Henry." Her baby sister's grin peeked out. "I'll try to be less offensive next time we talk. I can share tons of dirt."

Henry snorted, shook his head, and proceeded to the kitchen.

"Ollie, you have no idea." Tracking his swagger, Alice revisited the decadent luxury of her morning wake-up call. "My smoldering art guy knows more about me than I do."

"A challenge. I'll think up good stuff to share when I visit." Tongue wagging, Ollie sassed the camera.

"You do and I'll— You're coming to Boston?"

Ollie nodded with jack-in-the-box vigor. "Presenting a paper. I assisted on a big case, and now I get to attend the conference. Okay, I'm not the main person, but I'm going!"

"That's fantastic." Three years since she'd gone out for Ollie's college graduation. Lots of missed hugs to make up for. "When are you coming? For how long? Where are you staying?"

"August seventh, three days, and, uhh—" A guilty grimace crept over Ollie's face. "I kinda hoped with you. Before I knew about your move." She shrugged. "I'll figure it out."

Shit. Mr. Nagel had rented her old apartment. The new tenant would take possession in July, which started tomorrow, and she hadn't written Henry a rent check or even raised the money issue again. The spare room wasn't hers to give away. If she paid for Ollie's hotel and spent the evenings—

Steady tapping drilled into her head. Henry, rapping his forefinger on the breakfast bar. "You're over-thinking, my dear. You need only ask."

"But it's not—" Keenly aware of Ollie's stare, she refused to initiate a discussion of how they handled sexual requests and whether the rules applied to non-sexual ones. Ollie had heard enough.

"This is something you want. Ask."

She licked her lips and took a breath. "Henry, would it be all right if Ollie stayed with us while she's in town?"

"Certainly, Alice." His smile, combined with his direct gaze, warmed her. "It's no trouble. You'll have to make sure Jay is aware and able to meet your standards for hosting a guest in your room. I'm sure he'll enjoy that as well."

He would. Hell, Jay and Ollie would get on like a house on fire. Prankster babies. She grinned at her sister. "Done deal. You'll stay with us."

"Thanks, Allie." Ollie tipped her head back. "Thanks, Henry."

Alice rolled her eyes. "Don't make me regret having you here."

Ollie stuck out her tongue. "Better hide your kinky stuff from my poor virgin eyes."

"You really wanna play the virgin card? Because now I think about it, I haven't told Henry about your adventures with Bobby Sa—"

"Allie!" Olivia's screech shoved Alice back. "You wouldn't."

"You thought I wouldn't get into a sexual relationship with two guys, either. You definitely thought I wouldn't move in with them." Alice flicked imaginary lint from her shoulders. "Who's to say what I might do?"

"Oh, you're gonna get it now. First thing when I get there, I'm gonna tell—" An emergency siren blared. "Shit. Hospital ringtone. Gotta go. Love you."

She called out her love as the connection blipped closed. At the breakfast bar, Henry gathered items from the fridge and cupboards. Her rent money waited in her bank account. *You need only ask.* He'd asked her, with a straightforward plea, to allow him to provide a home for her and Jay. "If I wrote you a check for July's rent, right now, would you use the money to pay the rent?"

Henry halted his prep work. Mise en place, he called it. Functional design. His face softened from concentration lines to a slight smile. "No, Alice."

About what she'd expected, but if her checks sat uncashed in a drawer—in her folder, even—she'd notice the imbalance on her bank statement. "What would you do with it?"

"A trust, in your name. I'd ask Will or my brother to investigate high-yield opportunities while protecting the principal."

His overprotection wavered between attractive and aggravating. At least he hadn't lied to her face. "If I hadn't asked—if I'd just given you a check—would you have told me?"

"No, Alice." He cradled her name in gentle tones, but he watched her with a heavy, assessing stare.

"Because you wouldn't trust me with the truth?" No, he trusted her with Jay, his most precious possession. "Because I wouldn't have wanted the answer."

"That you've asked suggests you knew the answer you'd receive. You are—" He flattened his hands on the counter. "You are conflicted but open to negotiation, perhaps?"

The tremor in his fingers came from her imagination. Nothing made Henry nervous. Except—maybe—the moments when he feared she'd choose some other life. "So this hypothetical rainy day fund. What if I wanted to use it to surprise you with a vacation? Or a new car?"

Years of saving.

As Henry straightened, his chest broadened and his hands steadied. "I'm satisfied with my vehicle, but should we require a larger one in the future, or even a second car, the money would be yours to spend as you like."

A car. A house. A honeymoon for three. A college fund. Exciting, frightening possibilities glimmered on the horizon. "Would an account earn more money than putting the rent toward my student loans would save?"

"I don't know." He extended his hand, palm up in invitation. "Shall I ask Will to set aside time for us to discuss your options with this new flexibility in your budget?"

"Yeah." She crossed the kitchen. "Let's do that." Wrapping her arms around his waist, she pressed herself to his warm back. "Have I told you I love you yet today?"

He rested his hands atop hers. "You did make incoherent sounds this morning that I might have interpreted as a declaration of love."

She squeezed. "I love you."

He raised her hand to his lips and kissed her softly. "I love you as well." Blowing out a breath, he rocked her along his back. "I was about to put together a hearty casserole for supper. I expect Jay will return with an appetite. Would you care to help?"

She nodded, rubbing her face against his shirt before she let him go. Appetite was one thing Jay had in spades—for food, for sex, for affection and approval. She wasn't so different.

She and Henry worked together quietly, comfortably, weaving around each other from task to task as if they'd done so for years. Every so often, their gazes met.

Smoldering. Yeah, she'd totally called that one right.

* * * *

The deadbolt thudded into its unlocked position, the sound almost obscured by the radio's swelling piano. From her perch on the couch, Alice waved toward the kitchen.

Setting his tea aside, Henry nodded. As he strode past the dining room table, the front door swung open.

When Jay stepped inside, duffel slung over his shoulder, he came toe to toe with his immovable master. The slump in his posture disappeared.

Advised not to interfere, she kept to her cozy scrunch, though the article on the benefits of machined springs over coiled wire in lateral bending attracted a whopping zero percent of her attention. The dark, curling strands of hair falling over Jay's forehead, those merited at least fifteen percent.

"Welcome back. Are you pleased to be home, my boy?" Henry, projecting his neutral dom-voice, fell into the questioning rhythm of a scene opener. "Did you have fun?"

"It feels good." Clutching the strap across his chest in both hands, Jay kneaded and rubbed the black canvas. His shoe squeaked on the hardwood. "Peggy had lots of stuff planned for me."

He'd missed so much this weekend. The return of her flogger, her first games with her new toy, their night at the club. Two days had wrought so many changes in her. How different and unrecognizable might he be after his time away?

With a single soft hum, Henry suggested he believed in Jay's purported comfort even less than she did. "Do you need the restroom?"

"No, Henry." Shadows clung to the underside of his eyes. Must've been a wild birthday party.

"Lovely." Henry stepped back. Squaring his shoulders and lifting his head, he completed a simple but unmistakable transformation. His silence held the power to pin Jay in place. No doubt he delivered an intense green-eyed stare. "Strip down and present yourself to me."

The bag plonked to the floor. Jay hauled his shirt over his head, dropped it, and started on his fly. Obedience came swift and unquestioning, accompanied by a massive smile. A scant three feet inside the apartment, he stood naked and vibrating before their master. His tentative clutching and shifting dissolved into an at-ease pose.

Henry prowled, ruffling the sparse hair on Jay's chest and rubbing the muscled curves of his arms. "Did you complete the homework I assigned you?"

Jay's cock jerked. "Yes, Master Henry."

Henry had been right. Jay's pull to submit after his time away altered even the way he instinctively responded to a dominant tone. The formal "master," not often in use at home, suited his need to reconnect.

"Excellent." Massaging Jay's shoulders, Henry shot her a slight smile. He'd missed Jay as much as she had, though he'd muted his emotional responses in some dom-certified version of reassurance. "You'll provide a demonstration for your playmate and me after dinner."

Breathing deep, Jay bowed his head. "Thank you, Master Henry."

With a predatory swoop, Henry grabbed his cheeks in a vise grip and snatched a kiss.

Jay topped out on the hardness scale, his cock near vertical. His crooning, submissive whimper escaped their fused mouths. As their liplock ended, he gave a jaunty bounce and wag.

"Go and put your things away, please." Henry pushed hair back from Jay's forehead, his love no less in the commanding baritone than in the gentle caress. "When you've finished, you may set the table. Bring a clean towel from the linen closet to sit on for dinner."

"No clothes?" Sweet, wide-eyed Jay poured lilting hope into his voice.

"Not for you." In flattening his hand against Jay's chest, Henry re-attuned himself to the speed of Jay's heart and reminded them both of his mantle of responsibility and protection. "I've been denied my boy's beauty for more than forty-eight hours. We'll require extensive nudity to balance the scales."

"Thank you, Henry." Staring at the hand on his chest, Jay grew quiet. He swayed forward.

Henry enclosed him in an embrace, tucking Jay against his neck and stroking his hair. Jay'd get to blow off sexual steam in his after-dinner demo, but bedtime would be a story and snuggling. Maybe part of why Henry had worn her out this morning.

Jay sure needed the TLC. Weird, how a guy who loved his family to pieces and dropped everything to visit home so often returned more ragged and emotionally frayed than when he'd left.

"You're always welcome, my dear boy." Henry kissed the top of Jay's dark head. "However far you go, my arms wait for your return."

* * * *

A low moan hit Alice as the apartment door swung open Monday night. A second answered—muted, and at a slightly higher pitch. Jay. Apologizing, probably. Good. He ought to.

She allowed the nastiness rather than shoving it down, and recovery came easier. Fading without effort or tension, her anger dissipated in the time it took to lay her phone in the charger and slip off her shoes. Jay was too sweet to hurt them intentionally. If he wasn't ready, he wasn't ready. He knew his family. Maybe they'd flip out about his relationship with Henry. Bringing two lovers along might've been impossible to explain.

In stocking feet, she entered the dining room. The table had been set. The thick aroma of tomato and garlic told her Henry had pasta in the oven. Both normal Monday homecomings, neither competed with the unexpected beauty her men presented.

Back to the kitchen wall, Henry stood with his pants hanging open. As Jay buried his face between his legs, praise and encouragement fell in equal measure from his lips. Henry met her gaze and moved his mouth without a sound. *Welcome home.*

Unwilling to break Jay's rhythm, she nodded in silence.

Head bobbing, cheeks hollowing, Jay had gone past the point of licking, teasing variation. He jammed his splayed hands against the wall beside Henry's hips. Maybe his "punishment" included using nothing but his mouth to touch Henry—or himself. Safe bet Jay's pants stretched tighter across his erection than they did his delectable ass.

Thrusting shallow, Henry gripped Jay by the hair. A harder thrust, a low growl, and Jay's throat rippled as he swallowed.

Their game ended too soon for anything but the faintest stirring of her arousal. Bad timing. If she hadn't hit the T stop as a train pulled away and had to wait, she would've been home fifteen minutes sooner. Might've gotten a floor seat for the entire pre-dinner show.

With tender strokes, Henry smoothed the clumping mess he'd made of Jay's hair. "Well done. You do beautiful, passionate work." He patted Jay's hands. "You're free to move these now, so long as you don't touch yourself."

As Jay let go with a soft suction-pop, he wriggled his arms around the back of Henry's thighs and burrowed against his stomach. "Thank you, Henry. I am sorry. I know I need to tell them. Next time. I promise."

Rather than inform Jay she stood listening, Henry slid into a crouch and cradled him. "Not until you're ready, my brave boy. You've nothing to apologize for, though you do so with much-appreciated attention to detail. Your love is evident in your smallest actions. You needn't give up your family's love to enjoy mine, dearest—nor Alice's, either."

In a shared glance, she confirmed his belief, his faith in her. Even if years passed before she met Jay's family, she wouldn't stop loving him. Hell, her parents weren't lining up for introductions. Of course, she spoke to hers a few times a year, and Jay seemed stuck in perpetual college-freshman homesickness.

"Was she mad? She didn't act it yesterday, but I ditched you both." Jay's thin tenor didn't belong to a man who'd just celebrated his thirtieth birthday. "Do you think she'll accept an apology?"

Silly to get upset over a core element of his personality, especially one she loved. His submissive need to please hadn't appeared from nothing. Felt so to him because he hadn't discovered how to satisfy those desires sexually until a few years ago. Exploring his needs had exposed him to predators. But he had Henry now. And her. And probably an overprotective family, which answered why he didn't want to explain his lovers to them.

"I think you might ask her yourself." Henry waved her forward. "But I doubt our lovely girl feels she needs an apology any more than I did."

Eyes wide and dark, Jay lifted his head as she crossed the room.

"Henry's right, sweetheart. No apologies needed." Joining them on the floor, she curved around him and kissed his cheek. "But I won't turn one down, if you're handing them out for free and Henry doesn't have other plans for us."

Apologizing would ease Jay's fears. When he thought he'd done wrong, he needed to make it right. And Henry always found a safe way to let him.

Chapter 8

Bent over the foot of the bed, her legs spread, Alice practiced patience. Poorly.

Jay's gleaming steel toy had disappeared inside him while he issued no protests and more than a few pleases. Hers waited in her cupped hand, its smooth weight secure in her palm. Two Saturday afternoons in a row with her Intro to Anal Pleasure workshop. New for her, but continuing education for Jay.

"Now you're properly attired for the day." Henry trailed a finger down the curve of Jay's ass. "Quite handsome. Quite"—he cupped Jay's cheeks in both hands—"tempting."

Mirroring her pose, Jay flashed dark eyes and grasped the sheets. When they'd lain in this position last fall, he'd shaken with nerves as Henry tested her responses to impact play. His swirling confidence and happy whimpers today belonged to a different Jay. On this road, he traveled faster than her. But she'd finally started catching up.

Jay squirmed backward, wiggling his hips off the bed.

With a last squeeze, Henry stepped away. "Our girl will make a lovely match."

"Sorry I missed your first playdate with your new toy." Jay folded his elbows underneath his chest and scooted closer. His shower-fresh earthy pine tickled her nose. "Can't wait to see it in you."

"I can't wait to feel it in me." Uncurling her fingers, she offered up her plug. Half the heft of Jay's, but thrill-size for her.

Henry plucked the toy from her hand.

Jay swiped a kiss, his apologetic tug on her lip paired with shiny-eyed sincerity.

Palm heavy and digging in, Henry rubbed a circle along the top of her ass. "You gave your toy an enthusiastic welcome last week."

Fuck, he parted her lips and delved deep. Thick and hot as an extra winter blanket, he induced fever-chills with his strokes.

"And your excitement hasn't ebbed, I see." He slipped free, humming, and dragged his fingers across her ass. A drizzle of lube slicked her for him. Relaxing her ass, pushing to draw him in, turned her legs wobbly. Sturdy-hipped Jay shored her up.

"Very much in sync," Henry murmured. "Thank you, my boy."

Between the new game and the praise, Jay had to be burning a hole in the bedsheets with his cock.

When Henry swapped his fingers for her toy, the wide flare stretched her with ever-present pressure, demanding and satisfying and occupying the space meant for him. The one she'd give him soon.

"Stand up straight, my dears." Circling the bed, Henry cleaned his fingers and tossed the used cloth.

As she copied Jay's at-ease pose, metal grazed her thigh. She jammed her cheeks together. Jesus. In her hand, the weight hadn't felt nearly so heavy.

"Such a well-behaved pair of pets deserves more extensive play." Steeped in power and presence, Henry surveyed them from his post beside the nightstand. Though he'd stripped and toyed with them—literally—he retained his dress slacks, his button-down, and the tie he'd worn for her birthday last fall. The tie's leaded lines and colored panes had etched into her wrists, a permanent but invisible tattoo of his ownership and Jay's devotion.

"A reward for their diligence." As he passed them, Henry caressed their asses.

She sneaked a peek—though Henry smiled, because he knew, he always knew—at the lean line of Jay's cock, firm and proud. He held his pose with only the obvious betraying his excitement.

The slow glide of wood rasping on wood inflamed her imagination. Opening a drawer in the special dresser meant Henry had more planned. She sucked every drop of sweetness from the idea. Bondage? For her or Jay. For her and Jay. But Henry had filled them with toys. If he let them play with each other, where would he fit himself?

Jay. His full lips and sleek tongue. The image seared her with simple beauty, Jay hollowing his cheeks in eagerness, Henry reshaping Jay's throat with his length.

Henry stroked the top of the open drawer. "But I'll need something from them both first."

Anything. Her carousel of rewards flipped too fast to follow. In making her wait for him to name one, her smoldering artist scattered embers under her skin.

"Run along to the living room and clear the furniture from the rug, please."

Do what now?

"Go on." A smile tugging at his lips, Henry waved them ahead. "I'll be just a moment."

Bounding to the living room with carefree excitement, Jay flashed silver between his ass cheeks. She took dainty steps, and not only because following him offered a spectacular view. She'd never been so aware of her ass in her life. With each step, her toy shifted, rubbed, and reminded her to squeeze and lift.

In short order, the chairs and the coffee table hugged the big wall. The couch remained, the gray behemoth so often a cozy cuddling spot for three.

Jay struck a fierce pose, muscles straining, lips pulled back in a teeth-bearing grimace. Grunting, he play-heaved the couch with a mighty shove.

God, he had a fucking fabulous ass. Almost dimpled when he tightened up.

"Alice, you forgot to push." He flicked a boyish smirk her way. "I can't convince Henry he's working us hard if you're standing there staring at me."

Sure enough, Henry stood beside the dining room table. Damn light-footed dom-silence. Their stealthy lover delivered the best surprises—and if a way to fool him existed, she hadn't found it yet.

"I was on a break." Her favorite kind. She devoured Jay from his flexible feet to his tousled hair. "My staring-at-Jay break. If it's not an hourly perk, it oughta be written in."

Pinking with pleasure, he copped weightlifting poses. For all his sexy strength, he truly seduced with his sweet smile and his send-me-to-my-knees stare.

He'd captured Henry's attention, too. Henry smoothed his tie to his belt and beyond. Trapping his cock, his dress pants outlined his growing interest. Behind him, her usual chair hid all but an indistinct black handle. Too dark and thin to be her suede, and a crop wouldn't be a reward.

"This is a union job, right?" She nudged the couch with her knee. Her end glided three inches back. Despite its size, the behemoth floated featherlight on the non-scratch pads protecting the hardwood. "Henry's given us contracts and everything."

The last time they'd cleared the rug, he'd set them at each other in a pillow fight. Today's reward might be another test. She'd proven herself ready last weekend, but Jay's reaction to impact play remained a mystery.

Sighing, Jay gave up the muscleman antics and pushed the couch with a palm on the armrest. "And killer benefits."

Agreed. Though she didn't relish trying his workout. She clenched as if the toy in her ass would slip out with every step. Hadn't yet, but she'd been careful. And hyperaware.

He poured on the puppy eyes. "We still get our reward, right? Even if Alice is a shirker?"

Sticking out her tongue, she conspired to get him back with a solid pillow swat, straddle his naked ass, and ride his cock like a goddamn boss. See if he called her shirker then.

"I'm well convinced of your work ethic." With his low-toned purr and sweeping gaze, Henry curled his love around them. "But the sooner you finish, the sooner your game will begin."

Square pillows sat in each corner of the couch. Closest weapon at hand, but a draw—Jay had equal access. His gaze flipped past her. Damn. He'd spotted the floor pillows under the front window. As the couch slipped the last few inches and settled into position, she rested a hand on her weapon.

He boosted the pillow at his end and fluffed it with spread fingers, the way he held a basketball poised for a pass.

She'd have to toss a distraction pillow, dodge his throw, and dive on Henry's mark if she meant to beat Jay to those floor pillows. Tension traveling up her legs, she braced her feet and tugged. Not losing her toy might be part of the rules.

Henry spread his arms wide. "Welcome to your dance studio."

"Our what?" Her repertoire encompassed two kinds of dancing—the swaying and shuffling of ninth-graders in a sweat-scented gym and the grinding frenzy of the over-twenty-one crowd in a sweat-scented nightclub. Henry didn't belong in either picture, and where he didn't belong, sex didn't belong. The weight teasing her ass insisted sex belonged here. "Are you joking?"

Pillow abandoned, Jay faked a fanciful ballet twirl, arms flying and cock bouncing.

"I am utterly sincere." Henry stepped onto the rug and laid his hands on Jay's shoulders, settling their hyperactive lover with his long-fingered hold. "Dance is grace and beauty in motion. The both of you are, as well."

The both of *them*, maybe. Fluid, supple, and silent. Henry always
moved like a dancer. Jay powered through on the athletic grace of
strength, balance, and speed.

"I should think you'd enjoy dance, Alice." Henry released Jay,
raised his arms to an invisible partner, and executed a three-point pivot.
"Precise patterns, replicated into infinity, movement dictated by a
predictable rhythm—"

"But it's not predictable." Dances meant gawky adolescents stumbling
over each other. Too-small, pinching heels borrowed from Mom's
closet. That or alcohol-fueled abandon, and those patterns weren't worth
replicating. "I never know which way to go."

"Then you've had inelegant partners." He scooped her chin up and
tapped her lips. "Properly, you resisted giving control to them, as your
body did not trust them. Do you trust me, Alice? Do you trust Jay?"

"You know I do."

He kissed her forehead. "That's all I ask." As he positioned her and
Jay facing each other, he skimmed their bodies with fleeting touches. "I
expect neither of you learned formal dancing in school?"

She shook her head. Only if square dancing counted. No team sports in
gym for a whole week. What a waste.

"Not in school." Jay tilted toward Henry as his arms were raised and
his hand pressed above her waist. "At my sibs' weddings. Last one, I'd
just hit the boner-popping years." He shuddered, head to toe. "Dancing
with your new sister-in-law is the wrooonnng time."

Henry caught him in a swift embrace. "I doubt our girl will mind."

"Not one bit." Trying for a smirk, she probably came closer to a leer.

"She's more likely to consider your interest an added bonus." He
rubbed Jay's hip. "As do I."

He left them poised to move, hands clasped. Middle school dance
sounded about right, minus the sweaty palms. They had room enough for
the Holy Ghost between them and then some.

Henry clicked on the stereo, and orchestral music filled the air. "My
own school required attendance at dance lessons weekly."

Yum. Adolescent Henry. Sensitive, intense, all studious and charming,
with flawless manners—

"Half the class took to finding private time for release beforehand. The
male half."

—frantically jerking off before class in a desperate bid to stay in
control when it mattered. She rearranged her mental image from *how
sweet* to *fuck yes* as her body furnace cranked.

Cock twitching, Jay whimpered and swayed.

"The others, well. Girls were such mysteries." Henry maintained an unaffected tone, but his eyes crinkled with kind laughter. "Their signs invisible to us uneducated louts. Gasps and blushes. Thighs pressing together." He teased her with a swipe below the curve of her ass. "Surely they didn't entertain persistent visions of bodies writhing in unison on less vertical planes."

She had, a time or two. They might, sooner or later, depending on what Henry had left on the table.

"This is a waltz, but you needn't worry about the exact steps." In a graceful glide already attuned to the music, Henry slipped away. "We'll begin by having you gain an appreciation for your own bodies before you attempt matching the music or each other."

Jay cracked a wide grin. "Like masturbating. My favorite homework assignment."

Snorting, she ducked her head. Not helpful. With his muscled abs and half-hard cock, he filled her vision.

Henry chuckled. "Exactly right. Dance is a socially acceptable form of foreplay."

Not their version, with her and Jay nude and Henry their hands-on instructor.

"Follow your instincts." He waved for them to begin.

Her instincts sent her crashing into Jay's shin on the downbeat. As he hopped backward, she went along for the ride. With a quick spin, he kept them both from tumbling.

"Nice save." Plastered to his chest, she bonked her head against his shoulder. "I think we skipped the masturbation lesson and went straight to the dry humping."

Jay squeezed her waist and hoisted her. "I'm good with that."

Her feet dangled, her toes brushing the tops of his, as he shook them both with his laughter. Euphoric. That encapsulated this almost tipsy high. Naked, pressed tight to Jay, the weight of her toy shifting between her legs. She slung her arms around his neck and kissed him.

They'd gone off course, but Henry issued no reprimands. His silence, his stance, all stayed easy and relaxed as she slithered back to her feet. He smiled on approach and ruffled Jay's hair. Slipped behind her and nuzzled her neck. "Allow me to cut in, dearest."

He unspooled them and glided off—with Jay in his arms.

They made a gorgeous couple. Slim and tanned, his ass a splash of pale milk, Jay followed Henry without hesitation. And Henry…He commanded.

Wordlessly. His eyes gleamed. His arms formed a framework rigid but flowing. His steps powered their movement and determined their path.

Dancing was his basketball.

She and Jay stood on Henry's court. He meant to teach them an activity he enjoyed, but he wanted them to enjoy it, too.

In the privacy of their home, Jay poured his energy into learning his lesson and pleasing his master. Gazing adoringly, he glowed brighter as praise fell from Henry's lips. Jay's trust and Henry's leadership blended smooth and sweet. As their song spun into silence, Henry delivered Jay beside her.

She clapped with gusto. They deserved more. "Pretty slick, you two."

"All Henry." Loose-limbed, Jay flaunted an orgasmic flush. "I didn't think about a thing. It's just"——he wriggled as Henry released him—— "letting him move me."

"Beautiful understanding, my boy." Henry reeled her in and kissed her lightly. "It's all right if this proves more difficult for you, sweet girl. You so delight in conquering each challenge I set for you."

Determined not to miss his commands, she gripped him tight. His slacks, concealing his legs, made the shift in his weight hard to discern.

"Easy," he whispered.

Three sweeping steps per foot, boxy with diagonals. Plug jouncing with her, she missed the beat. As he dodged her knees, the music passed them by. Henry slowed, and she landed on his toes. "Sorry."

"You're fine." He rubbed warmth into her spine. "Elevate your chin. Watching my feet is counterproductive, strange as that seems."

He started again, in time with the music. His gentle eyes threatened to pull her away from counting steps. Seeing had to be easier than deconstructing the tug-o-war going on with their hands.

"You're making yourself cross-eyed, dearest. As adorable as you are, I've just the thing to redirect your energy." Halting their dance, Henry cradled her and sent Jay scurrying to the table. "Bring me both, please."

On her tiptoes, she peeked around Henry.

Jay waved his finds like victory flags. One black, padded blindfold. One feather-tipped teaser.

Her blindfold hadn't made an appearance in months. As her nipples hardened, Henry's dress shirt chafed in an oddly appealing way.

"Even your faintest moans add to our symphony." Henry stretched past her and accepted Jay's hand-off. "Precisely what I require, thank you. Our girl needs a narrower focus." Massaging her ass with his free hand, he set off rolling pleasure. "Not to worry, Alice. We'll widen your aperture as we go."

Her ass clenched and her throat opened, spilling another of the moans he praised her for. Graduation waited when she'd mastered her small plug. Henry waited.

"You haven't worn this for me in far too long." As he slipped the blindfold over her eyes, darkness descended. "How wary and uncertain you were then."

Her pulse grew loud. Her skin tingled.

"But some delights are unchanging." Tracing her ears, he swept back hair caught under the band. "You still tremble with such sweet anticipation."

Between her thighs, she tightened from her thudding clit to her toy. Floaty and loose everywhere else, she drifted, with the weight the sole anchor she needed to keep her steady and balanced.

"You feel the difference, don't you?" Voice flowing, he stayed close but on the move. "I see how you adjust your posture." He grazed her hip. "In tune with your center of mass." At the base of her spine, he laid a fleeting warm palm. "Anatomy is artistry. Even the smallest weight"—he teased her with a split-fingered tug on the handle between her cheeks—"creates new and beautiful forms."

His ability to find beauty in the big picture and its finest details seduced her. He'd break this down for her, present the components until she mastered them.

"Your body is always a dance, Alice. Allow me to sketch the lines in your pattern."

With pleasure.

"The rule of the game is…"

As a breezy tickle brushed her stomach, she bolted back and laughed at herself. Adrenaline and excitement made a potent mix in Henry's court.

"Excellent. Simply step away from the tease."

"Action, opposite reaction." Teaching her could've been as easy as papering the floor with shoe-shapes and letting her study, but he hadn't done that.

"Just so." With the wisp of a caress along her ribs, he drove her left. "Dancing is about understanding your body."

What he wanted to teach her wasn't dance steps at all.

"Knowing what feels pleasurable." Forward, a graze between her shoulder blades. "Transforming directed motion into natural, inevitable joy."

He talked of dancing the way he talked of sex. The act of creation, seductive and powerful. Maybe he got as euphoric manifesting ideas in his mind as she did when he flogged or fucked her.

"Consider how much you've learned about your body's capacity for sensual pleasure in the past year." He brushed the same side, again and again and again, twirling her with his touch. "These steps are as natural to you as breathing."

He intended to teach her what Jay understood instinctively. To let go of thought and embrace movement. To follow the feather.

"You're making the shift from thinking to experiencing."

A kind of hyperaware subspace. None of the decisions hers.

"You live in this moment."

The feather drifted away. If the pattern held, the tease would land at her back.

"Anticipate the next too quickly—"

He circled her navel, and she flew back two steps.

"—and you miss enjoying this one."

A tingling mass of sensation, she focused on the long signal in the noise.

"If you are always chasing, you are never feeling."

Only Henry mattered. If she followed where he led, the rest would fall away.

"Feel the glide in your body." With feathery touches, he prodded her calves. "Your exquisite muscles melting into new shapes and forms, the confluence of flowing curves."

So soothing, his voice. So gentle, his touch. Shedding the confusion, the worry, the guesswork, she floated into act-without-thinking escape. "We had to get naked for a dancing lesson?" Not that she minded, but needling Henry came with its own joys. Growly, possessive joys.

"We mustn't allow anything to interfere with the signals." His dry amusement accompanied a feather stroke on her back.

She flowed forward. His guidance was native, not an alien here.

"Nor with the beautiful sights." He hummed, soft and lilting. "Do you imagine how I'm looking at you now, Alice?" Using the feather, he sent her left and back. "Can you envision my hunger and approval?"

Hell yes. His flashing green eyes greeted her in her dreams. Picturing them required no more than the suggestion.

"Your nude form before me, rapt and attentive to my every cue? My voice has guided you for months, but here, in our dance studio, I need only my touch."

Cradling her, he placed his fingertips where feathers would have fallen. He laid her left hand down gently, his shirt crisp and his shoulder broad, and folded her right hand in his. The slight tug at her clasped hand, the solid pressure at her back, and her own shifting weight made each move memorable. Repeatable. Predictably glorious.

"Good girl. You needn't see your partner. Only feel the direction he wishes to move."

A hush fell between them. The music guided Henry, and he guided her. She didn't stumble, not once.

Bringing them to a stop, he clasped her cheeks and traced the bottom of the blindfold. "You see so clearly in darkness, dearest." As he raised the shield from her eyes, he kissed her. His lips offered pressure to sink into rather than run from. He waved Jay up from the couch. "Let's begin again, shall we?"

* * * *

When the stack of Sunday breakfast waffles had dwindled to two, Alice stabbed the top one and hoisted it over to her plate. No sense waiting 'til she finished hers, or Jay'd claim both.

Eyeing her half-eaten waffle and her new, untouched waffle, he pinched the serving plate and dragged the lone survivor to his end of the table.

She pointed her tongue at him.

Henry crossed his fork and knife on his empty plate. "I'd like to discuss a change in our routine for this coming weekend."

As if anything had been routine lately, with the classes at the club and Jay's birthday. Yesterday had been as close to normal as they got. Maybe he'd take them out and show off their new dancing skills. With toys.

"Is it a good—" Jay popped his head up. "Ohhh. 'Cause July." Dropping his attention back to his plate, he dredged crumbled bacon in his syrup-pond waffle. "Okay."

"July?" Visions of a summer arts retreat replaced the sexy-times movie playing in her head. First Jay, now Henry. Shit, she should hightail it to a continuing ed conference, disappear for a few days and see how they liked it.

"Saturday will be a difficult anniversary for a close friend." Henry nudged his fork into a straighter alignment. "I've traditionally provided support in helping her through it."

His close female friends could be counted on a single finger. "Emma."

"Yes."

"So you want to take her out to dinner or something?" God, let that be it. Henry wore his neutral face, impossible to read, which meant he was busy reading her. "That's nice of you. Gentlemanly. Jay and I can scrounge up our own for one evening. right. Jay?"

Mouth full of food. Jay glanced her way with puppy eyes.

Shit.

"In previous years, I've prepared a meal for her at her home."

An anniversary dinner. She'd gotten one last year. splayed beneath him across the table. She closed her teeth on her tongue. Fuck, that hurt. "Oh."

Jay had accepted this state of affairs for years. Henry wouldn't be the man she loved if he didn't take care of the people in his life. One dinner. No sex.

"Because you and Will attended dinners there all the time." Acceptance. Nothing to it.

"Yes. My presence is a familiar comfort for her." Laying his hand on the table, he patted his impeccably folded napkin. "I've also stayed to be certain she would be all right."

Her churning stomach no longer held room for the food on her plate. "Stayed the night, you mean."

"Yes."

Henry, thoughtful and solicitous. smiling as he asked Emma to fetch him the tarragon. Henry, kind and considerate. draping a blanket over her shoulders before he lit a fire in her fireplace. Because of course she'd have a fireplace. That she'd want lit. In July. Henry, tender and sweet. cradling Emma to his chest as he carried her to her bed. Where he'd stay. All night.

The waffle begged to be fork-shredded. Irrational fears should drown as easily in syrup. She unstuck her mouth. "I know you're not asking my permission."

"No." Hands folded. he extended his fingers like crossbeams in a saddle notch and tapped his thumbs together. "But I am opening the subject for discussion. because I recognize this might be a more difficult issue for you than it is for Jay."

"It might." Swallowing hard didn't alleviate her dryness. "Might be a pistachio for me."

Jay's fork screeched across his plate.

"I don't know if—" Sometimes being the submissive sucked. Henry would do this with her blessing or without. "If I can have this conversation without being your equal."

Jay would. Emma would. Individual molds for individual people. Henry would say. She could only be herself and hope he understood.

"You are always my equal, even when the final decisions are mine."
Eyes pinched, he covered her hand. "Share with me the root of the
difficulty, my dear. Allow me to help you."

Safewording wouldn't change anything. He'd remain bent on doing
this, and she'd hate every second, and they'd argue just as hard. Shaking
him off, she shoved back her too-confining chair.

"So say Santa's wife is out of town, and he's had a lousy string of
weeks. He's lonely and depressed, and a club temp isn't gonna deliver
human connection." She paced in bare feet across the floor they'd danced
on yesterday. "And I say to you, 'Hey, I'll go sleep at Santa's for the night.
It's just cuddling and emotional support.' Are you gonna say, 'Hell yeah,
go for it'?"

"I trust you both." He spoke softly, but the hand she'd rejected curled
into a fist.

"Not what I asked, and you know it." This ran deeper than trust,
or parallel, but it growled with a possessive stirring unaffected by
trustworthiness. "I trust you, too. And even if I don't know Emma well,
I trust you enough for both of you." The damn answers never came easy,
not with emotions involved. He'd opened her to the truth. All those
times she'd severed love from the equation hadn't stopped feelings from
existing. Hiding kept her from admitting and working through them.
"You want me to do this, but could you? Could you smile and drop me
off at his house and pick me up the next morning and never once have a
twinge of discomfort?"

In his silence, the blood rushing past her ears thundered with doubts. She
should've said nothing. Kept the peace. Stopped using logic as a weapon.

He rapped his knuckles. "No."

She sidled up to her chair. Under her hands, the wood top rail rose and
fell in a smooth wave.

"This night is a ritual, Alice. I cannot pass such a sacred trust off to
another, and I cannot ignore the anniversary and leave her alone." Like a
draft horse straining for that first inch of ground in a pulling contest, he
leaned in, bowed his head, and exhaled in a whoosh. "He was my friend
and mentor for fifteen years. Their boy was my godson. I, too, need to
honor and remember them."

The chair anchored her wobbly arms. "Emma had a son?"

"Thomas." He hummed, the notes falling flat as a grimace twisted his
lips. "Victor drove up to collect him from summer camp. Their joke of the
season had been how strange it felt to play spontaneously at home for the
first time since his birth."

Syrup soured with bile in her throat.

"Even now, I doubt she's forgiven herself for enjoying that freedom."

"They both died?" She hushed her voice to match his, a whispering echo in a vault he'd never opened to her before.

"An evening thunderstorm." Rubbing his fingers, he drew shapes on the table. Or erased them. "A tree across the road. The car—" His fingers stilled. He shook his head. "So I listen to her stories, and she listens to mine."

He could tell those stories to her. To her and Jay. They'd listen. "You—" But not remember.

When he reminisced with Emma, they bonded over shared experiences. The love and the laughter and the grief that followed.

"I what, dearest?"

God, he had the softest eyes. Not always. He did flinty and hard with the toughest minerals. But just now, she drowned in him the way she drowned in Jay. Henry trusted her with his vulnerability.

"You should be with Emma." One night. She and Jay had him three hundred and sixty-four nights out of the year. He deserved this. Someday, they'd all toast the memory of the boy who'd died too young and the man who'd helped make Henry what he was. But she'd leave this tradition to Henry and Emma. "So you can remember the people you both loved and respected."

Inhaling deep and slow, he leaned back in his chair. As he exhaled, he released the tension in her, too. "I see two people I love and respect in front of me, sweet girl."

Jay returned to cutting his waffle. "How come you don't bring Emma here? Maybe staying in the house with the reminders makes it worse. Sometimes talking about stuff somewhere else helps. Or with someone else. Like it's okay to. You don't have to lock it all away like you're ashamed to be sad or scared."

Jesus Christ. She and Henry needed to learn to shut the fuck up and let Jay solve the world's problems.

"What?" Stopping his fork at his mouth, Jay glanced down. "Did I get syrup on my shirt? I can take it off."

"You may remove your shirt if you like." As faint, lilting wonder lifted his voice, Henry stared unblinking at Jay. "But you are perfect as you are."

Shrugging, Jay popped waffle into his mouth. Two seconds, three seconds—his fork clanged on the plate and he wrestled with the bottom hem of his shirt.

Henry turned his gaze on her. "Alice, would that—"

"Yes." Oh hell yes. Have them both here instead of some nebulous otherwhere.

"You're certain you'd prefer another woman here, on your territory? You'd be displaced for the evening."

Like Mom and Dad's dinner parties. Hustled off to bed early with Ollie, the two of them creeping down the hall to see what was so funny that adults had to sit around a table of beer bottles and cards and laugh so loud all night. Now she had a nobler purpose, choosing to stay away and not eavesdrop. "I'm sure."

"Alice and I can go on a date." Slinging an arm around his chair back, Jay comically puffed out his bare chest. "I'll take her out on the town for a night she'll never forget."

She snorted. "Arcade-style virtual reality kayaking is not unforgettable."

"Think of the pizza." He mimed scooping up a slice and biting down. "All dripping with gooey cheese."

"You ate a hundred waffles. How can you be hungry for pizza?"

"I wouldn't be if I had that waffle trapped on your plate."

She scooted the plate down the table and dropped a firm kiss on his syrup-sticky lips. "All yours."

With a swipe behind her knees, he dropped her in his lap. "*All* mine?"

She campaigned to tweak his nipple.

"Thank you both."

Play paused for Henry's smile.

Chapter 9

Fully dressed, Henry teased her with the tips of the apron strings. Nubby, knotted ends dragged over her naked back. Cousin to her suede, a shudder-worthy reminder of the power he wielded for her pleasure.

"These tails are much too long." He stroked downward in a feathery fingerslide on the path of the bow tie dangling from her waist. The ends swung below her ass. "We'll have to try again."

With gentle pulls, he unknotted the thin ties against her back. Thin like the strong ropes in the suspension they'd watched with Santa, sliding along nerve endings and folds of memory. Raising her tingling nipples and cascading goose bumps to her elbows, where her forearms bathed in hot, soapy water. No dishwasher on this Friday night. They'd work by hand, she and Jay.

Looping the apron around her waist, Henry passed across her pubic bone in a fleeting promise. Playtime had begun with trading dishes for clothes. The clothes, unwanted, lay folded on the table. Stacked in the sink, the dishes sat ready to hand.

"All right, Alice." Henry's wraparound bow girdled her hips and settled in the small of her back. "You're properly attired for your position." He scooped up the tails, his knuckles weighty and warm, and let them fall. They bounced against her ass and rolled, dangling along the inner curve of her cheeks. "You may begin."

Fuck, the dishes. The washing she'd been assigned before Henry stole her breath with his apron play. Blinking away blurry distraction, she refocused on the white foam embracing her wrists. A cup, low and round, fell prey to her questing fingers. She pulled the mug above the suds and sponged inside and out.

"How convenient. This accessory leaves you"——Henry slipped through the open apron sides and cupped her breasts——"exquisitely accessible."

His smooth, knowing tone. Those sure hands lifting and tugging. The sink front a fine, sturdy pressure for bracing herself. For rocking. The cup tumbled from her fingers and sank. *Chunk.*

"Best begin again." Burying his words in her ear, Henry withdrew. Cooler air swimming into the gap inspired tighter peaks on nipples he'd stiffened with his roving touch. "Something less slippery?"

Fumbling, she grasped a plate and led the sponge along the winding green ivy on white ceramic. The plates hardly needed the cleaning. Dinner had been a light affair before Henry began their safeword ritual.

Matching her circular swipes, Henry grazed her shoulder blades. She switched to the sprayer and gave the plate a quick rinse. Kisses rained down her back.

By her side, Jay cradled a drying towel in his open palms. As his apron skirt jutted out with his rising interest, his bare bottom peeked out behind.

She extended the plate toward his waiting hands. Up, down, left, right, somewhere in the general direction of thick cranberry cloth. Christ, he had gorgeous ass cheeks. Sleek, round, and flexing.

Weaving along the pale break in Jay's tan, Henry grabbed hold of a firm, muscled cheek.

Jay, taking the plate with an oh-God-don't-drop-it grip, pushed back and shuddered. The plate received a flurry of swipes.

"Alice is rather more interested in scrubbing clean flesh than dirty dishes." Henry followed the curving arc beneath Jay's ass. "More work awaits, yet her hungry gaze hasn't left you."

"You think she didn't get enough dinner?" Ferocious drying attack finished, Jay popped the plate into the cupboard. "Maybe she's a picky eater." As impossible for him to hide his smile as hide his erection. His honesty poked through any façade. "We could make her another meal."

"Make her a meal." Henry sank to his knees behind her, shirt buttons catching and tugging her apron strings. He rumbled with baritone beauty between her legs. "What a lovely thought."

Sweeping his vibrations inside, she poured out a moan. Serendipitous synchronicity: He whispered his arousal, and her body amplified sound waves into sensual swells. The dishwater left her almost cool compared to the heat he inspired.

"Carry on with your responsibilities, please." Teeth grazing the top of her ass, Henry exhaled hot breath. "Your rewards are commensurate with your performance."

The dishes ran out too soon. Awash in arousal but far from climax, she dredged the sink, hunting in every corner. No magical multiplying forks or spoons. Unstoppered, the drain invited a spiraling exodus. She rinsed soap film from her skin and braced for the kissing and fondling to end. "All done."

"Oh?" The ass massage ceased. "Are you?"

She trembled, holding her arms up surgeon-style, waiting for an unknown. Henry strewed variables like wildflowers, in brilliant fields of awe-inducing color.

"I don't believe Jay's finished his task entire." Hand to hipbone, Henry coaxed her into a quarter-turn.

Jay greeted her with his plush towel in cupped palms. As he captured water droplets seeking escape at her elbows, he waggled his brows. "Not done yet."

Heat pulsed between her thighs.

He dried her with unwavering focus, the dark pools of his eyes hidden beneath lowered lids and thick lashes. His vigorous rubdown thrust the tendons in his forearms in and out and rustled the towel, but underlying Jay's inexhaustible energy, Henry's measured control acted as a brake. The lessons of a lifetime together.

Slowing once he reached her wrist, Jay gave each finger firm, patient attention swaddled in terrycloth. Reverent kisses landed in her palms. The towel reclaimed its wall hook. He stepped back, spread his feet, and clasped his hands behind him. "Done."

"Remarkable work." Rising, Henry laid claim to her with a multitude of tiny touches. "Such care you take with our girl." He skimmed the bare undersides of her arms. "My prize pupil."

She shivered. Jay, with his firmness, had primed her for Henry's floating caresses. They worked together, her men. Her own combo meal.

"Jay, we've one last dish to put to bed." Henry left behind the tingling pleasure of his dress shirt against her back. "I trust you know where this one belongs."

"On the highest shelf?" Jay sprang into a crouch and hauled her over his shoulder.

The world flipped and twirled. As the apron tangled in her hair, she pushed the neck loop free, laughing. A playful Jay and a teasing Henry turned her nights into climbing, swooping, physics-exploiting roller coasters, with the only promise a safe return. God, what a ride.

Arm clamped around her thighs, Jay paraded down the hallway. He moved his flexing ass and muscled legs for her alone. Mmm, no, not quite. When her hair swung away, Henry strode through her horizon, his crisp, tailored hem flashing above silent and bare feet on the hardwood floor. Jay's beauty belonged to him first.

With one hand wedged between her thighs, Jay drove her clit into a thumping proximity alert. Wiggling up, he arrived between her lips as he passed into the bedroom. "Uh-oh. I missed a spot with the towel."

She clenched. Firm fingers stroking deeper, he deserved her warmest welcome.

He eased loose with a pseudo *tsk*. "Can't put dishes away wet."

She flew. The bed caught her on a soft bounce. The landing rippled through her breasts, dislodging the apron top, and tossed her skirt askew.

Jay licked his lips. "I'd lose my prize pupil status. What would Henry say?"

Striding straight to the bed, Henry scanned her with eyes dark and forbidding as a primeval forest at dusk. His hands, closing around her ankles, hinted of bonds more weighty and permanent than leather and buckles.

The room spun, leaving her ass-up and quaking. The comforter cocooned her shaky breaths, warm and trapped against her face.

As he tightened his grip on her, Henry descended into a rumbling growl. Maybe he truly meant to make a meal of her. Dress her in a red hood stashed in the special dresser. My, what big teeth he had.

He wrenched free of her ankles. "Another time."

Self-denial. Her careful planner had something in mind for her, and he wouldn't change his design to sate his own hunger.

He whispered to Jay, masculine murmurs familiar and soothing as a lullaby. In a slow glide down the soles of her feet, Henry signed off with a ticklish, toe-curling flourish. "See what you might accomplish by other means, my boy."

The bed dipped as Jay crawled, his apron flap dragging along her calves and into the sensitive hollows of her knees. Head lowered, he skidded his nose against the small of her back and joined his tongue to the game. His meandering nose-rub jostled the apron strings. On the third pass, they slid with purpose. Nuzzling and sliding, he unknotted Henry's work with his teeth. His teasing nips and head-shaking whimper-growls lulled her arousal into pleasant neutral. Nudging with hands and knees and mouth, he maneuvered her onto her back, leaving the apron spread beneath her.

He straddled her thighs by the glow of the nightstand lamp. Darkness swallowed the room, blackout curtains shrouding them from the faded strength of sunset. In the lamplight, the damp patch on Jay's apron glistened.

She fingered the hem. Tugged.

His cock bobbed behind a pale blue sky. He bent and kissed her, their mouths crashing in a too-short frenzy. Breath heaving, he shot upright and pressed against her mons. Fuck, right on her clit. She bucked.

Holding her in place with his weight, Jay rolled the heel of his hand in slippery circles. "I think I'm just spreading the wetness around. This dish isn't drying."

"Shall I assist?" A swaying shadow behind Jay, Henry loosened the apron and left the strings slack. "Some puzzles are best approached from multiple angles." Lifting the loop over Jay's head, Henry exposed his own nudity. His dress shirt must've found a different home. Like Jay's apron, falling to the bedspread.

Jay's cock, freed from draped fabric, sprang forward. He presented a tempting invitation, a three-dimensional focal point cantilevered from a beautiful base anchored between his strong, curving thighs and rippling abdominals.

Settling behind him, Henry dropped a kiss at Jay's shoulder. Jay's wriggling reply juddered down his arm and out his hand, passing through her as if they played a variation on telephone. Or monkey in the middle.

"I want to see you come." She rasped like she'd downed a flight of whiskey shots. And somehow she'd gotten her hand around Jay, her fingers slim and pale against his ruddy flush.

Whimpering, Jay pushed in her grasp, but the decision wouldn't be his.

She sought Henry, arbiter of right and proper behavior, dispenser of justice and orgasms alike, and begged for a favorable judgment with her eyes. "Please."

His benevolence manifested in a nod, but his not-quite-suppressed smile suggested she'd asked for a gift she would've received either way. "I suppose the application of another liquid"—he idly surrounded her hand and stroked Jay's cock with her—"might prove beneficial in solving this stubborn puzzle."

As if Jay were a solvent to dry up her free-flowing arousal. Fat chance. Well—salt was a drying agent, and he did produce the tang of sea salt on a caramel treat. Meeting his gaze, she extended her tongue in a corner-to-corner sweep and fondled his balls.

As his cock gave a gratifying bounce, he stuttered his thanks.

Taking control, Henry steadily worked Jay toward climax for her viewing pleasure.

Heat splashed her stomach and breasts. She'd forever love Jay in orgasm, from the dazed wonder in his eyes and the curving pleasure of his mouth to the hoppy jerks of his cock and the curling pressure of his feet. He welcomed sex as a full-bodied joy. With his nuances and delights, he guided her down unmarked paths she'd miss on her own.

"Our dish needs a new bath." Comforting as a blanket, Henry draped love and approval around their shoulders. "Jay, my good boy, is your tongue fit for the task?"

"I'll fit my tongue to Alice however you want." Jay smirked with sloppy, post-orgasmic pride. "Chief Dish Bather, at your service."

Chuckling, Henry relinquished Jay and nudged him forward.

Jay fell on her with hungry devotion. Using his mouth and hands, he traveled a nonlinear route, a tour of Jay's favorite Alice bits, which covered the full scope of the territory but for one exception—he never crossed the boundary of her pubic hair.

Belly, licked.

Inner thighs, nibbled.

Arousal, rolling like a prairie grass sea.

Aching pressure built in her for more substantial caresses.

Jay tumbled them sideways and claimed a true kiss. His collarbone flexed in her clutch as she rocked her waist in his, but he held his hips back in a Henryesque tease. Fuck, she'd fling her leg over him in half a second and ride—

"Let's not do that, my sweet girl." Nestling behind her, Henry clamped his hand above her knee and pulled her leg straight. "We'll need a matching set to hold your toys."

Her toys. Toysss, plural.

A slender rod slipped between her thighs. Two fatter companions settled alongside. No swoops or bulbs in the bunch.

Henry stroked the top of her thigh. "Legs together." He exerted pressure on his return stroke, and she tightened around her guests. "Keep these warm, and you'll be pleased you did."

Waiting to be used, the toys acted as their own bondage. Henry's command and her always-present desire to please him tied her more tightly than nylon or leather. She'd gotten a full demonstration with Jay weeks ago. Her turn to play the model and reap the rewards. "A more advanced lesson."

"My students move at their own pace." Henry slicked lube between her cheeks. Excess drizzled down one side of her ass to the apron beneath. He left nothing to chance—and she only ever needed obey and enjoy. "Lessons come when they're ready, Jay?"

As Jay lifted his head, the nuzzling, sucking worship of her neck and breasts came to an end.

Henry massaged her with the broad pad of his thumb, a blunted pleasure she attempted and failed to draw deeper in. Damn patient, unhurried master. "The out-of-bounds marker is erased, my boy."

Waggling his brows, Jay teased a strand of her hair across her lips. "Have fun, Goldilocks."

Three toys of varying sizes awaited testing. Henry meant to find her *just right* tonight.

Jay dotted her with kisses until at last he lay level with the one place he'd overlooked. With his breath rushing in hot pulses, he closed his mouth over her and created a humid slice of heaven, his heat and her wetness mingling.

Thank Christ for permission to go out of bounds. As she bucked into Jay, the narrowest rod slid backward. Her reflexive squeeze failed to catch hold.

Henry, humming his amusement, patted her hip. "I've a better place in mind for this."

Smooth, round, and slimmer than his thumb, the toy entered without the jolting, popping, shudder-worthy stretch her plug caused. But the vibrations Jay created in her clit with his fluttering tongue gained echoing strength. She thrust into both. The rod plunged forward, and Henry smacked into her ass on either side, his knuckled grip setting her jiggling.

"More." Fuck, she'd avoided this pleasure far too long. *Dear younger self, so sorry for the wait.* "Please, more."

"Just so." Rubbing her ass, Henry gripped her cheek high. The toy faded in a slow glide until only the prodding tip remained. "Draw your desires deeper."

She chased the tip, her hips rocking, Jay sucking, and satisfaction thickening Henry's moan. With his hold on her ass, he'd displayed her for himself. He watched her swallow this slim stand-in for his cock.

The glowing bedside lamp cast him in high relief, his muscular curves and angles defined and sharpened by shadow. Kneeling behind her, he surveyed his design in a state of omniscient intensity. His lips seemed the only softness about him, their corners upturned in unfettered delight.

Thrusting backward, she buried the toy all the way to Henry's knuckles.

Jay tugged hard in the opposite direction, his tongue flattened across her clit.

Nuclear fission. As her atoms split outward, energy raced through the next and the next. The world dropped away. She swayed in a hammock of Henry's smile.

Slipping the toy free, he made her body his accomplice. Her orgasmic shudders pushed out the thin steel. With that much power, how much stronger and echoing would her contractions be around a man not so easily dislodged?

She fumbled behind herself, finding his thigh and following the inward curve up. Soft skin rippled as she brushed his stiff erection.

He clasped her hand, preventing her from closing around him. "You have other toys to play with tonight."

"Smaller toys." His hard heat tantalizingly close, she flexed her fingers. "I want you."

Jay, with a muffled laugh, bathed her in gusting warmth.

"Incremental adjustments." Flattening her hand on his leg, Henry pressed hard in warning and let go.

She obeyed out of respect, though desire for his possession overrode other thoughts. Personal possession, not only his toys but him, declaring her ready and claiming her.

"Think of them as stretching exercises." As he coated the second toy, turning it round and round, the metal shone in the lamplight. "A torn muscle would delay this game for you indefinitely." He rubbed the tip between her cheeks. "Push."

Wider than his thumb, the toy delivered an unfamiliar stretch. This thickness, unlike her plug, never plunged into a narrower neck. Squeezing, she sucked in a breath. "Wow."

As he steadied the toy, Henry massaged her in a rolling rhythm of grip and release. "Did your eyes deceive you, my sweet? Are your toys not so small after all?"

She wiggled into his hold. "Okay, this one's a lot larger than the first."

"Is it?" He bent and kissed her hip. "Jay."

At his whisper, Jay raised his head. Henry took a deep taste, the men sliding their mouths together, muscle running in taut, elegant lines down their necks. "Ambrosia. Thank you."

Released, Jay sighed and nestled his face between her thighs.

"Isn't it?" She squirmed further onto the toy. The similarity ended with the thickness. The weighted fullness of her walking-around plug invited anticipation. Foreplay. This toy mimicked intercourse. Thrusts held her open and Henry's knuckles provided a depth guide prodding her with every controlled slide.

Tongue stiff and pointed, Jay flicked her clit.

Sparks rippled around and through her, colliding with her new toy from both sides. Like a tuning fork, she vibrated.

"A quarter-inch." Henry upped his pace from teasing to leisurely Sunday morning fuck. "Added to the diameter."

A slight change. Minuscule, and yet—a quarter-inch on the diameter, multiplied by pi on the circumference, more than three times that added to the overall girth. In his hands, such a tight fit came with smooth penetration and incredible sensation.

"I do delight in making you moan." He wrapped her in warm amusement, his chuckle not altering his rhythm. "Perhaps I ought to set you a full array of geometry problems before I allow you to come."

Too late for that. Her urgency echoed between his thrusts and Jay's rapid flicks. "Please." The threat of a *no* dangled. God, if he denied her, she might lose control anyway. Holding back tensed her from temples to toes. Her breath stuttered. "Permission, please."

"Come, Alice."

Liquid, flowing command unleashed her. She shook herself limp and only afterward recognized Jay's strength, his palm spread atop her thigh as he braced her with the length of his body. Her dedicated sweetheart, so quietly busy, made her enjoyment effortless. He and Henry must've run through their game plan more than once. Having two thoughtful, caring men was the best damn gift. Fucking sexy, too.

Thrusts slower but unceasing, Henry led her through climax and onto a mellow plateau. Nestled behind her, he branded her with his cock: a thick, tantalizing stripe of heat rubbing her on each pushback. Reason enough to keep her muscles in motion.

"My lovely girl." He drew out the toy, all the way, and lifted her ass cheek. "So pink and open, her pretty petals unfolding."

Pushing, she waited for his return. He mastered her again and again, his patience a fraction greater than hers as she chased the rounded tip and welcomed the toy home. The pauses grew longer and the thrusts firmer. Not leisurely now but with driving purpose.

Jay and his hard-working tongue cast a spell over her clit. Devoted to his task, he helped Henry raise her from the plateau in a steeper climb.

She strained for each thrust, for the stretch, the slide, and the clenching pleasure.

"So eager and wanting she is." The lower Henry's baritone slid, the higher her arousal ascended. "More than accepting."

The delay lasted forever, creating hours in the space of a second and days in the space of three.

"Craving."

M.Q. Barber

Pressure, finally. Pushing the way he'd taught her, she thrust herself onto the probing tip. "God, that's amazing."

Toy switch, for sure. He delved with a broader, blunter, hotter tool, the best yet. Changing the angle alone couldn't account—the toy popped through like the fat end of her plug.

Shuddering, Henry groaned and clenched her hip in both hands. Toy-free, neither guiding. The flare squeezing past her muscled ring was the ridge of his cock.

Henry. Inside her.

Belly fluttering as she craned to watch him over her shoulder, she eased onto his shaft. Slow, lest he tell her no, but she'd damn well take him in full and rejoice in their snugger-than-snug fit.

"My bold Alice." In his kneeling position, he refused her access to more than incomplete thrusts. He kneaded her side, sending ripples and swells through her, turning her into an oscillating wave, and he and Jay the opposing shores. "Would you have more of me?"

"Always." Covering his hand, she wedged her fingers underneath.

He tucked her fingertips in his palm. "Do you see yourself? You embrace this new facet of our love with exquisite form. What a sweet, tugging joy you are."

Slow-rocking, he teased her with the head of his cock. Lube gleamed along his exposed shaft and distended veins, Henry firm and thick and holding himself back. He dragged his gaze over her in a stare as measured as the sweep of his charcoal pencils across a sketchpad. Deep, deliberate breaths broadened his chest.

"I see you." Her lover. Balanced between power and restraint. Worthy of hushed confessions, of whispered truths and infinite trust. "That's all I need to see."

"What you see"—he drew back, slipping free, his cock jutting toward her—"is what you inspire in me."

He lay down behind her and re-entered before the moan of his loss reached her lips. His plunge met her push. As he sank fully, the heat of his groin and the sway of his balls greeted her. Biting her shoulder, he scraped the edge of restraint, the pressure deep but blunt.

Cast in silhouette and shadow by the bedside lamp, he rose above her. Light skipped off his rounded shoulder and the thick, corded tension in his neck. "Give me your mouth, Alice."

Twisting her neck, she offered herself up.

With his kiss, he drove her into the mattress. He caged her between his bent elbows and savaged her mouth. He tugged her lips and tongue with strength enough to make her nipples ache, as if he'd spliced some shared circuit. His thrusts growing less measured, he snapped against her on every downstroke.

She stretched with an awareness different from the unthinking acceptance of her usual embrace. Her inner squeeze rippled differently, too, tight and gripping at the base but not revealing his length or depth. Those first inches, though. Fuck. As sensitive as her clit, and every point of pressure tickled by smooth, sliding heaven.

The bedspread resisted her grasping hands.

As she curled tight, orgasm building, Jay draped her leg over his shoulder. His slender, muscled back gave great leverage. She drove her foot flat and rocked harder, snugging her ass in the cradle of Henry's hips.

Parched and panting, she reveled in quenching Jay's thirst. He guzzled her down as Henry filled her up.

Her climax burst with the power to shift continents. Tremors echoed in emptiness and broke along new fault lines. Legs churning, heart pumping, she cracked in Henry's sheltering arms.

Behind her, he matched her quaking with his pounding hips. His chest met her shoulder. His stolen kiss cut off her wavering moan. Pulling his mouth free, he loosed a growl as she dragged in a breath. His hips stilled.

She lay shaking and sweaty with his growl reverberating in her ears and his cock buried in her ass. He'd climaxed without holding back as he often did to demonstrate his control. God, what a powerful thrill.

He clenched her neck in a teasing bite. "You're so beautifully unbound when you come, dearest."

She squeezed his cock in appreciation. Thank fuck tomorrow was Saturday. Sitting at a desk wouldn't agree with her in the least. "I'm glad you didn't feel like waiting."

"Eleven months seemed wait enough." For all the wryness in his tone, he delivered the words with tender care and ticklish kisses. "Thankfully, my Alice is worth every second." As he shifted his weight, his hips drifted backward.

She grabbed his forearm. "Don't go just yet?"

"Shh, my lovely girl." He finger-combed her hair, peeling sweaty strands from her cheeks. "You've no need to worry. I'll stay a while longer. As long as I'm able, hmm?" Planting a kiss on her nose, he bathed her in his satisfied musk, the leather note deeper and the citrus sharper. "I'd insist you tell me how sore you are, but I expect your body's hormonal response is obscuring any tender spots." He deposited another kiss at the arch of her top lip. "We shared a more enthusiastic workout than I'd planned. Though I wouldn't alter a moment."

"Me neither." She counted Jay and his talents in her estimation of perfection. Her thigh-squeeze netted a return pat on her belly, but he rested content with his face hidden and his breath a gentle breeze across her lips. "Guess we'll save that third toy for another night. More incremental adjusting." The steel cylinder must've rolled away when Jay had wrapped her leg around his head. Jesus, she'd turned his hair into a bird's nest with her gyrations. "Did I lose it?"

"Lost track, perhaps." Chuckling, Henry cupped the underside of her ass and rubbed circles. "I employed it during your distraction. The mid-size model ceded to its larger sibling as pleasure overwhelmed you the second time."

The difference had slid under her radar. With his widening regimen, he'd prepped her to take him without pain, to revel in him and embrace each moment. Her closest brush with vaginal penetration all night had been Jay fingering her lips while he carried her to bed, yet she'd come three times. If Henry always made anal sex this much fun, she'd never turn him down. "Sneaky man."

"I'll take that as your appreciation for my varied skills, shall I?"

"Most definitely." She gave an impish wiggle. "Sir."

Swatting her ass, he landed a teasing smack in the sweet spot.

She served him a dessert-swallowing moan. The sort Jay would make for chocolate cheesecake. That man needed a proper thank-you, a hug, and buckets of praise. She tugged him by his haphazard black locks.

Jay tipped his head back. She'd made a mess of him, an utterly gorgeous disaster with his broad smile at the center.

Leaving off his caresses of her hip and ass, Henry smoothed the strands for him. "Did you enjoy your feast? I'm more than certain Alice gloried in furnishing the menu."

With a wide stretch, she snagged Jay's discarded apron. "C'mere, stud. Let me dab your glow."

"She's delicious." He wriggled up her body, kissing as he went. "You know me—I love to eat." He nibbled her stomach. "And eat." His brief suck at her nipples sent a shiver through her. "And eat." Arriving in front of her face, he ran his tongue around his lips and gazed past her shoulder. "Washcloth?"

She dried his cheeks and chin with tender swipes.

"No need. A hot shower is in order." Inhaling and circling, Henry ran his nose along her neck. "And the sleep of the well-satisfied."

Chapter 10

Brash and beautiful in his post-orgasm haze, Jay hooked one arm over the subway car's top grab rail and slung the other around her waist. "I got you, babe."

"You have such weird musical taste." With Henry's permission, she'd taken Jay in the shower before their date as his weekly room inspection reward. Water beating down her back and his oh-so-fucking-firm abs under her hands. She clutched him now, ostensibly for balance as the T swayed toward Copley. "You're a decade-blender."

"Nope. I just lived in one." Stealing a kiss, he left minty freshness behind. "Blame my four older sibs."

With a hop through the square—literal, as she rubbed the bronze hare's ears and Jay leap-frogged the patient turtle—they hoofed it down tree-lined Clarendon toward the trendy club where Henry had made their dinner reservation.

They merited a cozy table off to the side of the crush before the stage. The walls bled artwork, splashes of color on canvas in styles she'd be hard-pressed to name.

"This is a total Henry pick." Artsy types congregated by the bar. Five bucks said the menu entrées started at thirty a pop. The stage show promised some big-deal Cuban jazz guy up next. She leaned across the table to make herself heard. "Did he leave an audio file on your phone to narrate the décor for us?"

Even sending them out for the night, he'd wrapped them in his presence. Noisier and filled with more hipsters than he'd tolerate himself, the restaurant merged his taste with Jay's energy level.

"Think he's got cameras?" Jay shuffled his place setting, dragged his chair around the table, and draped his arm across her back. "I better bring my A-game or he's not gonna let me, what's the"—he snapped his fingers—"squire you around town again."

She laid her hand on his thigh. "You're a fantastic date."

He proved himself sharing his entrée, raising the gooey, fancy grilled cheese in two hands and curving the corners up with his thumbs. "Smile, Alice. Say 'cheese' for Henry."

Laughing, she chomped the center and flashed him a cheesy grin. "Eeese."

"I like a girl who bites." As he waggled his eyebrows at her, he tore a huge hunk of sandwich free. Swallowing, he settled back in his seat and squeezed her shoulder. "So?"

"Sooo?" She washed her food down with sparkling water, having switched after one glass of wine. The surrounding tables emptied bottles with panache, but she and Jay, well—the last time she'd gotten drunk, she'd made stupid-ass decisions. And who the hell knew when the last time Jay'd gotten drunk was, but he'd never do it while escorting her. "It's good. Bet Henry could make this at home."

Knocking his forehead against hers, he chortled. "Not the food. What do I think about twenty-four seven?"

"Besides food?"

He nodded, flopping shaggy black hair over his uber-serious face. "Sex."

Their simultaneous singsong drew glances, laughter, and a few eyerolls from neighboring tables.

"Last night." He wore his kid-at-Christmas expression, wide chocolate eyes and white teeth. "Was I right? Did you love it?"

Hand clamped to his knee, she stretched up and nuzzled him. "You mean when Henry stuffed his cock in my ass? Damn right I loved it."

They high-fived, drunker on each other than their neighbors on over-priced cocktails. She fizzed and floated through a world of bright colors, smooth jazz, and sweet, sexy Jay.

With full bellies and giddy spirits, they ducked out after midnight. By unspoken agreement, they avoided the Fenway bars, even with the Sox out of town for the weekend, and the tourist bars crowding Faneuil Hall, because nobody needed that headache.

"Home?" Shirt sticking to her back, she debated options at the Green Line entrance. Too muggy for a walk up to the common or down through the fens.

"Home."

The night grew quieter with each stop, until the train disgorged them on a silent street and trundled off. Heat swarmed in thick bands, the sluggish breeze hoisting a white flag of surrender.

Jay slipped his hand in hers. "You think they're okay?"

Optimum believable outcome, she'd open the door on Henry and Emma laughing over happy memories. "Maybe he took her home." Yeah, if the night hadn't been as rough as Henry implied it'd be. So no. "Or she's asleep."

"I dunno." Jay swung his head. "The club's busiest at night. She's used to staying up."

Probably true, but not what she'd meant. The night might've knocked Emma out with an emotional punch.

"I met her husband." He dropped his foot off the curb and kicked a stone. "At the club. When I——when the board——"

Squeezing his hand, she slowed to match his restless amble.

"He seemed stern. More serious than Henry at his seriousest." His half-hearted smile faded with the breeze.

"Tough guy?" She'd pictured the class and refinement Emma breathed.

"Not a hulked-out linebacker. Different tough."

"Intense." The sort of man Henry would respect and emulate.

"Yeah." He stared up into the cloudy darkness. "Wish it'd rain."

Though his feet knew the route by heart, she guided him down the sidewalk and around the corner. He plodded beside her like a puppy heeling left.

"She took me shopping." *Tap tap tap* went his fingers, a jittery Morse code in her palm. "Back then, I mean." *Tap tap.* "So I could impress Henry."

Their building sat across the intersection. The living room windows glowed behind drawn shades. Emma's influence touched both of her men.

In a quick head turn, Jay cast her a glance and tugged his lip.

"I'm glad." She meant it, too. No faking required to reassure her sensitive submissive. "She must've seen how good you are for each other." He'd been her jovial playmate twenty minutes ago, but each step toward home added a pound on his shoulders. Funny. She'd expected to be the foot-dragger. "You make him so happy."

"I think she knew how hung up on him I was." He hopped to and opened the doors for her. "She never said he was out of my reach or, or, or that guys shouldn't be subs."

She pulled him into a hug. "Of course she didn't."

As the inner door clicked shut, he clung to her in the middle of the lobby.

"Henry decides who can reach him." Whatever weighed on Jay had settled like a yoke. His muscles refused to yield to her kneading. Abandoning the attempt, she backed up. "He let you in because he loves you."

Head bowed, he dropped his gaze. His knees twitched as if he meant to slide into a waiting pose, but he grabbed her hands. "She taught me how to set the table for him."

Table, sure. He was traveling all over the map, and she'd lost her set of directions. "That was nice of her."

Even years later, he prized that task. The nights when she'd gotten home and Jay hadn't set the table numbered so low they wouldn't register outside a margin of error.

"No, I mean, she did it herself. Taught me." Shuffling his feet, he swayed their linked arms. "For him, 'cause she wanted it done right, I know, but she didn't—she could've—she gave me her time and answered my questions."

"She gave you advice. Like"—the fucking light bulb erupted—"a friend."

He didn't want her to resent Emma. He'd dragged his feet and babbled because he'd watched her wage a mental competition for weeks against an opponent she should've considered a teammate.

"She said she'd learned the same way I was, one step at a time." He carried her left hand to his shoulder. "She didn't wonder anymore what made her dominant happy." His hand landed on the swell of her hip. "They'd grown together and she just knew."

Alice had a responsibility to protect him, and she'd made him uncomfortable calling Emma his friend in front of her. As if liking Emma would be disloyal.

"I said I couldn't picture her husband happy because he looked so scary." Raising her right hand, he nudged into her space.

She slipped backward. He'd dipped his head, and the dimmed night lighting in the common areas limned him in a faint glow. "What'd she say?"

"Confidence looks intimidating when you haven't found it in yourself yet." With a near-imperceptible tug, he guided her two steps forward.

Emma'd intimidated her from their first meeting. Her poised perfection, her close association with Henry, her—confidence. Emma danced in a world where she'd only begun to master crawling.

Jay swept her backward. The restaurant had been too crowded, but in the silent lobby, on refinished boards between the laundry and the stairs, he glided her through Henry's dancing lesson. "She said confidence and arrogance weren't the same, especially in a dominant, and I'd know I had the right dom for me when he was—" He flicked his tongue between his lips. "When he was intimidating enough to be arousing, wise enough to keep me safe, and caring enough to help me grow, even when the right choices were hard ones."

"Smart woman." Admitting Emma had been a friend to Jay cost her nothing. Understanding what Jay needed reaped rewards she'd see in him every day. Resentment slipped away, so much grit ground into fineness. "That sure sounds like Henry."

Jay halted their dance. Brown eyes steady and deep, he grazed her mouth with a kiss. "Like you, too, Mistress Alice."

Her heart ticked and the world spun as if she were a clock rewound. Her gears given purpose, she reached a rhythm no longer stuttered into by accident but arrived at by precise calibration and choice.

This place, this time, this bond belonged to her. And the bond she shared with Jay, of accepting his submission, was one shared with Henry, too. A fulfilling, meaningful puzzle, a responsibility and trust, staggering and awesome but so beautiful.

Framing Jay's face, she finger-combed his hair. The humidity-curled tips clung to her skin.

He closed his eyes and leaned into her touch.

"You're a good boy, Jay." Nuzzling his cheek tickled her nose and carried his woodsy musk into her lungs. "You have the kindest heart of any man I know."

Their quiet communion infused her with calm.

When he opened his eyes, their placid depths mirrored her feeling. He wore the sweet look he gave Henry when their lover's dominance led him into the untethered joy of subspace.

"Here, sweetheart." Whispering, she gripped his hand and headed up the stairs. "It's time to say goodnight."

* * * *

"—submit to anyone else, not as I could to him. We were one person. I'll never have that again."

The super should've been less diligent in keeping the old building in tip-top condition. Creaking floorboards and squeaking door hinges prevented all kinds of awkwardness.

"You don't know that, *sverchok*." Back to the door, Henry sat in his curving chair. "If you imagine it every time a would-be suitor tries to coax a smile from you, you aren't allowing him the chance."

Huddled on the couch, Emma shook her head at each word. The tea tray gleamed silver on the low table between them.

Jay at her heels, Alice dropped her keys on the hall table.

Emma stiffened as if the clatter delivered an electric current to her spine.

Henry rose, unhurried, and brushed her shoulder before he came to greet them. "Welcome home, my dears. How was your evening?"

Their puffy-cheeked guest swiped at her eyes. Her dark hair, hanging down, hid her pearl choker. Acknowledging Emma seemed ruder than ignoring her presence. A proud, poised woman wouldn't want them gawking at her pain.

"You picked a great restaurant." Replying on autopilot, Alice divested herself of phone, wallet, and shoes while Jay did the same. "For the food and the music both." But dinner paled beside all Jay'd shown her. His unshakeable declaration. Mistress Alice. "It's good to be home, though."

"I'm pleased you enjoyed yourselves." Henry pulled her into a light hug. She inhaled his scent, familiar, fragrant, and unchanged despite their evening apart. "Jay and I thought it was time to say goodnight."

On the couch, Emma shook. Her eyes widened. A thin gap appeared between her lips.

Fuck. Last time they'd invited Emma to dinner, Henry had ushered her out when his submissives' needs took precedence. Home field advantage. The power she wielded over Emma pinched her lungs and stole her breath.

"Of course." Henry released her and hugged Jay.

Pressing a trembling hand against the arm of the couch, Emma uncurled her legs and dropped her feet to the floor.

In less than a minute, Alice would lose her window. Her actions now would determine the woman she'd be. Petty and jealous, causing pain for the men she loved, or gracious and compassionate. "We'll ready the guest bed for Emma."

All movement on the couch ceased.

Pulling back from Jay, Henry raised an eyebrow.

"And we won't wait up." Her confidence flowed strong as the mighty Mississippi. "You two still have a lot to talk about, I'm sure."

Eyes screwed shut, Emma covered her mouth in both hands and bent almost double, her head at her knees.

Jay quivered. She'd do her loyal, empathetic submissive a disservice if she limited his outpouring of love.

"Go on." She patted between his shoulder blades. Approval would unravel those knots where massage had failed. "Give Emma a hug and say goodnight."

Jay bounded forward and sank to the rug at Emma's feet. His urgent whispers elicited soft sobs. Feminine arms emerging from the tangle, Emma hugged him with a ferocity that flexed her forearms in stark relief.

"Alice." Murmuring her name, Henry sent a shiver all the way to her toes. "They haven't yet invented a word for your magnificence."

* * * *

Waking in darkness, Alice fumbled toward rustling to her left.

Henry, warm and naked, rolled against her and breathed out a laugh. "Jay's possessive tonight."

Their sleeping lover had pinned her. His head rested on the upper slope of her breast. Curving his arm across her stomach, he clutched her ribs.

"He missed you, I think." She stretched, pointing her fingers and toes. She didn't normally sleep on her back between the men, and Jay usually went from clinging to sprawling. "But we did fine on our own for the night."

They'd left him home with the harder task. All the tricky emotional stuff she shied from.

"More than fine." Plucking her arm from between them, he draped it around her head on the pillow. "You've grown since you left for dinner."

Jay's doing. He never craved her dominance so much as when he lacked Henry's. Not a stand-in, but a lieutenant. He didn't imagine her as she saw herself, crawling through the mysteries of relationships and submission and love. To him, she danced.

"You wear your power with greater comfort." Humming, Henry teased the underside of her arm with gentle fingers. "Your confidence and strength are closer to the surface. Your belief and trust in yourself and your lovers has never been more apparent."

Henry had recognized her potential. He'd attuned the three of them physically—sexually—first because she wouldn't have accepted greater commitment. Now he demanded more of her. Emotional calibration.

"I feel stronger." Smarter. Better equipped. Every step she mastered added to Henry's pride in her. She'd always been a dancer. She'd just needed Henry to show her the moves and Jay to make her believe. "Did you get Emma settled in the guest room?" The phrase floated like helium, heady and light, the best name yet for the room she and Jay treated as a closet and a sometime playroom.

"Yes. The pajamas you left out were a thoughtful touch." In a slow sweep, he grazed her neck. "Thank you, Alice, for your generosity and perception tonight."

The sheet slipped off Jay's arm and tickled her stomach.

"Sending her home to an empty house would've been wrong." Rubbing her cheek against Henry's hair bathed her in his scent better than the pillow she'd borrowed. "And you're too much of a gentleman to leave her on the couch." A great quality, gentlemanliness. Attractive. Sweet. Sexy. "It's a good trial run for when Ollie visits, anyway."

Hosting guests taught patience and restraint. Loud, demanding sex would be a slap in the face when Emma lay alone on the other side of the wall.

"Mmm." Mouthing her neck, Henry massaged her breast. "I'm not of a mind to discuss our guest or your sister just now, my sweet."

As Henry jostled his arm, Jay snuffled and tightened his grip on her ribs. The sheet swept south to her thighs, carried on a wave of finger currents.

"Lie back and let me love you." Cock hardening against her hip, Henry palmed her sex.

"Are you—"

"Shhh." Kissing her, he took the lead with firm strokes. "Silence but for one word," he whispered. "If you intend to use it, speak now."

Or forever hold your peace.

She shook her head. *Pistachio* wouldn't pass her lips. Whatever he needed, she'd give gladly. And learn about her lover in the process.

Growling low, he nipped her jaw and throat. Bee-sting kisses raised tingles and tremors.

Jay lifted his chin and gave them a groggy-eyed blink. "Wha—"

Henry kissed him. Jay's cheek worked against her breast as he welcomed Henry's invasion with the same white flag she'd raised.

"One word," Henry murmured. "Nothing else."

Jay held his tongue.

Henry turned to her breasts, lapping at her nipple between Jay's chin and his bicep.

Easing back, Jay created room for Henry to work. Or a better view for himself. God knew the man harbored a breast fixation guaranteed to leave her swollen and needy.

Grabbing Jay by the back of his neck, Henry dragged him to his original spot.

Jay shot her a glance. He held her with an arm thrown across her chest and a leg atop hers, and his sleepy cock bounced against her thigh.

She shrugged. Henry hadn't shared his agenda with her, either, but he pursued his desires with single-minded focus. His kisses burned, deep and intense. Her breasts would bruise for sure. Parting her lips with more delicacy, he swung his finger like a pendulum. On each pass, the farthest point grazed her clit.

Jay's arm and her stomach earned softer kisses, but Henry wreathed Jay's hips with his fiery touch. Jay squirmed and panted, his breath hot on her breasts. His cock stiffened for all the attention bypassing it.

Teases turned to slow, steady finger fucking. Henry pinned her clit with his thumb while he worked his fingers inside. Her pulse pounded against him, begging for movement, but he delivered constant, aching pressure.

Her head grew heavy. The headboard spindles blurred and doubled. Jay crushed her breast in his grip and dug into her ribs.

She jolted off the pillow. *What the fuck*— Christ, no wonder. Henry'd taken Jay's cock between his lips.

He captured the head, sucking a thick straw with an even thicker milkshake waiting at the bottom of the glass. His cheeks hollowed into dark caverns. Hypnotic movement, the deep, greedy pull with an extra tongue flick beneath.

As Jay buried his face in her breast, muffled groans vibrated along her skin. He closed his mouth over her until even sound disappeared and he puffed out nothing but quick, heated breaths through his nose.

His stiffening body told her when he came, unaccompanied by his usual whimpering chorus. He jerked against her in silence, three hard thrusts and boneless shudders after.

She'd have an imprint of his teeth in her breast tomorrow, but he'd have an imprint of her nails in his back, and neither mattered when Henry hadn't stopped finger-fucking her.

He surrounded her clit with his tongue and tugged her hips off the bed. But his kiss was hello and goodbye in one. He pulled clear, knelt above her, and pumped his cock in his fist twice.

She bent her leg in unmistakable invitation.

Squeezing the base, he aligned their bodies and lowered himself over her. He refused to let Jay move away, and he hadn't entered her more than the slightest push. Enough to keep them on target. Enough to focus her tingling anticipation, the urge to grip him, the wait for spreading pleasure. Shivers rattled her, the burning chill of overheating need.

Pressing his forehead to hers, he sank inside. And didn't move.

Balanced on one forearm beside her head and his opposite arm around Jay, his grip tight at Jay's neck, he rocked his hips, slow and experimental.

With her leg wrapped around his thighs, she clutched him close.

He fucked her deep, never drawing back, heavy and solid and moving as if he meant to wedge himself far enough to stay forever. He kissed her with Jay's salty musk on his tongue. Even in her submission, they shared the flavor of ownership.

The grinding pressure of hips and pelvis carried her to the peak. Her orgasm erupted long before his. A dreamy haze descended. The world itself rocked, and stopping would mean its end.

Nothing but silence, and rocking, and the occasional heat of Henry's tongue in her mouth, probing above as skillfully as he did below. She lay half-asleep and coated in sweat when the rocking ceased, though echoes throbbed and Henry hadn't left her.

With wordless care and gentle kisses, he shuffled her and Jay. Rolling them all sideways, he tucked her between them with her leg slung over his hip and his cock reburied inside her.

Jay, curled at her back, yawned against her neck. After a nice orgasm and proof of Henry's appreciation, that man could sleep anywhere. Even in mid-July heat, sticky and sweaty and covered with sex-scent.

Not her. Too hot. Too sticky. Two male bodies surrounding her and adding to both conditions.

But Henry didn't seem inclined to let them go. He lay with his lips against her forehead and his cock filling her as if release eluded him, for all that he'd given them theirs.

She held her silence. He'd asked only that one thing of her since he'd come to bed. He'd brought her to orgasm, relaxed her body, and if she lay unsleeping all night, she'd take no lasting harm from the shortfall. Closing her eyes, she drifted.

What might have been minutes or hours passed. Time failed to penetrate her warm cocoon. But Henry sighed, rustling her hair. His loving hum, tempered by some unfamiliar note, prodded her to awareness.

"Don't ever leave me, my loves." He buried his whisper, fierce and all but inaudible, in her hair. "I couldn't bear the loss."

Chapter 11

Her back had become a ladder. Traffic traveled up either side of her spine in shuffling steps. She followed the climbers to faint light and steady thumping.

Chest hair tickled her cheek. Rubbing Henry with catlike affection, she forced her eyes open in stages.

Seven forty-seven. The bedside clock glowed with cheerful blue abandon. The clock hadn't gone to bed at one or woken up in the middle of the night for delicious, erotic, confounding sex.

When the ladder-climbing fingers halted their trek, Henry clasped the upper curve of her ass.

Fumbling with tangled limbs, she folded her arms on his chest and raised her head.

Jay slept beside them in a stomach sprawl. With the sheet kicked down and twisted around his calves, his toned ass begged for nibbling.

Henry followed her glance and chuckled, but at least part of him agreed, if his interest stirred beyond male morning mechanics. "You won't wish me a good morning? Has our beautiful boy stolen your breath?"

Shaking her head, she delivered teasing Eskimo kisses between his flat nipples. "You did. 'Silence but for one word.'" Her imitation carried more rasp than baritone depth. "Still not using it, but I kinda fell asleep along the way. Rule might have remained in effect."

Putting pressure on her ass, he prompted her forward for a proper kiss, growly and lingering. "That particular provision has elapsed." With tenderness, he dropped smaller kisses across her cheeks. "Though your obedient adherence is noted and appreciated."

His approval lodged in the lizard part of her brain. She'd starved the whole region for years, feeding herself a diet of work-related performance evaluations. Good ones, but they came so infrequently as to be anorexic.

Henry stuffed her full of praise and then some. Praise: A new name for his toolkit. She'd have to save that one to share with Jay.

"I'm delighted to see you smiling." Nudging her curtain of hair aside. he peeked at Jay. "The two of you are a heavenly vision to wake to each day." A sliver of a smile curved his lips. "My favorite vision."

I couldn't bear the loss.

His whispered confession belonged to darkness, to post-midnight melancholy and memory. After hours of supporting a friend in need, he'd come to bed with needs of his own. Immersed himself in their bodies. In their living, breathing presence.

Santa had been right. Henry carried solemn responsibilities on broad shoulders. His intensity needed respite. Joy.

Jay.

As running water hummed through the bathroom pipes, Henry pressed his thumbs against her back. "I ought to check on our guest."

"Let me." The words escaped without planning, but she wouldn't retract the offer. "Give us girl time."

Drops of terror squeaked through her heart valves. Building a friendship with Emma would take hard work and diplomacy. Bring on the former, the more the better, but the latter she'd have to tiptoe through without a schematic.

"You're certain? You needn't rush yourself. dearest." All intent eyes and even lips. he studied her from behind his inscrutable dom-face. "You've already proven yourself capable of exquisite compassion. a regal mosaic."

If he hadn't started sketches yet. he had to be planning them. Picturing in his mind's eye images less tied to her physical world of engineering than to his metaphorical one of shapes and colors imbued with meaning.

"I want to."

He supported her weight with warm, sturdy muscles. He supported her heart with graceful prodding toward growth. Getting to know Emma better. she'd support Henry in subtle ways of her own.

"I need to."

Accepting Emma's friendship wouldn't diminish her share of Henry's love and attention. The freer he felt to take care of his obligations without strategizing responses for her unhappiness, the more energy he'd have to devote to her and Jay. To showing them his love.

"Besides, that'll give you boys some quality time."

In his sleep, Jay curled vulnerability and trust around him like a blanket. His unlined face and parted lips invited kisses. His dark lashes rested against tanned cheeks. No wonder Henry took every opportunity to wake him slowly.

"I bet he'd love to return the favor you gave him last night." An unexpected outpouring of dominant giving. One she'd never tire of watching.

"Peace." Henry pecked her lips. "You've convinced me, sweet minx."

"I'm an excellent arguer." But now she'd have to tear herself away from her two musky men. Fuck. She'd better hustle through a washcloth bath, because no way in hell would she greet Emma with a dusting of sex on her skin. "I just talk until you give in."

His hum held a note of amusement.

"I do."

"If you like." He swatted her ass at quarter-strength, a solid, comforting claim. "Or I, in my patient wisdom, allow you to speak until you find yourself at the place we would have arrived all along." His chuckle jostled her. "Your journey is spectacular, and I quite prefer the scenic route."

She made sure to show off the scenic route between the bed and her bathrobe.

* * * *

Emma stood beside the front door, her hand pressed to the wall as she stepped into her shoes.

If their guest slipped out now, she'd never get this friendship off the ground. "I hope you aren't leaving so soon."

Emma froze. "Alice."

"At least let me get you coffee." She walked past, striving for casual, and turned the corner into the kitchen. "Caffeine is just the thing to start the morning."

Not her normal breakfast, but Emma'd been drinking coffee at the club. Henry kept a basket of teas and gourmet coffee beside the countertop machine. Shoulders tight, she started the brewer.

Footsteps. Soft padding on the hardwood, not the tap of shoes. Her invitation hadn't been rejected.

She rolled her shoulders and stretched. "It'll be a few. You sleep okay?"

"The room was exceedingly comfortable, thank you." Hands clasped behind her back, Emma gazed out the window. "Immaculately kept."

"Jay'll be happy to hear it." Impressing Emma required some doing. She'd have to praise him during her next inspection.

"The room is his?" Emma stiffened. Her frosty edge cooled the morning's warmth. "He gave it up for me?"

"No, no." Brewing coffee took all of five minutes. She must've set a land-speed record for unknown fuck-ups. "It's the guest room." She grabbed mugs from the cupboard and set them, clanking, on the counter. "He's in charge of keeping it habitable."

"Ah." Emma thawed. "He's done a wonderful job. He's a delightful boy."

"He is." Especially sleep-tousled. Or slinging her over his shoulder. Or sliding to his knees and staring up at her with soulful puppy eyes. "The best."

When the coffee machine chirped its readiness, she poured the first cup. *Evicted.*

Coffee sloshed over the side of the second. Missed her hand, thank fuck. The meaning behind Emma's chilly response lodged in place. As if she'd kick Jay out of Henry's bed. As if Henry would let such a thing happen.

"Alice? Are you all right?"

"Just made a mess. It's nothing." She set the full mug on the breakfast bar. "Cream or sugar?"

"I've upset you." Red-eyed, Emma reached across the speckled granite top. "Please accept my apology." Closing her slim hands around the mug, she brushed Alice's knuckles. "I jumped to a hasty conclusion completely unsupported by what I've seen of your relationship."

"No, I get it. Not a problem." She slipped free and snapped a paper towel off the roll. "The way Jay tells it, you did some matchmaking to help him out." No coffee stains on Henry's pristine countertop. "You don't want to see him supplanted." Coffee soaked up, she scrubbed at nothing. "Neither do I."

Coming out here had been a shitty idea. She should've let Henry play diplomat or Jay play comedian. Either would've done a better job.

"I shouldn't have spoken so carelessly." Pin-straight and shoulders back, Emma stood as proud and poised in yesterday's tunic and leggings, her face scrubbed clean of makeup, as she did greeting players at the club. "You've been a more than considerate hostess, and I've insulted you with an unconscionable slur against the clear love you bear. Forgive me."

Maybe the pearl choker did it. An invisible hand guiding Emma while Alice made do with clomping about, bigfooting the wrong words, the wrong actions, making friendship with this woman so fucking hard— "How'd you get to be so gracious and wise all the time? It's damn intimidating."

Yeah. About like that. If she'd thrown back some coffee, she wouldn't have opened her mouth and let accusations fall out.

Emma parted her lips. Eyebrows drawing together, she blinked.

Alice waved to clear the air. "Sorry. It's not you, it's—"

"No, it *is* me." Leaning on the island, Emma ducked her head and sucked in a breath. "I've misread you entirely."

Unlikely. Emma deserved a PhD in reading people. Her and Henry both.

Smoky blue eyes wide as she looked up, Emma teased a smile. "Here I've been, nervous as all hell, trying to project the perfect image of placid, nonthreatening submission, thinking it would reassure you I'm not out to steal your master. I've accomplished the opposite, haven't I?"

Emma, nervous? But *she* was the nervous novice, the one on unfamiliar ground—the new variable. Emma didn't know what to make of her any more than she did Emma. The power she'd felt last night had been in her hands all along, except Emma had recognized the truth and she'd imagined Emma held the cards. Christ, what a mess. Scooping up her mug, she leaned back against the counter. "I let jealousy blind me."

"I well remember that rush of territorial need." Emma gripped her lower lip in her teeth and shook her head. "It's more fundamental than desire, the urge to claim him and have others acknowledge that claim."

"All I could think about was how you're a better submissive." The coffee gave off a wisp of steam. Too hot to drink. Almost too hot to hold. "I thought I was doing it wrong. Jay hasn't got a jealous bone in his body. I forgot my own strengths."

"I'm the perfect submissive"—Emma rubbed the pearls at her throat—"for a man who died four years ago and left me alone."

"A man who mentored Henry." They had to be similar. "You like the things he does. You talk intelligently about art. You like cooking—you brought him a cookbook." A gift he used often and handled with care. "A handwritten cookbook. Who does that?"

"You carry yourself so well I forget how much you haven't encountered." Emma drooped, shoulders sagging before she firmed them. "He called the book a tremendous gift because he understood why I needed to present it." Raising her head, Emma trapped her with a steely stare. "I'm a masochist, Alice. A whipping is more pleasure than punishment. Victor used to make me write lines when my behavior displeased him."

The gorgeous book with its intricate detailing and precise penmanship on unlined paper—a punishment. An apology tucked away on the kitchen shelf beside the wood and tile box of file cards with family recipes. Emma's apology for the pain and confusion Alice and Jay had experienced that night in May. "That's why your handwriting is so perfect."

Emma laughed, not in her lilting feminine tone but a startled chuckle as she bent forward and settled her forearms on the island. "I got plenty of practice."

Greeting card companies needed to work on their thank-yous. Bet they didn't have one for her situation. *Dear fellow submissive, thank you kindly for exposing your private appetites to make me more comfortable.*

"I would've, too. Don't tell Henry——my handwriting's atrocious. The last thing I need is to be writing *I will stop putting my foot in my mouth* a hundred times. It wouldn't work, anyway. Sometimes they're surgically attached at birth."

The ice shattered beneath Emma's laughter. The thing Jay did, the jester act, had incredible power. Tapped into place at the right angle, shared humor collapsed barriers like nothing else. She owed him for teaching her that one.

"Alice, you've been exceedingly gracious, and I've been leaning on Henry more than I should." Tilting her mug, Emma tapped the rim. "Please believe me when I tell you I'm so happy for him that you've found each other."

"It's difficult for you, though." She tried mimicking Henry's calm, unthreatening delivery. The one that always told her he accepted her emotional confession without judgment.

"No more so than for you, I imagine, having me trying to hold on to something that isn't mine." Emma spread her hands on the island, pale palms up in a starry black sky.

Abandoning her mug, Alice gathered Emma's hands and squeezed. "Is that how you see it?"

"You don't?" Emma's slim hope stung like a metal shaving caught under a fingernail.

"Henry's friendship *is* yours." She wouldn't entertain arguments on that count. Her insecurity had driven a wedge where none belonged. "You're an important person in his life. And I think——" She waited for eye contact and held it. "He's a very important person in yours."

Mouth twitching, Emma pressed her eyes shut. Not fast enough to hide the shine in the bloodshot storm. "It's so easy," she whispered. "I look at him and memories greet me." Her hands trembled. "There's no danger. I don't have to expose myself to someone new. He knows who I was and who I am. And he listens."

"He's good at that." The comforting and familiar fit alongside the mysterious and strange in the puzzle of Henry. He passed her pieces as she needed them. "It's good for him, too. Sharing. Remembering."

Pulling her hands back, Emma fiddled with her wedding ring. "The romantic in me sees you filling a place left empty at Henry's side for twenty years. He's been waiting for you." She radiated brilliant, girlish joy. "Jay is a perfect fit for the place at his master's feet. You fit effortlessly between."

"Not effortlessly." Henry and Jay had put in huge amounts of effort to draw her in. And even as deeply as she loved them, she struggled, still, to understand and navigate their relationship.

"Not yet, perhaps." Emma slid onto a seat and sipped her coffee. "Finding your balance is a delicate dance at first."

Henry's dancing lesson. Jay's reminder. The metaphor—Victor's? A man she'd never met influenced her life in unpredictable ways.

"But I see it in you." As she reclaimed the mothering, advisory role, Emma's voice firmed. "You hear Henry's tune. You have an instinct for the steps."

"Hardly." Swiping her coffee from the counter, she took the seat beside Emma. "I've been at least a step behind all year. Sometimes a whole tune."

"As you see it." Emma took a lengthy drink and studied her mug, one of Jay's picks emblazoned with *I live to serve*. A tennis ball filled the *o*. Jay didn't play tennis. Emma smiled.

"Outsiders view the three of you as one unit. The more you and Jay obey Henry without violent displays of power, the more you irritate Calvin Gardner and his ilk. They see Henry and his kind as service tops, not dominants at all." Wrinkling her nose, she tapped her manicured nails on the ceramic. "As if power existed only in the deliverance of unwanted attention."

Service top went on her list of things to ask about. Jay would know.

"Henry's powerful without being obvious." His subtle commands aroused her as much as his blatant ones. The combination of mental and physical seduction tied her up just the way he liked her. "Jackasses shouting about how powerful they are kinda seem like they're proving the opposite."

"*Salut.*" Emma clinked their mugs. "Victor would have approved of you. I told Henry so last night. And you've charmed Will."

Family. Hers had expanded in unexpected directions. She'd always been the big sister for Ollie. Struck out on her own for college. Found male mentors at work. But thanks to Henry, she had something like an older sister by her side, sipping coffee at the breakfast bar on Sunday morning. Her new sister had to be wishing for a different Sunday morning with a different family. "Will you tell me about them?"

Mug gripped in both hands, Emma stretched for a smile. "You want stories of Henry and William strutting around with the brash confidence of boys, leaving admirers in their wake?"

"No." The light tone Emma'd used wouldn't throw her off. Diversionary tactics, architectural facades and fancy finishes. "Your husband. Your

son. You miss them, and I don't know them, but I do know you——or I
will, because you're Henry's *sverchok*."

Emma bobbled her coffee, bringing the mug in for a swift landing.

Hell, even if she'd mispronounced the nickname, she'd at least gotten
Emma's attention. "Nothing will erase that." She'd forge this friendship
not only for Henry, but for herself. Emma's place in their family didn't
slight her. "You don't have to tell me if you don't want to, or if you
aren't ready." Heart pounding, she put Henry's examples of pushing with
kindness to use. "But they don't have to be forgotten. Locked up in your
head or in mementos you treasure."

Emma sat motionless. She didn't seem the type to ride the babble train
to Foot-in-Mouthsville.

"Tell me how your husband took his coffee. How your son topped his
pancakes." Squeezing her mug, she tucked her feet on the chair rung.
"All the little details you remember that no one else knows." She forced
herself to shut the fuck up. Henry used silence to his advantage. He had
to have learned the skill for a reason.

Cupping her hands, Emma stared straight ahead. Safe bet she hadn't found
the backsplash behind the hammered copper farm sink fascinating. "It's——"
As she shifted, the pearls at her throat gleamed. "There are so many."

"I have time." The doors in the hall had opened and closed not long
before. They had thirty minutes, minimum, before the guys would
be presentable by Henry's standards. "And I want to know you better.
Understanding the people you love is a good start."

With narrowed eyes and pursed lips, Emma gave a slow nod. "You
truly are perfect for him. Each time we meet, I see it more and more."

The corollary hadn't gone unnoticed, then. Understanding the people
Henry loved would be a good start to understanding him, too.

"Where to begin. Victor." Breathing her husband's name with a wealth
of passion, Emma captured startling depth in two sharp syllables. "He
was everything to me from the moment I met him."

* * * *

Almost untouched, Alice's coffee lingered in a state of lukewarm
social lubricant. "You seriously told him that?"

"Absolutely I did. I challenged him like the dickens. At times he
agreed and at times he didn't, but never once did he raise a whip in
anger. It's a different——"

"Omelets, then." Jay led with his voice, half-shouting in the hall. "Or
those super-thin pancakes Alice likes."

His generous volume suggested an intentional warning system. Probably Henry's doing. Alert: Two men incoming.

"Dynamic." Emma finished. "But it seems you're overdue for breakfast." Tossing a glance over her shoulder, she squeezed Alice's hand with her slim, soft fingers. "Thank you."

"Anytime." Not an idle answer but a promise. Her imagined foe made a more than decent friend when understanding outweighed jealousy.

Athletic shorts hanging to his knees, Jay swaggered into the kitchen wearing one of the joke shirts he'd gotten Henry as a birthday present. *I have Manet things to do today.* The laundry had faded the swirling lines of the paint-by-numbers style picnickers.

"Morning, Emma." Bypassing their guest, as casual as if she appeared in the kitchen every morning, Jay spun Alice's chair and kissed her cheek. "Alice, you gotta tell me what's for breakfast. Henry's vetoed waffles, pancakes, omelets, and more pancakes. I'm out of ideas."

"Oatmeal?" She wrinkled her nose to mimic Jay. "Nah. Too wintery."

Hands bracketing her, Jay swiveled her chair back and forth at dizzying speed. "He said we get to help, but he won't say what we're making."

"Parfaits?" Emma offered her guess with a gentle smile. "Layering fruit and cream lends itself well to helping hands and to summer."

"Could be. He'd sound an alarm if we didn't have fresh fruit." Her frozen food diet hadn't impressed him much. But Sundays typically started with a big meal. Of course, usually they'd have expended a lot more energy Saturday night. "French toast? I dunno, I'm low on ideas, too."

Fiendish grin in place, Jay clamped her waist. "We gotta get you higher so you'll think better."

She swatted his shoulders, but he plonked her on the granite island top anyway. *Behave, sweetheart,* came close to passing her lips. Her brain engaged with split-second timing.

Jay tapped her head. "Is it working? Are you filling up with ideas?"

Behaving belonged to company manners. Family got the as-is experience, and Emma needed to know she qualified. Using emotion over analysis, Jay'd gotten to the conclusion twice as fast. That or Henry'd told him to be playful.

"The air's too thin up here." She stuck her tongue out. "Explains where your crazy ideas come from. Oxygen deprivation." Nudging forward, she gripped his shoulders for balance. "But if Henry wants the island for breakfast-making, he doesn't need my ass on it."

He might, Jay mouthed, waggling his eyebrows. But he swung her down so her feet touched the floor.

"Good morning, all." Striding into the kitchen, Henry collected attention like a magnet pulling in metal shavings. "I hope everyone slept well. July is giving quite the sales pitch for central air this year."

No silk lounging pants today. Henry commanded authority in solid navy slacks. But the top button on his crisp white dress shirt stood undone, and his bare feet exposed a touch of familial playfulness.

"The window fan was a wonderful help." As she straightened her back, Emma turned her seat in an arc matching Henry's progress, a move Alice would've labeled covetous before understanding the trained habits fueling the woman. Now her behavior seemed natural. "The humming white noise dragged me into dreams." Emma sipped her coffee. "Morning arrived before I'd realized."

She filed Emma's comment under *classy ways to suggest I didn't hear you having sex.* Who knew when she'd need a similar answer in her arsenal. The fan, of course, fell under *deliberate Henry moves.*

"I'm pleased." Rounding the island, Henry reached for Alice. "Dreams are a delightful way to occupy one's time." With the back of her neck cupped in his hand, he kissed her forehead. "Good morning, sweet."

Murmured approval, gentle warmth in his voice, his body fresh from his shower. As she swayed into him, she ordered her fingers to stand down. Henry's belt didn't need opening, no matter how tempting.

"Emma, lemme refill your mug." Jay, breezing by them, scooped up his target.

"Kind, but unnecessary." Emma eased out of her seat. "Henry, thank you for the hospitality. Your home is lovely, and your pets are more so. I've stayed in hotels that weren't so neatly appointed as your guest room."

"Yes, Jay does a wonderful job." Henry stepped away, taking the scent of his crisp, fresh maleness with him. Gaze straying to Jay, he allowed a rare broad grin to dominate his face. "He's taken on more responsibilities of late and excelled at them all."

Pouring the coffee despite Emma's dissent, Jay bounced in place. Goddamn, but he made an adorable praise-hungry wriggle-puppy.

"Sounds like a reason for waffles." Jay pitched his voice falsetto. "Every good boy deserves waffles."

As Alice's laughter mingled with Emma's, Henry tweaked Jay's nose, drawing him forward and shaking his head. "I ought to send you to piano lessons so you'll learn the mnemonic correctly. The scale contains no waffles, my boy."

Emma brushed nonexistent lint from her tunic. "And I ought to leave you all to—"

"Em. if you needn't rush off, I have ingredients for *pirozhki* waiting."
Reaching past Jay. Henry brushed the spine of a slender cookbook housed
on the open shelf above the sink. "Would you care to give us a lesson
from your kitchen?"

Hurried blinks fluttered Emma's lashes in a storm.

"Chief taster," Jay crowed. "I call dibs on first out of the oven."

"Don't burn your tongue," Alice teased, with dignity befitting the lady of
the house. This house, anyway. The dough Henry had made yesterday must've
been for this. Suspecting Emma would stay, he'd planned the outcome in
advance. Or he'd intended to teach his lovers the recipe either way.

"Never." Garbling his words, Jay waved his outthrust tongue. "Gotta
keep my gear in tip-top shape. I know who's got dibs on it."

Henry tapped the cookbook on Jay's head. "Fetch me the baking sheets
and rolling pin, please. The sooner we begin, the sooner we'll have an
appropriate stuffing for your mouth."

With a grin fit to bust his cheeks. Jay dropped his gaze. If only Henry
had picked a less roomy pair of slacks.

Their guest stood like a casting waiting for another's hand to crack
the mold.

Alice slipped between the seats to Emma's side and hunkered over the
island on her elbows. Shoulders brushing, she delivered a light nudge. "Stay."

Eyes bright, Emma nodded.

"Good." She gave a firmer nudge. "Sunday brunches are for family.
Now, tell me what we're making."

They swept into motion, an oddly coordinated foursome rotating
around the island. Cherries, apricots, and cream lined the sweet side.
Mushrooms, cheese, and onions lined the savory side. Emma guided
while Jay provided muscle power for shaping the dough.

Shirt uncuffed, sleeves rolled to his elbows, Henry worked the bench
knife with commanding precision, but with a flow, too. His casual happiness
wound around her with mellow ease. Their lazy Sunday morning rhythm
accommodated this, too. Her place had never been in jeopardy.

Jay rolled, Henry cut, and she and Emma filled and pinched pastry
after pastry. When they finished, they'd have a feast beyond what the four
of them could eat.

"Even Jay can't pack away this much food." She settled the last *pirozhki*
on one tray, and Henry swapped in an empty. "Too bad Santa's not here."

"Alas, Will's Sunday brunches are with his in-laws." Henry kissed the
top of her head. "Penance for his debauchery, as his wife assesses it."

Frowning, Emma pinched too hard, puncturing the dough and spilling filling out the ends. "He sent flowers and a note Saturday morning, the sweet boy." She scraped the mess clear and began again. "He's giving up his next Friday playtime to escort me to the symphony."

"Tanglewood?" Henry focused on his work brushing an egg glaze over the finished tray.

"Mm-hmm. Like old times," Emma murmured.

More history she lacked. The summer music showplace lay a two-hour drive from the city. But Santa's cabin, that'd be much closer.

Talk of composers carried them through the last of the dough. Jay, after trading his rolling pin for spoons, delivered what he insisted was a flawless rendition of the best classical music ever. *Chopsticks.*

The feast of conversation and companionship lasted the morning. The contentment lingered long after Emma had gone.

Chapter 12

Jay bounced through the club's lobby Friday evening despite the weight of Henry's duffel slung over his shoulder. Whatever props Henry had brought, he'd kept the packing list to himself. A pair of panties for her to wear later, maybe.

Her basic black dress flowed to her knees, concealing private joys. The garters holding up her stockings and their thin belt circling her hips swayed and tugged with her steps. Hidden to sight and hidden to awareness parted ways between her thighs. The free flow of air created a tiny but powerful underskirt breeze across her bare lips. She floated on the same thrill Jay did, except with deeper knowledge of the layers beneath their buoyancy.

Standing before the desk, the source of their excitement betrayed no hint of what the night held. Though Henry wore a sharp suit, the black a match for her dress, what cloaked him wasn't fabric but confidence. Yet even his unruffled calm carried an expectant air. "Good evening, Caitlyn. I trust all is in order?"

"Yes sir, Master Henry." After stowing their phones in Henry's numbered box, Caitlyn dug under the desk. "She handled everything upstairs herself before she left. You're all set."

She could only be Emma. The details would be exact, crafted however Henry wanted them. Reliable friends made for wonderful nights.

Caitlyn slid two red ribbons across the counter. "May I provide any other service?"

"Actually, yes." Henry pushed a single ribbon back. "You may exchange this for yellow."

Jay jerked in a stuttering sideways step, hair flying and duffel banging his hip. "Who's wearing yellow?"

"Easy, stud." As she snuggled against him, she triggered his automatic hug-back response. "The yellow's for me, but I'm still all yours and Henry's."

"Ours." His exhale heated her scalp.

"Entirely, wonderfully so." Lending weight to their embrace with a firm caress down Jay's back, Henry raised the red in his other hand. "Keep hold of this, please, my boy. We'll dress you properly upstairs."

Ribbon gripped tight, Jay followed each motion as Henry shaped the yellow one into a floralesque corsage and pinned it to her dress. When they both wore red, they were equals. Co-conspirators. Tonight, Henry granted her a different role.

He took them each by a hand, and they climbed the stairs three abreast.

Wearing a yellow ribbon, she could tell off a pushy dominant——politely——if necessary without needing to shout for a play monitor. The lack of red on her chest marked not a downgrade in Henry's claim but an upgrade in her autonomous power and his trust in her to wield it well.

Not spilling what she knew of Henry's plans grew harder the closer they got. But she wouldn't miss Jay's expression for anything.

At the top of the grand staircase, Henry paused. They had the broad second-floor landing to themselves. The salon lay to the right, the changing rooms to the left beyond the auxiliary reception desk.

"All right, my dears." Henry swept a disobedient strand of Jay's hair from his forehead. "Jay and I have the matter of his apparel to consider."

Speculative glances traveled from the duffel to Henry to her, strong evidence of Jay-mapping. He'd see the options Henry had packed first. She'd have to wait until he emerged in them.

Kissing her right cheek, Henry fortified her with grazing knuckles down her left. "We'll see you soon, my dear." In an intimate rumble, he added, "Think of the salon as your room."

Adrenaline poured in to meet——and exceed——the challenge he'd set. With his encouragement of her spot checks and rewards for Jay in the second bedroom, he'd put them on this path. Jay bestowing an affectionate title on her had paved it.

"See you soon." She broadened her smile for Jay and his curiosity-laden brows. "I'll be waiting."

Henry collected Jay with an arm around his back and led him to the changing rooms. Whispering, he tugged the strap over Jay's shoulder.

With his boisterous laugh filling the space, Jay cast a final look her way before he disappeared.

The closing door unstuck her feet. She had minutes, not hours, before she'd see them again. Inside the salon, a few players clustered in chatty knots of twos and threes. Fifteen, give or take. Two in yellow ribbons anchored cozy seating areas and raised expectant faces at her entrance.

"Sorry, boys." Muttering under her breath, she turned right and kept count of her steps. Jay would be delighted she'd remembered his retelling of his first date with Henry. "I'm not the partner you're looking for."

Twenty-seven. She took shorter steps in heels than Jay in sandals, or used a less direct route than Henry had taken five years ago. But her twenty-seven steps brought her to the same place, two cozy blue chairs on spindly, curving legs. The curves gave them strength disproportionate to their slender design, spreading the weight of the high chair back and solid arms outward and down to the floor.

Nestled between the chairs, a tall table held two cork coasters and a neatly folded card reading *Reserved* in Emma's elegant script. The paper rasped under her fingernail, a rough weave with a feathered fiber edge.

The chair, embracing her in its flaring sides, angled her gaze to the wide-flung double doors. As she smoothed her dress, the garter clips beneath bumped her palms. She shivered, once, the last kick before sinking into dreamland.

A flash of black crossed the doorsill. A brown-haired man in a decent suit, but not Henry.

Closing her eyes, she tucked laughter behind her teeth and let amusement crowd out all else. To the nameless man in the nice suit, she would've looked as sweetly attentive and eager as those yellow-ribboned men had to her. The stray urge for the approach of a stranger tickled. Just one, one excuse to tell the room she had plans, that she both cared and was cared for.

She breathed out emotional overabundance and held tight to a kernel of calm. Pictured the low-slung vanity in the second bedroom. Pulled open the shallow center drawer. Extracted her Jay-book and jotted the date on a fresh page. As the proper mindset cascaded into alignment, she opened her eyes.

Henry stepped into the doorway. The crisp cut of his suit showcased strong shoulders above a broad, bold chest—her powerful lover when above her and the perfect resting place when below. Smiling as he spied her, he lifted his chin and spoke over his shoulder. Jay would be waiting at his heels.

She scuttled the urge to stand or present her submission for evaluation. This room belonged to her.

Her men flowed inside with measured steps. Bare, tanned skin flickered beside Henry, Jay a gently offset shadow shielded by his body. Wearing wide-eyed delight, Jay craned his neck and gazed at her over Henry's shoulder. His mouth hung open, his full lips round and pink.

Worth waiting for. Five years before, Henry had sat with Jay in these chairs and taken the initial steps toward a relationship. This first date would be one all three of them could treasure.

Even as Henry closed his eyes and pursed his lips, he navigated the room with ease. He made the same face when savoring a perfectly seasoned meal. The reason sharpened as they neared—Jay's panting enjoyment carried whimpers past Henry's ear. A tenor soloist singing for his supper.

They made a striking couple. Their passage turned heads and lowered conversation levels, but only she would get to claim them. Her thoughtful, sensitive dominant, with his insistence on transforming every moment into some memorable design. Her sweetly astonished submissive, touched by the simplest gestures and overjoyed to follow into any wonderland of Henry's making.

Rising to her feet, she wobbled not from the height of the heels but from the force of their love. Henry paraded his in a cloak thickened by confidence and unsullied by jealousy. Jay's longstanding assertions of non-jealousy manifested in more than abstract notions. His satisfied pride lived in her now, the meaning and purpose guiding her life. Bonds they each shared as pairs added depth to the relationship they built as a triad, a truth shaped by all of their needs and desires.

Her men halted in front of her, and Henry's sidestep threatened to put her on her ass.

Jay was naked. Full-on, bare-ass naked.

The tails of his red ribbon dangled from a bow tied above his right bicep, and plain sandals covered the soles of his feet, but nothing decorated the beautiful body between. And his smile. God, his smile covered his whole face in the sort of holy bliss reserved for witnessing miracles.

Henry extended his hand. "Mistress Alice?"

She tore herself from admiring Jay's—belonging. This was Jay at his most natural, content to be petted and admired in meaningful service.

Inclining his head, Henry quirked his lips as he swept her with his gaze, undoubtedly sketching her in memory. "It's a pleasure to meet you in person."

"Master Henry." She lingered in the handclasp, in the warm approval he spread with a thumbstroke. "I'm honored you responded to my request." Sinking into the role-play framework she and Henry had agreed on, she settled her voice in a deeper, slower rhythm. Words carried the weight of meaning and choice here. Consent. Trust. "I've heard you have a knack for finding perfect pairings."

"It's something of a hobby. Graciously accepting perfection when its bounty is laid at your feet is the difficulty." In his exploration of Jay's toned chest, he paused his wandering palm at his sternum. "I'm grateful my boy Jay offered with such persistence."

Cheeks flushing pink, Jay bowed his head.

Henry surveyed the grouping of chairs and table. A slender ring of empty aisle, wide enough for two to stroll or pass, gave them privacy from neighboring arrangements. "May we join you?"

"Please." As she reclaimed her chair, she gestured opposite. "Have a seat."

Unbuttoning his jacket, Henry took the pale blue chair across from her. "Waiting pose."

Jay folded with the billow of a bedsheet coming off the line, his head back, his chest thrust forward, and his knees dropping into rounded, generous pleats.

Nearby conversations blipped into silent appreciation, and slight smiles spread in a graceful, widening fan. Whispers chased the silence. *First meeting ... I remember mine ... what a beauty ... poised and attentive....*

Henry rested his hand on Jay's head. "Have you a thought as to what you're seeking in a pet, Mistress Alice? Beyond compatible sexual desires. The bonds anchor themselves in mysteries hidden far deeper than genitalia, wouldn't you agree?"

"I would." In the last year, she'd turned the full one-eighty and left her mistaken beliefs about love rotting in a barren field. With the right people, those bonds had brought her to places not on any maps. The promise of adventure and the thrill of discovery created their own age of exploration and invention. Secret worlds inside them all, beautiful worlds, like Henry's quiet understanding and Jay's generous heart. "I want...."

What was Jay to her? The real question swirled beneath Henry's veiled inquiry. Get the answer right—be truthful—and she'd bring pleasure to both of her men.

"I want a playful pet who makes me laugh."

The way Jay scooped her up at any opportunity, or made goofy faces, or dished out over-the-top innuendo.

"A happy boy who's proud to serve his mistress."

The way he organized their room how she liked it, and in return he only asked she notice his effort. Acknowledge that his love brightened her life.

"I want to look in his eyes and see the confidence of a man who knows how loved he is."

His melted-cocoa stare, his subby-drugged happiness in a scene. The way he stared now, pleasure quivering from the depths of his eyes to the tip of his cock.

"I want a pet who'll work hard at his lessons, respect himself, and trust me enough to tell me when he needs more from me."

Because Henry was right, finding the balance didn't always come intuitively, even with years of practice. Jay guided them as much as they guided him. If he spoke in ways different from her blunt questioning, she'd learn to decipher his native tongue.

"And it wouldn't hurt if he were dangerously attractive." Licking her lips, she shot him her best sexy ogle, her eyebrows dancing.

"Dangerously?" As Henry tugged Jay's hair, Jay tilted toward his master.

"Mm-hmm." She captured and held Jay's gaze. "The kind of guy I almost can't keep my hands off of, whose clothes I want to shove aside while I'm nudging him onto his back on the couch on our first date. People say good girls don't want that—but I'm a good girl and I do, so people can say whatever they like and I won't care because I have what I want."

Rumbling approval, Henry shifted his knees wider. The cut of his suit hid his arousal, but Jay's stood in as a fine symbol for both.

"It just so happens—" Henry rubbed Jay's shoulders. "I may have what you want, as well."

"You know a good match for me?" Oh hell, coyness, right there. She'd have to remember that tone next time she wanted to wheedle a favor out of Henry. Like a nice flogging. Or anal sex.

His slanted smile said he'd deliver. "I have an excellent one with me tonight."

Including Jay's squirming hips and outthrust cock in her lazy survey, she settled on his sweet face. His grin rounded his cheeks, softened his sharp, masculine angles. "He looks well-equipped for satisfaction."

"As he appears, so he is." With his hand clamped at the back of Jay's neck, Henry rattled free an eager, moaning whimper. "This is my boy in his purest form, his truth running clear as a mountain stream."

"He has beautiful skin." The intimate lighting and low chatter in the salon crafted a newness, as if she hadn't run her hands over Jay a thousand times. Focusing her awareness on him fine-tuned the crowd to a low-level buzz vibrating in her blood. Henry had warned her about the fishbowl effect, but the *reserved* sign seemed to dissuade interruptions as much as encourage observers.

"Sun-kissed." Stroking Jay from shoulders to ass, Henry got a cat-stretch and wiggle for his subtle pride. "My boy shifts with the season, constant in his affections and ever-changing in his palette."

"It'd be a shame not to pet him." She extended her arm, palm up. "May I?"

Henry bent and kissed Jay's forehead. "Go and let Mistress Alice examine your charms, my boy."

Ribs swaying, cock swinging, Jay crossed the three feet separating them on his knees and resettled himself in his waiting pose directly in front of her. Hot breath washed over her calves as he bowed his head. "Command me if it pleases you, Mistress."

Jay's trust. Henry's trust. They balanced on a yoke across her shoulders, and yet the weight never bogged her down but lifted her up.

"Up on your knees, then." She cupped his chin, pulling him with her lightest touch, and he rose with trembling joy. "Let me look at the frame of this fascinating machine."

Desire pounded her fingertips with the constancy of the tide, tingling need flowing in and demanding she trace Jay like an unfamiliar blueprint. She couldn't grant him permission to come, not in the salon, though the need already made itself plain in his straining cock. God, so much trust in him as he watched her every move. She ached to topple him back and drop her pantyless self on top.

Not here.

Henry must contend with the same urges. But the war for control almost never showed on his face.

Mapping the ridges and hollows of Jay's throat set his cock jumping. His balls tightened.

"Jay." Her responsibility to see his cues and deescalate. "I have a task for you." As soon as she thought of one. God, don't let her look as desperate as she felt. Her heart thudded double time.

Coasters. Empty.

"I want you to fetch me a drink. Something sweet from the kitchen." Releasing Jay, she leaned sideways. "Anything for you, Master Henry?"

"Yes, thank you, that's a lovely thought." The intensity in his green gaze gentled, and he inclined his head. Confident in her abilities, he hadn't even unfolded his hands. "Water with lemon, my boy. A tall, slender glass. A fresh wedge, cut from a new lemon if one is available."

"Yes, Master Henry." As Jay bowed his head, his cheek brushed her arm. Almost her breast. "Thank you, Mistress Alice."

"Go on. I'd like a peek at your sexy behind." She gestured toward the kitchen, the entrance obscured by the steadily growing crowd. "Bring me back something nice—aside from yourself, stud."

With a broad grin and a grace balanced on the fine edge of humble and cocky, Jay sauntered off.

As he disappeared, she let out the last of her breath. "Jesus. How do you stop yourself?"

Henry perched on the front of his seat and steepled his hands below his lips. "From grabbing your waist and flipping you around on that chair? From tossing your dress over your ass, clamping my hands atop yours against that high cherry back, and taking what's mine?"

Her throat went dry. She'd need that drink now. "Uh-huh."

Eyes flashing, he returned to a neutral posture. "Because I enjoy the anticipation—and the denial. And I believe in the value of the rules in place here."

"He needed a breather." She had, too. The tight knots dotting the room bulged with players in the same game, a free-flowing mesh of glances and caresses and departures. They'd better make theirs before she missed a cue and caused Jay embarrassment. "The praise and attention had him on the edge."

"Mm-hmm. We'll sip our drinks enough to make his service worthwhile. You do seem parched, dearest." With his smirk, Henry offered a rare glimpse into his amusement. "And then we'll take him upstairs, where we might find a relief valve for his excitement."

Without questioning her assessment, he accepted her read of Jay's needs. Bringing their game outside the second bedroom, into a public-ish space like the club, challenged her skills—but she'd never shied from a challenge.

"You're doing well, Alice." Henry soothed in his rumbling baritone. "You found a method to give him space to calm himself, and you presented it as a command he desired, to allow him to fulfill his need to serve. I would have done the same. Have done, in fact." With no more than a green-eyed stare, he pinned her to the seat. "I'm finding it exceptionally difficult to refrain from rewarding your brilliance with an orgasm or three."

She clenched her thighs against the rush. Her readiness would seal her lips until one of her men parted them and unleashed an unstoppable flood.

Tilting his head, Henry lifted one eyebrow.

She followed his cue to a flash of bare flesh heading their way. Back in character. Jay's mistress. Not a fake role, but one with specific priorities.

"Of course——" Henry raised his voice, not truly overloud, but pitched for ears a dozen steps away and buried beneath black hair. "I would never send my boy off for an unsupervised play date."

"No, I understand." She matched his aloof tone, as if Jay's approach passed unnoticed. The salon's growing flock of players, too, she ignored, even as some strayed closer. Faces familiar from classes. Watching Henry work a negotiation, they'd paused their own extracurriculars. "He's a wonderful find. I'd be protective, too, if he were mine."

"If. Two tiny letters with a wealth of meaning. For the right woman, Alice—may I call you Alice?" He caressed her name, a long, licking 'L' and a melting "ice." She must've nodded, because he carried on with a flicker of a smile. "I'd consider a shared custody arrangement. Assuming the initial games are mutually satisfying."

A glass secure in each hand, Jay stepped between them and knelt.

"Shuttling your poor pet back and forth would promote instability. All that friction wearing him down." She plucked her glass free and drank deep. Sweet, wet, and cooling. "Excellent choice, Jay, thank you."

"I'm happy to serve you, Mistress." Relaxed and smiling, he preened under their attention. Despite his safely soft cock, his eyes shone. The club gave him something impossible at home—a quasi-public audience for his submission. Everywhere else, he buttoned up his need for Henry's dominance. "However you and my master see fit."

In a sensual slide, Henry trailed his hand down Jay's arm and claimed his drink. "I suspect we'll manage to find a frictionless fit, with suitable incentives." Tipping the glass and sipping became performance art closely watched by their adoring server. "The proper care of one's submissive is a tremendous responsibility. Thankfully, the joys in return are tenfold."

Henry took so much care balancing Jay's needs. His more blatant domination at home helped Jay power through the hours when he wouldn't let himself accept what he needed. The things he'd be ashamed to ask for.

"I can see you must take excellent care of him." The protected space here gave both of her men something they needed—the ability to show their true relationship without being judged. Without being shoved into boxes of masculinity that could never contain all they were to each other and to her.

"It's lovely when one has the leisure to study a potential partner, to learn their behaviors and quirks before extending an invitation." As he ruffled Jay's hair, his gaze never left her. "Yet still they surprise and delight us."

He'd catalogued her from the day they met. Assessing the purpose of each piece in her design, he'd determined the best shape for their three-sided relationship. The one he'd deem aesthetically pleasing, she'd call functionally efficient, and Jay'd name the smoothest ride.

"I took the liberty of reserving a room upstairs." Henry lifted the *reserved* tag from the table, creased the heavy paper at the fold, and tucked it in his breast pocket.

A courtesy, to let others claim the space once they'd left, but a memento, too. The sole question was whether the card would end up in her contract folder or Jay's—or if Henry had created a joint one for them as well.

Rising to his feet, Henry buttoned his suit coat. Command clung to him tighter than tailored fabric as he extended his arm. "Shall we adjourn to ascertain the exactness of our fit?"

She slipped her arm around his. "I'm honored, Master Henry." Pouring her impish joy into the title, she laid her head against his shoulder. "I have an idea or two for sampling your boy's charms."

"I thought you might."

* * * *

At a red-carded door, a nook tucked in a quiet corner of the third floor, Henry stopped. Blinds covered the viewing window. Releasing her arm, he turned to Jay, who'd trailed them with silent steps, up the stairs and through the halls, past countless others enjoying their service. The threshold of new adventure waited.

Henry clasped Jay's shoulders. "This room belongs to Mistress Alice tonight. Tell her your safeword, please."

"Tilt-A-Whirl. I promise to use it"—he shot her a sly eyebrow waggle over Henry's shoulder—"if Mistress Alice is too much for me."

She circled him and grabbed a handful of ass cheek, prompting an indrawn breath and a bobbing thrust. "I plan to be just exactly enough for you, stud."

"Will you obey Mistress Alice tonight, my boy?" Sweeping down Jay's arms, Henry coached him loose and easy, prepping his prizefighter for the improvisational thrill of the ring. Santa Will had claimed to be a boxer as a kid. Surely Henry had been his stalwart ringside support. "Will you treat her commands as if they were my own?"

"I will, Master Henry." As Jay craned around and peered down at her, he poured love and respect into his gaze. "Thank you for accepting my service, Mistress Alice."

"I couldn't ask for better." She kissed his cheek. Once the door opened, they'd be different people. The private people they always were and yet weren't. More fully the people they were all the time. Just—freer.

Henry's assessing stare slid into a crinkle-eyed smile, a match for her pounding heart.

She nodded to him. "Let's play."

Knob in hand, Henry gave the door a push. "Ladies first."

Once she flicked the light switch, her quick scan showed about what she'd expected—their classroom on a small scale, two rows of three desks. Henry's bag sat beside the teacher's desk. He must've sent a runner after Jay had changed.

"Everything appears in order, I trust?" Henry held Jay in the hall.

Her pet shuffled his feet. Shaping the scene with Henry for his approval, she'd been equally bouncy and impatient. Thinking on her feet. Wanting to start right away.

"You and Jay both," he'd murmured as he kissed her nose. "So eager to be teacher's pets."

"All good," she called. Deep breath. Spin. Smile. "Thank you so much for coming." She tugged Jay inside, his hand warm and comforting as he absorbed her jitters. "I'm kinda nervous about passing my practical. Having you as my practice student will crush those worries."

Henry entered last, shutting the door behind him.

"I'll need you to follow my directions through a few assignments while my adviser"—she gestured to Henry—"evaluates my performance." Enough detail to lay out a scenario for Jay, but vagueness, too, to leave room for the excitement of the unknown. "You'll help me look good in front of my teacher, won't you, Jay?"

"Yes, Mistress." He took the front-row seat she directed, folding his long limbs beneath the attached desk. Either aiming to impress her with his posture or bowing to Henry-ingrained habits, he sat straight and clasped his hands in front of him. "I have lots of experience with homework." He flashed his sweetest smirk. "If your in-class assignments are anything like those, you should get an 'A' out of me."

"Mm-hmm. We'll discover what I can get out of you." Tipping her head, she peeked under the desk and passed him by. Space would calm her racing heart. She paced a count of ten behind him, clicking her heels on the hardwood.

Henry leaned along the side wall, far enough to fade from Jay's awareness. This was her show. He'd unbuttoned his coat and pocketed his hands, a casual bystander, enjoying a performance he hadn't scripted. Unless she invited him in, he'd hang back and watch her work.

"Attendance first." She clicked to a stop at the back of the aisle to Jay's left. "Stand when I call your name, please."

A coiled spring of readiness, he vibrated in his seat as she rattled off three fakes.

"Jay."

He shot up. "Present, Mistress."

"You are, aren't you?" Crooning, she sauntered up and crossed rows. "Not like those tardy students who can't be bothered. You actually"— standing before him, she dragged a finger from his navel to his neck— "show up."

He breathed into her touch, pressing forward without demand.

"My star pupil." She tapped the desk. "Sit, please. Geography lesson first." An easy subject for Jay. A gamble for her, the chance for a pop quiz in case he stumbled and she needed to correct without punishing. "Who can name a state that borders Massachusetts?"

Jay thrust his hand in the air. He didn't wave for attention, but his arm trembled nonetheless. His taut body shouted a silent *pick me*.

"We'll hear from the front row on this question. Jay?"

"New Hampshire, Mistress." The pride filling out his tenor might have been for his home state or his pleasure in giving a correct answer. Maybe just for being her first choice.

"Excellent." Unable to stay away from him, from the strength in his shoulders and the misaligned strands of dark hair brushing his neck, she crept closer. "Stand when you give your next answer, please." She finger-combed his wayward hair and drifted down his sloping back until she hit curving wood. The seat confounded her need for him, blocked her ability to run her hands and her eyes to the last margin of her territory. Smart in theory, lousy in practice. "Beside your desk will be fine."

Murmuring assent, he chased her touch. The desk squeaked in a rubber-footed backslide with his shifting weight.

She drummed the honey maple under her fingernails. "Can you also name a state many people think borders Massachusetts but doesn't?"

With a jackrabbit leap, Jay launched to his feet. The desk rocked. "Maine, Mistress."

"Much better." The view, too. Ever-playful Jay flexed his gorgeous tight ass for her. "And still with the correct answer."

His squirming excitement deserved to be shared. Despite her in-charge declaration and the thrill of playing the lead role, Henry's silence registered as an absence. "He's a quick learner, isn't he, sir?"

Coat discarded, he watched them in his shirtsleeves, his pants rippling across a familiar thick outline. "I've always found him so. Particularly when he's in competent hands."

Jay, sighing, echoed her bliss.

"Such powerful legs he has." She crouched, near enough the heat of his arousal warmed her face, and squeezed her thighs against the urge to open for him. "Fluid movements." Tickling the backs of his knees, she set him prancing in a minuscule dance. "Are you a runner, Jay?"

"No, Mistress, but I'll run if you want me to." He had the energy. Running a 5K wouldn't soften the steel in his cock when he'd set his mind on a reward.

"Running's so hard on the knees." She palmed the insides of his, working upward along trembling muscles and taut tendons. Sturdy, studly Jay could go the distance. "A swimmer, then?"

"No, Mistress." He spread his feet by millimeters, a graceful slide pushing his stance wider and presenting his cock as if she hadn't noticed the beautifully plump head inches from her lips. "I ride my bike a lot."

The backs of his thighs earned a final stroke as she stood.

He whimpered, high-pitched and needy, but held his position.

"Speed and endurance." With tender affection for her well-behaved puppy, she scratched his stomach. He'd proved he had the stamina to wait and the faith to let her decide when and how he would be touched. When and how he'd receive his release. "What a perfect package you are."

His cock bounced. Did he think he could will himself into her palm? His urgent desire put him right on target for her plans.

"Let's see if you're as excellent at spelling as you are at geography." Stepping aside, she waved him forward. "At the board, please."

He took his at-ease pose, legs spread and hands tucked behind his back, wrists clasped above his ass.

Chalk pinched between her thumb and middle finger, she pressed the short stick into his right hand. "Writing implements up."

In unquestioning obedience, he gripped the chalk and raised his arm to the board. "Ready, Mistress."

"Good boy." Her arm fit snug around his hip as she closed her hand around his shaft.

Gasping, he jerked his hips and won a free stroke.

"I need a solid, reliable pen for grading." Soft and squirmy, all of him, except the rigid cock she teased with an almost-there massage. The short-trimmed, fuzzy hair surrounding him tickled her palm. "One that won't spill any ink until I'm ready to judge your work. This is just the one I want."

As if steeling himself for a marathon ride, he blew out a breath. "Thank you, Mistress."

"First word." Channeling his energy into mental work would distract him from coming too soon, but if he got out in front of her, she'd shorten the quiz. "Breathe." She matched action to speech, emptying her lungs beside his ear. "Breathe."

Chalk scraped and clacked as he shuddered. His swaying hips dragged her dress back and forth, so close they stood. The chalk fell silent. "Finished, Mistress."

"Good. That's good, Jay. Second word." She swept her nose along the top of his shoulder. "Nuzzle."

The crisp, woody scent of his post-work shower layered with his earthy musk. The sharp freshness lured her in with the demand to dirty him up, to make the lush depths of their combined arousal smother all else.

"Finished—" Her reward stroke caught him mid-word, and he stuttered into a tenor whimper. "Mistress."

"Wonderful. You're such a thoughtful student, Jay. Third word." She sealed her lips to his skin at his high-water mark, the divide between what his shirt covered and where the sun beat down on his neck daily. "Kiss." A second. "Kiss." A third. "Kiss."

As his cock twitched, she gave a quick, encouraging squeeze.

Chalk screeched. His second "s" gained a lengthy tail. He swiped his fist across the chalky trail and left a blur behind. "I'm sorry, Mistress."

"Penmanship under pressure." With slow strokes, she soothed his anxiety. "Would you like extra tutoring, Jay? More time with me to practice these skills?"

He moaned, quiet but unmistakable. "If I'm worth your time, Mistress."

If. Christ. She laid her cheek on his shoulder. Love by osmosis, hers soaking into him while she refilled from Henry, his understanding gaze landing on her and oh-so-worthy Jay.

"You're worth my everything." Her kisses morphed into gentle nips. "Fourth word, now. Are you ready?"

"I am, Mistress." Strong, slender, and eager to please her, he vibrated in the circle of her arms.

"Nibble." Warm. muscled shoulders fell beneath her tugging teeth. "Are you a nibbler, Jay? A long-legged jackrabbit like you, you must enjoy nibbling whatever slides between your lips."

His heart thrummed under her left hand, and the echo pulsed through his cock in her right. Pressed behind him, his nudity coursing prickling awareness everywhere they touched, she drew his excitement into herself. Stepped out of herself, as if her ownership granted her access to every wheel and lever controlling the flow of his arousal. As if they shared the same skin, the same mind.

"I do when it's yours, Mistress." He executed the slow, unfinished circle of the "e." "Or my master's."

"You do good work." Countless nights, now, she fell asleep in the aftermath of powerful orgasms he delivered with rolling waves of his tongue. "All that talent." Mornings, too, when she woke not to the alarm clock but to Henry's rumbling growl as he climaxed in Jay's waiting mouth. Her clit pounded, hot and needy. Time to skip a word or two. Jay didn't need drawn-out foreplay any more than she did. "Do you know what I like to work with, Jay?"

Henry perched against the teacher's desk, his lips pursed and his green-eyed gaze intent. Her game had reeled him in. Pride nestled alongside her arousal, a pair of spooning partners waking and stretching.

"No, Mistress." Clutching his chalk, Jay stood poised to write, to kneel, to come—whatever pleased her whims. Her pauses became his. Her desires, his.

"My hands," she whispered. Power at her fingertips. "Fifth word. *Caress.*"

She swarmed him. The sparse, swirling hair on his chest slipped between her knuckles. Abdominal muscles like finely embossed metal rolled and swelled and dipped with his breath. Narrow hips gave way to thick arrows pointing toward his pleasure. Skirting his cock, she gripped his thighs.

He flexed, unconscious alternation, as if he pedaled in place. A drop of pre-come splashed hot against her wrist. Three letters in, and his hand no longer moved.

"One 'r.'" Tracing the shape alongside his cock unleashed a whimpering chorus. "Two 's'es."

"Thank—" He shuddered, and his handwriting suffered, but he finished the word. "Thank you, Mistress."

"It's my pleasure to help you succeed." Fluttering her fingers around his cock, she raised invisible sparks on contact. "My privilege to show you what I want from you." Privileges Jay had granted her and Henry had allowed—no, encouraged. She grew into the spaces between them, tracing her own desires deeper in each expansion.

"Almost done." She firmed her hold. In Jay's sexual blueprint, forcefulness equaled security and desire. "Sixth word." She'd take care of him the way he needed. The way she wanted. "Stroke."

As she demonstrated, he scrawled the letters in a shaky hand. The chalk flashed up and down, and she matched the pace on his cock.

"I'm real close, Mistress." An unnecessary but adorable admission. The rich earthiness of his arousal surrounded them with thick, humming tension.

"I know. I know you are." Hunting for his ejaculatory edge, she upped her rhythm in a calculated push. "You're my dedicated student. I'm so pleased with you."

Cock trembling, he poured out an urgent whine. His balls tightened.

"This last word is a command, not a vocabulary exercise." Air flowed across her lips in a trickle, time slowing as Jay waited on her word. "*Come.*"

The chalk snapped between his fingers. Gasping her name, he bucked his hips. White jets streaked the blackboard.

She pumped with purpose, draining all he offered. Enough to spatter his grade, a sloppy but recognizable A+, below his list.

"I got an A?" Breath sputtering, Jay pressed his forehead to the board and slumped on wobbly legs. Relieved he'd held out so long, or cooling. She'd served his spelling lesson with a side of phys ed.

"Top of the class. Time to take a seat." Nothing soft showed itself. Her dress, but that was thin and she meant to keep it on. Hard desk, hard seats, hard floor. Shit. She should've planned better, because she wanted him on the floor but not uncomfortable. "A nice, soft seat for our star pupil."

Henry nudged the duffel beside the desk. "I've a reward here that ought to suffice."

Gratitude swamped her. Henry, bringer of the best gifts. Maker of the best plans. A challenge and an example, one she'd push herself to match every time Jay dropped to his knees at her feet, until she deserved his trust and devotion as much as Henry did.

She steered Jay toward the bag. "Go ahead, sweetheart." Pressing on his shoulder set him sinking with his customary grace despite his still-heaving lungs. "Take your prize."

As he opened the bag, he sagged against her, his weight a tingling reminder of her own deferred climax. Once she'd gotten him settled, his first touch would be explosive.

Jay raised his hands with a delighted laugh. Familiar, navy blue cotton silk trailed through his fingers. Mumbling thank-yous, he plunged his face in and inhaled.

Henry'd brought along their sheets, the ones she'd awakened wrapped in this morning. Nothing special, except Jay hugged them to his face and chest like he'd won the lottery.

"Good reward?" She tousled his hair.

"Us." Tipping his head back, he lifted the sheets, silky blue sliding over his arms.

Sure, okay, but he could have that any—— "Home."

He rewarded her understanding with his sunniest smile.

Their games were part of their relationship, but *they* were a them, an us, together, lovers, family, always. They'd go home to the same bed tonight after they'd wrung each other out. The secure constants Jay craved and maybe—no, almost certainly—the reason Henry had devised a lengthy, low-pressure approach to adding her to their relationship.

"Build a nest here, please." Tapping a spot directly against the class-facing side of the teaching desk, she bent and slipped off her heels. She'd never keep her balance in them once she put Jay to work. "I want my best boy up front with me."

Whatever Henry had wanted from her and whenever he'd wanted it, he put responsibility for Jay's needs first, and Jay needed a woman unafraid to dominate him. Gently, and with love, but one who wouldn't walk away, push him aside, or jealously compete for Henry's undivided attention.

"Yes, Mistress." He folded the sheets in a neat square, one of a hundred ways their expectations shaped his actions. "I like being near you."

Henry had held off until *she* was certain. Until she'd come to him and made the commitment—asked for an expanded contract, told him she loved them, felt ready to move in, agreed to try dominating Jay a little at a time. Where Jay rushed in, Henry tested every step with unobtrusive thoroughness, right down to packing their sheets in his kit.

"I adore being near you, too." Praising his folding skills, she sat him with his back to the desk and his face upturned. "In fact, I saved a snack to share with you." She swayed to her feet, dragging her dress across his face. "Are you hungry, Jay?"

"Starving, Mistress." He ruffled her little black dress like a warm summer breeze.

Positioning one stocking-clad foot with care, she wedged herself against the outer curve of his hip. "You'll eat whatever's put in front of you?"

"Uh-huh," he moaned. "I mean, yes, Mistress, I will, please."

"Good boy." As she straddled his face, she dropped her dress around him. He gripped her calves, palms kneading before he jerked away. "I'm sorry, Mistress, can I?"

"Use your hands? Of course you can. Thank you for asking." Squeezing his hips and ribs between her legs, she aimed to provide the powerful security Henry would in her place. "Hold your snack in both hands while you lick the center."

He stroked her legs as if the stockings mesmerized him. Under the dark veil of her dress, touch mattered more than sight. Touch, scent, and taste.

"Go ahead," she whispered. Tremors born of her long anticipation built and spread. "I'll tell you—" Christ, he'd found the borders of the stockings with his fingers and tongue, and his hair teased her thighs. "I'll tell you when you've had your fill."

Strands of hair dropping back in a gentle *whoosh*, he inhaled with the ostentation of an overzealous wine steward. A long, slow, pointed lick parted her. His satisfied groan vibrated as he sucked her clit inside his mouth. She was Jay's hard candy, and he'd melt every sugar molecule on his playful tongue.

The surge of heat sent her slumping to the desk and left her gasping for breath. A chemical reaction, Jay's tongue and her clit. Bringing the two together sent her soaring—and Henry loved watching them in flight. Recursive arousal, the three of them building lift and thrust in an endless circle.

Jay lapped at her thighs, her stopgap measure for containing her arousal after Henry hadn't allowed her panties. Teasing, he twined fingers and tongue around her garter straps and let them snap back. A bee sting, or the pressure of a hickey forming at the center of a burning kiss.

She tried to praise him with words as Henry did, but pauses and panting punctuated her love letters. Cradling her ass in both hands, Jay stuffed his mouth with her slippery lips.

While he devoured her with devotion, she repaid him with shaking knees and near-collapse. The desk's broad, flat surface kept her from smothering him between her thighs or sending them both to the floor. Verging on a new peak, she stiffened.

As Henry passed her, the hissing slide of his tie echoed her sighing satisfaction. He tapped the blackboard beside the last of Jay's work. His ink, her penmanship. "I see our boy's grade writ large. Is Mistress Alice"—Henry wrapped teasing warmth around her title—"ready for her evaluation?"

His tie dropped beside her, the thin end unrolling across her wrist. Scrabbling uncoordinated fingers, she snatched the rest. Jay and his flicking tongue sent her into climax with Henry's tie crushed in her fist.

Fabric fluttered. Henry's dress shirt, crisp and warm, dragged across her bare arm. Her cheek. Her closed eyes. Left behind as a makeshift blindfold, his shirt enveloped her in a Henry-scented fog. His belt jangled and rasped.

With sweet tenor growls, Jay shook her garters in his teeth.

The hem of her dress lifted. Exposure let in currents of chilly excitement, the heat of her thighs and Jay's breath no longer a secret exchange. Longer feet nestled alongside hers. Muscled legs wrapped her own. New heat grazed her ass.

Henry's shirt captured her unsteady breaths and fed them back to her. She didn't dare move, not an inch, not an anything, but Jay's unceasing attention rolled waves out from her center.

Knuckles bumped her inner thigh. Strong hands with a dusting of hair on the backs. Unmistakably Henry.

He gently separated Jay from her throbbing clit. Fleeting touches teased her with flesh on flesh, trembling anticipation of the unknown. Henry hadn't revealed his plans to her, only listened to her suggestions and helped her shape her scenario. They'd gone beyond that now.

As he slid his hand in a half circle, Jay whined, soft and low. Cupping Jay's cheek, maybe. Rubbing his thumb across those full lips, rubbing *her* in like a lip balm made for him alone.

"My good boy." Henry swept his cock down her ass and along her thigh. "Share with me."

Fingers curled under her stockings. Jay worked his jaw rapid-fire between her legs, but the lens of his attention had shifted. No need to guess where.

Henry, undulating without thrusting, rocked her hips against the desk and ran his hand up the back of her dress. The button edge of his shirt skimmed her ear. Whisked away, the fabric revealed Henry's deep green eyes before he captured her in a tender, melting kiss.

Her jittering arousal and orgasmic aftershocks coalesced in a sensual ball pulsing to his rhythm.

"Jay feasts on his fantasies." Bent over her back, Henry spoke in a low rumble. "You gave him the lovely, brilliant mistress he needs."

He toyed with the zipper at her neckline.

Tick.

Tick.

The teeth unclenched at an agonizing crawl.

He splayed his hands, spanning her back, and peeled the dress aside. The high neck and sleeveless fitted top became bands around her upper arms. Stroking her spine, he leaned in, nude and solid and with a weight, a presence, beyond size. "But that isn't what you are for me, is it?"

She shook her head, a nonverbal 'no' the best she could manage through ratcheting excitement at passing him control. Pinned by Henry, she lay exposed, her legs shaking as Jay worked magic with his tongue and crept up her thighs with groping hands.

"No, you're my good girl, my bold Alice." Sweeping her hair aside, Henry twisted a tight ponytail in his fist and heated her neck under an open-mouthed assault of nips and growls. "Shall we finish this night together?"

Her attempted nods pulled his grip tighter, reminded her whimpering, trembling atoms of the elemental truth of his power. Even as he reduced her to tumbling arousal, he lifted her up.

"Have you tasted a sufficient slice of dominance?" He nudged her thighs, the head of his cock slick and sliding along her lips. "Submit to me, my sweet girl."

Her half-moaned *yes* earned her a long, slow penetration. Two thrusts of solid heat, and on the third he pulled fully out.

She choked back her begging denial at Jay's moan. Henry jostled her to the same rhythm, twice, three times. He sank inside her again on the four-count. Again. Sweet fuck, he drove her to the brink with deep thrusts and denied her the release, feeding Jay his cock and the taste of her in between. She met him with arched hips. Anything to drive him further, faster.

Rationing his thrusts, he roused her greedy anticipation. Silent count, a chant in her head, one, two, three times their hips danced while Jay swallowed the prize. Four, five, six, Henry rattled her to her toes, his chest hair scraping her back, his breath thundering in her ear.

"Please." She welcomed the man who freed her from worry and doubt until only love and faith remained. "Please, sir."

Blanketing her, he closed his hand around her tight-fisted grip on his tie. Forehead pressed to her temple, he kissed her cheek. "Shatter," he murmured. "Let me feel you, beautiful girl, your vibrancy, your incoherence"—he nipped her lips—"your utterly divine moans and your quaking heat with every"

——one——

"delightful"

——two——

"plunge."

Three.

She jolted into climax on command, the signal racing through tingling lips, ringing ears, and aching breasts.

Growling, Henry chased her peak with his own. He jerked hard, their bodies slapping together, and held himself still. Christ, she praised the day they'd abandoned condoms.

"One last gift." The urgency of his whisper snaked through her luxurious haze. He spread his hand at the nape of her neck and adjusted his grip. "One he needs from us. One he'll love."

No question, then. She wiggled her ass. "Do it."

As he swept her back with a powerful pull, the desk flashed past beneath her. She stood upright in the nanosecond before he dug his knees into the backs of her legs and dropped her into Jay's lap.

Eyes rolling back, Jay thrust with jouncing hips.

She hurried to align their bodies and take him inside. Refilled. Bending backward, she planted her hands beside Jay's outstretched legs as he sang out his joy. She'd gone too far past orgasm to scale that peak again, but damn if she wouldn't enjoy the ride——and the view.

Henry muffled Jay's whimpers with a mouthful of cock. All hesitancy and public persona forgotten in the rapture of serving his master, Jay gulped him down.

"That's it," Henry murmured. Hands flat on the desk, he played her inverse, thrusting forward with his ass clenched and his thighs taut. His cock held firm, his erection slow to fade post-climax. "Take us both. Do you taste her, Jay? The same sweet wetness gripping your cock eases mine into your throat."

With Henry weaving his spell, Jay came quick and hard. She squeezed him tight, welcomed his thrusts, and rejoiced in his unconstrained enjoyment. Henry had been right. Boosting her confidence with a trip to the club had prepared her to set the example. To let Jay see her strength and find his own.

Fingering her hem, Jay cozied his head against Henry's shoulder as Henry settled beside them on their bedsheet oasis. "Thank you for tonight. I won't forget how special you made this."

Henry kissed his hair. "You deserve every moment, my dear boy. And Alice outdid herself in planning and execution."

As if he hadn't set the whole thing in motion. Framing Jay's return around the fifth anniversary of the night Henry had accepted his service, making it coincide with her own induction as his mistress, had been a stroke of genius.

"Oh, I missed a few things." Like not remembering a soft seat for Jay. Gotten more than a few right, though. She sashayed her dress over Jay's stomach. "Guess I know why my panties got banned."

"I merely provide tools for your imagination." Henry tugged her dress down her arms, collapsing the fabric to her waist, and idly stroked the breasts he'd bared. "How you play with them is your choice."

Subtle control. The thinking-five-moves-ahead dominance she'd begun to recognize and appreciate—and emulate. As if he'd handed her a toolkit and invited her to tinker. Henry opened her eyes to new strategies on his chessboard and fresh brushstrokes in his masterpieces.

Snuggling atop Jay, she tucked her head under Henry's chin and let him wrap them both in his strong embrace. She'd hold Jay in hers, at least a little while longer. "Happy first-date-iversary, stud."

Henry sure knew how to make a match.

Chapter 13

On Saturday morning, Alice nudged the last desk into alignment and joined Jay as he swung Henry's duffel over his shoulder. The second intro class for dominants had gone more smoothly than the first, with vigorous discussion and no outright assholes.

One persistent questioner remained, a stocky thirtysomething man co-opting their place at Henry's side. "She appreciates his assets. He's been the perfect occasional third for us."

"Occasional and permanent are vastly different levels of involvement." Henry steered the conversation into the hall. "Assuming he's interested in making such an enormous change, is she secure enough in your affections to tolerate the adjustment period?"

As she wrapped her arm around Jay's, he snapped off the classroom lights behind them.

"All secure," he whispered.

Giggling, she pecked his cheek.

The questioner jumped and glanced back. "Mine both already know how to obey me. They listen well."

"But do you? You plan to fulfill both submissives equally going forward, do you not?" Henry took long strides, his pace brisk. "How long has she enjoyed your undivided attention? How much time will fully integrating his needs require?" As he started down the stairs, his voice gained a hollow echo. "What will her role be in bringing him along?"

"Henry's making my mouth water with the analytical approach." By unspoken agreement, she and Jay stuck to a comfortable meander. Better to give the poor guy space than spook him with another giggle.

"You sure it's not his departure making you drool?" Jay swiped a finger across her lip. "Those dress pants tightening across his ass when he takes those big steps?"

"That too." Hitting the stairs, she dipped her hand in his back pocket. "I can multitask."

Jay wiggled his ass but held his tongue.

"I hadn't—" Mr. Clueless scratched his proto-beard-scruff cheeks. Compensation for the bald spot he had going. "I mean more should I tell them together or order him to pack his shit and get his ass to our place pronto and surprise—"

With one glare, Henry cut the guy off mid-word at the second-floor landing. "You're under no obligation to consider my advice, let alone follow it, but you owe your submissives the courtesy of giving this idea more deliberation."

"I have." A whiny, affronted edge accompanied the quick reply.

Henry resumed his descent.

The questioner hurried to catch up. "I've been thinking since the last time we had him over."

She and Jay, trading eyerolls and nods, moseyed along behind. "He's so missing the point."

Caressing the banister, Henry rounded the last curve and stepped into the lobby. "Ideally, you'll involve both of them in the discussion as equals."

He glanced up at them, his languid blink the lone indication of his suffering. Leap-before-you-look dominants made his teeth grind twice as hard when they wasted his time. This guy wanted a seal of approval for his awful idea, not an interrogation about its lack of merit. Henry'd try anyway. He wouldn't be the dom they loved if he didn't.

"Perhaps the occasional sessions are all the two of them require—and desire—together." Skirting the lobby proper, Henry led the guest straight toward the exit hall.

"But I want more." The questioner trotted alongside, disappearing under the arch. "You've got a great setup, with those two hanging on your every...."

"Just now?" Emma's alto floated up the grand staircase. Standing at the front desk, she spun and eyed Henry. "How many?"

Jay would want to say hello. Henry, too, once he'd politely disposed of the guest. Besides, they hadn't been the only ones having a special night out yesterday. Curiosity—and Jay's bouncing enthusiasm—carried Alice across the lobby.

Behind the desk, Daniel waved at the numbered boxes and mumbled answers. Their security staffer hadn't gotten the fun of throwing anyone out of class this morning.

Emma caught her lip between her teeth. "Did he say——" Spotting them, she tossed on a hasty smile and let the conversation die.

Well wasn't that a fun puzzle. Alice leaned against the desk. "Morning. Fair warning, Jay's gonna hug you twice as hard now to make up for not seeing you when we got here."

Arms wide, Jay offered himself up. The duffel swayed at his hip, the strap slung bandolier style. "I'm the chief hugger. Test hugs dispensed daily."

"Lovely to see you both." Emma locked Jay in a bear hug with slim arms turned to corded steel. "Is Henry coming right back?"

"He's schooling some guy with more sensitivity than I would." Thank God he didn't expect so much diplomacy from her. "He'll just be a minute."

Though why saying so added to Emma's nervous disposition didn't clear up the mystery. The older woman patted Jay's back with motherly affection.

A night out with Santa should've relaxed anybody. Hell, he laughed as often as Jay and with deeper gusto. "How was your concert? Last night, right?"

"Yes, it was wonderful." With a final pat to Jay's forearm, Emma slipped free. "Warm, but the clear skies sang with beautiful stars, and the orchestra was exquisite as ever." She smoothed her skirt. "Will's a thoughtful escort."

"Must be a long drive back in the dark." Not her subtlest fishing job.

A flush sprinkled Emma's cheeks. "I'm sure the drive is the same length no matter when it's made."

"I'm sure." Okay, maybe the adage was true, and people in love saw love everywhere. Emma's attitude toward Will didn't differ much from her attitude toward Henry——a big dollop of affection, a moderate one of deference, and an indiscernible amount of attraction.

"You should've stayed the night." Flashing his sly charm smile, Jay swaggered into the conversation. "He's got a huge"——he spread his hands wide——"shower. I know, I've taken lots of showers in my life."

Emma labored at a shaky laugh. "With the way you zip around town all day, I shouldn't wonder."

If Will and Emma had spent the night at the lake, the agenda tilted toward talking, not flogging. Still, Emma's legendary poise showed uncomfortable cracks.

Leech discarded, Henry reappeared in the lobby. What she wouldn't give for a psychic connection to tell him he'd walked out of one vexing conversation and into one equally confusing.

"Em, I wasn't certain you'd be in." Grazing Emma's arm, he pressed a light kiss to her cheek. "How was Tanglewood? Such a lovely night—did you bother with seats under the shed?"

"The lawn." For a moment, Emma's stormy blue eyes softened. "But never mind that." She nodded toward the exit. "Did you convert another to the church of Henry?"

As Jay snorted, Alice idly thwapped his chest. Better than opening her mouth and pointing out how often he attended worship services.

He snatched her hand and kissed the back.

"That one would need more than a few moments after class to bring around." Henry smiled at the two of them. Polite patience with lackluster students might drain his energy, but their playfulness restored him. "If he goes forward with what he has planned—and I use the term generously— he's likely to lose both of his partners in spectacular fashion. He'd do better to lay the groundwork than to spring such a momentous decision on them unilaterally."

Shoulders stiffening, Emma shot Henry a grimace. "We should talk in my office. Daniel, Master Henry needs his mail, please."

Daniel slid their cellphones across the desk. He raised two square-ish envelopes with a card dealer's panache. "The other, or...."

"Both directly to him, thank you." Emma's fleeting glance at her and Jay boded ill.

As Daniel passed over the cards, the top envelope revealed *M. Henry* in shining, embossed script. Fancy as a formal invitation.

Henry shuffled the invites. The tip of his thumb whitened, and the corner of the second envelope bent under the pressure. "In your office, then." Winter swirled in his tone. Stepping past the desk, he led the way.

The look she and Jay shared, following, didn't carry half as much amusement as their conspiratorial camaraderie five minutes before.

* * * *

Scooting into the office behind Henry, Alice pulled Jay along. Henry stalked toward the bookshelves lining the far wall.

Emma dawdled in the doorway. Of her own office. "You're certain you wouldn't rather—" Frown lining her face, she gripped the door handle. "Jay could stow that heavy bag and bring your car around."

The duffel hugging Jay's hip sagged from the lack of filler items to hold its shape. Heavy didn't describe the floppy canvas and leather by a long shot.

Henry jangled the keys in his pocket. A wealth of green-eyed intensity, he focused his dominant gaze on Jay. "No."

Jay transformed his lanky, loose-limbed stance into military precision. Back straight. Shoulders squared. With his bowed head, he revealed the submission, rather than confrontation, guiding his posture.

As inevitably as a magnet swayed a compass needle, the attitude drew Henry closer. Claiming the space in front of Jay, he rough-cupped his cheek. Their tension spilled over, raising the hairs on her arms.

"He's not a child, and I won't send him from the room while the grown-ups talk." A short slide brought his hand to the back of Jay's neck. Tight knuckles revealed the measured force in his grip. "My boy contains an immense inner strength."

A well refilled daily by Henry's love—and now hers. Bolstered by praise and control, Jay stood steady amid the swirling currents.

Henry tapped the envelopes against his thigh. "Tell us all of it."

As the door closed with a click, Emma pressed her back to the dark wood. "He insists you're poisoning subs against him, and he wants to demonstrate that he's what they need."

Jay's tormenter. Their efforts—the tea, the classes, the unexpected encounters at the party—had rattled Cal.

"Unacceptable. His greeting alone tells me the kind of example he intends to present." Releasing Jay, Henry raised the white envelopes. "You cannot allow him to infect this community any further, Em."

Did the satisfaction fluttering in her stomach make her a sadist, too? They'd come into Cal's playroom and transferred his toys to a higher shelf. Christ, she'd laugh her ass off watching him try to reclaim them with increasing desperation if those toys weren't people he'd hurt in the past or would in the future.

"Do you think I don't know that?" Emma worried the lines of pearls at her throat. "What do you expect I can do?"

"Stall him." Henry slid his finger under the seal. "Broken equipment." A loud, jagged tear opened across the flap. "Scheduling issues. A misplaced reservation." Extracting the note with two fingers, he bent his head. "A backlog of requests. Too many activities for the month. Put him off long enough, and he might redirect his attention."

At each suggestion in Henry's gruff recital, Emma shook her head. "I've run through those excuses in the last two months."

Since the night Henry first brought her to the club, when Jay's reappearance ignited the long-banked embers of Cal's cruelty. Maybe no "long enough" existed to make the jackass quit. Even five years later, Henry stopping his scene with Jay stuck in his craw.

"He refuses to be dislodged no matter how many inconveniences I contrive, and he complains to sympathetic board members at the smallest slight." Pinching a pearl, Emma took a deep breath and shed the speed her voice had gathered. "Him running afoul of Master Andrew in that business with Leah and having his priority privileges suspended was a stroke of luck."

After seeing Leah's well-behaved submission in the salon, he'd thought her a mousy target. Spectacular backfire.

"Enough rope to hang himself." Henry scanned the note he held. "He's become obsessed."

With reclaiming Jay. With getting back at Henry.

"He wanted the eleventh." Bowing her head, Emma wrapped her palms together. "He always does."

Jay jerked. Eyeing the cross-beamed ceiling, he trembled as if the floors above might collapse and crush him. Three stories pancaking until he stood alone in his fourth-floor nightmare.

With a low growl, Henry ripped open the second envelope.

"Every year. He——" Emma twisted her face with bitter too-much-coffee not-enough-cream distaste. "Discussing details of room and equipment reservations members make or why they might choose specific dates would be a breach of ethics."

Oh Jesus. Henry celebrated the good anniversaries with them. Cal obsessed over imagined wrongs. In the week before Henry and Jay had sat in the salon on their first date, Cal had been ignoring Jay's safeword and laughing. The idea of him marking the occasion every year——an acidic burn rose in her throat.

The second note crumpled in Henry's grip. "He can't seriously entertain the notion that the board will allow him to parade his misguided attitudes as teaching the other side of the argument. Consent is sacred. His 'other side' is assault and abuse and has no place here."

"I agree, but nothing can be done about it now." Pushing off the door, Emma waved at the notes. "His full privileges have been reinstated. He charmed the board into giving him the main platform for his show."

"You're the operations manager, Em." Incredulity or frustration might've lurked beneath Henry's neutrality. Impossible to tell when he went all dom-faced. "You make the assignments."

"And I didn't hear about this debacle until I walked in this morning." Coiled in on herself, Emma made a tiny target but one supercharged with potential energy. "This is the mess I get for taking a night away." Voice rising, she clipped her words between sharp teeth. "I'd have an easier time if you'd agreed to sit on the damn board. I told you——"

"And I told you——" With his no-nonsense tone, Henry commanded silence. "Will would do a fine job in my place. I cannot—I will not—put anything ahead of my responsibilities to Jay and Alice." Thick paper rustled in his fist. "They come first in my life."

The foundational, rock-solid tenet of their three-sided relationship. Alone or with friends or addressing a crowd of strangers, Henry never shied from vocalizing the depth of his commitment. Strength and honor weren't party tricks he donned to impress vulnerable submissives. He lived his beliefs.

"I would never challenge that, Henry. You deserve every happiness with them, the joy of a full house, of——" As her voice cracked, Emma shut her eyes. "If I can't protect the people I love, if I can't maintain the integrity of Victor's vision for this community, what use am I?" High-pitched anguish dwindled to a whisper. "I've allowed all I have left of him to crumble to pieces."

Cal infected more than those he abused. With his entitled attitude and his unwitting enablers, he splashed collateral damage. He slithered into the sanctuary and spat venom on the commandments. Weakened enough, they'd fall.

"I see." Henry stared beyond Emma, across the desk to the wall behind, where a whip hung looped with care over bronze hooks. "This is your confessional."

The office bathed in masculine elegance, a dark and heavy den of mahogany, walnut, and leather. The same as Emma's husband had left it, maybe. She surrounded herself with the pearls and the whip, with objects and images that spoke to her as her husband once did. Cal draped an oily shadow over the loving dominance venerated in these halls.

But Jay——surrounded by love and praise, kept busy with tasks, he let go of the mountain of hurt. Henry's love had ground Jay's insecurity to a fist-sized stone. To expel the betrayal forever, they had to crack the stone. Confronting the place had begun the work. Confronting the betrayer would crush the remnants to dust.

Two problems, two dominants to grasp them. Emma needed Henry's support now. For Jay, who carried Henry in his heart, Alice would be enough. She extended her arm.

Stepping past, Henry laid the envelopes in her palm as if they'd rehearsed the motion. The flicker in his eyes and the trailing brush of his thumb showed all the gratitude and praise she needed.

She skimmed the top sheet, a message written with a pen dipped in scorn.

...hiding behind your morning kindergarten for weak-minded fools ... wouldn't dare approach true practitioners of the art ... your fragile mastery couldn't withstand a challenge ...

"The window for discussion has closed." As Henry clasped Emma's shoulders, her indrawn breath rasped with the intensity of the first on a frosty morning. "You seek an outlet to expiate your guilt and frustration. To deliver Victor's judgment."

Henry's decision to make. Her faith in him raised no petulant, childish objections. However he handled Emma's pain, he would bring sensitivity and skill to bear. As she would, holding her tongue while Jay inched closer and peered over her shoulder.

Shuffling the first letter to the back exposed the second envelope.

To my craven, disobedient cockslut.

With one greeting, Cal'd set the tone for the demonstration he intended to give.

Dipping into her waistband, Jay rubbed the swell of her hip. Back and forth, in time with his breathing. A stroke of security, a reminder of his present circumstances, maybe, keeping him here with her and not tumbling into memory.

She ached to crack a joke——express surprise at Cal's ability to use the word *craven*, laugh at the ridiculousness of him applying *my* to Jay at all, or declare her cockslut solidarity and reclaim the slur with pride. But laughter, in shattering surface tension, left deeper hurts untouched.

"I cannot punish you as he did, *sverchok*." Henry's gentle baritone floated in stillness. "It's not my place, nor is it yours any longer."

Flipping the envelope to the back, she tipped her head against Jay's cheek. Cal's venom didn't burst into flames under the office light's yellow warmth. Pity.

You fear me, slut. I see it in your avoidance. You fear me because you know you long to submit. Your pathetic safe haven will never satisfy you. Does he make you scream, slut? Do you cry apologies and beg at his feet? Take the rest of your whipping like a good slave and someday you'll earn back the privilege of sucking my cock. Bring your little pussy and present her to me. She might gain you a reprieve. Does she cower as well as you do? No matter. She'll learn.

The note ended with a command to attend the demonstration Friday night. Cal's letter to Henry had couched the demand as an invitation to "honored guests," but the one to Jay made no attempt at pretense.

Jay, trembling, cleared his throat. "Are we going?"

If they didn't, Cal would control the conversation. He might reestablish credibility with the club's unattached submissives. Attending could be their chance to shut him down.

"Cal likely intends his offensive letters to prompt me to decline on our behalf." The low murmurs had stopped, but Henry held Emma in a one-armed embrace.

In a simple gesture, Henry anchored forgiveness and apology to swallow up panicked emptiness. Emma'd gotten struck by Cal's fangs. He'd gone around her and secured the slot through the old boys' network. She'd returned to the unexpected and out of control.

Alice had thrashed in a similar panic at Jay's departure, choked by uncertainty. With unrelenting questions and a well-timed flogging, Henry had driven out her fear. Emma needed a trustworthy dominant who would do the same for her. A discussion for another time.

"Not a pathetic attempt at goading you to show up?" Alice lifted the letters. The crisp, heavy paper ought to feel unpleasant, full of sweaty desperation. "He's hitting the testosterone bottle pretty hard."

Insecure bullshit wouldn't work on Henry, but macho posturing matched Cal's style. The jackass lacked Henry's patience and subtlety for waiting, watching, and predicting outcomes. He overstepped. He would again. But the right overreach, in a public setting? Henry was right. If they gave Cal the rope, he'd hang himself.

"He'd do better to try that on a man who hasn't the opportunity to prove his manhood whenever he desires." Henry encompassed her and Jay both in his smile, and his green eyes held a depth defining *manhood* miles beyond mere bedroom antics. "But I expect he knows that, which implies he wishes to achieve the opposite."

Jay plucked the letters from her grasp. Holding them in two hands, he read with eye-scanning absorption. He'd be fine. Fine. Henry's love, her love, had immunized him from the venom seeping from the ink. He needed her faith, not her coddling.

"So you decline, and he taunts the crowd with your absence and waves your return letter like a white flag." Wouldn't that get Cal's rocks off. Bragging how he'd bested Henry. "He'd woo them to his side by saying you were afraid to meet him on equal footing."

Attending lent legitimacy and power to Cal's challenge, but so did not attending.

"Precisely." Henry maintained an even tone, but his focus strayed to Jay, who stood oblivious to anything outside the margins of the pages. "In my rejection, I would cast him as a child playacting in his father's clothes, unworthy of dignifying with an appearance. He, in turn, would decry me as a coward."

Rocking in silence, Jay shifted in the rhythm of a hill climb, dogged and unyielding.

Emma ceded the comfort of hiding in Henry's arm. As she stepped away, she raised her chin and dragged a finger under each eye. "The membership would fracture, divided over how to define a master's strength and where to cast their contempt."

Surely Cal would have a backup plan in case they showed—hell, Henry would have half a dozen contingencies—but their presence might push him off the ledge. They should go.

Henry would never force Jay into this confrontation. He'd foster a safe atmosphere for Jay's growth, and he'd wait patiently until Jay understood what he needed to heal and asked for it. If Jay—

"I want to go." The letters fluttered to the floor at Jay's feet. "I want to go."

Yes. She held her breath.

Henry edged forward and stopped. A twitch exited his left pinky, as if he'd compressed every drop of excitement but couldn't contain the concentrated result.

"You believe we ought to attend the demonstration?" In using his bland testing voice, Henry demanded willful choice instead of blind obedience.

"You said—" Jay ducked his head. "A long time ago—" He shook off in a full-body shudder and stilled. "You said you needed to know how I'd react, seeing Cal. If I'd panic." Shoulders slumping, he fisted his hands and knocked them together. "And I did. Two months ago I did, and Alice stepped up like a boss, but I didn't. I let her down."

Bullshit. "You didn't—"

He waved off her half-formed objection. "You say it's fine, but it's not fine to me. I want to be the best me. The me who submits to you both because we all want our life that way and not because I can't do anything else."

Fuck what their attending did or didn't do for Cal. Jay deserved the chance to face his tormenter and shut the door on the worst point of his life. He needed to confront his fear and recognize down to the subatomic level, to every spinning quark, that Cal would never control him again.

"I want to be a strong submissive. A proud submissive." He drowned them in his dark eyes, in rich soil nurturing new strength. "I've felt that way at our apartment since the first time I walked inside and knelt at Henry's feet. And I felt it again here at the club last night, serving you both." Squaring his shoulders, Jay raised his head. "I want to go."

They couldn't protect him from this.

"I am—" A gruff whisper choked Henry's smooth, rolling baritone. "I am so very proud of you." He reached out, and Jay crashed into his embrace. "Though this won't be easy, you are more than man enough for the challenge. Who are you, Jay?"

"Yours." Forearms straining across Henry's back, Jay spoke fierce, swift, and low. "I'm your sleepy-eyed morning kisser and your sweaty-limbed afternoon showoff and your dinner-table setter and your unbreakable masterpiece. I'm Alice's teasing sweetheart and her horny stud, her personal heating blanket and her favorite speller. I'm a million and one things, and all of them are *Jay*, and all of them are loved, and I won't forget this time."

"Our Jay." Henry claimed him with the raw power he saved for moments when they overwhelmed his passion, an intense, dam-breaking kiss punctuated not by cracking concrete but by Jay's urgent, eager whimpers. Henry's gentleness crept in with comforting nips, tiny promises of a deeper claiming to come. "The unsurpassed pinnacle of Jay, because with each choice you summit a higher peak." Smoothing back dark hair, Henry kissed Jay's forehead. "Thank you for taking this journey, dearest."

"I love making you proud." Jay snuggled in tight. "That's Jay, too. I love knowing I'm safe, that I won't be ridiculed or rejected. That's the me I want to show. The confident me."

"Do you know how we shall accomplish our goal?"

Jay shook his head. "Show up?"

Henry chuckled. "Yes, that, but we shall leave the ribbons at the desk. Let your conscience rather than my commands guide your behavior. Say all you need to. Reject him wholly however you wish."

The longer she stayed with her men, the more her conscience sounded like Henry. Safe bet Jay's did, too.

"No ribbons." Jay squeaked. Wide-eyed terror streaked across his face. With hard-won determination, he narrowed his gaze and chased it off.

Beautiful. So fucking beautiful, Jay mastering his fear and choosing the hard path.

Jay nodded. To himself, to them, to his ever-shrinking insecurity. "No ribbons."

Chapter 14

"Red, sir?" Caitlyn reached under the counter.

With a sharp slashing gesture, Henry cut the air. "No, thank you."

The young staffer sneaked a glance at Alice. "Of course, sir. I should have remembered. Yellow?"

"No ribbons tonight."

Despite a week of preparation, with nightly interrogations and quizzes, Henry's words cranked her pulse. Jay had to be shaking in his skin. But he had to confront Cal without restrictions. She blessed her fidgety lover's knuckles, one leisurely kiss at a time.

"Graduation," Henry murmured. Damn straight. Jay'd made valedictorian, and he'd fucking ace this ceremonial sendoff. "Alice and Jay have attended the dominant ethics class twice. They won't be granting anyone control over them this evening, Caitlyn." As Henry tapped the counter, two hard clicks echoed off the high ceiling. His bare left wrist edged out from his cufflinked dress shirt. "Please mark them as my guests without the submissive notation in the ledger."

Wide eyes flashing toward them, the green-ribboned girl inclined her head. "Master Jay, Mistress Alice. Please accept my apology for not greeting you upon your arrival."

"An unintentional oversight." At least she sounded cool and collected, for all the frenzied adrenaline pooling in her muscles. Kicking the shit out of Cal and stepping over his fetal body would've been her preferred opening move. "No apologies needed."

"We'll overlook it, of course, Caitlyn." Jay, voice rolling naturally after hers, poured out sincere understanding. Henry's watch glinted on his wrist. "You couldn't have known."

A sigh escaped the girl's parted lips.

Alice held in a laugh. She'd sighed, too, when her men had exited the bedroom in their matching stone gray suits and Henry-green flourishes coordinated with her dress. *"If you like the ties"*—Jay unzipped his fly and waved his favorite green undershorts at her—*"check out my extra layer of protection."* She pecked his cheek. No ribbons, but hers and Henry's all the same.

Caitlyn pivoted at startled-bird speed. "May I render you another service, sir? Sirs? Madam?"

"No, thank you, Caitlyn." Ushering them aside, Henry delivered a fond smile. "Your service has been carried out to perfection as usual."

"Have an enjoyable evening, sirs, madam." A wistful twinge lightened her tone.

Halfway up the curving staircase, Alice caught Caitlyn staring after them. "Poor girl." As the bend led them out of sight, Alice exaggerated her sigh and squeezed Jay's hand. The more lighthearted they started the night, the less nervous Jay would be. "You've given her another fantasy. Now her crush isn't only on Henry."

Jay snorted. "If she wants me to dominate her, she'll have better luck with fantasies than the reality."

Nudging his hip, she dropped into a sultry purr. "And if I want you to dominate me, sir?"

"Yes, ma'am." Sly-voiced and straight-faced, he managed a credible Henry impersonation. "Just tell me exactly what you want me to do to you. In great detail." He hung back a step and gazed up at her. "Then order me to do it."

Straight faces collapsed. Her giggle spurred Jay's smirk into full-blown laughter and converted Henry's smile into a chuckle.

She patted Jay's chest. "You got it, stud."

A shared glance filled her with Henry's pride in them. He'd been extra firm with Jay all week, demanding and challenging, and put him to sleep wrung out and relaxed nightly. Shared Jay's shower tonight, her men's growls and whimpers vying with the pounding water for her just-home-from-work soundtrack.

Arriving on the third floor, she schooled herself to seriousness. Greetings and introductions blurred. Henry presented her and Jay to every face he recognized in passing, and he recognized a solid eighty percent. By the time the hallway opened up into the main demonstration room, she'd offered two dozen gracious hellos in as many feet.

Jay held up beautifully, confining his fidgeting to a respectful handclasp. If his strokes across his watchband stood out to her and Henry, no one else would know.

Henry'd gotten the old-fashioned timepiece from his grandfather at his prep school graduation. Fastening the watch around Jay's wrist, he'd shared the advice that had come with the gift. *"A man of honor keeps his word, even in so small a thing as arriving on time. Truth ought to be as quick as the minute hand, trust as hard-won as the hours. When little truths grow into large trust, the satisfaction of a life well-lived is sure to follow."*

The demonstration hall teemed with players. Rows of chairs lined one side of the main platform, where the spotlight beamed down on an empty X-shaped frame. The spillover grazed a trio standing nearby.

"I see Emma." A distraction might break Jay's staring contest with the padded wood. "Do we know those guys with her?"

"Board members." Henry's dry tone added *in Cal's corner* to the plain pronouncement. "Those two will expect an impressive show, particularly when they've granted him the night as a personal favor after Emma's repeated refusals."

Emma tugged her ear. The men with her laughed, one gesturing at his brow.

"Are they talking in secret code?" Maybe Emma wanted them to ride to her rescue. "Is someone stealing second base?"

Gaze straying to Jay, Henry hummed soft and low. "Talking shop, most likely. Victor scarred his ear in a single-tail accident. He always said he was lucky he hadn't lost an eye. He insisted on safety gear for anyone he trained."

She scanned the crowd for a non-whip-related topic. Jay hadn't bolted, and Henry kept a subtle watch over him, but still. Cal would show up with whips soon enough. If the jackass invited Jay on stage, she'd need more than Henry's strong arms to hold her back.

"Santa's here, too." Much closer than Emma, he stood chatting with a gray-haired man the size of a toothpick beside the North Pole. "We should say hello."

Ending his staring contest with the equipment, Jay raised an instructive index finger. "Ah-ah, he's Master William tonight, Mistress Alice."

She claimed his arm, linking their elbows. "As you say, Master Jay."

He giggled with her. Giving him time to acclimate had been a smart decision on Henry's part. She offered Henry her other arm, and he gamely joined their promenade to Santa's side.

Turning, the gray-haired stick revealed himself.

"Master Laurence." Henry dipped his head. Protocol prevented him from greeting Will first. Courtesy, or seniority, or something else in the complex web of etiquette in play. "The board appears well-represented tonight."

Santa William eyed her with unusual care. Not ogling, though the teardrop cutouts in her pine-dark dress left her back and stomach bare. Will's tie made a subtle show of solidarity, its cheeky pattern of golden nautical knots resting on a deep green background. While Henry and Master Laurence exchanged small talk, he scanned Jay with searching intensity.

He knew. His pursed lips and rounded cheeks held back a jest—she'd stake her dress on it.

"And your pets, of course." Like a stone skimming still waters, Master Laurence skipped his gaze across them. "I see you're traveling with both today."

She slipped her arms free and extended her hand. "It's a pleasure to see you again, Master Laurence."

The old man's stuttering eye-dance almost ruined her straight-faced determination. She clenched her tongue between her teeth.

"Ah." The gray-haired master stiffened. "Mistress Alice." With a quick tilt, he shifted her hand from shake to lift before grazing the back with papery lips. "An unexpected pleasure."

Expelling a jolly laugh, Will grabbed Henry in a burly, backslapping hug. "You've armored up your little ones. I must say, they wear it well." As he twinkled sea-blue eyes at her, he greeted Jay with a solid handshake. "How does your new power feel, Master Jay?"

Jay, grinning, shook his head. "It chafes a little, sir. I mean—"

Will hugged him with the manly embrace he'd given Henry. "You're a credit to your master, Jay, in any guise." Gruff whisper delivered, he released a blinking Jay.

Ostensibly brushing out wrinkles in his suit, Alice rubbed Jay's back. "There you go. That's better."

Jay rocked to equilibrium, his gratitude tucked beneath his sheath of charm. "It's a night for the emperor's new clothes. Just my luck, I got stuck with real fabric."

For now. They hadn't discussed the night's end, but Henry undoubtedly had plans for every outcome. In the best, Jay's courage would be rewarded with a full weekend of heavy submission and plenty of exercise.

"Master Laurence, if I might ask—" She scuttled the question she most wanted answered, about why the board would allow Cal to present, as nosing too far, too fast, into club affairs. "What are your thoughts on proper attire? You wear such handsome vests."

As the older man launched into his answer, Henry graced her with an eyebrow salute. Master Laurence took roles seriously. Gender roles, maybe—he carried old-fashioned women-are-children notions—but mostly lifestyle roles. She'd presented as a submissive at their first meeting, and he'd accorded her less status. Now she presented as a mistress, and he spoke to her with an accommodating, if pedantic, attitude.

"My guests of honor have arrived," Cal called. With black leather pants, a whip holstered on his belt, no shirt, and a wide-brimmed hat, he overshot sensual power and landed on cartoon ringmaster.

Jerking to attention, Jay returned to fidgety watch stroking while Master Laurence halted his dissertation on patterned socks.

"The emperor himself," Will muttered. "Someone ought to burn his closet."

Snickering with Jay, a welcome crack in his tension, she sidled closer. He'd have to project his strength in front of Cal, but she could buttress him.

"How exciting." Cal approached, his shark smile gleaming. "I suppose you simply couldn't stay away."

"No, not with your thoughtful invitation, so painstakingly worded." Henry studied Cal. "Though I do apologize. I missed the directive to don costumes."

As she bit her lip, Jay ducked his head and Santa turned a chortle into a cough. Only Henry and Master Laurence maintained polite neutrality.

"You miss many things, Henry." Cal sneered with pretty-boy ugliness. "But I'll demonstrate them all." He flung his arm in a grand sweep. Toss in a handlebar mustache and a red coat, and the ringmaster illusion would be complete. He probably thought he looked fantastic. Blind to his flaws—in dress, in mannerisms, in recognizing the basic humanity and dignity of other people. "I've reserved you a place so you'll have an unobstructed view of the proceedings. I know how you love to watch me work."

How dare Cal bring up the night he'd assaulted Jay as if his grotesque betrayals belonged amid casual chatter over cocktails. As if Henry hadn't castigated himself over and over again for not stepping in sooner.

In silence, Henry weathered the jab with a stone's equanimity.

"Do try to keep your jealousy in check tonight." Sneer reappearing, Cal glanced at Jay. "Stealing is bad form."

"So is continuing without consent." She darted into the conversation with more righteous anger than conscious thought.

"You've brought the kitten who clipped your balls." As Cal ogled her, his slippery ice-blue eyes threatened freezer burn. "Is she growing a cock now?"

Palming her back, Henry lent her his calm. Goading Cal would be ineffective if she lost control. She had to keep hold of herself if she meant to keep hold of her men.

"Don't need to." She slid her hands past the edges of tailored suit coats and cupped Henry and Jay. "I have two perfect specimens right here."

As Henry kissed her temple, Jay brushed his lips against her neck. Warm breath and nuzzling noses eased her surging blood pressure.

"I've always been an overachiever." Dual twitching cocks more than gratified, but she chased other quarry tonight. Releasing her gentle hold, she pasted a bored glaze on her face. "Not everyone has"——she eyed Cal's skintight pants with disdain—"impressive enough qualifications."

"Your pets are bold, Henry." Irritation flickered in Cal's eyes and rippled through his voice, but he held himself together with frequent glances at Master Laurence. Impressing the board might rank higher in his goals than knocking her, Henry, and Jay down a peg. "They've forgotten their manners."

Someone had. Sniping at Henry and her without so much as a hello for Master Laurence, Cal had misstepped. But the older master issued no reprimands, answering with bland neutrality all but the initial surprise she'd handed him in her ribbonless state.

Narrowed eyes and lowered brows suggested Cal had caught on. "And you've forgotten to tie pretty ribbons on your pussies. How will we know they're yours? You're too soft for anyone to know you're a dominant otherwise."

Emboldening Cal with his silence, Master Laurence sharpened her hunger for details of the master's talk with him after the business with Leah.

"They're dominants in training today, Cal." Henry, naturally, ignored the slur against his own skills. Only jabs at his lovers merited attention. The rest flowed beneath his concern like so much sludge to the sewer. "May I present Master Jay and Mistress Alice?"

As Cal's amusement crumbled, his lips twitched in a proto-snarl. "Are you making a joke?"

The old man might support Cal——or he might be observing how far Cal would go if no one steered him back. Master Laurence hadn't objected to Will's characterization of Cal as a naked fool. But he sat on the board, and the board had agreed to tonight's demonstration.

"Speak to my partners all you like." Warning scraped along Henry's neutral lilt. "You may be assured they'll respond in kind."

Equal footing. A hard place for Jay to stand, but a necessary one. The freedom to recognize he owed nothing to Cal beyond the barest courtesy required of all club members.

"You make a mockery of dominance. True masters would be appalled." Cal's scowl deepened, his twisted mouth an angry red scar beneath the glass-sharp shards of his eyes. "The cunt maybe has fight in her worth beating out. But this bitch?" He waved at Jay with five fingers she ached to grind beneath her heel. "He was born to live on his knees. He's a whining, cock-hungry fuck-slave, and that's all he'll ever be."

Rage darkened her vision, turned the lights fuzzy. An iron band enclosed her wrist.

Henry.

Sweet Christ, she'd almost hauled off and decked Cal.

Fist pinned to her side, she unclenched trembling fingers. Henry had silenced his cutting insights. Will had muted his diversionary humor. She had to settle her anger and let Jay shine. If he stumbled, they'd all be in place to help—but they had to let him go, first. To feel his worth himself, not handed to him in others' praise. To acknowledge his value, real and distinct from their love.

Jay stood unbowed. Quiet sincerity flooding his deep brown eyes, he met ugliness with faith. "I'm not a slave."

"You're a slave dressed in a master's clothes." Cal fingered the whip hanging at his hip. "Purely because your so-called master enjoys being dominated by his fucktoys."

"I decide what I am and who I'm with." In his unblinking stare, Jay carried Henry's implacable grace.

Like a defensive dog expecting the snap of teeth, Cal raised his chin sideways.

"I made the wrong choice a long time ago." Hands clasped behind his back, Jay measured his truths by the minute hand. Slow, steady strokes. "I respected someone unworthy of my respect."

Leather flicked at Cal's hip. A single brass snap kept his bloody threat holstered.

"I know better now."

Henry threaded his fingers in hers.

"And when I choose to serve—" Jay breathed deep and thrust his shoulders back. "It won't be you, Calvin Gardner. It'll never be you."

Elated, she throttled the urge to thrust a triumphant fist into the air. To shout until her throat went raw and her cheers dried to a rattle.

The whispers of nearby eavesdroppers would have to suffice. Jay
hadn't raised his voice, but he hadn't tempered his tone, either. A low roar
raced away, fueled by the perpetual motion of the rumor mill.

A red flush ruined Cal's icy composure. "You aren't fit to lick my
boots." Pitching his voice overloud, he spilled adolescent insecurity, a
thirtysomething who'd never grown up. "I have a better class of slaves
waiting. It's time to prepare them for their debut." His abrupt spin slapped
his whip against his thigh. "Master Laurence, I appreciated your vote of
confidence at the board meeting." With his sidelong sneer, he targeted
Henry. "It was well in keeping with my father's wise decisions when
he ruled here. If you'll excuse me." Scurrying off, he pushed his way
through the crowd.

Henry, glancing after him, hummed quietly. "How like Cal to believe
the board rules rather than serves."

Wrinkles overtaking his face, Master Laurence pursed his lips. If God
were gracious, the just-enough-rope approach dangled in his head. He'd
seemed disappointed over the Leah situation. Maybe he'd grown tired of
managing an old friend's sociopathic son.

"That was—" Like autumn leaves fluttering to ground, tiny tremors
rippled through Jay. "That was *amazing*."

She flung her arms around him. Fuck the watching crowd. Impetuous
and eccentric could be a good look for her. "I'm so goddamn proud of you."

Over her shoulder, Henry claimed a rough kiss. Brief enough for
decorum, long enough to send relaxation cascading down Jay. As Henry
drifted back, a wisp of happy-Jay-whimper floated by her.

The lights flickered, two times. The milling crowd shuffled toward the
waiting seats.

Henry squeezed Jay's shoulder. "We may go if you like."

Tucking his lip in his teeth, Jay eyed the platform and its St. Andrew's
cross. "The victory would be just mine. He'd target other people here."

"He would." Low-toned and serious, Henry smoothed Jay's lapel from
the mess her clinging embrace had left. "Whether his bad behavior is your
responsibility to obstruct is a question you must decide for yourself."

Fidgety nods escaped first. "I want to stay."

They claimed seats in the so-called place of honor the staff had roped off.
Delicate short couches acted like box seats to the front and right of the filled
rows of sturdy wooden folding chairs. Master Laurence and Santa William
claimed one couch, and Emma and her board-member escorts a second.

When all had settled, Alice sat between her men. Henry laid his arm
across the sofa back in a masterful stretch. As tight as the men hedged her

on either side, Henry's hand rested square against Jay's back. She'd have rather snuggled Jay between them, but the appearance of independence benefited him. He'd get his snuggles at home.

The overhead lights dimmed. Striding into the spotlight came Cal, his booted feet thudding up the three steps to the platform. Behind him trotted two hooded figures on leashes.

He blathered on, playing the ringmaster in a showy, arrogant speech devoted to a litany of his own talents. "And, of course, hold applause until the end, lest your appreciation impinge upon my concentration." He strutted to the front and tipped his hat toward them. "Welcome to our honored guests from the board, who require no introductions. If I may, I'll dedicate tonight's demonstration to Henry—excuse me, *Master* Henry, our beloved coddler, who prizes safety over pleasure. What a wonderful mother he makes."

Henry remained unmoved. A handful of chuckles spilled in a crowd approaching a hundred, ten rows of ten seats of awkward shifting and silence.

As if he expected a cape to swirl behind him, Cal spun about and stalked away.

"Cal's mother wishes she had such a hard cock for her pleasure." Will's whisper heralded low, spreading laughter as the quip traveled.

Back stiffening, Cal clicked his heels to a stop. "Not all appetites are so tame." Standing between his subjects, facing the crowd, he spread his arms wide. "There's pleasure in danger when I hold the whip."

He stripped the subs' cloaks to the floorboards.

Snatching her hand, Jay wrapped them together on his knee. "I'm not leaving."

The man on stage shifted lean, muscular legs, the lanky strength in his calves and thighs leading to a trim waist and firm abs. Sparse hairs dotted his chest, and he boasted a thick, shaggy mop of black strands falling across his forehead. With his soft brown gaze, he surveyed the crowd in a state of attentive calm. His waiting pose.

Jay looked out from those eyes.

Oh God, she was going to be sick.

Henry tightened his embrace. A deep inhale brought her the gentle bite of citrus, light and fresh and oh-so-welcome.

"Not leaving," she echoed. But Jesus Christ.

Flickering beyond Henry's solid bulwark, audience members rotated their stares between the stage and their resolute trio. No fucking wonder. The woman, dark blond and curvy, carried attributes a smidge more generous up top than her own, but Cal more than made his point with the pairing.

"Step forward and be seen, slave." Cal scooped up a short crop and slapped the man's thigh with it.

Yelping, he skipped front and center. His brown eyes flashed below the fringe of his hair before he bowed his head.

"Seen, I said. Not heard." With the crop, Cal prodded between the slave's legs. "Spread." When the man widened his stance, Cal drew back the crop. "Be still."

Balls swaying from the hit, the slave confined his flinch to a silent grimace.

"What's this? No thank-you for your master?" As Cal switched him, rapid strikes on his inner thighs, he targeted Jay with his stare. "What an ungrateful slut you are."

Though the slave shuddered, his cock rose. "Please, master, this slave is sorry and thanks—"

"Too late. You've been ruined by impotent masters who dole out praise when punishment is deserved." Cal's shit-eating grin at Henry made adding *fuck you* redundant. "Retraining is a must."

As Cal delivered punishing slaps, the crop whirred like playing cards tucked into bike spokes. Jay'd shown her on his spare bike one Saturday. They'd ridden up and down the street, building up speed, fake-revving their "engine" as the turning back wheel snapped the cards over and over. A fun sound. Sickening, now, when thighs glowed exit-sign red and tears streaked the slave's cheeks.

"Proper order must be maintained. Slaves are a carpet of bones and flesh for my amusement. When they rise above their station?" Twirling his crop, Cal glared at Jay. "Well, it's the cross and the whip for you."

Jay turned her fingers white, but his face masked the distress leaching from his grip. He and Henry sat unmoved as matching bookends, a mix of boredom and faint disapproval graven in straight lips and slow blinks.

Scowling, Cal circled his slave and studied him face to face.

Anticipation. Henry mastered them with their own excitement most days. His murmured promises—

Cal straight-armed the slave in mid-chest. Grunting breath billowed out, and the slave stumbled back. His shoulders hunched as he sucked in air.

Arm extended, hand raised like a stop sign, Cal laughed. "To the cross, slut."

The biddable Jay-copy complied. Cal manipulated him into position with flicks of his crop. Red splotches rose along outstretched arms and legs.

Henry had taught her to follow his tune with teasing feathers and gentle hands. When they played, her heart sang a giddy harmony with his and Jay's.

The man strapped and padlocked to the heavy frame met his master's training methods with gritted teeth and wide, rolling eyes. Skittish as a horse confronting a prairie rattler.

Cal unsnapped his whip. The coils thumped at they dropped to the boards, and the slave flinched. Stepping closer, grasping handfuls of muscled back, Cal grinned. He raised the whip handle—a fat, foot-long leather-wrapped club—and extended his arms over the bound man's shoulders.

"A slave serves at his master's pleasure." Jamming the handle against the slave's throat, Cal throttled him with a two-handed grip. "The animal's own enjoyment"—he kneed the gagging slave in the balls—"though sport for laughter, is unnecessary, and ought to be strictly controlled."

The whip hung around the slave's neck, the weighted handle and stinging tail dangling down his back. His breath came in pained wheezes.

Cal abandoned him. At the corner nearest their seats, he slowed his swagger and stroked the bulge in his fancy pants. "A master, of course, is free to indulge his appetites where and when he will."

He must have trapped Jay long ago with the seductive charm he poured into the smile he targeted her with now. His lone trick, useless when he couldn't resist showing the serrated teeth waiting to tear into fresh meat.

As he leered, his eyes lit up. "He compels obedience from mouthy bitches using every tool at his disposal."

Calling on her is-this-boring-ass-lecture-over-yet face, she gave him no edges to gnaw or scabs to pick. Audacious jackass. As if she'd jump out of her seat and beg to join him.

Cal worked his jaw sideways and stalked away.

A *humpf* sounded behind their couch. "He cheapens his gifts—"

Holy shit, the quiet, gentlemanly resignation was coming from Master Laurence.

"—with such a distasteful attitude."

The nude woman on stage remained in the spotlight. She'd watched the cropping and binding with nonchalant interest. Either she'd perfected her mask of indifference the way Alice and Jay had at home all week, or she truly didn't care about her co-submissive.

Cal passed behind her. Without a word, he yanked her by her hair, twisted her neck until she faced him on her knees, and ground his crotch against her cheek.

Nothing of Jay's worship or her own love for sucking Henry's cock came through the woman's dead-eyed gaze. She allowed Cal to mash himself against her, but she wore the vacant stare of a clock-counter. How many minutes until her shift ended and her life would be her own?

In Cal's hands, a pile of leather and buckles became bonds for the woman. Sleeves captured her forearms behind her back, and straps secured her wrists to her ankles. She rested on her haunches, immobilized.

Cal kicked her knees wide. "The animals must know who is the master here." He dragged his boot, a scuffing rasp on the boards, and probed her sex with the black leather toe. Grabbing her by the hair, he jammed her face into his groin.

The woman uttered muffled groans and swung her shoulders, a pendulum out of balance.

"Their fear and struggle is the master's reward for his toil." Paying no attention to the woman at his feet, Cal reserved his sadistic glee for eye-fucking Alice. No telling how often he'd jerked off to this scenario with her in the key role.

But anger lived in the growing furrows across his forehead. He pumped his hips, violent thrusts rattling the rings on his slave's gear and knocking her knees against the platform.

"They quake in terror, as they should." Cal glared. The jackass had loved her quaking and crying the night they'd met. Her indifference almost seemed to offend him. "Their fate is mine to command."

She faked a yawn and leaned into Jay. "Smile like Henry stepped into your shower."

Jay laughed. He sure as hell hadn't expected her whisper, and his surprise bolted through an all-natural grin. "He did."

With a low hum, Henry declared the recollection a happy one.

Cal sealed his slave's nose and mouth.

Escalating violence. Every time she and Jay refused to respond with pain and fear, Cal upped his cruelty and lost another piece in his powerful image. He couldn't safely control partners. He barely controlled himself.

Oxygen-deprived, unable to wrench free, the woman writhed in futile, awkward jerks.

Cal's truth ticked by. Thirty seconds. A minute.

Murmurs washed through the crowd. A striking redhead in steampunk chic, leather-and-buckle Victorian, stood and snapped her fingers. The man beside her jumped up.

"We're going." Leading him by a leash attached to his collar, the mistress exited the row. "This isn't the brand of obedience I want you to learn. We'll stop at the desk and sign you up for Master Henry's next class."

Squealing, Cal backhanded the slave at his feet. She landed sideways, thumping in a heap on the hardwood stage, and spittle flew as she choked.

"Try that again, and I'll knock every tooth out of your smug-bitch mouth."

Holy fuck. In her struggle for air, his scene partner'd left teeth marks in the crotch of Cal's leather pants. She didn't act near as cowed as the man he'd left tied. Part of imitating the "fight" Cal ascribed to Alice? The insolence he was so damned determined to beat—or fuck—out of her.

"Fuck you. You didn't say fuck-all about choking." The bound woman wheezed and rasped, her voice raw. "And I like air in my lungs."

Cal dragged her back to her knees by her hair. "You'll take what I have for you, wherever I put it, and if air can't get through, you'll learn to breathe cock."

Wresting her head back, the woman laughed. "With that?" She nodded toward his groin. Her bite had deflated Cal's interest.

"His cock must be allergic to laughter," Alice whispered. "He's melting like a wicked witch in water."

As Will's bass guffaw boomed behind her, Jay laughed and Henry snorted. He'd been reading them *The Wizard of Oz* on storytime nights for the last month.

Cal swept up his cast-aside crop. "This is *my* show. I will have proper respect."

The woman flinched from Cal's slapping strikes at her breasts. "Knock it off, asshole. I agreed to this submissive role-play shit and the hair dye because the money was—"

Cal belted her with his closed fist.

Gasps rippled from the front row to the last. Henry tossed a pointed glance at the board members behind them. No money exchanged hands at the club. Professionals played elsewhere, by different rules.

"Calvin, did you pay this woman?" Master Laurence's words came creased with disappointment, a napkin folded around a distasteful bite of a dish better left uneaten.

"A thousand bucks." Rocking on her bound arms, the woman managed to roll sideways. "Three hours' work, he said."

Membership fees covered upkeep for the building and equipment. The charter forbade payments between individual members for activities inside the club. Pay for play violated the community spirit.

Behind her, hushed voices rose as board members argued. "——appalling lack of judgment."

The whole place operated as a nonprofit social club. The philanthropic arm supported programs to end sexual assault and domestic violence. Too bad they'd taken so long to cut out the spreading rot in their own house.

"No, no, Master Laurence. All part of the scene." Face flushed. Cal turned his back on the woman and stalked toward the cross. "Surely my word of honor has more worth here than that of a poorly trained submissive." He unlooped the whip from the male slave's neck. "She's been coached, of course, to be deserving of punishment. I meant to show the sort of behavior other members' submissives get away with." Glaring at Henry, he cracked the whip. A testing stroke.

Locked to the cross, his slave shuddered. In a worm-wiggle of hip and elbow, the woman crawled toward the far side of the platform while eyeing Cal.

Alice battled the heart-galloping urge to interfere. "I don't think she's lying."

"Nor do I." Henry swept his knuckles down her arm and squeezed her fingers.

"——childish grudge turned tantrum." The whispering among the board members intensified. Cal'd fashioned his own noose.

Cal raised his voice over the growing din. "But some few still understand what it means to submit."

The whip snapped.

Moaning, the slave drove forward and sagged back. "Th-thank you, master."

Jay, pressing hip to hip and knee to knee, stared unblinking as the whip fell. Cal's strikes outpaced the slave's supposed gratitude. Distinct thank-yous grew into a droning mumble.

The flood left the slave cringing from the onslaught, each *crack* the impact of a tree trunk, the slamming pain weakening a tenuous hold on safety. In his destructive nature, Cal cared nothing for limits. He smashed his toys and reveled in the pieces.

Blood beaded on a long diagonal.

The whip fell again, and the slave's scream broke the chain of chanted thanks.

Cal bared his teeth in a fierce smile. Panting and sweaty, he raised his arm.

Tears and spit dripped from the bound slave's chin. "Please." He gulped for breath. "Please, I didn't know."

"I give it what it deserves." Cal flicked the whip and raised a fresh cry. "Its fear spills forth. Submission is weakness——"

"Please, no more." The slave's shaking suggested a precursor to shock. "Please, master."

"——suitable for animals who cannot attain mastery." The whip descended.

Acid seething in her stomach, she forced herself not to look away. Jay hadn't. The demonstration needed to end. The woman's admission should've been enough. What more did the board members need to recognize Cal didn't play by the rules?

Swinging his head, the slave squinted with dark, pinpoint eyes. "Please." His voice cracked.

Cal laughed. "The fun has only begun. Do you imagine you have a voice here?"

The slave sagged. Cracks caused by Cal's chilly disregard and stinging games might be racing through him, hidden stresses surging to the brittle fracture point when a final touch would shatter him. Once broken, a man——

Shooting to his feet, Jay attracted a hundred gazes. "There's no shame in stopping." On a cautious slant toward the stage, he approached the slave from the side. "Whatever he told you, whatever he promised, the choice is still yours."

——only found himself again with hard work. And so much bravery.

"Do you see this interference?" Playing to the board, Cal swung his arm toward Jay. "This time is mine. Granted to me."

"A master with true control doesn't fear pausing to check his partner's health and safety." Hands clasped tight behind his back, Jay rubbed Henry's watchband. "He understands safewording isn't cowardice or a slight against his skills."

Cal cracked the whip. The tip danced shy of the front row. "Eyes on the stage. I'm the one you came to see. Unless you'd rather watch me peel the arrogance from this fuck-slave parroting his owner's philosophy."

Sidelong glances and low retorts spread.

Raising his head, the shaking slave stared at Jay.

"You can say 'red' when you've had enough." Jay dominated the hall, the crowd quieting as though he spoke to them all and not his curious mirror. "He won't admire you for taking a beating. He won't listen for what you need. But we're listening."

The whip shot between them. Braided leather curled around the slave's ribs from back to front and scored his stomach. He screamed. *"Red."*

"No. No, that's not fair." Cal yanked the whip to his side. "It doesn't get to say. My slaves don't have safewords. I haven't allowed that babyish whining in years. I decide when the game ends. I decide."

Will vaulted onto the platform and ripped the whip from Cal's hand. "No, you don't."

The leather thumped to the boards.

Emma issued commands in a low alto, and black-banded play monitors took charge of unbinding the woman huddled on the platform and the man draped over the cross.

The man fixed his gaze on Jay.

"Do you see, now, how deep the insubordination and disrespect run?" Stepping away from Will, Cal spread his arms for the crowd. "I demand redress."

"Paying for submission? Disallowing safewords?" Will gripped Cal's upper arm and jerked him to face the board. "That's two stains against the fundamental tenets every master and mistress here commits to follow in their membership agreement."

Unable to shake loose, Cal struggled. Wild panic showed in his darting eyes.

Will clamped a second hand on his shoulder. "I'm satisfied with Calvin's demonstration of his own unsuitability for continued membership. At least one of his partners will require medical attention, and neither appears to have been an entirely willing participant. Gentlemen and lady of the board? What say you?"

Cal's laughter reeked of hysteria. "It's not enough for Henry to jump up his fucktoys and flaunt them in my face, now he has his bulldog interrupt my demonstration without cause. He can't stop my show. He can't—"

"He can." Master Laurence pushed himself to his feet. "He is obligated to do so, both as an honorable master in this club and as the newest member of its governing board."

"What?" Cal's screech reached the rafters.

"Master Jacob's retiring," Will drawled. "I've been appointed to fill the remainder of his term until the next election cycle. The board finalized the decision this afternoon. Did I neglect to mention that? Silly me."

The crowd roared with acclamation and congratulations. Henry's suggestions to Emma hadn't gone unheard. The board seat had gone to Santa, and the power and prestige—and responsibility—had gone with it.

With gracious thanks, Will nodded even as he kept a firm grip on Cal. Hell, his smile probably owed more to having the bastard's arm twisted behind his back.

Beside the platform, Jay helped his lookalike into a robe. Henry's steady competence showed in his smooth motions. Calming the skittish colt he'd once been. His lips moved, though his voice didn't carry. Two black-ribboned monitors stood by and let him work.

Grasping Henry's hand, she turned up his palm. The lines traveled far. Eyes on Jay, he hummed a rising note as she traced them.

"You've been playing chess." Tinkering with the guts of the machine, in her parlance, an infinite machine with uncountable and intricate moving parts. "Long game."

His dark gaze grew less opaque, as if he'd invited her into the green wilds and she'd stumbled onto a cleared path. He pressed his lips to her brow in blessing. "The most satisfying ones always are."

Henry set pieces in motion and found satisfaction watching others step into positions he'd cleared for them. Jay discovering his strength, Will joining the board, and Cal being removed. Henry didn't demand a place in the spotlight for any of it. He'd mastered invisibility.

"You could've been the one standing up there." Though Santa had a good handle on the situation. And on Cal. Sulky, struggling rage was fast becoming her favorite look on him.

"Victor would have had it so." Henry glanced at Emma, who stood conferring with the other board members on stage.

"Not you, though."

"Had it fallen to me in years past, I might have taken up the mantle. Running the club has never been my dream, though I might have settled for the task had you and Jay not come into my life." Standing, he smiled broadly and offered her his arm. "Will has long desired this, and the timing is right. He deserves the leadership role. He'll make an excellent guide."

"He just needed to be seen as one." Taking down Cal made for a hell of a first day on the job. Santa would build a reputation as a decisive but fair governing master.

"Appearances." Henry tucked her arm into his elbow. "Real or illusory, much rests on them. Over time, the image one projects may sink deep enough to become the person instead of the role."

Following his gaze to Jay as he shared his deep well of compassion and wisdom, she basked in the reflected thrill. "And they finally see the strength and beauty in themselves that others see in them."

The robed slave threw his arms around Jay. A nanosecond of surprise flashed in Jay's eyes and stopped his mouth before his empathetic reflexes took over. He shot the pair of them a brilliant grin.

Wandering closer, Henry chuckled. "Our boy does take after you, dearest."

"Me? What'd I do?"

"Inspire others." He nodded toward Jay and the man huddling against his chest. "He has his own Leah."

Yeah, he kinda did. The younger man clung to Jay for stability the way Leah had done to her until her master had arrived. He'd be adrift until he found a Henry like Jay had. "You know this means you'll have to find him a nice playmate who isn't Jay."

"Actually, I believe that responsibility falls to Will." Humor lurked in Henry's eyes. "We'll simply offer a suggestion or two."

"——me through the front desk." Disentangling from his unexpected embrace, Jay chattered like they were at home. Comfortable and safe being himself. "Emma will make sure I get the message. Do you shoot hoops? I know some other subs you should meet. We might start a regular pickup game."

Radiating self-confidence, he shone brightest in the room. Jay took fucking fantastic strides with adorable swagger. Maybe the day when he'd kiss Henry courtside in the park had grown closer.

"Immediate expulsion, then." Master Laurence's declaration wafted over the crowd. "A unanimous decision."

Will marched Cal to the stage steps. "Walk or fall, I don't care which."

With noisy, booted disdain, Cal clomped down the risers. His sweeping glare encompassed them all.

She shot back a sunny grin. Emperor's new clothes. They'd pantsed the bully and paraded his flaws. Word would spread to those who hadn't attended. And the best part was that he'd done it to himself in a Henry-engineered design.

"We'll have your belongings boxed up and delivered. You've forfeited your privileges." Handing Cal off to a pair of play monitors, Will stared him down. "You're no longer welcome here."

"My father——"

"Your father." Command swirling, Henry dropped into his dominant voice and paused the world. "Your father was an arrogant but respectable man with an enormous blind spot for the flaws of his offspring. Your behavior caused his rift with Victor. You cost him the goodwill of his friends and drove him from his home, and still he defended you. You're a disgrace, Calvin."

"I am a master." Cal ground out the words between clenched teeth. "You will treat me with respect."

"You were never a master." Jay, his hand on the former slave's shoulder, mimicked Henry at his blandest. Delivering facts so obvious they needed no emphasis. "Your title is as empty as you are."

With Emma's wave, the play monitors hauled Cal away. He hurled invectives and pleaded for a hearing but received turned backs and silence. Fitting for Jay to utter the definitive statement of Cal's tenure at the club. He'd earned his right to pass judgment in blood.

Emma, Master Laurence as her escort, gathered up Cal's demonstration partners and sent them on their way. Medical care and statement-giving awaited them downstairs.

"Well done, Master Jay." Emma straightened his tie with a teasing smile and a touch of fussy mothering. "Master Henry." She inclined her head. "Mistress Alice." The smile she shared with Alice and Henry carved a harsher edge of grim satisfaction.

With Cal ousted, his clique would follow him into exile or learn to play by the rules. The club would regain its balance. Santa would reinvigorate the board, and Emma would reclaim her place shepherding submissives.

Master Laurence patted Emma's arm. "Time to tend to the last of this nasty business." With farewells for them, he steered her toward the exit. The other two board stalwarts fell in behind. "Will's been telling me he has some thoughts for making certain this ugliness isn't repeated. I thought we might fit in an extra meeting."

The crowd thinned as the excitement ebbed. The area behind the stage had quieted to the three of them and Santa William.

"Plenty of good ideas." Will clasped Henry in a bear hug. "I wonder where I got those."

"I'm sure I haven't the slightest notion." Henry hugged back, hard, and disengaged. "It does me good to know you'll be at the helm. Your guiding hand is sorely needed. You'll do wonders for Em."

Will snorted and shook his head. Stepping in front of her, he threw his arms wide. "Mistress Alice, may I?" At her nod, he boosted her off the ground in a hell of a hug and planted a bushy beard kiss on her cheek. "You keep these men in line, now. I don't want complaints about them running wild in this club."

"Oh, they know"—she landed in the gentlest of set-downs—"when to be wild and when to be gentlemen." Her glance at Henry met his. "Might be what I love most about them. They're both a two-for-one deal. I never have to settle."

Jay got the same polite inquiry and hardy hug with less floor-leaving.

Shrugging his suit coat into place, Will sighed. "I hate to run, but I have shiny new responsibilities waiting downstairs."

"And I've a date with two deserving submissives at home." Henry draped a dark, hungry net over them with his gaze.

Will winked. "I'd offer to trade, but I doubt the world holds enough of anything to sweeten that deal."

Not for her. She reeled in Jay and claimed a kiss. Threading her fingers in his hair, she pushed every ounce of her love into him.

"No, not anything." With an intimate murmur, Henry wrapped them in boundless affection. "I possess exactly what I want."

Chapter 15

On Friday afternoon, Alice plowed through her third straight hour of searching for the magic numbers to push the Frellinger project's fail point into the safe zone on the stress sim analysis. In a blur, a pine-green lunch sack settled beside her elbow.

Eric the humble stood by her desk. "Bike messenger left this. I told Nancy I'd bring it up."

"Thanks." She projected a professional, asexual impression at work. So no asking if the messenger had been a whippet-thin tower of muscle with shaggy black hair and a charming grin that covered every expression from Bashful Boulevard to Cocky Lane.

"Welcome." He shuffled off. Uncurious guy for an engineer, with zero creativity but a solid baseline for their design pod, married, dependable, and completely uninterested in teasing her about a secret admirer. His deskmate would've announced the delivery to the room and asked if her bang boy could send him lunch, too.

She swiveled the insulated bag. The pink delivery tag bore Jay's logo and listed the sender as *available upon request.* Two taps would put her on the phone with Henry, requesting he make himself available. Inappropriate at work, but tonight was a play night. He'd cooked up a new way to tease.

Fingers tingling, she tipped out a bento box and a sealed envelope. The heavy cardstock held a nap like velvet, rough and smooth. *Miss Alice Colvin* graced the center in Henry's neat, swirling hand.

She sliced the edge with her letter opener. A trifolded paper landed in her palm.

Alice,

This note comes frightfully late, but I do hope you recognize the sentiments behind my missives arrive with a wealth of forethought and deliberation. Please enjoy all of your mid-afternoon snack, as dinner will be flexible—shall we say fluid?—this evening.

Not to worry, all is taken care of. I believe you know your dual responsibilities by heart. We shall see tonight.

Yours,

H.

The computer simulation ran merrily along as she resolved to obey and enjoy her almond granola mix, peanut butter, and tightly wrapped apple wedges. Every bite of the slow-burning stamina treats sparked anticipation of Henry's sure intention to wring the energy from her later.

At quarter to six, as she slid her key in to enter Henry's domain, the apartment door swung open without her push.

"Gear drop, please." In formal dress pants and a button-down, Jay gestured toward the side table. "If you'll leave everything here and follow me?"

Henry had started the game an hour early. With a shiver, she abandoned the day and the outside world with it. "Is the master of the house otherwise occupied?"

"You'll meet him when you're properly prepared." From the way Jay's eyes danced, his solemn tone and unfidgety stance qualified as marvels of Henry's engineering. "He's very particular about his guests' comfort."

"Is he?" No Henry occupied the living room, and no shouts of greeting came from rooms beyond. Memory overlaid milieu, night after night of surprises, the risk of the unknown and the body-shaking rewards of the courage to submit. "I could go ask him."

"No peeking." Jay took her arm gentleman-style and steered her to the bathroom. "Your instructions are inside. If you have—" Gazing up, he silently repeated himself.

"Take your time." Whatever Henry's plans, Jay would insist on executing them to perfection. If she rushed him in her excitement, she'd twist him between the desires of two masters. She rubbed his forearm. "I'm enjoying myself on the arm of a handsome escort with excellent manners."

He leaned in, warmth emanating through his thin shirt, and his tension eased. "If you have any difficulty requiring further explanation or wish to cancel your reservation, please open the door and inform the host with a single word of your choosing." His natural smile emerged. "Do you have a word you'd like to use, Miss Colvin?"

"Oh, I don't think I'll care to use it—"

He snickered.

"—but I'll go with 'pistachio.'"

"Very good, miss." He snapped his feet together and raised his chin. "I'll relay your sentiments to the master."

"You do that." Stretched on her toes, she planted a kiss on him. "You made me leave my wallet, so this'll have to do for a tip."

As she descended, he chased her lips. "Way better than money."

She pecked his cheek. "And that's for bringing my afternoon snack."

"Who, me?" Flashing a too-innocent blink, he shooed her into the bathroom, where dimmed lights over the mirror created a shadowed, sensual atmosphere. "I'd love to collect more tips, but you're supposed to be relaxing. Kissing me'll get you all rowdy." With a slow pull, he narrowed the gap, an ever-thinning slice of Jay smiling at her until the door landed in the frame. "I'll be back to knock when it's time."

Alone.

Two syllables so different when she no longer cut herself off from their relationship with every closing door. Her anticipation grew untainted by the fear that tonight might be the last night.

An envelope propped on the counter bore her name in Henry's script. A second new note for her collection, treasured all the more for their recent rarity. For ten months, they'd graced her door every other week, but in the last two, sharing a home and a bed, Henry had delivered her instructions in person. She pressed the invitation to her nose.

Rose petals. Not Henry's leather-and-citrus, but the sachet he'd used to support the note scented the envelope and ivory cloth.

The sweep of a washcloth between her legs, a lifetime ago. Warm water, fading inhibitions, Henry encouraging her to surrender herself into his care. From him, she'd learned to slow time, to crystallize moments in contemplation, just as from Jay she'd learned to exist in the pure joy of those moments.

Heaviness settled in her breasts. The silk of her bra, so comfortable all day, grew into chafing confinement.

With a soft rasp, the note slid free.

Breathe, Alice.

Her laugh broke the silent spell. She'd kiss that arch tone from him, take him inside and not let him loose until she'd transformed him into the fucking-hot pure dominant who growled and gripped her neck when he came.

My bold love. In the last year, you've granted an uncountable number of my wishes. One might endeavor to catalog the stars in the sky or the sands on beaches the world over and finish the task before reaching the limits of your wonders.

Sensitive, revealing-himself Henry melted her, too, turned her insides to sticky syrup and heated her over a steady flame.

Tonight, my desire demands your indulgence. Indulge, Alice. This next hour is yours. I recommend a warm bath to heighten the rose scent and raise the temperature of your toy—

She flipped the washcloth back. Her heart-shaped plug waited with the black bottle of silicone lube. A fiery rush coiled around her legs and under her ribs and out her mouth.

——as you play, but the choice is yours.

It always had been. Henry's confidence came from knowing what he wanted and showing his pursuits the not-insubstantial benefits of agreeing. He hadn't forced her down this path.

I'll send Jay to you with further instructions. For now, enjoy your playtime. Use your toy to reserve a place for me. I intend to press my claim later.
Until then,
H.

"I love the way you press." The letter carried a whiff of citrus. His darker notes, the rich leather clinging to musky male, she'd have to retrieve from the source.
With her new letter tucked safely aside, she ran the bath as she peeled off her work clothes. The rose scent drifted up from the water. Nude, she breathed deep. The mirror mimicked her motion down to her flaring hips. Breasts lifted, stomach rounded, she held for a ten-count and let go.
A different woman than she'd been a year ago. Then she'd needed to hide and regroup. To rationalize her desires and push away her uncertainty over Henry and Jay's interest, expecting the thrill to fizzle out too soon.
The woman in the mirror today believed in love. She'd lived with love's gentle caress and breath-stealing truth. She no longer wondered what her men wanted from her but rejoiced in what they built with her.

* * * *

A shave-and-a-haircut knock interrupted her floaty daze.
"Delivery," Jay called with a cocky tease.

"Come in." As the door opened, she mustered an imperious wave. "You can put it anywhere."

Jay waggled his eyebrows. "I'll leave that to Henry."

Water sloshed as she struggled to hold in her giggles.

"Damn, that's not my line. Forget I said that." He swung a black dress inside, hanging it on the door hook, and laid sandals on the counter. "The master wishes you to dress and present yourself in the dining room when you're ready."

"Then I won't keep him waiting." She stood. Water sluiced down her body. Courtesy of a gravitational assist, her toy tugged. Her breasts throbbed in the steamy, scented air.

Surveying her, Jay dissolved into breathless, open-mouthed appreciation. He swiveled the door handle up and down, his fingers clenched around the antiqued bronze. He met her gaze boldly, his eyes round and dark, as he dipped his head. "I love you, Alice."

Flashing his widest grin, he dashed away.

Rather than investing in new extravagance to mark their anniversary, Henry had pulled out a memory, her backless halter dress and summer sandals. Last year, she'd donned them in her studio across the hall, wondering all the while whether she'd be overdoing things, trying too hard to be sexy for her uninterested neighbors.

"God, was I wrong." She slipped on the lightweight cotton and spun. As the hem teased her knees, she clenched her toy. "I'm a lucky, lucky woman."

Hair shaken free of its loose bun, she tamed the steam-frizz. Henry hadn't left makeup on the counter, and Jay hadn't delivered any. Best to go without, then. Clamping her lips for color, she stepped into her sandals and opened the door.

Her footfalls echoed on the hardwood. Snapping strides, but slower than her heartbeat. Relaxing her ass, she let the weighted toy dangle and shift with her swaying hips.

Jay maintained a perfect waiting stance beside the table, his stillness rich with potential energy. A command from Henry—maybe even one from her—and he'd take her here on the floor however she asked.

But beyond him, Henry examined her with a regal tilt to his head and a devouring hunger in his slow-sweeping eyes. "Hello, Alice."

Fuck pretense. She returned his once-over, from his shiny shoes to the black dress pants covering powerful calves and thighs but not fully hiding the bulge at his groin, and onward, to the classic white dress shirt and the gleaming cufflinks above his artful hands.

"Hello, Henry." She took her time at his face, tracing the strong curve of his jaw, the straight line of his nose, and the growing curl at the corner of his mouth. A man she loved lived behind those bold green eyes.

He extended his arms, palms up. "May I offer you a seat at my table?"

"I wouldn't say no." Covering the distance, she left behind the uncertain novice she'd been. Laying her hands in his seemed a meeting of equals.

"So often when one is beset by incredible beauty, the moment passes more quickly than the eye can capture. The opportunity is lost." Kissing her cheek with European flair, he brought her the scent of his mastery.

Rich, dark leather invaded her senses, an oil slicking her desire for his dominance. Gathering his fragrance, she imitated his kiss too late to brush his cheek.

"But occasionally——" He nuzzled her nose as he switched sides. "If one is supremely lucky, fate presents the chance to revisit the composition." He kissed her opposite check, and she reciprocated. "To offer an alternative form, one once limited to fantasy now made possible."

He handed her into the chair. Plates stacked on the island suggested dinner would be coming, but the dining room table held only an ivory linen tablecloth over a cushioned table pad.

She rocked in the slipcovered seat, toying with herself and letting her satisfied sigh escape. Henry loved to hear their pleasure. "Are you offering me a fantasy, Master Henry? I've been a good girl. I followed all of my instructions."

"Perhaps I'm offering you a fantasy of my own." He gripped the corners of her chair back. Looming, imposing, he raised the fine hairs on her arms with his proximity. "But if you wish to play, you'll have to say so explicitly."

Jay's shuddering breath beat her own by half a second.

Share a fantasy of Henry's while he played out their first night together with a new script? Christ yes. She licked her lips in a bid for time to collect the scattered atoms pretending to be thoughts in her head. "You mean you want to fuck me?"

Humming, he teased her bare shoulders with tiny spirals. "I mean we intend to fill you up, Jay and I, until you've no room left in you and still the words spilling from your lips are all *more*."

Her belly burned so hot her toy ought to be liquefying. "I understand the game, Master Henry. I want to play in your fantasies."

Fuck, he growled his fucking power growl and Jay whimpered and the room flickered like flames, shifting in and out of focus with her breath.

"If you're able to stand in the morning, my sweet girl, I'll consider it a personal failing."

In the morning, hell. Her legs wobbled in the chair, and he'd done no more than kiss her cheek and talk to her.

"But for now—" He bent and placed his mouth at her ear. Exhaled, slow and controlled. "You know what I want from you. Do it without being told."

Bondage. Tighter than any cuffs could safely be, firmer than any flogging, his belief in her obedient submission got her on her feet despite her unsteady knees. She stepped to her right. The hem of her dress floated between her fingers. Raising the black cotton in the back, she exposed her ass to the air and Henry's heavy stare.

Jay twitched.

She draped her dress at her waist and stretched across the table, curling her fingers around the far side.

Silence, but for their breathing.

She slipped off her sandals and spread her legs, her feet shoulder-width apart. Her toy settled lower, its weighted reservation securing Henry's place.

"Good girl."

With two words, he brought her near to begging for his touch.

Thank God he followed up with a graze along the curve of her ass. "Your pink-cheeked beauty proves your adherence to my directives. Did you enjoy your bath?"

"Very much, sir." Much as she loved her boys, sometimes a girl needed unsupervised playtime. Her hands had been the first to investigate her body. Learning to manipulate her toy as Henry did had been a privilege. "Thank you for trusting me to explore on my own."

"You've earned my trust. So patient you've been, when your adventurous nature would have sent you charging forward." He wiggled the handle between her cheeks.

Aching for a firmer tug, she strained toward him. Her dress dragged the tablecloth beneath her.

Chuckling, Henry squeezed both halves of her ass. "For authenticity, you ought to have your embroidered black panties, but I couldn't bear to part with them."

The pair he'd taken their first night. They'd disappeared, never to be seen again—by her, at least. "I'm glad, sir."

He swept his thumbs along her sweet spot, the crease beneath her cheeks. "Such a lovely sight." Cupping her in full, he pressed fingers to either side of her clit. "The first night my Alice surrendered herself to me."

Rocking his palm gave him rudder-like control over her toy. She followed the sideways swells with her hips.

"You gripped the table so tightly." Bringing his fingers together with her pinched between, he increased the pressure on her clit. "Almost as tightly as you gripped me." He rubbed her own lubrication over her nerves. "How much tighter, I wonder, will your grip be tonight as you embrace us both?"

Pleasure lashed her from the inside out, her contractions cascading. "Please, sir. I need to come. Please."

"Not yet." His low command left her shaking and raw. "You'll wait. My good girl. My sweet Alice." He stole away and took her orgasm with him.

She cried out. The wavering note folded into a needy, hungry moan.

"Let go of the table and stand for me." He tugged her upright so fast she left finger-folds in the tablecloth. With greedy caresses, he stripped off her dress. "Jay."

Jay's gaze had never left them.

"Such exquisite bearing and perfect form you've shown. You, too, have earned my trust and greater rewards." Clasping her shoulders, Henry held her back from the table. "Your waiting is done, my boy. Take your place, please."

"Thank you, Master Henry." Jay hopped on the table and sat with his legs dangling. His cock distended his formal black pants. Unlike Henry, he wore no tie, and the top button on his shirt hung undone.

She stood nude between two fully dressed men, one with his arousal obvious to her eyes and the other with his nestled against her ass.

Henry squeezed. "You'd like to unzip him, wouldn't you, Alice?"

"Yes, sir." God yes. So damn fuckable, an arm's length away, and her denied orgasm gave her body a head start. She hummed at a higher-than-usual speed.

Grasping her wrists, he brought her hands to Jay's waist. "I've seen how you watch my lover, how your gaze has followed his lithe muscles since the day you moved into this building. Do you think I haven't noticed?" Henry teased out his words in a flowing, hypnotic rhythm. "See the beauty he offers."

Jay leaned back on his hands and pumped toward her.

She worked belt, button, and zipper in rapid succession, until his pants gaped and his cock stood unencumbered. No underwear for him, either.

Henry dragged her knuckles down Jay's shaft. Furnace heat ran through taut veins. Jay whimpered, and she throbbed with sympathetic anguish. Waiting would drive them both to the brink of need and insanity before Henry let them go.

"I see you in the mornings, armored for your day at the office, taking powerful strides on slim legs, and do you know what I imagine?"

All those times they'd passed in the lobby or on the stairs, he'd nurtured her attraction without giving a hint of his own. A fiery chill revved her arousal. "Tell me, sir. Please."

"I envision those same legs, bare and grasping as you mount my Jay with your purposeful, unyielding determination."

Jay stared with bottomless brown eyes drunk on Henry's storytelling and her exposed body.

"I envision the strength you would demand of the man who sought to master your wild beauty." He stroked the tender undersides of her arms all the way up and transferred his grip to her breasts. With the pads of his thumbs, he raised her nipples to hard points. "I see you sealed between us, fluid and writhing, enjoying the best of both worlds, given freedom to pour yourself into forms of your own choosing and accept those given to you. Your place is here, Alice. A place prepared for you. Are you prepared to accept it?"

"I am." How she managed the rock-solid delivery with her heart surging out of rhythm, she'd never know. "I want what's mine."

Henry kissed the pulse behind her ear. "Take him."

Permission. Room for her strengths alongside his. The stage shifted, teetering from foreplay and formality to the improvisation of co-leadership, an informal balance they perfected every day.

With a lift from Henry, she knelt on the table and straddled Jay. Her body demanded he satisfy her, the sooner the better, but she tempered her passion with self-control. Jay belonged to her. More than his physical needs resided in her hands.

"He's right, you know." She devoured him with a harsh kiss as her fingers mastered the buttons on his shirt. "I watched you." Fabric pushed aside, she dragged her breasts over his bare chest. "All the time."

Weight on his hands behind him, supporting them both, Jay offered her his neck. "We watched you, too." He rocked his hips, and his cock scorched her thigh. "First night you slept across the hall, Henry talked about us having you while he fucked me. I came so hard."

Jesus, fuck. She scraped her teeth on his carotid and apologized with a string of kisses. "Funny." Taking him in hand, she glided his cockhead between her lips, coating him with her readiness. "You know what I was doing that night?"

Legs flexing along her calves, he whimpered and strained.

She breathed out and sank, careful not to rush. She had the weight of her toy to consider—and the weight of their master's gaze. If he meant to paint this moment, and Christ why wouldn't he, she wouldn't hurry his perusal of their joining.

"Killing the batteries in my vibrator," she whispered. "Burying my fingers imagining the two of you fucking."

With curling fingers, Jay formed hills and furrows in the tablecloth. "How were we?" His sweet tenor settled in a low rasp between heavy breaths, and still he tried to shoot her a charming grin.

"Fuck, I love you." She rose and fell on his cock. He seemed harder. Bigger. Her toy at work, or the anniversary excitement, or the anticipation of having Henry alongside him soon. "The real thing is so far beyond fantasy. Beautiful. Amazing."

The descent of a zipper pitched a stutter in their rhythm, a shivering excitement beneath Jay's urgent whine and her plunging hips. His cock kicked, and her toy got a strangling.

Jay drew back, breathing hard. "Jesus, that's close. Like a dinner bell, right? Henry opens his pants, and our asses pucker up for a kiss."

Laughter took the edge off, but the wildness stayed in Jay's eyes as he scanned her thighs surrounding him and her swaying breasts. Meeting her gaze, he sucked in a breath. Their stare flickered. His attention darted past her.

A solid hand splayed across her back. "Spread our girl for me, Jay."

She shuddered. His voice. Fuck, even better than the ticking zipper and the slick squelch of lube was the unconditional command in Henry's voice.

Parting his knees, Jay exposed her in a wider vee, tilting her toward his chest.

Toy handle in hand, Henry grazed her shoulder with a kiss. "Push, Alice."

She obeyed. As the toy's flared center slipped free, her moan and Jay's mingled. He wouldn't last long, but neither would she.

A heartbeat, a lone empty embrace, and new pressure nudged her. Thicker now, more insistent, but she no longer braced for intrusion. Pushing into the stretch, she greeted fresh joy with a saucy buzz. "Hello, beautiful. Where have you been all my life?"

"Waiting for you." Resting one hand on her hip, pinning her between her men, Henry penetrated her in a steady thrust. He wrapped his other arm around them both, over her shoulder and Jay's, and grasped the back of Jay's neck. "Preparing you."

She attuned to her lovers like sonar, her pulse revealing their size and strength clasped tight inside her. She contoured to their ridges and textures. Shaped for them, and them for her.

"Alice." Groaning her name, Henry squeezed her hip. "The singular woman who balances our composition with exquisite grace."

Trembling, his eyes unfocused, Jay supported her. "I feel you." His voice shook. "Both of you."

"Me too." God, did she. Hands on Jay's shoulders, knees on the table, she lifted and sank, a half-inch at a time, a slow, dizzying ride with her filled and aching for release.

As her head dropped back, Henry claimed a kiss. At once rough and tender, he turned fucking and making love into a unified whole.

Shaggy locks tickling her jaw, Jay nipped her throat. Henry's thrusts found their answer in him, a solid backstop jerking with her shifting body.

Dueling sensations strengthened with every collision. Reinforced. Halves of an arch collapsing together, their weight sealing the keystone in place. Her orgasm would demolish the whole structure, but the rush wouldn't stop. Too close, tension and pressure sending fault lines to the surface. She babbled against Henry's tongue.

He allowed her a breath.

"Please. Can't stop." She cascaded energy in both directions, or maybe her men only seemed to vibrate because the whole world did. "Please, Henry."

He poured power into his thrusts, but he traced her cheekbone with the lightest brush of his lips. "Come for us, Alice. Take us with you."

"Love." Fighting for the words through a gasping cry, she spiraled into agonizing bliss. "I love you."

Their triumph echoed hers, a chorus surrounding her, burning three vibrant notes into a single pure flame.

* * * *

Snuggled deep in a bed of pine boughs, Alice hummed at the sunny sauna heating her back. A warm breeze tickled her ear. She rolled her shoulder, and the breeze conjured up a soft whistle. A dim sun wore a white halo. Impossible, when the sunshine hit her on the opposite side.

Opening her eyes, she transformed her warm bower into a gently snoring Jay curled at her back. The bedside lamp glowed on its lowest setting. Henry lay propped on his elbow, watching her. Draped over his hip, the sheets teased her with the muscle sloping toward his thighs.

She eased clear of her dark-haired playmate, who slept with his nose buried in her hair, and wriggled toward Henry on her elbows.

He tucked her hair back and cupped her chin. "I've water and a snack for you on the nightstand."

Dinner had been hours ago. A light meal, sandwiched between their first go and the second, a teasing, lengthy game of who's on top as Henry encouraged her to play with angles and momentum in his big bed. Her repertoire held a handful of positions to embrace both men at once now.

Complimenting Jay on his staying power, she'd gotten a sweet confession. *You played with your toy for an hour in the bath. Henry played with me for an hour in the kitchen. I would've shot the second you bent over the table if I hadn't unloaded twice already.*

Her yawn refused to be contained. Stretching, she treasured the soreness in her bones. "You aren't sleeping?"

Henry rolled away and returned with a pineapple cube he pressed between her lips. "I'm indulging in one of my favorite pastimes."

She chewed slowly, letting the sweet juice flood her mouth, and questioned him with a lilting hum. His sketchpad, closed, leaned against the lamp. If he meant drawing, he'd already finished.

Running his thumb across her lip, he captured a stray drop. "Watching my lovers enjoy peaceful slumber, their minds and bodies equally exhausted."

She smoothed a whorl of hair above the flat circle of his nipple. For all the care he took and the praise he delivered, she could improve at reciprocating. "You do good work. The formality, Jay butlering, everything special from the second I got home. You made it so easy to let go of the outside world and concentrate on the three of us." Rubbing his chest, she warmed her hand on his muscled planes. "The dress was a beautiful touch. Thank you for thinking of it. And for——" His sternum, so solid and broad, protected a heart unlike any she'd known. "For not giving back my panties." If the time ever came, she'd know it now for the end of their relationship. "You'll keep them forever?"

"On the day I'm laid to rest, they shall occupy my inner breast pocket." Combined with his unblinking gaze, his words held the weight of a vow. "Your first act of submission, not merely in the giving but in the courage to accept their absence and thereby begin exploring your boundaries." Feeding her a second piece of pineapple, he lingered while she sucked his fingers clean in a promise of her own, love and service bound together. "I'm a visual creature, my dear. Your clothing is an integral piece of your landscape."

"The things you choose for me to wear, they're meaningful to you." And the ones she'd been dressed in only once more so, maybe treasured and put away, maybe inspiration for his next creation. She'd suspected, but black-box guessing paled beside going over the blueprints with the inventor himself.

"To an extent." He peeled the covers back, dragging his hand down her ribs as he revealed her. "On some occasions, the intended meaning may simply be to appreciate your beauty in an exotic cloak."

"Exotic like the red dress for your gallery show?" She leapt on the chance. Her question had gone unanswered for months, and he seemed in an accommodating mood. Mellow and pleased, as they'd all been since last week's success at the club. "The one with the Chinese-style collar."

"So you've finally returned to your interrogation on the subject." Teasing, swaying, he kissed the tip of her nose. "Have you found the right question yet?"

"I think so." She picked through her phrasing with care. "What gave you the idea to put me in that dress, and why did you choose it over the others you had me try on that night?"

He wagged his index finger. "Still trying to get away with two questions, I see."

"Just one. The 'and' makes it one sentence." She followed his chest hair on its downward trek to his navel. "Are you gonna tell my English teachers they gave me bad information?"

"No, Alice." He slung his arm over her. With his hand flat between her shoulder blades, he dragged her closer. "But perhaps it's time Jay and I gave you another lesson in the difference." His intimate murmur gained weight as he nuzzled her cheek. "Counting when you feel one item and when you feel two will help fix the notion in your mind."

God yes. "I'm game for a remedial class or two." Even her sore muscles uncoiled with eagerness. "But you're going to answer my *one* question first, right?"

"I am." Eyes dark and serious, he exhaled with steady precision. "Several years back, I attended a lovely ceremony at which the bride revived a generations-old custom and wore her grandmother's wedding gown."

Bride. A vise compressed her chest. Her throat closed.

Light and easy, he stroked her spine. "The dress was a deep, rich red, a traditional symbol to bring boldness and blessings upon the marriage. An auspicious beginning for the happy lovers."

With his gentle delivery and comforting touches, he unlocked her voice. "You wanted our date to feel like a wedding?" Henry had chosen the clothes for all of them, the red dress for her and matching ties for himself and Jay. Jay, who'd called the night a renewal of vows. "Was that when you knew you wanted me to stay?" For good, she meant.

Shaking his head, Henry resettled himself a hair closer. "I knew long before then. The dress was merely a subtle reminder of that feeling. One I had intended to enjoy without discomfiting you with the implications."

She'd listed her college boyfriend's proposal on her contract answers. Henry would've considered how gun-shy she'd gotten about serious relationships. At every turn, he'd shielded her from the depth of his love, even when her hesitance pained him.

Voice as hushed and tender as his, she nestled nearer. "When did you know?"

"You can't guess, sweet girl?" His lips twitched, his crooked smile fleeting. "A special night."

"They were all special nights for me." Her mental survey failed to pinpoint when his treatment of her had changed once they'd embarked on sexual adventures. "Every time you touched me was a new thrill. It still is."

Closing the thin gap, he muffled a groan in her neck. "November. You'd role-played so well with Jay on our previous night, instinctively offering what he needed without knowing the source of his nerves." His ticklish investigation of her spine ended with her ass cradled in his palm. "I was certain, then, you would be able to handle our unconventional situation. That in having two men in love with you, what frightened you was never the number but only the love."

"I didn't recognize it at first. But I knew something was different." She muted her laugh to avoid waking Jay. "I came up with excuse after excuse and convinced myself every one was valid."

"As I watched and worried. November was an indulgence." He brushed kisses at the corners of her mouth. "A night to have you to myself after allowing Jay that freedom. To carry you over the threshold and claim you, as much as you would allow."

Not even figuratively, but literally. He'd swept her into his arms and carried her from the bath to his bed, and she'd bled on his sheets. Old traditions in keeping with his bent toward artistic theater and history.

"Our wedding night." The darkness beyond the lamp swallowed her up, blinding and incomprehensible. Henry considered her his wife. No way divorce existed in his lexicon. "I didn't have a clue."

"Would you have stayed then if I'd told you?" So gently he asked, with acceptance and not blame in his voice.

"I would've run far and fast. I wouldn't have let myself get this involved." Foolish. She'd given men less consideration than design projects, marking them all under failed tolerances and refusing to re-run the simulation. Until Henry and Jay had wedged themselves into her life with their undemanding friendship and their structured arrangement. The warm security of their love flowed all the way to her toes as she pressed them to Henry's legs. "I would've missed everything that came after."

With one searching kiss, he poured his soul into hers. She succumbed, letting him overwhelm her senses and race through her blood.

He grazed her forehead before drawing back. "Then the time was well spent, even if success required we remain apart for longer than any of us would have liked."

Staying apart had disturbed Henry, but her confused circling must've crushed the man asleep behind her. Henry would've borne the brunt of his boyish enthusiasm and adorable persistence. "When did Jay start nagging you?"

"With a desire to have you move in?" In a near-silent laugh, Henry puffed air through his nose. "The day after your birthday celebration. Mere moments after the door closed behind you, in fact."

"That soon?" Thanksgiving, God. Less than four months into their relationship, and both Henry and Jay had been certain. Her heart had taken half a year more to convince her head.

"Only because Henry'd already said kidnapping you was off the table," a sleepy Jay answered from over her shoulder. "A move-in invite sounded like a good compromise."

"Holding her captive in the apartment until she agreed seemed a tad overdone. Though the thought did occur." Henry pressed his hardening cock to her thigh.

Laughing, she encouraged him with a firm grip on his ass. "You're as incorrigible as Jay."

"As insatiable as well." He rolled her on her back and rested a share of his weight on her. "Your counting class will be in session momentarily."

She twisted in his arms, reaching out and brushing Jay's chest. "Were we too loud? Did we wake you, sweetheart?"

He shuffled closer, blinking the sandman from his eyes, and stole a kiss. "Sleep is overrated."

Gripping Jay by his hair, Henry claimed a kiss of his own. "How fortunate we are to have forty-eight hours to indulge our fantasies on this anniversary weekend."

True. Their next class at the club was two weeks away, she had no overtime projects demanding her presence at the office, and they'd planned no dinners with friends, no basketball outings. A weekend to recuperate would do them good, especially with next week's challenge on deck.

"Let's enjoy it while it lasts." Her mental tally of things to do and chant of *please let this go well* kept track of the hours already. "My baby sister will be here in five days."

Meet the Author

USA Today Bestselling Author **M.Q. Barber** likes to get lost in thought. She writes things down so she can find herself again. Often found staring off into space or frantically scratching words on sticky notes, M.Q. lives with one very tolerant, easily amused husband and one very tolerant, easily amused puppy. She has a soft spot for romances that explore the inner workings of the heart and mind alongside all that steamy physical exertion. She loves memorable characters, witty banter, and heartfelt emotion in any genre. The former Midwestern gal is the author of the Neighborly Affection contemporary romance series as well as several other standalone romance novels. Pick a safeword, grab a partner or two, and jump in. Visit her on the web at mqbarber.com.

Be sure not to miss M.Q. Barber's contemporary small town romance

HER SHIRTLESS GENTLEMAN

Her heart is in his hands…

After her marriage ends in betrayal, Eleanora Howard finds herself
struggling to navigate the dating scene as a thirty-one-year-old divorcee.
But feeling undesirable, and living alone in the house she once shared
with her ex, is hardly the recipe for finding new love—until she meets
Rob. He's just the kind of charming, old-fashioned guy she needs—but
he's also eager for intimacy…

Chapter 1

Dead last. Again.

The four of them went out after work every Friday, and every Friday Eleanora sat and smiled while guys bought drinks for Sharilyn. Hit the dance floor with Amber. Chatted up Chelsea's breasts.

Even the sidekicks—wingmen, whatever guys called themselves—refused to give her a second glance. She couldn't blame their lack of interest on the ring. She'd taken off the meaningless metal circle before the divorce had been finalized.

But to the endless crowd of broad-smile bar-hoppers, she rated five seconds of stilted conversation between texting or checking sports scores or playing Angry Birds. The highlight of four hours of boredom. Single life almost matched the worst tedium of married life.

That's what she got for saddling herself with David and galloping through her twenties with his ring on her finger. He'd been her first. Her only.

Now she performed rotating roles as babysitter, chaperone, and charity case. She didn't belong at a too-small table packed alongside tight-skinned and perky-breasted girls who flashed their IDs with the affected nonchalance of twenty-two-year-olds.

She downed the final sip of her third beer of the night. She didn't dare hop in her car and head home yet. Given her luck, she'd end up pulled over and facing a drunk-driving charge. David would love any excuse to point out her idiocy. Hiring a lawyer without him finding out would be impossible in this town. She'd never live down the humiliation.

"—and it's deep, too."

Chelsea laughed along with what's-his-name. Dog Collar Dude. Not attractive, but he had deep pockets. Probably thought he'd be getting in deep with Chelsea tonight, payment in exchange for buying round after round of drinks. God knew he hadn't taken his eyes off her breasts.

Laughter came dangerously close to making Chelsea spill out of her silky, sleeveless v-cut. Eleanora's closet didn't hold a shirt anywhere near so revealing. Boring and staid, as much an accountant in her fashion picks as in her career choices. And in her bedroom habits.

She tilted her brown bottle. All gone. No magical extra swallows remained to knock David's voice from her head.

"Whoa." An unknown quantity stumbled to a halt beside her chair. "Your friend's hot."

Fantastic. The newest Mr. Drunk-and-Horny leaned in close and drenched her nose with the scent of teen body spray. Probably the same disgusting brand he'd used in high school. Probably lived in the same bedroom, too.

"Oh? Which one?" She'd come to this lousy bar with three friends— well, acquaintances—and he didn't have a chance with any of them.

The skinny blond kid blinked as he scanned their table. Jesus. He looked barely old enough to buy the three beers he held, and she'd celebrated thirty-one six months ago.

Sooner or later she'd have to inform her coworkers she wasn't going out with them anymore. They were twenty-four, twenty-five, and poaching college boys was fine for them. For her, the whole scene smacked of desperation. Three months of this bullshit added up to quite enough.

"Uh, all of 'em?" He presented a dopey smile.

"Damn, Ellie. Picking 'em young tonight, aren't you?" Sharilyn swung her martini glass upward, sloshing vodka over the rim. "Good for you."

"Yeah, no, I'm not——"

The kid wobbled into her chair. "I don't feel——"

Vomit splattered her shoulder and rolled down her chest. Ugh. Should've dodged faster. She shoved him back.

Stumbling over his own feet, he landed on his ass, spilled his three beers all over himself, and retched. The acrid stench of puke replaced the flood of body spray in her nose. A toss-up, really.

She laughed over the chorus of oh-my-gods from the rest of the table. At least the night wasn't boring anymore.

* * * *

"Oh, fuck."

Rob swallowed the last of his beer. Lucas had better hurry up with the refills. "What now?"

They'd hit a handful of bars already. Brian had found trouble with every damned one. With Lucas staying at his place for the summer, he'd been playing mother hen for the last three weeks.

"I think my baby brother's puking his guts out."

"Take him home. Happy beer-buying birthday and all, but he's done for the night." He'd celebrated his own twenty-first on base with a pack of fellow tech geeks. Good guys, including Brian. How had fifteen years gone by so fast? "Pour him into bed."

"Yeah." Brian grimaced. "Soon as I figure out what to say to the woman with puke running down her shirt."

"Try an apology." He shoved his chair back and stood, scanning the tables for Lucas's god-awful sea-green pullover. "Where is he?"

He spotted the vomit-splattered woman about the same time Brian answered, "Your four o'clock."

Shit. Lucas had spewed at a full table, and he couldn't get eyes on him. Man down. Threat?

No punches thrown, so far as he could tell. A circle of horrified and disgusted faces clustered to one side, their owners staring at the floor. One guy held his phone up. On the far side of the table sat a laughing woman with a beautiful smile and a stained shirt. Damn. He hadn't taken a woman home in almost four months, and Lucas had party-fouled the first to catch his eye. "C'mon, let's go rescue Lucas and get out of here."

Looked like tonight wouldn't be the night to break his sexless streak.

* * * *

"Oh my God, Ellie, seriously, how can you laugh about this?" Light glinted off glitter-speckled fingernails. Amber pushed back from the table. "Yuck. Danny, take me dancing." She dragged her boy of the night away with a theatrical flounce.

"You do kinda reek, Ellie." Sharilyn wrinkled her nose. "Not your fault, but eww."

Waving in front of her face, Chelsea nodded.

Dog Collar Dude flipped through his phone. "Fuck, I missed the kid's first splash. You think he could upchuck again? The visual'd make the video so much better."

Eleanora glanced down with care. The regurgitated beer soaking into her shirt quickly lost its amusement value. The kid had added a puddle beside her chair. He barked out coughs like a hoarse dog.

"No, I don't think he's got anything else in his stomach." She poked his knee with her foot. "Kid? You all right? You got somebody we can call for you?"

No answer, unless she counted more retching. Between the sound and the smell, her stomach started to turn.

A second man with the same pale hair as the first dropped to the floor beside the kid and laid a hand on his back. "Shit, Lucas, I thought you might've passed out."

"Are you all right, miss?"

Sex on a stick. Thick thighs encased in denim inches from her eyes. She launched her head back and her chin skyward. Eyes up. Ohhh, bad idea. The stranger loomed over her with his strong jaw and his short, dark hair and his no-nonsense eyes.

"No, of course you aren't." His aborted hand movement stopped short of her shoulder. "Ugh, he did a number on your shirt. Let me give you a hand."

He slipped around the other side of her seat. Cupping her elbow in one hand and pressing against her back with the other, he coaxed her to her feet. Large hands. Warm hands.

Her body jangled like a change jar spilling on tile.

"Look, he's really sorry, or he will be when he's sober." The stranger glanced down, shaking his head. "He's twenty-one today."

She nodded. The blond guy picked the younger one off the floor. First legal drinking day. Okay. She filed the data under *don't care* and waited for details about Mr. Tall, Dark and Handsome.

"You can't wear that home."

Her chest had snared more attention in the last five minutes than in three months of flaunting herself at bars. She'd found the secret of dating. When introversion and modest assets failed, distress attracted the good guys. Not how she'd hoped to find someone.

The man with large hands squeezed and let her go. Peeling off his shirt, he revealed a to-die-for body. Solid, toned muscles from top to bottom. Too bad his jeans came almost to his waist. Denim blocked the enticing slope heading into his pants. God, David had never reached such nonchalant bare-chested perfection.

Her rescuer held out his shirt and gestured her toward the back of the bar. "Here, let me give you mine for tonight."

No fucking way. This guy couldn't be for real. She stumbled over her chair.

He steadied her with a quick hand on her clean shoulder.

"Thanks." Oh, hallelujah. She'd started thinking she'd never find her voice. "That's, umm, I appreciate it."

"Least I can do, miss." He guided her in front of him past the line for the ladies' room and stopped at the door.

"Yo, man, you gotta put your shirt on." A beefy guy in a black shirt with the bar's logo over his chest held out an arm. "Carrying it don't count. You can't be shirtless, not in here."

She disagreed with strenuous, silent objections. Her gentleman deserved to go shirtless wherever he liked.

"You wanna run around half-naked, you gotta head down the street to the Lazy Eight."

Making that man put his shirt back on would be a crime. Her skin heated at the slow slide of excitement between her legs. Thirty minutes of fantasizing and foreplay with David left her dry as a desert compared to three minutes of standing next to Shirtless Gentleman. The longer she lingered in his orbit, the harder her lungs worked to serve up oxygen.

Lust walloped her with embarrassing swiftness. She lacked the looks and flirty attitude to pull a guy without adding a vomit-soaked shell to the mix. Riding off into the sunset with Shirtless Gentleman glinted so far out of the picture the location didn't exist on her map.

"Yeah, I get that." Shirtless Gentleman raised a hand. "You can toss me out in a minute. Right now, this pretty girl's got someone else's puke on her clothes, and I'm going to make sure she's safe while she's changing."

Gripping his shirt, she ducked into the ladies' room past the line of pissed-off, well-beyond-buzzed women. Shirtless Gentleman's presence seemed to deflect any cursing about cutting the line.

"No, ma'am," he rumbled over the din of music and chatter. "I don't wax and you may not touch."

Ma'am. Polite. Mannered.

She stuffed her shirt in the trash and grabbed a handful of paper towels. Fit. Chivalrous.

The damp paper towels scraped her neck under her hardy scrubbing. At least the kid hadn't destroyed her bra. The practical white soft-cup would serve.

Was Shirtless Gentleman military?

Tucking in the shirt didn't give her the fitted look it had given him, but she managed to minimize her resemblance to a child swimming in her father's clothes. Squinting hard almost made the outfit look intentional. A style choice to wear a black wide-neck tee with exposed white bra straps.

Yeah, almost.

She slipped into the hall, her skin electric. His bare chest greeted her from two feet away, his arms crossed and his feet planted in a wide, easy stance. A few hoots and drunken catcalls rose from the women waiting in line.

Shoving aside her embarrassment, she tipped her head back and met his eyes. "Thank you."

His attention stayed centered on her. The unsmiling bulk of a man sported solid pecs and a penetrating stare.

"Again." She fumbled for a classy conversation starter. "Your shirt's really soft."

Your shirt's really soft. What the fuck. Her brains had gone soft. Complete mush. Mashed potatoes held the edge in outthinking her.

His mouth twitched. "Must match your skin."

"Sorry?" She'd heard him wrong. No way had he complimented her skin. Men didn't say those things to her. "I didn't catch that."

He shook his head and dropped his arms. "Shirt looks better on you than it ever did on me, miss. Let me walk you back."

Turning, he swept his hand behind her and landed with a light touch. Five points of pressure, a half circle of fingertips keeping in contact as they returned to the table. More than a few whistles followed them.

"It doesn't bother you? Being"——she waved at the crowded tables——"stared at? Graded? Like you're on display?"

Stupid question. Of course, the attention wouldn't bother him. He had cool, calm confidence perfected. Anyone with his godlike body would want to show off.

"I got over any fear of public grading in basic training."

Military. Nailed it.

Not yet, you haven't.

Her face flamed.

"A'course, the opinions of a bunch of yappy drunks aren't worth all that much, positive or not." Shrugging, he tapped her back. "Being on display for the one woman who matters, well now, that's a whole other thing. That'll make a man nervous, sure enough, however cool he plays it."

Great. He had a woman who mattered. Smooth, too, about sliding the revelation into the conversation. No ring, but an empty finger didn't mean much these days.

"I think you've got cool down." Months of going out with the girls from work had taught her how to categorize the bar crowd. The unholy chaos broke into three groups, all ring-free, with the singular difference whether they were ring-free but committed, ring-free and open or cheating, or ring-free and actually unattached. Limiting herself to the third group hadn't done her any favors. "I hope your woman who matters sees through the facade and tells you what a great catch she's made."

He paused his tapping. "Oh, I don't—"

"Woo, I didn't know you were that kind of girl." Sharilyn slapped her hand on the table. "Swapping clothes in a stall?" Her nosy, flamboyant attitude owed nothing to the drinks she'd downed. She came by her perky personality naturally. "What else did he get on you, Ellie?"

Ugh. She smiled through her irritation. Eleanora was bad enough, thanks to her mother's obsession with family history. Every girl wanted to be named for the great-grandmother she'd never met.

Shortening her name to Ellie might as well transform her into a cow. Get along now, Bessie, Daisy, Ellie.

Sharilyn made her sound like a cow giving the milk away for free with a man she'd met ten minutes ago.

"I'm—we weren't—"